Also by

GENERAL G

THE SAVIOR OF CHICKAMAUGA AND THE MAN BEHIND JUNETEENTH

[Robert C. Conner] brilliantly uses a solid array of primary sources to paint a good portrait of this complex man whose military acumen was overshadowed often by his personal shortcomings. ... In this new book, we are introduced to a general whose self-assurance, boldness, and quick-thinking proved to be a major asset on the battlefield, but whose propensity to disregard cooperation with his peers kept him from Army command when his martial performance rivaled men who rose to that position. ... It's an excellent and long overdue addition to the historiography of the Western Theater of the Civil War, as well as to the Reconstruction movement and the relations of the military with the freed slaves of the Old South and the Southwest.

York Blog/Civil War Round Table

[D]etailed yet succinct ... thorough and concise throughout; not flamboyant—a smooth, easy, and interesting read. ... This book is engaging, informative, and an important resource for students of the American Civil War, as well as for anyone interested in command relationships during wartime.

Emil Posey, Tennessee Civil War Round Table

[Granger'] story casts much light on the civil war realities, including battles for political advantage and career advancement. Despite his exasperating nature, Granger proved relatively adept at this game, although his premature (though predictable) death in 1876 prevented him from outlasting his opponents or penning his memoirs. Conner's biography will ensure that Granger's military career will not be forgotten "warts and all."

The Journal of Southern History, Vol. LXXXI No. 2

THE LAST CIRCLE

OF

ULYSSES GRANT

ROBERT C. CONNER

Square Circle Press
Schenectady, New York

The Last Circle of Ulysses Grant

Published by
Square Circle Press LLC
PO Box 913
Schenectady, NY 12301
www.SquareCirclePress.com

First American paperback edition 2018.
Printed and bound in the United States of America on acid-free, durable paper.
ISBN 13: 978-0-9989670-1-1
ISBN 10: 0-9989670-1-7
Library of Congress Control Number: 2017960988

Publisher's Acknowledgments
Cover: ©2018 by Square Circle Press. Cover design by Richard Vang, Square Circle Press. Cover image: Gen. U.S. Grant writing his memoirs, Mount McGregor, June 27th, 1885. From the Library of Congress Prints and Photographs Division Washington, DC 20540 USA.

The author's personal and professional acknowledgments appear in the Author's Note.

For Barbara

CONTENTS

THE LAST CIRCLE OF
ULYSSES GRANT

PART ONE

THE BETRAYAL OF OLD FRIENDS

CHAPTER ONE

JULIA GRANT TRIED NOT TO THINK ABOUT MONEY. Not to think about bills to tradesmen, some of whom had cut off service, while others continued to supply the household, thus increasing her obligations and sense of guilt. The quickest way to overcome guilt was to wallow in grievance, anger and self-pity, which she knew was unworthy. Nor should she increase the burdens on Ulys by letting him observe her distress, which would make him feel guilt and worry on her behalf. She hoped he had not seen their daughter Nellie just now, walking downstairs in tears after the breakdown of what Julia had thought was a simple conversation. All she had done was ask Nellie about her husband and children back in England, whom of course she must be missing. But that separation could hardly excuse the younger woman's anger and rudeness. Julia knew perfectly well that there was more to it, some family trouble over there that hardly bore examination, something neither mother nor daughter wanted to open up in the current circumstances of the overall family crisis.

She took some deep breaths, and told herself she could now leave worrying about finances to her eldest son Fred, who, with his wife and two children, had moved into the Grants' five-story townhouse on East 66th Street, just off Fifth Avenue and Central Park. But Julia worried that Fred might be too deferential to her own supposed feelings, hesitant to suggest selling things despite the necessity of doing so. And his very presence reminded her of his own involvement in the collapse of the family fortunes, along with the deeper entanglement of her second son, Buck, who had actually gotten Ulys into the Grant & Ward investment firm.

Fred and Buck had both had to sell their houses to pay creditors, while she and Ulys had sold properties, too, from Galena to Washington. The younger children, Jesse and Nellie, also had invested money in the firm and lost it, along with other family members and many ordinary people, including veterans, who had had faith in the general's name, but were, along with him and all the Grants, swindled by Ferdinand Ward. Julia drew a quick breath in and out to release a little of her still hot indignation. For her and Ulys both, Ward's crime, deceiving and swindling the people who had taken him for a friend, was almost inconceivable, and that smooth young man was far worse than some violent robber on the street. This very house they lived in now, it turned out was not owned by them free and clear as she and Ulys had thought, because Ward had pocketed the payments leaving the mortgage still unpaid. She felt his concealed villainy as a horrible sign of a depraved modern age, inconceivably far removed from the West Point honor code by which her husband lived, or her own Christian faith.

Anyway, Buck and his wife Frances, who was more than eight months pregnant with their third child, had moved in with her father, Senator Chaffee. Jesse and his wife and daughter, along with Fred and his family, had moved into their parents' house on 66th Street.

The Grant & Ward Wall Street firm had failed without warning almost a year ago. It was on May 6, 1884, that Julia's—and the whole family's—illusions of prosperity were destroyed, when her husband Ulysses told her they had lost everything but debts. In those bleak days, the Grants' checks to pay bills had been returned because of insufficient funds, a mortification from which they were rescued by a $1,000 loan from their friend Matias Romero. At least, Ulys had insisted on treating it as a loan, although the check had just been left discreetly on their hall table by Romero, on his way out after a visit.

Ulys' insistence on paying debts was of course admirable, as was his commitment to earning back the money himself through writing a book. But Julia sometimes wondered how practicable it all was, and took refuge in the conviction (not necessarily shared by her husband) that the Lord would provide. They had survived poverty before, and calumny, and other slings and arrows of outrageous fortune. They were surviving now by selling property, and by this work of Ulys'. Although he had accepted and advance of only $1,000 from the new publisher, a drop in the bucket compared to their prior income of $3,000 a month, there was talk of much more money to be earned, if he were healthy enough to produce what was wanted—enough to pay every creditor and provide for the two of them indefinitely. But that was uncertain. Earlier this month, there had been something more solid when Congress for the first time provided the general with a military pension. It was much appreciated by the whole family, though Julia also detected in Ulys a trace of fastidious embarrassment at how badly they had wanted and needed Congress to act. It was humbling.

The reason for the family's financial disaster was the rascality of the investment firm's managing partner, Ferdinand Ward, who with a banker cohort in devilry, James Fish, had since been arrested and charged with fraud. Just last week, on March 26, 1885, Ulys had given evidence for the banker's trial, and was cross-examined at home. And then his health collapsed.

Ulys had, of course, been sick before. He had been hobbling with a stick for more than a year, since he fell on the ice the previous winter and hurt his hip, and then struggled with pleurisy. The family's butler, Harrison Terrell, had become then the general's constant companion and valet, helping him walk safely, a role that continued as there came further ill developments in Ulys' health. It was early last summer, at Long Branch on the Jersey shore, that was the beginning of the throat trouble, when he bit into a peach and thought he had swallowed a hornet or some other stinging insect, and then when he drank even water he said it hurt like liquid fire. But the family physician, Dr. Barker, was in Europe, and it was not until November that the throat specialist, Dr. Douglas, diagnosed cancer. At first they didn't tell her this, or even Ulys straight out, although he heard enough to guess the truth, and started treatment for it without telling her or anyone else. She had of course found out, although she had refused to believe at first that it was a fatal malady. She had kept on asking the doctors if they could cure him, but ceased at last when she perceived they avoided answering her directly.

Many years ago, after the war, she had received a similar verdict from a surgeon in the much less serious case of her strabismus, when he told her it was too late for an operation to correct her crossed eyes. She smiled in familiar recollection of Ulys' comment after she told him: "Did I not see you and fall in love with you with these same eyes?" he had asked. "I like them just as they are, and now, remember, you are not to interfere with them. They are mine, and let me tell you, Mrs. Grant, you had better not make any experiments, as I might not like you half so well with any other eyes."

Her smile faded away as she returned to the present, to the word cancer that no one wanted to use. Ulys seemed in a way glad of the diagnosis, it was better than being debilitated and tortured by a secret, unknown enemy. Meanwhile, he had knuckled down to writing the story of his life—writing for bread, she called it. Julia also knew he enjoyed the work, or had until recently, when it become too much for him. He wrote mostly in a little room at the top of the stairs, overlooking the street.

It was hard to keep hopeful, with her dearly beloved

faithful companion now sinking lower, weakened by fits of coughing. She, too, had lost her natural ebullience, though she made an effort not to let people see the extent of the loss. She could hardly deceive Ulys, and they still could comfort each other, but nothing was as before. It physically hurt him to laugh or talk. He had written less and less, day by day, until no longer able to manage even the lap board, then stopped entirely. Before, she had been a little hurt when he would smile, hold hands briefly, but see her as a distraction from the writing. Now, when she could take his hand for as long as she liked, and did, and knew it was a comfort to them both, it was much worse. When he flinched in pain, she would flinch in sympathy. People, even their boys—no longer boys—had stopped meeting her eye, not wanting to let her see how bad they really thought, or felt, his prospects were. She had had to steer the family's spiritual adviser, the Methodist clergyman Dr. John Newman, away from the state of Ulys' soul, keeping him focused on prayers for strength and recovery, for peace from pain in life, not death.

Despite their little flurry this morning, she thanked God that Nellie had come home from England on March 14. Ulys had brightened to see her, as anyone could observe, as he always had done. The good effect on his spirits persisted even as his physical decline continued. Nellie was both shocked at the deterioration, and impressed at how much of the book he had managed to write despite declining health. What only Julia saw was the night he stayed awake and wept for very joy at his twenty-nine-year-old daughter's presence in the house.

Grant had wept before over Nellie, in plain sight at the White House, and not from joy, at his only daughter's wedding eleven years ago. It was a match that Julia had more or less supported, in a rare case when she was not in complete accord with her husband, but had soon developed misgivings about after Nellie left for a new life in her husband's country, England. The young man had not fulfilled any promise he might have had.

In unspoken fact, Nellie was Ulys' favorite child. He had held her hand through his first inaugural address as president. While he loved the boys, too, Nellie was his favorite just as Julia had been favored by her own father, Colonel Dent, all the way from her childhood at the White Haven plantation in Missouri until his death in the White House. Spoiled was another word for it, how she and Nellie had been treated by their fathers, but Julia did not feel she had been ill-prepared for life. If Nellie's husband was now unable to appreciate his American wife—which Julia increasingly feared was the case—that made him the spoiled one, not her. Julia resolutely put aside thought of this morning's scene, vowing not to hold it against her daughter, and recalled that Nellie, like Julia herself and her daughters-in-law, was pitching in with routine daily tasks, as family members had to fill in for the much diminished and now overburdened domestic staff.

Julia knew traces of Missouri remained in her voice to this day, while Nellie's accent seemed to vary depending on where she was and whom she was talking to—and so was sounding more American these days. Now, of Julia's and Ulys' four children, only Buck was not living at their parents' home, which was perhaps just as well since he could be seen as a reminder—in fact the unwitting agent—of the family's disastrous comeuppance. And Buck's father-in-law, former Senator Chaffee, retained ample financial resources despite his own lost investment in Grant & Ward. But Buck and his own father loved one another, and Ulys was much too good a man to ever blame his son or want to make him feel guilty for the catastrophe—or any more guilty than his parents knew he already did feel.

Buck was a sweet-natured mama's boy, whose plight touched Julia's heart, although she could not help feeling there was something unmanly in the way he had entrusted all of their fortunes to such a villainous partner. And for all that Fred and his wife Ida had lost in the crash, and after he'd given up his Army commission and pay, Julia noted that they still managed to employ a nanny. Nor was her mind entirely at ease when contemplating her youngest son and child Jesse, who like the others had not settled into a respectable and successful career, and whose behavior and bearing were not always what she thought they should be. But her love for all the children overwhelmed any doubts, which she confined to the back of her mind.

Nellie sat with her father now, across from Julia, who had told the nurse and valet to get some rest, after they had changed Ulys' neck dressing and put back the silk scarf which covered it. "You need sleep," she'd told them, "at least a nap," and when Nellie said the same thing to her she replied, "I am not for sleeping now." It was only eight o'clock in the evening, but all of them had had their nights interrupted as the general's condition deteriorated. Now though, he was sleeping, half propped up in the bed, and his wife and daughter sat quietly with him.

Julia closed her eyes, too, for a moment, before discreetly shaking herself awake. Her attention was suddenly caught by the closed curtains in the window, the top of which seemed a little askew. What did they call that, a soft cornice or a valance? Was it scalloped, that pattern? She might adjust the cloth, or direct someone taller in the operation, but better not to inquire too closely as to what was behind it. There would be no money for frivolous structural repairs, even simple ones to caulked tiles. She shifted her position in the chair, pulling at her dress and wiggling her shoes. The latter needed a cobbler's attention and, as far as she recalled, it should not be a problem since they did not owe that particular tradesman anything, or not much. She did not feel in a position to throw away old shoes or much of anything else.

Nellie met her eyes, causing Julia almost to start in distress as her thoughts returned to the man in front of them. Both women knew the lump under the general's jaw was not going to stop growing, nor would his swelling neck. The little hole at the back of his tongue would get bigger, as would the ulcers. The sedative treatments of morphine or laudanum would continue, along with atropine and red clover, brandy and cocaine—the latter two of which, apparently, somehow, did not directly work against each other, nor stir Ulys' old craving for alcoholic intoxication. The pain in his throat would not let him drink any alcohol now, despite Dr. Shrady's regular removal of whatever secretions had accumulated there, so the brandy was injected. The neck dressing could be changed by a nurse or valet, by Nellie or by Julia, but no one could make swallowing any easier for Ulys. He could barely manage water or broth. Because it was so difficult, he tried on rare occasions to gulp a significant amount at once, incurring great pain and sometimes a reaction of choking and vomit. The brandy went into his veins, while the cocaine was dissolved in water and used with a cloth or sponge as an anesthetic swab applied inside his mouth. Between them, the drugs and alcohol cleared the lungs and dulled the pain enough to let him drift off into sleep, but that made his breathing more labored and raspy. Julian and Nellie found it a heartbreaking signal of the accumulating ruin within.

A recent choking and coughing fit, relieved only by hemorrhage, had scared them all, but Nellie thought the doctors did not appear to be surprised. Dr. Shrady, the new man, had seemed more surprised that the general had been able to hold up and keep working so long, when others might have taken to their bed and turned their faces to the wall. Shrady had also been the first to bluntly call the disease by its name, cancer, at least to his colleagues and Fred. Before he ever met the general, when he first examined tissue scraped from his mouth, he had pronounced him "doomed," and while nobody would use such language to

Julia, she was not insensible of the true course of events. Nellie held her father's hand now, and glanced across at her mother with a little sad smile.

Julia guessed part of Nellie's mind was with her three surviving children back in England; little Grant, her eldest, lay under a tombstone there. She had left them behind to be with her dying, ruined father. Julia knew Nellie's marriage had proved harder than the girl could have imagined when she wed the glamorous, older Englishman—Algernon Sartoris, whom Ulys never warmed to—in 1874, and went across the ocean to make a life among strangers.

She looked down from her daughter to her sleeping husband, but now remembered Nellie sick once as a young child, sick almost to death in that too rough Missouri cabin Ulys had built and they called "Hardscrabble." He sat with her then, and got sick himself of ague or malaria, in that place Julia had never warmed to. They were better off back at White Haven, her plantation home. Julia hadn't married as young as Nellie, who had been too young at eighteen, they all three had long since realized. But Julia had been that age when she first met Ulysses, her brother's friend from West Point, and had permitted him to talk her into a secret engagement. That was forty-one years ago, when he had been a very junior officer with dubious prospects. She thought of their life together as a sort of "Switchback Railway," which the newspapers said was the name of that new roller-coasting attraction in the Coney Island amusement park (to which she had never ventured).

She and Ulys had had a glorious ride of a life together, although in reality his prospects never seemed to stay solid. First they had that long engagement, lasting while he was away fighting in the Mexican War. He had talked about becoming a mathematics professor, at West Point or some private college—had certainly shown no ambition to be a general or politician. But instead of academic life, after their marriage, they lived in small northern Army posts where

she'd had to learn housekeeping on her own without her father's slaves to do the work. There were little dances gotten
up for Army wives in Sacketts Harbor, New York, on Lake
Ontario, and Detroit, Michigan, dances where she'd had to
lead without showing it because Ulys had no ear for music.
Then the Army kept them two thousand miles apart for two
years, until he resigned from it, which let them in for more
hardscrabble years in civilian life. They lived with her family
in Missouri for most of that time, as Ulys started off at
farming, for he was no grasping Yankee businessman like
his abolitionist father. But he'd had to beg work from that
father, Jesse, at last, and move the family in 1860 far upriver
to northwestern Illinois, where she had made it her business
to adapt to northern ways. In the war, Julia went with the
children to and from his camps, skirting the rebels, sometimes visiting Jesse and his wife, her mother-in-law Hannah,
who wore her hair in rigid curls. They thought her a too in-
dulgent and extravagant mother. But she had also learned,
better than Ulys, how to conduct the family's personal business—renting, buying and selling, traveling.

The White House was where they'd spent the longest
time together. Then more than two years of journeying
around the world, followed by semi-retirement in New
York. Their four children, and more grandchildren. What a
life to contemplate. But now in ruins of fortune and men's
eyes, and of Ulys' dear body, and him with the book-writing
not finished, stuck back again in the Civil War. Her cousin
James Longstreet had been stationed with Ulys (who called
him Pete) in St. Louis, after they left West Point, and before
they fought together in Mexico, and then against each other
in the Civil War. Pete Longstreet had wooed and married
Louise Garland at the same time that Ulys and Julia were
courting. Now, Julia mused, Louise still had her man,
healthy and hale despite his wartime wound.

Nellie said, "I hear General Parker was here this morning."

"Only a general by brevet," said Julia. "Really a volunteer staff colonel."

"I dare say he was, Mother," said Nellie, the expression reminding Julia of her Englishness these days. "But he served in the Cabinet, too. And Fred says he's been here before, and you won't let him in to see Father."

"Your father is in no condition for guests," said Julia, then continuing as if she couldn't help herself, "and the Commissioner of Indian Affairs is not of Cabinet rank."

Julia told herself to be patient with Nellie, who would remember Parker from her childhood, of course. Once on a tour with Ulys after the war, they'd let him take Nellie and her younger brother Jesse on an expedition to see Parker's sister, who was a Seneca like him but had married a Tuscarora and lived on their reservation in western New York. Meanwhile, Julia and Ulys had taken a romantic trip to Niagara Falls.

It wasn't Parker being an Indian that Julia minded, nor the strange fact that when they had first met, in Galena, Illinois, in 1860, it was Parker the federal engineer who was the more successful man than her husband. But now he brought with him too many memories. A great friend of General Rawlins, who was always dropping dark hints about Ulys' drinking, it was Parker himself who caused scandal after the war by being too drunk to show up on his own wedding day to a white woman—or girl, another eighteen-year-old in love. They got married quietly a week later, and Ulys insisted on going to that ceremony, too. He told her, irritatingly, that Abraham Lincoln had done much the same thing before his wedding to Mary Todd—with whom Julia, like many women, had had a tense relationship. On a visit to the Army of the Potomac in early 1865, Julia had seen Mrs. Lincoln fall into a prolonged jealous rage over a subordinate general's wife that did seem insane, so she was not surprised when, a decade later, Mary's surviving son Robert Lincoln had her placed in an asylum for a few months. Still, Julia was not of the opinion that the Lincolns had had a loveless marriage. And the Parkers' marriage, as far as she knew, had been more successful than the Lincolns', although falling short like all others to the Grants' own wonderful union.

At the Office of Indian Affairs Parker fell into one of the Grant administration's early scandals, not a bad one, not convicting him of anything, but enough to push him out of office. All the scandals had bewildered Julia, not least when they caught up friends and family, although never including Ulys or her or the children. They confirmed her determination to avoid all thought of money. Parker, however, had thought of it, had gone off to Connecticut, quickly making and losing a pile in the stock market. Then, she heard, he took a low-level municipal job that was controlled by Baldy Smith, a onetime Union general whom Ulys had promoted in the war, before they fell out. Julia reflected that she seemed to know a lot about Parker, too much. He came with too much baggage.

"I think Father would like to see him," Nellie insisted. Before Julia could decide how to respond, Ulys stirred, and her first thought was horror that he'd been listening to them talk about this Parker business, and it had woken and upset him. But that did not appear to be the case. His face was contorted as he gasped for breath, yet she forced herself to look on the bright side—he seemed far from a death rattle. "Water," he said, and she lifted the cup to his lips, and he was able to swallow some without an obvious increase in pain.

Into the room walked quietly another Julia Grant, the eight-year-old daughter of Fred and Ida, and a favorite of the general's. Julia restrained herself from wondering aloud whether the girl ought to be in bed by now. Ulys, stirred into consciousness, took the hand gravely offered by his granddaughter, and smiled at her with his eyes. He looked back and forth between these three people he loved, and was grateful for their presence.

"Do you know," Julia asked her granddaughter, "about the ancient Greek tale of Ulysses, by Homer?"

The little girl contemplated the matter gravely, and replied, "I think I've heard of it, but I don't really know it."

"Well," said the elder Julia, as Grant and Nellie happily looked on, "he had a long sea journey home from a long war, and many years later, your grandfather, my Ulysses, and I were on the same sea, the Mediterranean, which is between Europe and Africa. And we came to the island where the Sirens, who I think were sort of mermaids, tried to lure the first Ulysses ashore by singing to him, and they said I should stop up your grandfather's ears with cotton wool, but I said I feared nothing, and had learned from Penelope in that book to travel with my husband and not stay home. Then there was a real storm and I wanted to go back to Malta, but my Ulys reassured me. I fear no storms when we are together, and nothing can part us now."

Chapter Two

William Farrar Smith stared gloomily into the bathroom mirror which reflected the long established evidence that a comb-over had ceased to be even a faint possibility. His vanity in this regard had led most of the Army to refer to him as Baldy, but not to his face. Ely Parker would certainly make no such reference, when they met for lunch today.

Smith had spent part of the morning at a meeting downtown, at the south end of Manhattan which remained the business center of New York despite growing competition from more northerly precincts. He was staying in the Fifth Avenue Hotel at 23rd Street, and after breakfast had taken the Sixth Avenue elevated railway downtown. The steam-engine-driven elevated—or "the El," as the younger people were beginning to call it—was still a novelty to an out-of-towner, as Smith now was. It was a great improvement over the horse-drawn streetcars or cabs, which could get caught up in downtown's notorious traffic jams. New York, he observed, did not seem to have the new trolley cars yet. After his meeting, heading for the luncheon, he rode the elevated back above all the street traffic, while observing life through the third-floor windows of office and apartment buildings. Sometimes his gaze was drawn higher still, to the new skyscrapers as high as ten stories.

Ely worked in the city Police Department's five-story headquarters at 300 Mulberry Street. Smith was a little leery of the neighborhood, not far from the teeming slum tenements and the boisterous Bowery, but could hardly admit as much when he himself had worked there for several years on the Board of Police Commissioners, and was in fact the man who'd gotten Ely hired. Smith became president of the board in 1877 but left in '81, leaving the city, too. He was just visiting this week, doing some business, but mostly catching up with friends.

The police department had cut Ely's pay as an alleged economy measure soon after Smith departed. The fact that the Indian stayed in the job, which he now complained had little to do with engineering and architecture and was more clerical in nature, keeping track of supplies—the fact that Ely stayed on was, to Smith's thinking, a somewhat humiliating admission of need. When he'd been hired, Ely said he needed the police job because his engineering skills had grown rusty after his years away from the trade. He had been in the Army, in politics and on Wall Street, and before all that on the reservation to which he had returned when the new Lincoln administration found a more politically reliable person to fill his patronage job in Illinois. Smith himself, who was a few years older than Ely, was now making a good living as a civil engineer in Philadelphia. His children—those who had lived—were grown, while Ely had just the one child, a daughter, but she was young, only six or seven. Ely had married late and had his child a good deal later. While Smith could now afford to drift into semi-retirement, and for recreation engage in newspaper squabbles about the war, Ely had to work.

At one of the railway stops a middle-aged man got on the car who limped, with one of his legs held stiff and bent. Smith wondered if it was a war wound, but, gazing around at his fellow passengers, clerks and other working people, he reckoned they probably cared little about the history of the Civil War. Most were probably born far from New York, and were engrossed in their own preoccupations of making their way in the fast-changing modern world.

Smith would have liked to buy lunch, at least for Ely if

not for the passel of guests who were also likely to be there. But the Indian was touchy about accepting anything that could be construed as charity, even lunch—though he was enduringly grateful for Smith getting him the Police Department job. Ely had picked the place, a humbler spot than Smith would have chosen. The former commissioner had been known for champagne tastes going back to his days in the prewar Army.

Today's guests—at least the ones he'd been told about —should make for an interesting party. One was Francis Herron, whom Ely had apparently known out west before the war. Smith himself had gotten to know Ely in 1857 working on a lighthouse construction project in Michigan, and then in Chattanooga during the war, but had never met Herron. Like Smith, Herron had become a major-general in the war, but unlike Smith, who was a West Pointer, Herron had been a civilian volunteer in 1861, winning promotions when very young. He fought west of the Mississippi, at Wilson's Creek and Pea Ridge, and played a key role in late 1862 at the Battle of Prairie Grove. Smith remembered with a suppressed shudder what he himself had been doing on September 17 of that year, on the corpse-strewn fields near Dunker Church on the bloodiest day in American history, at Antietam.

Herron didn't seem to have amounted to much in the rest of the war, as far as Smith could recall, although he stayed in the Army until it was over. Then he went carpetbagging in Louisiana, and, as Ely had reminded Smith a few days ago, became the U.S. Marshal there, and later the state's Secretary of State. There had been some fuss, some dispute, about his role down there, hardly unusual in those days. Now Herron was lawyering or something in New York. Smith, too, had left the Army after the war. Ely, who hadn't been able to get in it until 1863, had stayed in longer than either of them, as long as Grant did.

Ely's other guests were Tom Sweeny and Vladimir

Krzyzanowski. Sweeny, whom Smith had known in the old Army, was now a retired brigadier living in New York, where their paths had crossed occasionally. On the most recent occasion, some reunion dinner Ely had dragged him to, Smith was introduced to Krzyzanowski. When Smith had first met Ely in Detroit before the war, the Indian was an enthusiastic Freemason. Now he communed more with his fellow veterans, or at least they formed one of his circles.

Smith would be the only West Pointer. Sweeny and Krzyzanowski were immigrants, from Ireland and Poland, respectively. Sweeny had lost an arm in Mexico with a New York militia company, then stayed in the Army fighting Indians, and rose quickly with the Civil War. He too had served under Grant, at Donelson and Shiloh, Iuka and Corinth. He'd lost his job under Sherman for brawling with a volunteer superior officer, Grenville Dodge, who was now a railroad tycoon. After the war, Sweeny was up to his ears in the Fenian "invasion" of Canada, but somehow managed to hang on to his Army commission and go back on duty in the Reconstruction South. Grant must have been looking out for him.

Krzyzanowski hadn't joined up until the Civil War, when he too had risen fast. He fought bravely and effectively at the end of the second day at Gettysburg, leading a night counter-attack against the Louisiana Tigers, a bayonet charge that drove them off Cemetery Hill. The night before Krzyzanowski's charge, Smith had been commanding Pennsylvania militia in nearby Carlisle, Pennsylvania, during his first military exile, before Rosecrans fetched him to Chattanooga and revived his career. Jeb Stuart's cavalry had shown up at Carlisle and demanded its surrender, but Smith's force there held out.

Krzyzanowski didn't quite make it to general, except after the war by brevet. General Carl Schurz, Smith recalled, another immigrant, complained that Congress hadn't confirmed a wartime promotion, which Schurz recommended, because the members couldn't handle the spelling or pronunciation of Krzyzanowski's name. In the Army, they called him Colonel Kriz. After the war, like Herron, Kriz had found government work, and he still had a job in the Customs House here. There was some postwar scandal, too, Smith remembered vaguely, as there had been with Ely at the Indian Bureau, but there was so much scandal and rumor of it these days that you often didn't know what was real and what was just being used as a political cudgel.

Coming into the restaurant, Smith noticed Ely's stiff-brimmed hat first, hanging on a peg, and then saw his friend sitting at a table with a younger, taller, thinner and more conventionally handsome man. That must be Herron. A copy of the veterans newspaper *National Tribune* was on the table. Smith had steered the meeting to this somewhat respectable, if interesting, eatery on Lafayette Street, opened by a refugee from the 1848 Hungarian revolution. It was a step up from the billiard halls and other dives by police headquarters to which Ely was inclined to gravitate, but the neighborhood was far from genteel. The Indian made introductions, and they ordered drinks—non-alcoholic in Ely's case. Smith knew he had given up drinking—or at least cut way back—several years ago.

"I've got to go back to the office," Ely felt the need to explain, a tad disingenuously, it seemed to Smith.

"I'm hoping to avoid that," said Herron, "or at least to make it tolerable."

Smith smiled indulgently. All three men—all five that would meet—were two decades removed from wartime glory, and now enmeshed in prosaic, ordinary lives. He asked Ely what he was doing for the Police Department, and got a quick response. "Work orders. Going over them could put you to sleep, especially if you added whiskey to it." Smith then brought up the subject of the recently deceased Police Inspector Thomas Thorne, whose funeral he knew Ely had attended, and they talked about Thorne's role in fighting the draft rioters of 1863.

Sweeny and Krzyzanowski arrived together, moving slowly across the room. They must be friends, Smith realized, presumably both cradle Catholics who in their youth had battled European empires, British and Russian, and both now New Yorkers. Sweeny was a stocky man in his mid-sixties, with a black beard like a shovel and a Cork accent seemingly little diminished by his many years in the United States. He had settled easily with his family into New York's vast and growing Irish metropolis. Krzyzanowski was a few years younger, slimmer and more debonair, but his health seemed fragile. Kriz's wife died a few years ago, which Ely had just mentioned to Smith and Herron.

There were more introductions, the men calling each other "Sir" indiscriminately. Herron and Sweeny weren't sure they had ever met, although in 1861 they had both been at Wilson's Creek, where the Irishman was wounded. They said enough now to establish that they knew each other by reputation. Herron and Krzyzanowski had run into each other down South after the war.

Smith brought up the somewhat touchy issue of Ulysses S. Grant, to whom he had not spoken since 1864. Most of them had known Grant during the war—at least he thought Herron would have known him—and they all shared the popular fascination with Grant's physical and fiscal ruin, and his struggle to write the story of his life, all of which was fodder for endless newspaper stories. Smith couldn't hold on to a grudge with this latter-day Grant, who in civilian life kept on stumbling into disaster—which didn't mean he would whitewash the man's many failings.

"I can't get in to see him," Ely said. "They say he's too ill, but I never was a favorite with Mrs. Grant."

"Aye," said Sweeny, "she's more receptive to millionaires now, is it?" And less receptive, Herron thought sourly, to Indians she held no longer of any account.

"I see they have goulash for a dollar," Sweeny went on, brandishing the menu. "Maybe I'll get brave and order it."

Ely smiled grimly and said, "The status of the general's health is such, I was told, that it is uncertain when he will be able to entertain visitors. But others do go in."

"I'm sure they are excluding most people, to give him a little peace," said Smith. "I don't think I'd be welcome there. But whatever our quarrels, I don't wish him ill. Did you know the general, Herron?"

"I met him at Vicksburg, but got there too late for the real fighting, just in time for the siege. Ely got there about then, too."

"In a more humble capacity," said Ely.

"Then Grant sent me off to take Yazoo City," Herron continued, "which turned out to be wet work as torpedoes sunk our ironclad. Luckily, the alligators we'd seen on our way up the Yazoo were not in evidence at that time. As for Grant, I got sick and he moved way up above my sphere."

"Didn't you come back to the Army?" Sweeny asked.

"I did, but not so you'd notice. They had me in Brownsville for a while, disrupting our rebels' cotton trade while supporting Juarez in Mexico, until we got pushed back to Brazos Island. Then on to Louisiana. At the end of the war I was dealing with surrenders, issuing paroles and such."

"He sent Buckner downriver to New Orleans to meet with Canby," said Ely, with a faint smile. "Then hauled in the last Confederate general, who was an Indian."

"Stand Watie," Herron confirmed. "In June. He was a Cherokee, but there were various tribes involved. They weren't straight surrenders; we had to start writing new Indian treaties. Actually, Ely took over that later in the year, after I'd left the Army." Ely's Indian service for Grant had begun then, long before he became commissioner or the general became president.

"But you know who else was taking surrenders?" Herron continued, turning to Sweeny and Krzyzanowski and answering his own question. "Your fellow immigrant and Union general, Peter Osterhaus, whose conversation managed to shock the rebel lieutenant general Dick Taylor, the son of the late president." The old Irishman did not seem impressed by this information.

But Krzyzanowski broke the pause. "Yes. He was a comrade from the revolutions of '48. As was General Asboth, who introduced me to Hungarian cuisine at a restaurant just a few blocks east of here."

"There are a few that way on Second Avenue," said Sweeny.

Smith realized that to these men, the war had been won by volunteers, and foreigners, outsiders like themselves. He, on the other hand, could not help viewing it from the perspective of his alma mater West Point. Yet George Washington had won the Revolution with the help of foreign volunteer generals, including the Poles Kosciuszko and Pulaski, back when West Point was a front-line fort, not a school. Smith was learning to bridge both worlds, like Grant, whom he'd been two years behind at the Point. Grant came from the people, for all his later acquired (and now disappeared) wealth. In 1861, he was a hard-luck civilian barely getting by. The war that followed gave the men around this table more in common than with any civilian. And peacetime civilian lives, including their own, must look trivial in contrast.

Since the war, out of the Army, Smith had prospered, while Grant became president and a friend to business interests. The men at this table did not identify with that side of Grant, although—or because—they and he lived in big-money New York. Many New Yorkers had been lukewarm about the war when it was going on, and since its conclusion most were ever more ready to forget it. Maybe Grant appealed more to these old comrades now that he'd lost everything, and was poor again.

"Do any of you want to see General Grant these days?" asked Ely.

"You mean his last days," said Smith. Unlike the others, Ely's service in the war had been only as a staff officer. But his close ties to Grant gave him status among them, even if those ties had frayed over the years.

"I would see him," said Herron, "though I can't pretend we were ever close. I feel for the man."

"I know you were close, Ely," said Smith. "So was I for a few months, as you'll recall in Chattanooga, in 1863. But Grant finds reason to find fault. I think he looks for scape-goats."

"I was at Chattanooga with Hooker," said Krzyzanows-ki, "the only time I served under Grant—if you don't count the last year of the war, when we all did. But I never met him, so won't intrude on him now. Why did the two of you fall out?"

"My corps was at Cold Harbor in '64," said Smith, "af-ter we'd gotten wrong orders and marched miles out of the way. We still had some success at the beginning, drove the rebs out of Cold Harbor that first day, which was the first of June. But the maps were wrong, and you couldn't see a battlefield, just trees and trenches. Then there was the big attack, with no coordination between the three corps. We lost thousands of men in minutes, because Grant ordered an insane assault on an impregnable position, a movement which neither he nor Meade bothered to coordinate. An as-sault just as stupid as Burnside's at Fredericksburg, where I also had served. The men were shot down in ravines, no support on our flanks. I refused to order another charge, and the commanders of the other corps, Wright and Han-cock, agreed with me. Then Grant and Lee left our wounded for four days to die between the lines. I won't sen-timentalize either one of them."

"General Grant hated the sight and sound of wounded

men," said Ely, "or dead ones either. He cared deeply for them."

"Yes," said Smith, "I've heard that, and I don't want to quarrel with you, Ely. But I think it's gush. Grant's great virtue was taking action, yet he didn't do anything to save those boys, because he wouldn't admit he'd lost the battle to Bobby Lee. And Lee waited, to make the point he'd won, that they were our boys laying there, not his. Our boys in Andersonville, too, Grant wouldn't exchange—though at least for that you could make a military case. Not for Cold Harbor. It was unforgivable."

"I heard," said Krzyzanowski, "that they hushed up the battle news because the Republican convention was in the middle of nominating Lincoln for a second term." Herron had heard the same thing. Lincoln's re-election looked like a long shot in June of 1864.

"Right after that," Smith continued, "when I came up to Beauregard's lines at Petersburg, damn right I was cautious and made sure to reconnoiter, maybe too much so. It's Grant's blundering tactics at Cold Harbor that made me do it. That was the end of my war. He just kept battering away."

"With more success than Burnside," noted Herron dryly.

"And prisoner exchanges were resumed," said Ely, 'before the end of the war."

"I was long gone by then," said Smith, "but Burnside was still there after Cold Harbor, until he blundered into the Crater. It was criminal to have men like him, and Butler and Sigel, still in service that late in the war. I suppose to do Grant credit, by the spring of '65 their lines at Petersburg were so weak his frontal attack finally worked, and led to Appomattox."

"Sheridan was on Lee's flank," said Ely, seeming to press for another concession. "Blocking the way south."

Smith ignored him. "Giving credit was something Grant

wasn't inclined to do. More than two years before all that, at the Battle of Williamsburg, my old friend Hancock got his nickname 'the Superb,' when fighting under my command." He suddenly stopped talking. He hadn't been looking to do what he and so many others were unable to resist, rehashing the war one more time.

"Grant thought General Thomas was too cautious," said Herron, making a concession of his own, "but his record looks pretty good to me. Rosecrans, too, except for one day at Chickamauga."

The waiter interrupted the conversation by bringing their orders, including Smith's plain pork chop—he'd decided against Hungarian cuisine. There was, however, what looked like red cabbage on the plate, a string of which he ate with a bite of boiled potato. Sweeny, with his empty right sleeve, industriously worked at his plate left-handed. Smith then continued from where Herron had left off, on Rosecrans, who had revived Smith's career by bringing him out to Chattanooga in 1863, just after the defeat at Chicka-mauga. Then Rosecrans was fired by Grant.

"I lasted longer than Rosecrans," he said, "but after Cold Harbor, I had no heart for it all." There was a pause, perhaps for continued eating or remembrance of the Union dead, but Smith could not resist adding, "The real reason I was relieved was not the attack at Petersburg, where my corps' gains were praised by Grant and Butler both. I didn't know how many or how few rebs were behind their fortifications, and no one blamed me at the time for not taking the city. But that's not why I was fired. It was because I warned Rawlins about Grant drinking on June 29. Butler had witnessed the drinking, too, and used it somehow with Grant to get rid of me."

They all looked at Ely, who decided not to wade into that particularly sensitive area of dispute. It was true, as far as he knew, that Grant had never been drunk in the heat of battle, but that didn't mean it didn't matter, his drinking.

Grant had told Ely once during a game of billiards in Gale-na about having been a member of the Sons of Temperance, and Ely too had opened up about drinking, how his ancestor the Iroquois prophet Handsome Lake had preached against it. Yet the two men also had acknowledged by word and action the appeal of liquor, the way it would cosset your mouth, jolt your throat and gut, yet soothe and warm you, too, and let you know you're alive. They'd done some drinking together, though without losing sight of the danger. During the war, Ely had supported chief of staff John Rawlins, another Galena man, in trying to stop Grant's drinking. Bringing Julia in was their secret weapon, and with the uxorious Grant, it worked. Julia's loving presence and their children's were what he needed, proving much more effective than the policing efforts of Rawlins and Ely, who became, you could argue, sometimes unwelcome reminders of Grant's less stable days. And Ely had to shake off his own drinking problems too. He didn't think Grant was sus-ceptible to blackmail, if that was what Smith was implying, but decided not to address the issue directly.

"Ben Butler was a character," Ely said. "A great rogue, and nothing of a general, but a great politician, too."

"He was a friend to the Negro after the war," said Her-ron. "And thus to Grant."

"Not a man well acquainted with the truth," said Smith. "And didn't the Supreme Court a year or two ago throw out Butler's civil rights act?"

"Grant's civil rights act, it might better be called," said Herron. "And that was to the court's discredit."

"Weren't they mostly his appointees on the court?" asked Smith. Herron coughed up a piece of goulash, what-ever that might be. He had followed Sweeny's suggestion in ordering.

"So I take it you won't be coming to see General Grant now," Ely resumed, steering the conversation and Smith away from military and political controversy, and back to the point. "How about you, Tom?"

"I've nothing against Grant," said Sweeny. "Nor him me. Though I did knock down his millionaire friend Dodge after the Battle of Atlanta, and later tried to start a war with England. He called me in after that," Sweeny continued with a smile, and his good humor spread to the company. "He read me the riot act, said he'd kept me out of prison, but that the Army could still use me down South if I promised to behave. So I did, and even got a promotion to peacetime brigadier, for my sins. I'd go see him now," he concluded, as the laughter died down.

Krzyzanowski had finished eating and was lighting a cigar, seeming to wave aside the notion of going to see Grant along with the smoke.

"If they won't let you in, Ely," said Herron, "I may as well not bother."

"You might have better luck going together," said Smith. "I'll be leaving town tonight, and though I wish him no ill, I've been on the outs with General Grant for twenty-odd years. But there's no reason why you shouldn't go."

"I don't like to go where I'm not wanted," said Ely.

CHAPTER THREE

ADAM BADEAU, WHO DURING AND AFTER THE WAR had served with Ely Parker on Grant's staff, was now helping the general write his memoirs. For five months he had actually been living with Grant, but a few days since he had to move to a hotel because the house on 66th Street was growing ever more crowded with relatives. The living arrangement had been useful to Badeau, who was almost as broke as Grant, but was hardly necessary for the writing project any more, as the general's workload was dwindling. With the recent and apparently irreversible decline in Grant's health, progress on the book had more or less ceased. This turn of events obviously alarmed everyone, not least the new publisher, Samuel Clemens, although he continued to talk big about the subscription sales he was lining up. Clemens and Grant had both taken risks in signing a contract on February 27, and it remained to be seen how it would pay off.

Badeau would have liked to be able to despise Clemens, whom he had known for years, as a boorish bumpkin. While he was severely envious of the younger man's highly extravagant prosperity, he had also heard Clemens was taking on debt for this new publishing venture, forming a New York company with a nephew who did the more tedious work of running the firm. It was subscription publishing, in this case with the product being pushed by door-to-door salesmen, and Badeau found it a lowbrow, rather disreputable enterprise. But he acknowledged the value of the money that it might earn, which he by no means despised or disparaged. Clemens had started the firm so he could get his own books put out the way he wanted, and make more profit off them, but now had become obsessed by Grant's. He seemed to envisage selling a lot of copies of Grant's *Memoirs*, and was also selling a lot of his own new book, *Huckleberry Finn* (written under his pen name, Mark Twain), which was the first to be put out by the new firm. Grant's book was in line to be the second it published.

The most alarming thing was that Badeau, at loose ends, had started reading Clemens' novel, and could not agree with certain dismissive, straitlaced New England reviewers. *Huckleberry Finn* shared some characters with Clemens' preceding book, *Tom Sawyer*, which Badeau regarded as essentially a book for children, and he had been expecting more or less the same thing from the new one. But he was coming to the appalling suspicion that the new book was some kind of masterpiece. He had been similarly shocked a decade before, as an underemployed U.S. consul in England, to discover Sherman's military memoirs were actually quite good, just as Grant now had turned out to be a competent writer—although at least Badeau could ascribe the latter phenomenon in part to his own tutelage.

The success of *Huckleberry Finn* was especially vexing as it had come out in February, and was excerpted in the same issue of *The Century* magazine in which appeared Grant's first article, on Shiloh, for which the general earned less than $1,000, which went to pay debts. Both pieces had created a stir, with many positive comments. Century published the best American fiction, and had also started a hugely successful series of Civil War articles, written by soldiers who had experienced the events, with Grant's recollections being the jewel in the crown (as Badeau's highborn English connections might put it). The present and future writings of these two very famous but, to Badeau's eye, rather vulgar Americans looked set to utterly eclipse his own literary fame. Further, Clemens was becoming increasingly

obtrusive in his role as master of ceremonies of the circus to which Grant's life—or rather its last stages—had evolved into. This flashy, white-suited celebrity had barely known the general until recent years. He had been the top-billed speaker at a welcome-home dinner for the returning hero in late '79, when the Grants were proceeding slowly eastward from their round-the-world tour. It was at the Palmer House in Chicago, where he had thoroughly engaged the assembled throng of middle-aged military, business and aldermen, causing them to collapse into gales of laughter at two o'clock in the morning. When Grant moved to New York City the next year, he and Clemens started seeing more of each other, and now were allegedly great friends.

Clemens had been off on a lecture tour for most of the winter with George Cable, another former Confederate turned racially advanced novelist. But now he was back, focused on Grant and with his finger in everything. He was much taller than the stout, fussy, bespectacled Badeau, a few years younger, and full of life and self-confidence, often in full lecture mode as his preferred method of conversation. Clemens was even taking credit for getting Grant to write his memoirs at last, although Badeau was quite certain that he himself had played a larger role last year in encouraging the general to get started—and obviously financial necessity was the real spur. Grant, he knew, was grateful for literary encouragement, and had proved eager to work when he could.

Currently, Clemens was fulminating against Century, which had been going to publish Grant's book before he beat them out on behalf of his and his nephew's Webster & Company. Fred had been Clemens' ally in winning over General Grant to the idea of leaving Century for the new publisher. Grant, typically, had expressed loyalty to Century, which reminded both Clemens and Badeau of him sticking by Civil War comrades who went on to run enterprises such as the Whiskey Ring. Century still had rights to a series of magazine articles the general wrote last year and which he needed now to include in the book. It was a matter more complicated than necessary, and Clemens had been pressing his strong views about it on everyone from Badeau to Fred to Clarence Seward, Grant's lawyer. Seward was the nephew of the statesman William H. Seward, with whom Grant had had an occasionally contentious relationship after the war; Clarence had been raised by his uncle's family. The elder Seward had been less hostile to Grant than his boss, President Johnson, and supported his election both in 1868 and 1872.

Clemens also took a keen interest in Grant's writing, feeling free to express views not necessarily coinciding with those of Badeau. Then there was the completely irrelevant and unnecessary contretemps stirred up by Clemens when he brought in a pet German sculptor by the name of Karl Gerhardt to do a bust of the general. Badeau had come in to confer with Grant and woke him up, which had purportedly upset the young German's concentration, and definitely incurred Clemens' wrath. Badeau acknowledged that Clemens, like any railroad or shipping tycoon, was entitled to play at being a patron of the arts, but nothing excused his downright rudeness.

Badeau was himself a literary man. Before the war, he'd had published a collection of theater criticism, including fulsome praise of the actor Edwin Booth, who had become a close friend. But since then, Badeau's wagon had become hitched to Grant's star. Clemens was punctilious in calling him "General Badeau," which was one more irritation since the title referred to one of those common-as-dirt brevet promotions that came to Uncle Tom Cobley and all after the war—an appellation which Badeau both appreciated yet disparaged, even as he used it on the title pages of his military history. Titles were fraught, for a sensitive man. Still, there was no doubt Badeau had become a soldier, a military and not just a literary man, who had been badly wounded at Port Hudson in 1863, and then served under General Grant in war and peace. His only other published work was a three-volume military history of Grant, the last two parts mostly written over the decade when he was a U.S. consul in the United Kingdom, and not overburdened with official duties. When he had arrived in England, early in the Grant administration, he had undermined the American minister, John Motley, by reporting accurately that he was taking his instructions from Charles Sumner, chairman of the Senate Foreign Relations Committee. Sumner opposed the policy of Grant and his Secretary of State, Hamilton Fish, regarding the highly sensitive issue of U.S. claims for damages done by Confederate naval raiders built in British shipyards during the war. Motley was recalled, but Badeau did not replace him, and was left in place to make the best of his consular appointment. The British preferred him, at any rate, to Sumner, whose very aggressive and unrealistic position was that they should give up Canada to the United States to settle the wartime claims, which if taken seriously would probably have led the two countries into a new war. Grant, by opposing Sumner, had turned out to be a peacemaker.

Badeau had parlayed that time into another as yet unpublished book, a study of the English aristocracy, a milieu far removed from *Huckleberry Finn*—although Clemens now seemed to live in the grandest style at his country estate in Hartford, to which, unfortunately, Badeau had yet to receive an invitation. Badeau had thought the English aristocracy book would appeal to American literary ladies, especially as he was throwing in a little gossip. But it had been heavy going, taking years longer than he'd planned, and, he had to admit, was duller than Clemens' new, vulgar book. One reason for the long genesis of Badeau's book on the aristocracy was that he'd been distracted by the large task of writing Grant's military history. Those three volumes had come out, and were praised by everyone including Grant, to Badeau's intense gratification. Then he had embarked on another book before finishing with the aristocratic saga. This new effort would be his first novel, based on his shorter consular service in Cuba. That work, too, was coming to fruition, but unlike the aristocracy book had yet to find a publisher willing to commit. Still, Badeau hoped to see both of them into print this year. He was excited and nervous, though able to conceal that, and hoped further that one or both of the new books together would ease his pressing financial deficits. He was embroiled in some legal difficulties, notably with the State Department, which had questioned his financial accounts. But any literary or financial success he might achieve would pale in comparison to Clemens', who seemingly went from strength to strength. Now the garrulous new publisher talked not of literature but of the business he had founded with his nephew, Webster, and a compositing or typesetting machine that he was investing in, which he believed would make him even richer.

There was no escaping the man. Badeau had tried to avoid him after the German sculptor incident, seeking to maintain a certain *hauteur*, but Clemens was oblivious, and barreled on regardless. That morning, Clemens had cornered him in a hallway, leaning his bristling moustache and cigar-bad breath in toward Badeau and saying, "If he dies now, we'll have to salvage the book."

"I can finish it," Badeau had replied.

"No doubt. Maybe I could, for that matter. But I want it to be Grant's."

Badeau still had complete access to the house on 66th Street, and remained a confidant of Mrs. Grant. Julia was always happy to hear about progress on Ulys' book and praise for her husband's writing, and occasionally had insights of her own. Just that morning, she had connected Grant's sometime horror at wounded men and undercooked beef with distaste for his father's trade of tanning hides. Badeau could have responded—but did not—that there was no virtue in such sensitive avoidance of wounded soldiers, as he well knew because he shared Grant's horror. Whatever the military or patriotic justification, it was Grant who had put them there, in the hospital and the grave.

Now, with the general's increased debility, Badeau was no longer burdened with so much of what he had come to regard as ill-paid, underappreciated drudgery. Endeavoring to buttress this positive thinking, and to escape a growing obsession with Clemens, he also dwelt on the reflection that Grant's written account had not even gotten through the Civil War yet. That meant the general's book of memoirs, if it could be salvaged for some kind of publication, would no longer be such a threat to sales of Badeau's own *Military History of Ulysses S. Grant*. The scholarly looking Badeau, his close-set eyes always under spectacles, was less stout and red-faced than he used to be, since he had brought his drinking more or less under control. He was unemployed, though, and every job he had held for the past two decades was obtained through Grant's influence, so it would be very helpful if the royalty checks kept coming in.

Not that he actively wished for the general's sickness and death. Sitting now in the parlor with Julia Grant and Fred, and the Methodist parson "Doctor" Newman, Badeau felt himself to be, and was, a friend of the family. As such, he was properly sympathetic, and felt genuine fondness for the Grants and for some of the children, although Fred was beginning to grate.

A few months ago, Badeau had successfully urged the general not to visit his doctors by taking streetcars around town as an economy measure, regarding it both as a humiliation for him, and a threat to his health in the cold fall weather—and had finally carried the point. For all the fuss people—including Clemens—made about the "Gilded Age," some saying Grant was too close to the rich, Badeau still felt the need to guard against any lapse back into the family's pre-war Midwestern vulgarity, which would reflect badly on all associated with them. Badeau did not share

Grant's love of horses, which pulled the streetcars, and the stink of their excrement, which he never quite got used to, was sometimes an aggravation to his temper. Now, Grant's increasing weakness made any quixotic gesture like riding a streetcar impossible. Badeau realized the Grants were focused on the general's health and their other troubles, and that they could hardly be expected to pay attention to his own concerns. It was every man for himself in this age of gilt.

Badeau agreed with Clemens about this much, that Newman was difficult to appreciate. Unctuous and orotund, his clean-shaven face framed by longish graying hair, the preacher was now engaged in informing the room at quite unnecessary length that they were at the beginning of Holy Week, which would culminate on Easter Sunday.

Julia, normally sympathetic to Newman, actually shared Badeau's feelings at this moment. The mention of Easter reminded her of Good Friday, and the death not so much of Jesus but of Abraham Lincoln, who had been shot on that day twenty years ago. She had persuaded Ulys not to go to Ford's Theatre on that Good Friday evening, and he had ever since been troubled by the guilt of wondering whether he might have protected the president from John Wilkes Booth. Badeau, Julia remembered, had actually met Booth in 1863, when he was recovering from a war wound at the home of Booth's brother Edwin, during the New York draft riots, when Irishmen were murdering Negroes—as no doubt Booth wanted them to do, and as the Ku Klux Klan or whatever they were called now were continuing on occasion to do in the South. Ulys' efforts to protect the Negroes seemed to have died away with his administration, and Reconstruction. More subjects hard to contemplate, for the slave-tended, doting daughter of Colonel Frederick Dent. But Ulys, too, had moved a long way from his opinions before the war, when he had been a Democrat who'd voted Buchanan for president in '56, and hoped Stephen Douglas would win four years later. They'd moved together in the way they thought about racial matters, she a little behind-hand.

Now, Edwin Booth was the greatest actor of his day, still the toast of New York. The world was full of things impossible to think about. Julia felt regret, surely, for Lincoln's death, and indignation at his murderer, but also relief that Ulys was spared, and that she had not shared the fate of Mary Lincoln. She was still unready to accept in her heart the diagnosis that her husband was dying, or to think about it much, at least just yet. Rising, she interrupted Dr. Newman and returned to the sick room.

It was the valet Harrison Terrell's turn to arise from his post at Grant's side, Julia taking his seat and nodding him off to take a break. She looked closely at Ulys, who seemed to be both awake and at rest, which she supposed were positive signs. But everything positive now had a negative side. His hand sat passively in hers, this man who until a few days ago had persisted in the act of copulation, which he had performed with enthusiasm at regular intervals whenever they were together, a circumstance he always desired, ever since their wedding night. The persistence was a secret, agreeable surprise to Julia as she moved all through her fifties, and while its vigor and frequency had been tempered by illness, its recent cessation had shocked her into the realization that he really might be dying.

Grant observed his wife sit beside him, and realized his head was clearer than it had been, his pain and breathing tolerable. But he seemed to be paralyzed, unable to smile at Julia or squeeze her hand. He supposed this was how death came, and would have smiled were he able as there occurred to him the obvious irony, that a man who had commanded the armies which won the Civil War, and served two terms in the White House, was now unable to order his own lips or fingers to move. He wondered if Clemens and Badeau would be able to cobble together the manuscript enough to make it publishable. There was no sense indulging in regrets, but leaving that book unfinished, in its current state, would be a bitter one.

Newman, Fred and Badeau remained in the parlor. They had all risen when Julia left the room, then somewhat awkwardly resuming their seats. Conversation floundered, as Newman did not resume his Easter week monologue.

Fred thought gloomily about his children, three-year-old Ulys still kept in long hair and girls' clothing by his wife Ida, conforming to genteel fashion, and their daughter Julia, who would turn nine in June, and was becoming increasingly fresh to her parents, and particularly to him. She was petted and spoiled by everyone else. Yet he could hardly ask his own parents, in their trouble, not to indulge his daughter.

Fred was taller than his father and more handsome at thirty-five, but the resemblance between them was strong. He had retired in December as a colonel from the Army. He was now working with Badeau on the *Memoirs* and increasingly had become acting head of the entire Grant family. But he felt his position to be ridiculous. The whole family was broke, all of them except Nellie ruined by Ferdinand Ward and James Fish. Nellie too had lost money in the collapse, with no real support from her unemployed, impecunious and unsympathetic husband—while Fred and Buck were drawing on the embarrassing benefits of their heiress brides. Fred felt that the world was laughing at them all. Before these recent dealings with Clemens, before the crash, when he was still in the Army, Fred and Ferdinand Ward had found time to talk to each other, seemingly on a confidential basis, as the swindler lured him into the web. Did he not deserve to be laughed at?

While his father had been devastated not just financially, but emotionally as well by the collapse and its aftermath, he had had something to fall back on, the greatness and splendor of his career, which led to his current work writing the book. The rest of them had no employment but as appendages to the general. Fred had been sounding out Clemens about going into the publishing firm, only to discover that his younger brother Jesse had made exactly the same approach, and that Clemens obviously was not keen on hiring either one of them, even though he had dangled the possibility of doing something along those lines before the general, when trying to lure him away from Century. Then Fred heard a rumor that Century had not gotten the book because they would not hire the other Grant son, his brother Buck, who unlike Fred had a civilian trade as a lawyer, but was not exactly in demand in that capacity. Jesse, on the other hand, had never graduated from law school. Ridiculous was a mild word for their situation.

If Father was about to die with the book unfinished, Fred would immediately and urgently need work, or at least money, to provide for his family. Maybe Clemens was right, there was enough done on the book that they could shape it after the funeral into enough of a money-maker to feed all the Grant family as well as all the publisher's door-to-door salesmen. One of the advantages of dealing with Webster, Clemens' firm, as opposed to Century, was that they were not charging costs back to Grant, but providing services including illustrations, maps, sales agents, editing and clerical assistance, free of charge. Still, Fred was worried, and jealous of any man who had the ordinary dignity of regular employment.

Nor, looking back, could he take solace from a distinguished military career. He'd been promoted fast on his father's name and reputation, but achieved nothing on his own. He graduated low in his West Point class, then served with Custer in Yellowstone and the Black Hills, but didn't get along with him. It was the providential birth of Julia in '76, and the leave he took as a result, which had saved his life by keeping him clear of Little Big Horn. But what was Providence sparing him to do?

The atmosphere was relieved by the entry of Nellie.

Nellie Sartoris had been in the study writing to her daughter Rosemary in England. It did not take her long, as Rosemary was only four years old, her youngest surviving child. Vivien would turn six in a week, and her present had already been dispatched. Nellie also wrote regularly to young Algy—with more spirit and unconstrained feeling than she communicated with his namesake, her scapegrace husband. She wrote to one of the children every day, and as she did, as had happened just now, her thoughts often went back to her first child, named Grant after her father, who had died in 1876 when less than a year old.

The closeness of the father-daughter bond, which was recognized by everyone and was the reason for Nellie's presence in New York, hardly made up for the absence of her own children. She had wanted to bring them over with her, but Algy—her husband—had objected, spitefully yet powerfully enough to prevail against her, and them. She was afraid the marriage was drifting into a war, one which she could not win, alone in a strange country. Now, back in her own land but in this strange city of New York, with her old family and without her children, Nellie felt bewildered, holding back tears. She wandered distractedly into the parlor, hoping to fall into the conversation there.

But after conventional greetings the talk sputtered and died until she said, "Well, Fred, let us see what Dr. Newman and General Badeau here, who is I think an old friend of Ely, say about him coming to visit this house. Would it not lift our father's spirits?"

"I hardly think we need involve ..." began Fred, while Badeau said, "Ely Parker?" to which Nellie responded, "Yes. Who has been turned away at the door, to my mortification, and apparently not for the first time."

"He is hardly the only one, Nellie," said Fred. "Father does not want the pity of people coming to see him in his current state. And when he can, he needs to work."

"I don't believe Father had anything to do with it," said Nellie. "Seeing Ely would do him good, would it not?"

"Well, we'd better not get too excited," said Fred. "What's done is done. I'm not going to quarrel with mother now. Or with you, I hope, Nellie."

"Who is Ely Parker?" asked Newman.

"Only the man who copied out the surrender terms at Appomattox," said Nellie, "and was at father's side in war and peace. And before the war, too, in Galena."

"A Seneca Indian," said Fred, "whom we have, as Nellie says, known for many years."

"Ah yes," said Newman, "I remember the name now. What is the difficulty?"

There was an awkward silence, until Badeau said: "Perhaps Mrs. Grant is not anxious to renew the acquaintance?"

"Perhaps not," Nellie conceded. "But I am."

"It may be as well not to introduce family conflict," Newman intoned.

Badeau threw in with the apparent majority view, saying: "Perhaps General Parker's time has passed."

But Nellie was not in the mood to be browbeaten, and said: "Dr. Newman: Surely it cannot be Christian to turn away my father's old friend in this manner, for either of their sakes? And even if he does not come back to see us, someone should tell him his good wishes have been welcomed, not merely spurned. As someone who can remember looking up to him at the age of five, I want to let him know that my respect has not diminished."

"I would hesitate to venture an opinion on so personal a matter," Newman replied, "and wish very strongly to do nothing to upset your mother and the family."

"Would you be prepared then," Nellie asked boldly, "to act as my chaperone and arrange for me to meet my old friend General Parker?"

"Is that quite wise, Mrs. Sartoris?" asked Badeau.

"The wisdom of this world is foolishness with God, is it not Dr. Newman?" asked Nellie.

"So says Saint Paul," he conceded, casting an inquiring glance at Fred, who shrugged and raised his hands in a gesture of surrender. "But why do you wish to do that?" continued Newman.

"We can hardly leave it as it is, when we have all but insulted a good old friend of Father's. At least I must seek him out and speak with him."

Newman smiled, and said, "Your feelings do you credit, Nellie. I will not argue with Saint Paul, or with anyone in your family, and am at your service."

CHAPTER FOUR

MARY AUDENRIED SPENT THE AFTERNOON with her best friend in New York, Mrs. Lucinda Hobbs, both of them wearing silk dresses and elaborate hats, engaged in investigation of the Ladies Mile on Broadway above Union Square. They resisted the temptation to go back to A.T. Stewart's vast and wonderful department store between Ninth and Tenth streets, a great temple of commerce with which both of them were familiar. Mary and Lucinda ventured uptown instead, starting at Tiffany's, then into Gorham's for silverware, to a hole-in-the-wall little milliner's shop, and Lord & Taylor at 20th Street for dresses and accessories. The theaters in the district were coming to life, some open for the matinee crowd, which sometimes halted their progress. But the ladies did not mind this enhanced opportunity for gossip and observation of the passing scene, while the stores provided their own versions of entertainment. Most of them also offered railway express postal delivery to Mary's home in Washington, D.C., where the retail offerings were fewer and less alluring. The prosperous widow of an Army colonel, with her own family money, Mary had left a difficult teen-age daughter behind in grandmaternal care while she took this short pleasure trip.

Lucinda's carriage and patient Irish coachman had followed the two eminently respectable ladies up Broadway and Fifth Avenue, and they took care not to stray too far west to the dubious Tenderloin district on Sixth. Still, Mary felt exhilarated by the undercurrent of muck, stink and dust in urban life, as well as the carriage which took her away from it, uptown to the Buckingham Hotel on Fifth. That was where she was staying, and where they took tea. Then Lucinda departed for home with her coachman, and Mary went to her suite in the Buckingham, where her maid Louisa was waiting. She took a leisurely bath. While many rooms even in good hotels did not have a private bathroom, Mary always made sure that hers did.

Louisa helped her to dress, which was a significant task since her garb included a whalebone corset and modest bustle beneath an understated, long-sleeved evening gown. This was not one of her new purchases, but a combination that Mary had reason to think was flattering to her forty-year-old figure. Louisa also did Mary's long brown hair, all as if her mistress were being taken out for the evening. The maid was of course aware that no respectable woman would venture forth by herself after dark, but did not inquire who might be coming to escort her mistress, or otherwise to see her. In fact, Louisa was acquainted with the visitor who was on his way, but that acquaintanceship would not be renewed tonight, for she was relieved from duty until the next day and dismissed to her own small hotel room upstairs among the gables, underneath the roof.

Mary had to wait a bit too long in the sitting room, desultorily inspecting *Harper's Weekly*. At last she heard a soft scratching knock at the door, to which she went up and said softly through, "Yes?"

The low grunt in reply might or might not have included the word "Cump," but Mary recognized the voice well enough. She opened the door, stepping back, and in came William Tecumseh Sherman.

Cump was a civilian now, having retired from the Army to St. Louis, where he often left his wife Ellen while traveling almost as much as ever, usually to engagements on the Eastern Seaboard. But Mary saw less of him these days than when he lived in Washington, and his embrace now was passionate, before he stepped away, saying, "You're all dressed and ready to go?"

"No," Mary smiled, "I wasn't planning on going anywhere." Cump's pockmarked face, when pressed against hers, had still been cool from the late March weather, and he smelled of brandy and cigars from wherever he'd been dining—and of himself, a familiar and not unpleasing scent to Mary. It was still early, and he would not have drunken much. In that regard at least, she was a wholesome influence. Nor had he gone to the theater tonight, his usual recreation, but not one where she could decently accompany him. He was not as thin as he used to be, but his eternal nervous energy drove him on, now coiled within as he looked out the window across 50th Street at the Roman Catholic cathedral, St. Patrick's. It was newly completed after what Mary gathered was many years of work. The prescience of the builders staking their claim so far north of the city center was proven by the buildings now grown up all around this Catholic pocket, which included a large orphan asylum on the next block uptown.

"Ellen or Tom might like the view," he said sourly.

Mary knew that Roman Catholicism, the religion of his wife and children, was a dangerous topic for Cump, especially since his favorite child Tom had deeply grieved him by becoming a Jesuit priest. Similarly out of bounds was the entire subject of Ellen, the wife from whom he seemed to absent himself as often as possible. Yet Cump showed no pride in his disloyalty. Mary was not bothered by discussions of his family life, which Cump often slipped into anyway— or of hers, as she sometimes sought his advice about the increasingly indecorous behavior of her rather spoiled daughter Florence. But she did not now want a cloud over their evening. Since no bright alternative conversational gambit immediately occurred, she said, "The bathroom is through there," indicating with a nod of the chin. He immediately went into it.

It was not long before he returned to find her sitting on the sofa, where he too settled down and took her hand, but to her slight annoyance put it down again and commenced talking about General Grant—how he, Sherman, was amazed and aghast at the great man's ruin. He seemed torn between contempt for the folly of the gull, and admiration for the courage of the dying writer, along with pain at the pain of his friend. Mary concentrated on keeping her patience and putting just enough life into her hand that Cump remembered to notice and commenced to kissing it. She knew her simple power to soothe the savage breast or beast, to tame Cump's normal fierceness. Later, he would fall asleep beside her, and might arise in the middle of the night to return to his own room on another floor of the hotel.

"Is it too bright for you here?" he asked, and Mary reached back to turn off the electric lamp. When their affair had started five years ago, six weeks after the end of her husband's lingering illness, it was lit by gaslight. She and Joe, her late husband, had once or twice spoken about the Shermans' marriage, and Joe's assumption that his boss sought extracurricular embraces. She had not dreamt of sharing them at that time, and had been taken aback at the general's absently tender yet rather businesslike approach so soon after her widowhood. But her shock did not prompt rejection. She could no more resist his advances than some Carolina town toward the end of the war, and was no more expectant that she would be the only party besieged by and surrendered to him. Yet, unlike the defeated rebels of South Carolina, she did not complain of his treatment all these years later.

The affair still suited them both, for the time being. Yet she had hopes, which presumed the death of his sickly wife, that she suspected he did not share. Five years ago, the gaslight had shown the red in her lover's hair, which by now had faded away almost completely to grey and white—and thinned a lot, too. And while he'd gained just a little weight over the past few years, he was considerably heavier than in his prime, or just after, when she first met him following the war, long before she had the remotest thought of their becoming lovers. Plenty of illumination now remained in the room for him to see her smile as she reached toward him, and they kissed mouth to mouth. Cump, urgent, improper, reached down to her foot, removing the shoe, then advanced his hand under her gown and petticoats to her left stocking, which he caressed with gentle vigor up past the French knickers to the garters attached to the corset—which he did not appear disconcerted to encounter.

Removing it and their other clothes was a production of continued, concentrated urgency on Cump's part, with which Mary happily cooperated, taking care to demonstrate no relief at being freed from the corset's constraint. One of the items of her post-bathing preparations to which she had personally attended was the careful insertion of a contraceptive sponge. A glance provided her the inopportune information that there seemed to be a few more moles and scars on Cump's fair skin since she had last beheld so much of it, in Washington, D.C. She expected that on a later occasion, perhaps tomorrow night, he would become more adventurous, seeking and dispensing delights to which she reckoned Ellen Sherman remained a stranger. But she was somewhat surprised when, in the bedroom yet still partially clothed, he moved to turn her over. She compromised by lying on her side facing away from him, lifting the skirts of her camisole to spoon him, and reaching back to guide his entry from that position. That permitted him some show of affection and perfunctory attention to her body beyond the vagina into which he thrust, and which was slick enough for both their purposes. His nervous energy reasserted itself as sexual power that belied his sixty-five years. She moved her hips quietly in familiar synchronization with his more vigorous movements, building to what she anticipated would be his all-consuming climax. While there might be stains on the

sheets, the dress, the camisole or other items of her clothing, there were limits to the demands that would be placed
upon her. Not for the first time, Mary concluded how fortunate it was that Louisa knew her place, which did not
involve asking indiscreet questions.

CHAPTER FIVE

LIKE BALDY SMITH, Ely Parker appreciated the elevated railway, which had a station on the Sixth Avenue line conveniently close to his apartment on 42nd Street. The world had changed so much during his lifetime, and with him now living and working in the very center of change, New York City, he felt he had no choice but to embrace it. Maybe that's what he'd always felt. He remembered his visit to Washington, D.C., 39 years ago, when, remarkably enough, he had personally negotiated with President Polk on behalf of the Tonawanda Seneca, who were trying to hold on to their reservation in western New York State. He was supposedly eighteen then, at the start of a dozen-year legal and political struggle for the Tonawanda which was ultimately successful—for the most part, although they lost some of the land. He might even have been younger, since all he knew was the year of his birth, 1828, but not the month and day.

The nation's capital had been a crude, poor, muddy country village in the 1840s, with pigs wandering the dirt streets. 'Root, hog, or die,' didn't Stephens report Lincoln as saying? Slaves were everywhere. Whereas this modern metropolis of Manhattan had millions of people of all races and classes, often dressed in bright colors, thronging and clamoring, briskly moving through the paved streets where every kind of abundant display was on offer for purchase. While Washington had grown up some by the time he came to live there after the Civil War, it was still being left far behind by New York.

In far upstate New York, though, the Tonawanda reservation hadn't changed much. It was as bucolic, and hard to make a living from, as ever. He'd hauled hay there all day as a young lad, for both Indian and white farmers, drinking big draughts of water from every well and sweating it all out, never needing to piss. Ely didn't suppose he'd ever live there again. He'd been glad enough to get away from it in the war, plunging back into the white man's world, in which he had often prospered, at least for a time.

When he was fifty, having burned through his youth and success, Minnie gave birth to their first, their only child, whom they named Maud. So now in his declining years he had a white wife and taken-for-white daughter to support. He had played his part under Grant getting the Plains tribes onto reservations and out of harm's way. But the two of them had really thought the Indians' proper course was to follow his, Ely Parker's, example, and become part of mainstream American life, like the immigrants. The Indians weren't immigrants, though, Ely thought to himself, smiling thinly as he walked from the elevated station past building sites and squatters' tents, goats and vegetable patches, from which came a babel of languages with which he was mostly unfamiliar—like the tongues of the Plains Indians. The poverty up here seemed considerably more benign than in the slums downtown, such as the notoriously squalid Five Points neighborhood, a few blocks south of the marble-fronted police headquarters on Mulberry Street. Up here, there were more of these poor squatters to the east and west, near the rivers. Many of them, like himself, had grown up in farm country, another world. Yet they found work in the city, most of these migrants, at least those who managed to keep their distance from alcohol, or more exotic drugs. They were meatpackers, garment workers, longshoremen and clerks, in machine shops and loading docks. Bleak enough trades some of them, mechanical, or the mere drudgery of a job, like his own, in municipal patronage.

Was this sugar-coating the desperation behind some of these camp sites, of people left to fend for themselves? One didn't like to dwell on the grimness of the mills and other places—such as the slaughterhouses of the West 30s—where many of them found work. He had come to believe that the Republican and Democratic parties were allied with business and the rich, each trying to exploit the immigrants in its own way. But then the other parties and agitators, the prophets of revolution, did the same thing.

Nor had the government done much, or was doing much now, for those trusting Indians who, like him, had come to Washington in suit and tie, often photographed like that in rows of respectability. Grant's peace policy was over before his administration, before Little Big Horn, and now the Indians, like the blacks, were left with broken promises. Ely remembered how Lee at Appomattox at first drew back, seeming to mistake the dark-skinned Union staff officer for a Negro, then acknowledged him as a "real American," meaning an Indian, to which Ely had replied, "We are all Americans" now. Even then, Ely had been lightning quick to follow Grant's new policy of peace.

He had come to value more the old Seneca culture, and the cultures of the other Indians, and no longer pretended to know that they'd be better off if they gave it all up—for what? For this world of billboards and barkers, a bewildering maze of overhead wires, and the constant hustle for money? Even uptown now, he could look up and see a small jungle of wires, although they were supposedly going to bury them here. They had laid a telegraph cable on the bottom of the Atlantic Ocean, all the way to England. Out on the Western plains, deserts and mountains, a few Apache under Geronimo still resisted; but the Lakota Sioux chief Sitting Bull, whose men killed Custer nine years ago, had now signed a contract for $50 a week to join Buffalo Bill Cody's Wild West Show.

Late middle age meant realizing what you don't know, along with what matters to you. All Indians were torn between two worlds. It was his ability to speak English that had made him a teen-age diplomat, and helped him and others save the Tonawanda reservation, with which he'd never lost touch. But had he misled his brother Indians, leading them into the white world, where now even he was just tenuously hanging on? Had he, had they, done it for a mess of pottage? Was he as guilty as Custer and Sheridan and others of his fellow U.S. Army officers? Guilty or innocent as Grant?

Not that the immigrants were all better off, or the more virtuous for being poor. The draft-rioters against whom Inspector Tom Thorne had fought were murderous Irishmen. But then most of the policemen who fought with him were Irish, too, as was their superintendent, John Kennedy, whom the rioters beat up badly and left for dead. Kennedy had been brought to the Mulberry Street headquarters, which officers fought vigorously to defend, while other police stations were burned along with churches and the colored orphan asylum. The mobs killed dozens of Negroes, but they killed Irish policemen too, like Colonel Henry O'Brien.

In the years before the riots, the Irish Dead Rabbits gang of thugs was paying obeisance to the mayor of New York, Fernando Wood, an Anglo-German Protestant of colonial stock, who was a crooked shipping merchant. Wood's municipal police force engaged in pitched battles with the state-run metropolitan force, while letting the gangs run vice. And the city's merchants had been brazenly engaged in the illegal African slave trade, right up to the Civil War. In New York now, the poor still lived cheek by jowl with the rich, but there was a growing chasm between them—which was maybe not such a bad thing, Ely reckoned, if it avoided Wood's kind of closeness. "Fernandy" Wood, as they called him, had gone on to serve after the war as a Democratic congressman fighting Reconstruction. Tammany, meanwhile, had extended its Gilded Age reach up to Albany and down to Washington.

Ely shook his head, away from the city's corruption and worse. He thought of his Red Jacket medal, given to that somewhat questionable Indian by President George Washington, and depicting the two of them. It was now owned by Ely is his capacity as a so-called grand sachem of the Iroquois Confederacy. Fernando Wood had had the same title; he was a grand sachem of Tammany Hall. But the Red Jacket medal was real, and it mattered to Ely. So did his copy of the Appomattox surrender, in Grant's own handwriting with Ely's addendums, dictated by the general. He had the two original yellow sheets of Grant's writing, framed on white backing paper, on which the document was authenticated and signed by him and Grant.

Red Jacket was his uncle and Handsome Lake his grandfather, but Ely's last name was neither Seneca nor American, being adopted by his Indian family from a captured British soldier, Gaylord Parker, whom they had befriended in the Revolutionary War. Last fall, in October 1884, Red Jacket's bones were reinterred in Buffalo, and Ely had spoken there in a service organized by the city historical society. He had taken to writing letters about the history of his people, hoping to put some of it on the record. But Ely had already told Minnie she could sell the Red Jacket medal, if need be, after his death, and the surrender document too, from Appomattox. They and a few other historical markers amounted to his savings account, all of which Minnie probably would need to sell because he had declined to participate in the widespread corruption practiced in the Police Department, and by its Tammany Hall masters. And, he pondered gloomily, because he'd lived high in Connecticut and gone broke on Wall Street, like a lot of other damn fools and onetime soldiers in the 1870s—not so far from what Grant had done now a decade later.

Ely wasn't as broke as Grant, but his golden touch was all gone. He'd already sold, to a *Harper's Weekly* artist, a rough sketch he had done at Appomattox setting out where the participants at the surrender were placed in the room. While his body was beginning to fail, he would have to work as long as it held out, wearing a stiff collar in wearisome routine. Nor did he have the heart to restrain the spending habits of Minnie quite down to the level of their current income. She had, after all, married and lived with him in his prosperity.

Ely's old friend Frank Herron had also had to accustom himself to earning his bread in this metropolis, since Louisiana became inhospitable after the collapse of Reconstruction. They both aspired now to hold on to their current position in society, which amounted to a sort of shabby-genteel state of clinging to the middle class. Herron had acquired a wife and stepchildren down South, and even though he was younger than Ely, like him felt too old and uninspired to seek his fortune again out West. Not that New York was necessarily an easier place to make a living.

For one thing, you had to keep up here. The modern word meant Ely had to ride in elevators and learn how to use a typewriter, and had one of those new telephones in his Mulberry Street office. This morning, to his astonishment, Nellie Grant—Sartoris, rather—had called him up on the new machine, and asked him to meet her and some Dr. Newman or other—a clergyman, he gathered—in Central Park. Walking up to the park now from the east, the heavyset Ely paused at the 65th Street entrance to catch his breath and consult a pocket watch. He felt well, no serious twinge from the rheumatic arm or dodgy back. New York was a good place to walk in, a healthy place, you might argue, if he could find the time to take the exercise, especially in one of its less noisome neighborhoods, like this. Across

Fifth Avenue was the white marble, mansard-roofed Astor House. Other mansions were under construction in the vicinity, around the corner from Grant's handsome row house. The street lighting in this newly prosperous area was electric powered, whereas much of the city was still lit by gas lamps. Reporters clustered on 66th Street across from the Grant house, which Ely glanced at from Fifth Avenue, having avoided walking by. The shacks of the poor that you used to see scattered around these northern neighborhoods were gone now, at least on the east side.

The park itself seemed to him a curious feature of the modern age, a massive construction and engineering project that produced the opposite of what such things normally came up with. Yet it was not an isolated achievement, for there was now a similar Prospect Park in Brooklyn, a few miles south of a more conventional but revolutionary engineering achievement of the 1880s, the new age cathedral of Brooklyn Bridge. Prospect Park was designed by Frederick Olmsted and Calvert Vaux, who had also done this Central Park in Manhattan, where picnickers, baseball players and families took the air at weekends. Ely breathed in its relatively fresh air now, strolling past some wooden swings, a few of which were in use, and a lawn where two couples played croquet. He noticed the absence of the fumes and smells which he normally took for granted in New York, the product of incinerators, solvents, sewage. (But even here there was no escaping the whiff of horse excrement.) The noise of the city fell away, replaced by children's laughter, and a sudden inhuman call from the Menagerie.

The park proved that not all the actions of Tammany Hall pols and the Gilded Age rich were turning out barren for the common people. Still, there was a bitter reality in how it had come about. Poor people had been cleared away from the area where the park now was by none other than Fernandy Wood, who took particular pleasure in destroying the mysteriously named Seneca Village, where blacks and

Irish had lived in surprising harmony. As Grant might put it, money could get things done. Should that buy some forgiveness, maybe even for Wood? And could it do the same for the slave-owning, Indian-killing founders of America? Ely had grown to doubt it. But it was complicated, and rich men were often better company than preachers, and he sang to himself some half-remembered lines from a Gilbert and Sullivan show that he and Minnie had seen a few years ago at the Fifth Avenue Theatre: "A paradox, a paradox, a most ingenious paradox, ha ha ha ha ha ha ha ha, a paradox."

In plenty of time, Ely took a winding trail going up to the Concert Ground, the designated meeting place, basking in the peaceful greenery, although he saw tennis courts had sprung up to cater to the new craze. He was not sure he would recognize Nellie now, and had never met her companion, but was confident enough they would know him. No matter his suit and tie, Ely's Indian features were enough to mark him almost anywhere.

Nellie Sartoris and the Rev. John Newman, though, while already at the Concert Ground, were not looking in Ely's direction. They gazed westward, where the grand new Dakota apartment building loomed in castle-like isolation at the edge of the park, with the Museum of Natural History also visible some blocks to its north. Newman stood by a bench where Nellie was sitting, as she declaimed, "Ely was always an exotic, not a savage but a grand old Indian, although that was a quarter of a century ago and of course he's really younger than father."

Newman grunted noncommittally. While he had granted Nellie's request to play chaperone for today, he was uncomfortable that she had asked him not to tell Julia about it. Julia had previously confided to him some of her own concerns about her only daughter's troubled marriage, and apparent willingness to wander unescorted in New York. Grant, too, he knew, was worried about Nellie's marriage and life in England so far away, but had been less concerned about her flouting the ladies' calling-card conventions of New York.

"In England, you know," Nellie was continuing, "except for people like Pitt the Younger, you have to grow old before you gain power. 'He polished up the handle so carefully that now he is the ruler of the Queen's Navy.' " Since Newman looked more baffled than usual, she explained, "Gilbert and Sullivan, you know," before proceeding: "Whereas Father was the youngest president ever elected, and Ely was not just younger than he and in his Cabinet, or almost in it, but a Red Indian to boot, which you would never see anything like in England, despite Queen Victoria's partiality for the Empire."

"An admirable woman," said Newman.

"Oh I quite agree," said Nellie, "and I'm not being the least bit ironical. For all my English flippancy, I am also like the English—or like my mother for that matter—in having no small regard for proper and right conduct. The trick, I suppose, is to determine what that is."

Newman had turned his head to see a well-dressed American Indian walking up toward them, and coughed meaningfully. Nellie, oblivious, was chattering on, but he interrupted and addressed the newcomer as he came up. "Is this Colonel, or should I say General Parker now?"

And Ely, arriving, replied, "Is this Doctor, or the Reverend, Newman?"

Avoiding the issue of military rank, Nellie turned to him smiling and held out her hands, while responding with what seemed to be continued prattle, in a heightened pace and key, "Ely, it's so good to see you after all these years, even if you were unchivalrously ignoring the lady, although doesn't Mark Twain equate the Confederates with the chivalry, so maybe that was why the English supported the South in the war, except for people like the cotton mill workers, but I suppose the chivalry doesn't think they really count. And this is indeed Doctor the Reverend John Newman, who is a

Methodist clergyman known to my parents, and not to be confused with the Englishman of the same name who is a cardinal of the Roman Catholic Church, although Mama"—she stressed the last syllable in the English fashion—"says our Dr. Newman may become a bishop, and almost did a few years ago, which I didn't even know Methodists had—bishops, I mean—and I don't think they have mitres or scepters and those long hats, whereas Roman Catholics do, I think, not that I suppose they travel that way, but Cardinal Newman isn't one—a bishop, that is, or is not."

Newman managed a smile and said, "It is the Methodist Episcopal Church."

"Quite," said Ely, smiling too and adding, "Good to see you, Nellie." Now that he had a good look at her face, he could see it was indeed the one he had known from years ago, all grown up. She had stood to greet him and he saw a dark, compact, lively and attractive woman, who he calculated would be about twenty-nine years old. Behind all the banter she looked at him intently.

As the three of them strolled in the park, Nellie kept up her nervous talking, pointing out a carpet of wildflowers, violets and crocuses mostly, in one spot and how she wouldn't have noticed them before she had children and became their teacher. Then she half excused and half apologized for her mother's conduct to Ely, while stating her own mortification and apology, and appealing to him: "My mother is not a bad woman," she said, gesturing to prevent interruption from either man, "although she has treated you badly. And often my father is not well enough to receive visitors. I mean, her excuse was not a complete fabrication."

"I never supposed so," said Ely. "I have often admired your parents' marriage. They were—are—in natural sympathy with each other. There is an ease between them that must be comforting."

"There is," said Nellie. "But I think Father would gain from seeing a good old friend like you."

Ely again assured her that no apology was needed, and Newman chimed in defending Julia while extending general benevolence. The pause that followed was naturally filled by discussion of Grant's health, which was in steep decline this late March. It was still chilly in New York out of the sunshine, Nellie lamented, and the fires in their house failed to warm the general sufficiently, or blunt his increasingly alarming fits of coughing. Newman trailed behind, still in earshot, letting her talk to Ely.

"We had been going out, Father and I, him wrapped up in blankets, in Senator Chaffee's carriage. He has a four-in-hand, and took us on rides around this park. No longer," she shook her head. "Father cannot manage it now. I thank God for the writing, for this book he is writing, although he told me it was wearing him out and maybe it has." She stopped, turning to Ely as Newman caught up, and saying, "I sometimes think of how hard his life has been, for all its grandeur since the war. Wasn't it hard too before then, back in Galena, when he, when we, met you?"

"One might think so," said Ely, "but I don't think that was your father's view, then or later. He thought he was doing then what most of us do, putting food on the table, and one foot in front of the other." A rare smile crossed the Indian's face as he reminisced. "I remember him reading Dickens aloud to all four children, although you and Jesse were hardly old enough to understand it. And while I'm sure things, circumstances, now are difficult, writing always came easy for him."

She said, "He used to read to mother, too. Sometimes poetry, Robert Burns. Writing the book gives him, I think and hope, more reason to live."

"Can he live long?" Ely asked, perhaps too bluntly, he thought, as Nellie caught her breath.

"I pray so," she said, her eyes straying to Newman with

the religious reference, and added, "I fear Dr. Newman does not think Father sufficiently a praying man." Ely grunted.

Newman said, "General Grant has participated in family prayers, and when well enough he often used to attend my church. But it's true that I would be glad of a more explicit affirmation of his faith, as would your mother."

"Yes, I do not argue with you," said Nellie, and resumed strolling along.

She thought suddenly of her husband Algy, along with his opera singer mother and actress-writer aunt, the whole amusingly sophisticated family whose irreligion had at first shocked her. But then, her father's daughter, she had found it easy enough to do without God, especially after her son died, when religion provided insufficient comfort. How could God let that happen? She imagined her father had found little comfort there after battle. Yet the surviving children must be taught the conventional pieties.

When her parents came to stay in '77, after leaving the White House, Algy was cautious and clever enough to pay them court, and promise her better days. He barely kept it up through their stay. Soon enough Algy, still handsome with his deep-set eyes, forceful sweeping moustaches and hair parted in the middle, unrestrained by religious or apparently any other scruple, had found it easy to stray into drunkenness and the arms of other women. As the unapologetic pattern continued, she found it less easy to welcome him back into the marriage bed. The dark, powerful, hairy face that once thrilled her had turned brutal, at least when turned her way, though unwilling to meet her eye. Nellie no longer felt inclined to laugh at a conventional cleric like Newman, whose loving wife Angeline was a close friend of her mother's. She shivered in the weak March sunlight, shaking off the memory of her husband's evaporated charms and again stopped, turning in the park pathway to face the stolid Indian beside her.

"Ely, you must come back," she said, "and Father must see you." Ely just stared at her.

Newman, standing behind them, suddenly interrupted. "Do you know General Sherman, Colonel Parker? I understand he has recently arrived on a visit to this city. Perhaps that might provide an occasion for a reunion between you and General Grant."

"I know General Sherman," Ely replied, "and would be glad to see him again."

"Then we must arrange it," said Nellie, smiling and then pointing, "Ah, look, the robins are back. It's good to see them, although I'm afraid I've come to favor our little English robins over your bigger red-breasts here. But I love the big American flowers, and miss the real summers."

"We have real winters in New York, too," said Ely. "Not your milk-and-water English weather."

CHAPTER SIX

THE GENERAL HAD TAKEN A TURN FOR THE WORSE on the twenty-fifth of March. The next day he rallied somewhat, enough to give testimony in the trial of James Fish, the sinister, older banker ally of Ferdinand Ward.

The judge had spared Grant from going to the courtroom, instead holding the proceedings at the family home on 66th Street. Fish's lawyer had suggested a postponement in light of Grant's state of health, but Clarence Seward responded that the general wanted to testify. So he did, seeking to clear his name, while admitting the likelihood that he had signed a letter presented by Ward without reading (or writing) it. He generally tried not to think about his defrauders, especially Ward, who had deceived him and everyone so completely and disastrously.

In recalling these events for the court, Grant took care not to let himself be stirred up into unproductive rage. He should have known to distrust a man, he thought wryly, who was known as The Young Napoleon of Finance (or of Wall Street), given that he'd never had any time for his own contemporary, the Emperor Louis Napoleon—or much in the way of sympathy for that emperor's uncle, the original Napoleon of France, despite sharing the latter's proficiency in mathematics and artillery. The general's testimony and that of others at Fish's trial, including Ward's, did clear the Grants of any role in the fraud, other than ingenuous folly. Fish and Ward were blaming each other for the disaster. To Grant it appeared that the younger man, who had not yet come to trial, was the worse villain.

Julia, while relieved that the testimony must make others believe in her husband's innocence, which she of course had never doubted, wondered if the strain of the deposition had been too much for him. She thought it might have reminded him of his testimony in Washington nine years ago, in defense of his aide Orville Babcock, as he began that gloomy last year in the White House. Yet those months, unlike this latter time, had not seemed so bleak to her.

In the days since Grant had testified against Fish, he had coughed harshly through the nights, otherwise drifting through the time, less and less able to write, sometimes playing solitaire, but ever weaker. When he had been thought just well enough to take a carriage ride in the park with Julia and Nellie, he was much fatigued by it, yet woke coughing worse than ever in the night, painfully retching and gasping for breath, which prompted Shrady to inject him with brandy. Because he tended to choke more lying down, on the 29th the doctors decided he should no longer go to bed. Now he would spend most of his time in the same two leather armchairs, turned toward each other so he could spread out his short legs, except when Harrison or the new male nurse, the bewhiskered Henry McSweeny, helped him use the bathroom. The two main doctors were Shrady —sharp-faced with his Van Dyke beard—and the taller, stouter, white-bearded Douglas, with strain visible around his eyes, who had served with the general in the Civil War.

On March 30, Grant suffered a ghastly painful choking fit, crying out, "I can't stand it. I must die. I must go"— which was a shocking break from his normal phlegmatic endurance to the few people who heard it. Julia was not among them. He would not speak so in front of her or the rest of the family, would have managed to restrain himself —but she was well aware of the bleak progress of events. One side issue disturbed both of them, although it was something few others probably thought of, and no one discussed. They had often been separated before and during the war. But now, for the first time in their marriage, she could not share his bed when they were in the same house.

Shrady and Douglas, Fred hinted to her, thought the end was near on the Tuesday of Holy Week, the 31st of March. Julia could not believe it, but through that night she sat by him, sometimes weeping. Fred ordered the children —his own two and Jesse's toddler Nellie, who were all liv- ing in the house—to be barred from Grant's second-floor sick room. (It caused occasional confusion that all three of these young children—Julia, Ulysses and Nellie—were named after previous generations of the family, three of which were now sharing quarters.)

Julia went to lie down briefly on the afternoon of the 31st, leaving Fred and Elizabeth, Jesse's wife, in attendance at the sick bed. Fred could not help feeling a mixture of titil- lation, guilt and dread as he admitted to himself the attraction he felt to his sister-in-law. She was younger, liveli- er and even prettier than his own wife Ida, with whom his relations were less free and easy than they had been. Ida had had a hard time with the pregnancy and birth of her younger child, and this continued to affect her health and spirits. Fred felt a spasm of self-contempt, which he knew was unhelpful in this circumstance. He wondered if his in- ability to escape destructive thoughts might be some intimation of incipient lunacy.

Pacing behind Elizabeth, who sat at Grant's side, Fred tried to calm himself down without sinking deep into gloom. He felt paralyzed by indecision, the acting head of the family who did not know how to act—not that there was anything to be done to forestall the event if his father's time had really come. He remembered how as a youth, rid- ing when not yet thirteen with the army in Mississippi, in the Vicksbug campaign, being sickened at the sight of dead men. He and Captain Cadle had been the first ones into Jackson, Mississippi, after Joe Johnston's rebel army pulled out. Then, in the siege of Vicksburg, sleeping in the general's tent, suffering from dysentery and toothache. It seemed then life was full of adventures, as he was swept along through the next few years in the warmth of the country's embrace, its love affair with his father. Nothing so simple again.

God knows he had tried. At West Point, he thought he was following his father's slogan, "Let Us Have Peace," by befriending the southerners, but instead seemed to have gotten tarred by association with a scandal, the constant harassment of the academy's first Negro cadet, James Webster Smith—although Fred had played no direct part in this. Smith never did graduate, Fred recalled, and then died young, and he now felt vaguely ashamed of not having stood up for him. Even after his father lectured him about it, telling him his ideas were out of date, that of course West Point must have Negro cadets, all Fred had done was avoid Smith and controversy. He had not harassed him, but never tried to like him, either. His father had chosen the better path, Fred knew now, and it was President Grant who made sure West Point admitted other Negroes, who did graduate.

After that Fred had served under the ever flamboyant George Armstrong Custer, who had been a great Northern warrior in the Civil War, yet one who shared the Southern West Point feelings against Negroes. So did Sherman, for that matter, as Fred discovered serving on his staff. Trying to be loyal to his father, he also discovered that Sherman, Custer and Sheridan (another of Fred's staff jobs) all opposed the president's Indian peace policy—although Sheridan, unlike the other two—supported Grant on Reconstruction. Sherman had gone off in a huff to St. Louis in 1874 to run the Army from there, but then had come back two years later when scandal had removed his *bête noir*, General Belknap, from the War Department—in what was another hour of need for Grant (and a scandal stirred up by Custer). Fred knew his father continued to honor and love Sherman. Like Lincoln, he was always portrayed in the

Memoirs in a positive light. While the endlessly talkative and indiscreet Sherman did not always seem to reciprocate, Fred knew that at bottom level he believed in Grant almost as a substitute for religious faith.

While Grant had remained close to Sherman and Sheridan, he despised Custer as a long-haired showman and glamorizer of war, who had led his men to their deaths for no good reason. Fred couldn't either agree or disagree. Custer's Civil War cavalry charges had been too dramatic and successful, praised not just by the newspapers but by hard-nosed commanders and military analysts like Sheridan. Apart from anything else, Custer had been extraordinarily courageous, but had also played a major role in crucial Union victories on the most important front of the Civil War, from Gettysburg to Appomattox. Until his last, disastrous blunder in the Dakota Territory, his record had been nothing like the sentimentalized image of doomed cavalrymen represented in some Civil War lore, or as in Tennyson's poem, *The Charge of the Light Brigade*.

But Fred had not agreed with Custer's Indian policies when they were in the Black Hills together, and had felt confident enough to say so. Possibly in reaction to that, Custer accused him of drunkenness. Nor was the charge baseless, adding a further burden of shame, even though in this behavior Fred was definitely following in his father's footsteps—at least that's what the gossip said. Fred's opinion about that, about his father's relation to alcohol, was more complicated. Then Custer had exposed Grant administration corruption—Belknap's—in Washington. Then he had gone off on his charge into glory or folly with the Seventh Cavalry, with the band playing the Irish air "Garry Owen"—but without Fred Grant—on into Little Big Horn. How was Fred to make any sense of Custer's history or of his own, the story of his life? How could he agree with his father about Custer, who had attended Fred and Ida's wedding in Chicago in '74? Now Fred's father trusted him, as did his mother and the rest of the family, but he felt himself inept and inadequate, hardly able to keep going through the motions of what they all expected.

Sometime before five o'clock in the morning on the first of April, Nellie had a note sent to Newman asking him to come to the house. She brought Fred a cup of coffee and a smile to keep his courage up, which she had often done before. Their new-old joke was that Nellie kept urging Fred to get some sleep while also bringing him coffee which would wake him up, but now they didn't think much of sleep or their need for it, except for the children's. Nellie took the nurse's job of washing her father's beard. The water became somewhat discolored from what he had coughed up, and she had washed away.

Newman soon arrived, for once not commenting to the reporters still hovering in the street, or to the three wire service "bulletin boys" whom Fred had been persuaded to let park themselves inside, in the hallway. Nellie thanked him as he walked in, and he smiled tightly and replied, "It is not a time for sleeping." Newman's career, like so many others, had flourished with Grant's patronage, but did not originate with it. A Methodist pastor and writer, his denomination sent him to New Orleans in 1864, during the war and the federal occupation, to tend to the freed slaves and reorganize Methodism in three Southern states. His five-year mission had been enormously successful. Moving to Washington in 1869, the same year the Grant administration began, Newman became a friend of the first family, serving as pastor of the Metropolitan Memorial Methodist Church they attended. Newman also became chaplain of the Senate, and was appointed by Grant as inspector of U.S consulates in Asia. Now, he too lived in New York, where the Grants had attended his fashionable church.

Newman stayed with Grant most of the day. The general was easy in his company, seemingly sympathetic to his religious notions, even saying "Amen" to his prayers. But

Newman knew perfectly well that Grant was not much of a praying man, and at least in part was indulging his pastor for the sake of the dearest person in his life, his wife Julia. Sometimes Newman had pressed the general on spiritual matters, and was met with what he regarded as evasive responses. Grant had told Newman he'd enjoyed the novel *Ben-Hur*, which had a Christian theme, noting that its author, Lew Wallace, had served under him early in the war as a subordinate general. Newman knew Grant had never been baptized, and Julia had told him she wanted it done. The question, though, was whether *he* wanted it. Newman did not raise the matter that day.

In the afternoon, Nellie brought in little Julia to the sick room, despite Fred's prior instruction, and smiled sweetly on the way in at her eldest brother, who was still on duty there. The little girl walked up to her grandfather and stood gravely by his two chairs, on which he was propped up with pillows and swathed in blankets. He looked kindly at her, and was able to raise his thin arm out of the blankets to put it around her shoulder. Young Julia did not flinch, but leaned into the embrace against him, resting there. Fred was benignly impassive. Later, she came back in with her younger brother Ulys and their cousin Nellie for a brief visit —cut short when Grant began to cough, grimacing in pain.

The elder Julia took her namesake and the other two youngsters back to the nursery, where Nellie, Ida and Elizabeth were taking turns reassuring and comforting them and each other—although Nellie spent more time than her sisters-in-law in the sick room with her father. While the world thought Nellie was pleasing enough to look at, with her dark face and deep-set eyes, a lively, full mouth and snub nose, she had sometimes felt intimidated by Ida's tall, chiseled beauty, as she had been by too many society ladies in England. She still felt rounder, softer, plainer than both these sisters-in-law, Ida and Elizabeth, but in this house they all got along, and Nellie's self-consciousness had fallen away.

She still sometimes wondered if she were as good a wife as them, and felt sure she fell short of her mother's standard in that regard. But she blamed Algy more for the failings of their marriage, even though she knew it was unfair to compare him to her father. She had finally come to realize how much she had hurt her parents, especially Father, when she went away across the ocean. Her children's existence meant she could not regret her marriage, but she did repent the thoughtless folly of her youth.

The immediate health concern for the general was twofold: That he would choke to death on his own phlegm, pus and blood—all of which together had a tendency to stick and harden if not constantly removed—or come to the same end from an opposite cause and die of a hemorrhage, with a last fatal gush from his mouth. All pretense of work had ceased. The fate of the unfinished book, and whether in its current state it could restore the ruined family fortunes, were rational fears, but now were overtaken by events. Most of those observing were convinced that Grant's death was imminent, and so concentrated on his immediate physical and spiritual concerns, or, when they did think about his life and legacy, took a grander view than that of word counts and publishing contracts.

Grant had sometimes turned down injections of morphine to keep his head clear for writing, but he wasn't working anymore and he needed the drug to sleep. So now he let them give it to him, along with the cocaine mixed in water which was used to swab the inside of his mouth and throat, gently applied on the cancer sores to dull the pain. He didn't much like the effect of that drug mixture, different from the old familiar dangers of alcohol. His mind seemed drifting beyond his control who knew where. Around the bedside, he could be heard muttering about the Battle of Shiloh. Julia talked to Newman again about baptism, but the minister told her he could only baptize an adult who had consented to the procedure.

Grant, struggling back into consciousness, could see Julia beside him, and realized it must be very late at night, or early morning, then saw Fred and Nellie, Douglas, Shrady, Newman, and others coming in and out, mostly one by one. When Julia asked, "Do you know me, darling?" he was able to murmur in response, "Certainly I do, and I bless you with all my heart." The valet, Harrison Terrell, like Julia, stayed mostly at the bedside. He paid close attention to what the doctors said on matters such as diet and pain management, and followed their instructions.

The two medical men went off to confer, and then returned. Grant was now able to detect Dr. Douglas seeming to defer to the younger—albeit balding—Dr. Shrady, who was a fairly recent addition to the medical team. He vaguely realized some crisis must be at hand. The drugs had quieted his coughing some, but still left him gasping for breath at times, breathing being something he couldn't just quietly give up. But it looked like he'd never finish the book, and there did not see much point in living without that work.

Newman was talking to him about religion—Julia must have asked him to. Grant agreed to whatever Newman seemed to be proposing, reasoning it couldn't do any harm, might be beneficial and would please his family. *Who knows, Newman might even be right, which wouldn't necessarily make him easier to take.* Grant's life had been, and remained, concerned with more practical, immediate matters. But then his father, like Lincoln's, had never thought him practical enough. When Newman mentioned baptism, Grant responded, "I thank you, Doctor. I intend to take that step myself." Then he felt a spray of water, saw a silver bowl in the preachers' hands and blurted out, "What have you done?" even as he realized that he had heard Newman say, "I baptize thee Ulysses Simpson Grant, in the name of the Father and the Son and the Holy Ghost."

"I have baptized you, General," the minister confirmed, in reply to Grant's question.

"You surprised me," said the general, who was also amused at the absence of his first given name, Hiram, in Newman's words. This baptism had confirmed an ancient—well, it dated from 1839—error in nomenclature committed by an Ohio congressman and confirmed by the inertia of West Point bureaucracy. Grant had accepted the change because he had always gone by Ulysses and had then preferred the initials U.S.G. to H.U.G. "I am obliged to you," he added now, seeming to tacitly acknowledge that he had probably consented to the procedure. Baptism was a ceremony which he and his parents had neglected to have performed in the preceding sixty-three years. His thin smile turned into another failed attempt at coughing.

While some people in the room were made a bit queasy by these proceedings, Julia was relieved that Ulys had consented to be baptized and happy enough at its accomplishment. But she was more terrified at the prospect it forebode of his impending death. She saw Shrady and Douglas conferring intently again beyond the doorway, and then Shrady went off. She gave Douglas an inquiring look, and he came over, bent down and whispered in her ear, "He needs an injection of brandy, as a sort of soothing stimulant." In other words, Julia thought, they are afraid he will choke to death as he loses the fight for breath. Shrady came back and had Harrison roll up Ulys' sleeve.

Grant observed these preparations dispassionately. The procedure might be successful, in which case he was willing enough to be stimulated back into life and work, to postpone the inevitable end. Curious that eating was now not just painful but dangerous, since it brought on choking. His throat muscles were impaired. And how odd that alcohol should be used in this way. For all the gossip about his drinking, it hadn't been a problem for the last twenty years, when he had been constantly in company with Julia. It was not that she rode herd on him, told him what not to do, but that he'd only wanted to escape into drink when Army life was keeping them apart, robbing him of the essential comforts of wife and children. He hadn't found it difficult to give up now, when drinking spirits was obviously out of the question because it would inflame the cancer in the back of his mouth and throat. Even swallowing water was quite painful enough. So was gulping for air. Harder than giving up alcohol, he had hated doing without cigars, the comfort of gloomy camps and glittering dinners, of work and of rest. He missed still the hit of tobacco fumes at the back of his throat, when he had half accidentally (yet not uncommonly) inhaled. Of course he realized that smoking had very likely contributed to the cancer. Betrayed by a friend.

Grant continued to struggle for breath until Shrady injected him with brandy for the second time. By now Newman, who had been saying the Lord's Prayer, had found out what was in the syringe, the minister's eyes growing round at the seemingly rather scandalous news—but he managed to hold his tongue. Grant immediately began to cough. Julia's response moved rapidly from relief to alarm as the agonizing coughing fit built. She moved behind him as he sat up, her arm around his grown-thin body, as he strained, hacked, then suddenly vomited profusely into the large tin bowl held by Harrison. He vomited so much blood and dark, foul-smelling, solid-looking tissue that even Julia quailed for a moment, drawing back, and the doctors looked alarmed, and she suddenly realized that the Angel of Death was right here, ready to take him away, and she carefully embraced him again, gently burying her weeping face in the back of his fragile, bony shoulder and neck.

But he didn't die, just drew back, dull-eyed, leaning against her embrace. Shrady injected digitalis to stabilize the heart. Julia continued to hold him as Harrison cleaned his mouth with the suction device, and then McSweeny applied a cocaine-and-water soaked sponge.

CHAPTER SEVEN

IT WASN'T THE BAD DREAM, not the worst of them, not the one about Prairie Grove. Nor was it Pea Ridge, where Herron had been wounded while striking heroic poses on a horse. The horse came out worse, killed by a cannon shot, while he suffered only a broken ankle, so was able to lead his soldiers for another hour of combat before being captured. No, this dream was about Wilson's Creek, the first real battle for him or anyone in the West. That one was quite bad enough, a Union defeat with the regiment taking heavy casualties. The losses were heavy at all three battles—blood, terror, death and maiming, each worse than the one before, and his responsibility for it larger. Before the war, he'd gone west to follow his brothers in the banking business, and joined the militia for fun. He was barely out of boyhood, it seemed now, when the war started, and he had found new, supposedly heroic roles to play, with dazzling success.

He shuddered to remember now that something of Pea Ridge was in the dream, the leaves catching fire around his wounded men, one Iowa farm-boy named Hawkins killed grotesquely by an exploding ammunition belt. But the dream hadn't been the worst one. Still, Adelaide was lovingly holding his shaking body as he came awake in a cold sweat, until he relaxed, swallowing tears, into the calmness of pleasant, semi-developed West 99th Street. Very used to this by now, she smiled tenderly and after a while got up into the early morning. He breathed deeply, grateful for his wife. He hoped he had not woken Augusta or the boy.

Yes, Pea Ridge was in the dream. Along with dead men, many of them boys, really, most at any rate younger than Colonel Herron, who had just turned twenty-five. Some of them had time to scream at their life blood rushing away. Boys dead these twenty-three years and so denied the hum-drum life of the middle-aged.

Eugene Carr was in the dream, his Fourth Division commander. He lived on still. Carr's division took most of the casualties in that battle. Those still alive were exhausted, heavily outnumbered, their position increasingly desperate, slowly falling back through hour after hour of Confederate attacks. Carr was only a senior colonel then who, like Her-ron himself, was wounded in the battle, at the Elkhorn Tavern part of it, to be precise, and promoted afterward to brigadier. Now Carr was still in the Army, a colonel again and an Indian fighter whom the newspapers called "the black-bearded Cossack." Herron as a young volunteer had modeled himself after the hard-driving, hard-bitten West Pointer. Now, despite the dullness of office work in New York that ate up his days, he felt no envy for Carr's life spent relentlessly pursuing the last Indian resistance. Not that there was much left. That Cossack beard was probably gray by now.

Herron got up, suppressing a final shudder from the night terror, and peered at his reflection in the mirror. No more bushy wartime whiskers—his sideburns had once ri-valled Burnside's in what he looked back on as a ridiculous bushiness, though he'd never had as fierce a beard as Carr. Now, his moustache was a gray shadow of its former self, and his head was going bald. People used to tell him after the war that his eyes seemed haunted, and perhaps some-thing of that quality remained, but dulled by time. Bending to look in the mirror reminded him of Ada's reminders to stop stooping as he walked; and while he wasn't as heavy as Ely, a middle-aged pot belly was growing. He shrugged the vision away. It was hardly a tragedy that his handsome ap-

pearance had faded. He looked what he was, a mild-man-
nered, middle-aged New York lawyer and sometime
businessman, a not-much glorified clerk, trying to pay the
rent and stay out of debt.

The family had not started as his own. In New Orleans
he had met and married Adelaide, a Roman Catholic widow
with three daughters. They never had children of their own,
which made for a sadness he had long since come to terms
with, as he became a father to the girls. The oldest of them,
Caroline, was now married out in California, and the
youngest, Augusta, was twenty-one and at home. Georgette
had died young some years ago after marrying a man named
Stark, leaving a grandson (or step-grandson) with Herron's
first name, whom he and Adelaide were raising. Young
Frank was seven now, and Herron had adapted easily
enough to raising a boy instead of step-daughters. Now he
did not hear Frank or Augusta stir. *Good. Let them sleep.* He
realized with a slight shock why the dream might have
come, overriding his usual dull fretting about money: Today
he and Ely would meet General Sherman. Herron had met
Sherman before, but didn't know him at all well. Nor, he
was pretty sure, did Ely have a close relationship, although
he must have met him often enough with Grant.

Frank Herron and Ely Parker had much in common.
Both were family men, renters who struggled like the mass
of New Yorkers to make a living. But Ely, with his government job, also had something in common with Sherman
and Grant, who had never prospered in the private sector.
Not that Herron had, either, but it was his bread and butter
now. Sherman, though, had ridden off into retirement with
what must be a healthy pension, supplemented by royalties
from his own *Memoirs.*

Maybe Grant could do the same or better with his book.
He must be breathing a little easier now that Congress had
finally granted the former president his first military pension, which the newspapers said Sherman had helped

arrange, vigorously lobbying in D.C. and overcoming his usual, well-advertised disdain for politicians. Even Ely still owned that place in Fairfield, Connecticut, in what you might call a railroad suburb, or a place in the country. He'd bought it in his Wall Street prosperity, and his wife and daughter used to spend summers there, although Herron thought he might have it rented out now.

Herron, distracted as he dressed and ate breakfast with a gently smiling Adelaide on West 99th Street, wondered about the difficulty of making money, especially for former soldiers—difficult, that is, except for outright crooks like Dan Butterfield and William Belknap, both of whom had somehow managed to escape conviction and punishment. Maybe James Blunt, his senior in the Prairie Grove campaign, belonged in the same category. Blunt had gone on fighting through the war, helping defeat Sterling Price's invasion of Missouri in late '64. He seemed afterwards to have had some dubious business dealings with Indian tribes, maybe taking advantage of them, although nothing was ever established. Then he became a lawyer in Washington, and died in a madhouse.

Those ex-soldiers were the sort of men who perpetually and unhappily surprised President Grant, and diminished his reputation. Still, Grant's current poverty spoke to his personal honesty, as Herron hoped his own lack of prosperity—and Ely's, for that matter—would be interpreted the same way. Ely had been ousted as Indian Affairs commissioner for supposedly paying too much for emergency supplies for the Western tribes who were starving on reservations, but was eventually cleared by Congress. Herron had more confidence in his innocence than in Blunt's. Herron himself had fended off accusations in Reconstruction, like every other carpetbagger, most of whom were innocent of crimes.

While Grant was loyal to ex-soldiers, with whom he identified, it was around businessmen, the captains of industry, that he got starry-eyed. *Were Grant and the rest of them, us, too unworldly, too virtuous to get our share of Gilded Age graft, or too inept?* Grenville Dodge, who served in Carr's division at Pea Ridge, and became a general close to Grant, was now a millionaire. But he'd always been more of a railroad man than a soldier. Herron had heard gossip the other day that Joshua Chamberlain, volunteer hero of Gettysburg, Petersburg and Appomattox, then governor of Maine and president of Bowdoin College, was fast losing his money in business. He thought of the Scotsman John McArthur, a successful Chicago iron-maker before the war, who fought at Donelson, Shiloh, and in the Vicksburg campaign, and broke the rebel line at Nashville—and who had failed in these after days at both public and private employment. Not to be confused with another onetime soldier, John McDonald, a crook in the Whiskey Ring. They were Grant's friends, too, although McDonald turned into an enemy.

Baldy Smith seemed to have done all right by himself, Herron remembered, recalling the last time he and Ely had met with Civil War generals. But despite the difference in fortune, Smith had more in common with Ely and Herron, the latter thought, as men who had served in the war with some prominence but were now more or less forgotten by the public. Sweeny and Krzyzanowski fit that pattern. Maybe most soldiers did. Sherman and Grant were different, great men in the eyes of the public and historians, while Ely and Herron were drones in the hive of New York.

He kissed Ada—Adelaide—reassuringly and picked up a letter on the mantel, his address on the envelope written in block letters, and put it in his pocket. He went outside, taking a breath to swallow down any hint of panic, and the self-disgust that could trigger it. The area was not long or far from country ways, so far uptown, although farmers were pretty much gone by now, and their abandoned fields (those not being builded over) were growing wild, or covered by squatters' shacks. In either case, the land awaited

new development. There was, though, a horsecar line on
Broadway, back in operation after a recent strike, so he
hopped on a car to get to the elevated railway station on
Ninth (or Columbus) Avenue. He rode further downtown
on the El, taking pleasure as usual in the cast-iron scaffold-
ing and well-built wooden cars, although the relatively fresh
breeze was mixed with whiffs of smoke from the steam en-
gine.

Getting off near his 32nd Street office, he was greeted
by the familiar, somehow reassuring, sour-sweet, wet
garbage smell of morning New York, an ordinary odor experienced by the living, as opposed to those left behind at
Wilson's Creek, Elkhorn Tavern and Prairie Grove. Nor, he
recalled bleakly, would that odor or anything else be smelt
by Emory Upton, the colonel who broke the rebel line at
Spotsylvania, and shot himself seventeen years later. Upton's brilliant tactical achievement, emulated by Grant and
Hancock two days later, plunged that battle into a long
bloodbath, which amounted to the closest thing to a Union
victory in the 1864 Overland Campaign. There were worse
things than money troubles.

It was not a day for the secretary to come in, so Herron
didn't have to keep up any show of prosperous activity. But
when alone and at rest he was subject to attacks of—what
exactly?—not usually a flashback of war, like in last night's
dream which he had not quite shaken off, but a sort of
free-floating anxiety, about more than just money and his
periodic lack of application in making any. He focused on a
photograph on the wall of himself and Ada and the three
girls, taken in New Orleans a dozen years ago. He should
put up one of young Frank. He breathed deeply and swallowed it down again, whatever it was, and won the usual
reward—a long way from medals or glory now, but grasping
the ability at some level to function. He managed to answer
a couple of overdue letters, in one case coming up with a
substantive response that might lead to a settlement. He

opened most of today's mail, which fortunately for his household finances included a check from a client, then unpacked and ate most of Ada's sandwich. Sherman had pointedly invited him and Ely Parker for two o'clock, meaning that unlike Baldy Smith, he wasn't going to be standing anybody lunch. Finally Herron fished in his pocket for the letter he had brought with him, which he already scanned hastily the day before.

It was from a man named Elias Watson, an inmate of the New York City Asylum for the Insane on Ward's Island, by Hell Gate in the East River. Until a few years ago, the Soldiers Home of the City of New York was located there, and Herron had visited it from time to time. The resident soldiers were almost all veterans of the Army of the Potomac, in which he had never served, but they and he had much in common. He had known the writer only slightly by the time the home had been closed to save money, and Elias was transferred to the asylum at the same location while most of his comrades went to the nearest federal soldiers' home, in Maine. But he had gotten to know Elias better in recent years, as he tried to calm down both him and the nurses—most of them rough men given patronage jobs by ward-heelers—and persuade the authorities to let him go and join his comrades in Maine. Reading over the letter, he felt guilty for not having visited recently, and more persuaded that the threat of legal action might be in order to secure the man's release. It would obviously have to be a *pro bono* case.

Herron strolled out and deposited the client check in his bank, smiling at the familiar teller, then walked uptown a few blocks to the Union League Club. While activity helped calm him, he remained aware of whatever it was, whatever he couldn't define and from which he needed to be calmed. It was not wartime memories or nightmares, but rather the reverse, the mundane horrors of ordinary life, of comfort, of bland existence which he could not seem either to master or to mine for sufficient meaning and ballast. At least Sherman would be a distraction.

As it was not quite two o'clock he hesitated on 37th Street, where he came upon Ely doing the same thing, so they walked into the club together. They hadn't invited Sweeny, remembering that Sherman had fired and court-martialed him in 1864 after the brawl with Dodge, and apparently the two fiery generals—Sherman and Sweeny—had not met since then. It was Grant who sent Sweeny south in Reconstruction, when Sherman opposed that policy and was happier fighting Indians in the West. Then Sherman had opposed Grant's Indian peace policy, too, even though he was named after an Indian warrior. (Herron wondered what Ely thought about that.) The two famous generals had not agreed on politics since the war, but no one doubted that Sherman still could influence the whole Grant family. Unlike Grant, Sherman was famously bigoted, and probably regarded Sweeny and Krzyzanowski as a couple of damned immigrants, maybe Reds, whom these days he could hate better than Red Indians.

When with Ely, Herron tended to become constantly on edge about some potential racial slight, since any fool might sneer at a cigar store Indian or latch on to some worse characterization. But the club porter hesitated for only an acceptable fraction of a second—like Lee had done at Appomattox—before letting them in. Few strangers recognized or remembered either one of them now. They found Sherman with his cigar in the smoking room, surrounded by a few middle-aged men who might have been old friends or complete strangers just drawn into the great man's circle. Sherman vaguely introduced them, but Herron was too slow to catch who they were—they were men unknown to him, anyway, probably to his commercial disadvantage.

Sherman was distinctly polite to Ely, Herron noticed, despite—or more likely because of—his reputation for lack of enlightenment in racial matters. About seven years ago, when Sherman was still head of the Army, Herron had somehow gotten himself into a discussion with the great man about his experiences in Louisiana politics after the war. That had prompted Sherman to go off into a tirade of racial epithets and denunciations against Reconstruction— against the policies of the former president and commander-in-chief who was supposed to be his close friend. Herron hadn't encountered Sherman since that memorable occasion. Now, as usual, it was Sherman who dominated the company, waving his cigar like a baton. Herron was at least as touchy as Ely about racial matters, and knew that despite his best efforts he might be provoked by Sherman, who despised carpetbaggers.

Herron was not ashamed of his service in Louisiana, of trying to carry out Grant's policies upholding the rights of the Negroes. When Reconstruction ended, in '77, he'd had to take his new family north, because he couldn't make a living in the new South. Nor could his black friends, any more. In fact, their lives had been in danger with Grant no longer in the White House to provide some protection. Very likely they still were, for those few who chose to continue the losing political battle.

"Grant," Sherman was saying, "may live after all, at least long enough to write his book. He was at death's door, they all thought, and he coughed his guts up, but it didn't kill him."

"God be praised," said Ely, conventionally.

"Never mind God," Sherman responded. "That's who that parson Newman credited—on All Fools Day, it was. But Doctor Shrady said it was more likely the injection of brandy."

"How did that help?" asked a fat man of fifty, with florid moustaches.

"Damned if I know why they did it," said Sherman. "But Shrady thinks he coughed up the tumor, or part of it, which since it didn't kill him turned out well, the coughing and hawking up, I mean. They hadn't cut it out because they didn't think he could stand the operation, and he almost didn't stand this. But since then, he's gotten better, sleeping through the night, starting up with the book again. A miracle that damned hypocrite parson called it. Grant just told me he thought he'd live a little longer." Sherman jabbed his cigar decisively into the ashtray, and looked fiercely at his guests.

Rather to Herron's surprise, Ely spoke up. "There's something to be said for hypocrisy, which is just as well since most of us are hypocrites about something. Some Frenchman with an unpronounceable name said it's the tribute vice pays to virtue." This got a laugh, including from Sherman, who said, "You are too loose for me, sir." But in the pause that followed, Herron considered Ely's point seriously, and agreed with its drift: that hypocrisy was preferable to naked, unapologetic evil, unless it masked and facilitated it.

Then Sherman abruptly changed subject. "Do you know Grant's Negro man Harrison? Terrell, I think?" Ely said he thought he had met the man. "Well," Sherman continued, "here's a funny thing. I knew he'd been in the war so I naturally assumed he was in the United States Army. So did Grant, it turns out. But then he discovered Harrison had actually been on the other side, serving with his Confederate employers—he was a freeman, whose masters had been travelling gamblers before the war. I think they were in a regiment under Lee called the Richmond Blues. Grant said when he found that out, he just laughed. Of course he—Grant—couldn't talk much. So I filled in for him, sort of apologized, even, for our old arguments about … darkies." Herron, who presumed Sherman was editing himself for the sake of propriety, was surprised to find the famous general looking directly at him, and realized he was remembering their fraught conversation of seven years ago.

"Did you know Grant owned a slave? In Missouri?" Sherman continued. Herron was baffled at where the mercurial general was headed on this sensitive subject, and shocked at the information he conveyed. He had not known this, that Grant had ever owned a slave.

"He freed that man," said Ely, who apparently did know. "Signed manumission papers before he moved to Illinois. When he was dead broke and could have sold him." This was another surprise to Herron. It occurred to him, although he kept his mouth shut, that Grant's actions contrasted favorably to those of Thomas Jefferson at Monticello. Yet Grant must have been more embarrassed at ever owning a slave than proud of freeing him, or why would he have kept it a secret? Like his drinking, and how he gave that up.

Sherman grunted. "It's these lynchings that have gotten to me," he said, off on a different, though possibly related, tack. "They made me see Grant's point. And damn fools like Jube Early with their 'lost cause' romancing and Jeff Davis with his endless apologia—is that a word?—of a book. I was the South's best friend, but find myself somewhat unappreciated there. The fools on the other side, the Radicals, are right about that much, about the lynchings. You can't have people taking the law into their own hands."

"I agree with you, General," said Ely.

"As do I," said Herron, rather surprised at Sherman's concession, however belated, and offering one of his own: "And I also agree with you and General Grant saying 'Let us have peace'."

Sherman grunted, seeming to signify, Herron felt, disdain for all slogans and *clichés.* "You know what I was saying about Grant's slave," Sherman continued, "well it seems to me it makes him a better man than Thomas Jefferson." Herron, becoming genuinely amazed that the turns of the old soldier's mind and conversation should echo his own thoughts, asked why.

"Well," said Sherman, seeming to veer off on yet another tangent, "you know how a certain class of people condescend to Grant, say he's a grubby little man not up to their intellectual or moral level? It's all nonsense. God knows we should all revere the Founding Fathers, but Jefferson's life proved his youthful abolitionism was cant. And unlike Washington, who died a generation before, he didn't even free his slaves in his will. Yet Jefferson lived his whole life in luxury, while Grant freed the only slave he owned. And that happened when he was trying to avoid accepting his father's charity, which is what that job offer in Galena amounted to, which he ended up taking. Not that I judge him. That was a rough time, before the war, for me too. I also relied more than I liked on my father-in-law. But if you want to talk morality, then I judge Jefferson lower than Grant." Herron thought of objecting that President Jefferson had ended the slave trade, but decided not to interrupt the flow.

"Not that Grant was any kind of damn-fool abolitionist. He didn't want war any more than I did; he was a Douglas man. Nor did Seward, when it came down to it, or Lincoln, either, despite all those speeches about an irrepressible conflict and a house divided they'd been flapping their jaws about before."

Seward, Ely recalled, had refused to help him get into the Army in 1861, despite their prior acquaintance, saying it was a white man's war. And he was too tight with Andrew Johnson after the war. Still, Ely had not shared the Radicals' disdain for the Secretary of State, and respected his memory.

Sherman rolled on. "But the war came, as Lincoln, a wonderful man, said later. Then we had no choice, as Douglas and even Buchanan saw, although McClellan seemed to think he could pick and choose all the way through it. As for peace," he continued, turning to Herron, "I was ready for that the day the war ended, or, as you may recall, the day

I tried to end it but Stanton and Halleck stabbed me in the back."

"I was never in love with war," said Ely, still remembering Seward, how he had restrained Grant from invading Mexico. Maybe Grant had learned something from the wily old New Yorker. "These days, as a civilian, I like it less than ever."

"I never loved it," said Sherman, a tad unconvincingly, Herron thought. Herron wondered if Ely might also have meant "as an Indian" when he said "as a civilian." Whether or not that thought had occurred to Sherman, he duly plowed into the next sensitive issue. "Not with the Indians, either. Grant hated to fight them, and the Mexican War, too, but we did what had to be done. We were allied with the inevitable, the facts on the ground. Nothing can stop the march of America, like the Army of the Tennessee, or our new inventions and settlements, the mines and factories, the forests cleared, the prairie plowed, the poor of all Europe hurrying here. You look at that energy, that locomotive of peaceful production, and for all the crooked dealing there's more good than harm, more men of all races advancing with it than crushed under its wheels. That's what Grant believes, and I've come around to his way of thinking."

Sherman's unstoppable conversation did not seem to require interlocutors, although Herron doubted that Grant was as firm a believer in Manifest Destiny as his friend made out. He also wondered if, by Sherman's logic, the demise of slavery, too, had been inevitable, thus arguably making the war unnecessary. Or had Eli Whitney's cotton gin entrenched slavery in the South, where it had become impregnable to what Sherman would call the cant of abolition? But Herron held his peace as Sherman's irrepressible bumptiousness carried the conversation.

"I'm a civilian too, these days, and Grant has long been one. He was in the Army less than twenty years, you know.

Spent more time in the White House than any other place. Really, that's why Julia was so upset when he didn't run in '76, and why she wanted to be first lady again four years later. She loved being queen of Washington, and carried it off pretty well. More important, though, she kept things together for them, as Grant well knows, in those rough years before the war. And he was grateful she married him despite her father's disapproval. They've always relied on each other. Makes you quite sentimental about marriage." Sherman's glittering eyes did not reinforce that sentiment. Herron had heard contradictory things about the strength of the Shermans' marriage. Unlike the Grants, they spent considerable time apart, by choice of one or the other, or both. "Anyway, the White House was the closest thing she's had to a home since she left her father's plantation."

"Not much of a plantation," Ely said. "Didn't the old man, her father, give it up at the end and die in the White House?"

"Yes. Colonel Dent," said Sherman, dragging out the first word to emphasize the illegitimacy of the title, for Julia's father had served in no army. "Did men like that support Reconstruction in Louisiana?" he asked Herron.

"No," Herron replied. "But Longstreet did."

Sherman grunted. "Longstreet needed the money," he said.

Herron, despite himself, felt his hackles rise. "We have enough corruption up North, even in this gilded city, not to drag General Longstreet into the mire," he said, trying to restrain his anger without turning it into pomposity. "Anyway, he seemed to me an honorable man, as I'm sure General Grant would agree."

"General Grant has thought many men honorable," Sherman said pointedly, before relenting. "And I'm sure in the case of General Longstreet he has made no mistake. And God knows Grant has been honorable, and needs money worse than anyone. I raised private funds for him this winter, but he wouldn't take a penny. Then I lobbied Congress to get him a pension—a pension he'd given up for my sake, so I could become full general in his place in '69, when he resigned outright from the Army. If he had simply retired, he would have had an income for life, but Grant was never a man to feather his own nest. Nor was he any kind of politician, should never have mixed himself up in that filthy racket, but the scandals of his administration did not dishonor him."

"No one doubts it," Herron said formally, although it did not fail to occur to him that Grant had accepted gifts of things as valuable as houses. But then so had Sherman. It would be impolitic to mention such matters.

"That man Ward," continued Sherman, "who swindled Grant here in New York, was simply a confidence trickster, the lowest form of criminal. One so low that Grant could not imagine his type existing, which is why he keeps getting surprised by them. Or else that it's so damned dull, this money-grubbing, that Grant could never concentrate his mind upon it, never paid attention, whether in Washington or in this Tweed-ridden New York City of yours which seems to have developed the lowest form of criminal politics, which democracy has turned itself into." Herron rather enjoyed Sherman's splenetic disdain for politicians, journalists, religious fanatics, quacks, tourists and others, although he was put off when the famous Union commander descended into simple bigotry.

"Of course politics is bad enough even when it does not involve theft, it almost always turns into an affront to any man's integrity," Sherman continued. "My brother John, you know, is a pillar of the Senate, and I have no reason to doubt is an honorable man in his dealings. But what can one say of a young man, who goes to work for him or any politician, and must cut his jib to his master's whim, or the party's changing line?"

What, indeed? thought Herron, somewhat ironically, but

restrained himself from any comment as Sherman drew himself up short and showed signs of remembering why Ely had sought the meeting. To Herron's relief, Sherman summoned sufficient discretion not to discuss such matters in front of strangers—or whoever they were—at the club, although these men had shown no actual inclination to open their mouths since Ely and Herron arrived. Sherman stood up, still vigorous (unlike Grant, his younger friend), and said to the two of them, "Come with me, gentlemen," bowing farewells to the others and leading the way into a private conference room. Herron shut the door behind them.

"I'm sorry, gentlemen," the great man began, and Herron thought the apology seemed genuine, something owed to fellow veterans of the Civil War. "I saw the general yesterday afternoon, and as you heard I think he shows improvement, but perhaps I painted too rosy a picture. You deserve the truth. His state of health is still exceedingly fragile, and will remain so. It is cancer, too far gone to operate on, so it must be fatal sooner or later. Whatever Dr. Shrady said he coughed up will not be enough to save him, and there is always the danger of a sudden downward turn, and *finis*. In these circumstances, I did not feel able to bring up anything controversial, about who should or should not have access to him. I'm afraid I did not do what I may have led you to believe I would."

"I quite understand, General," said Ely.

"Of course," agreed Herron.

Sherman made a point of shaking hands with them both in farewell.

Ely and Herron said their own good-byes outside, headed in different directions.

"I'm quite sure Sherman's right about Grant being an honorable man," Ely said. "But I've gotten so all this ... folderol," he waved a pointing finger at the club, and down the street, "this money, in what Mark Twain calls this 'Gilded Age'—it just makes me uncomfortable."

"Comes in useful, though," said Herron. "And even we poorer folk get to gaze upon the architecture. But it does seem kind of ridiculous, those stiff society folks, or even Sherman, thinking they rule the world."

"Don't they?"

"Maybe we're turning into Reds. I thought you policemen were supposed to protect us from them."

Ely smiled, saying, "I guess it's because I'm not part of it, the prosperity, anymore; it's not my world. Nor Grant's, I suppose, though Sherman's trying to hold him up there in it. It never really was my world."

"It is Mark Twain's, I hear," said Herron. "Though Sherman probably thinks he's a Red, too."

Chapter Eight

To many people's surprise, with the possible exception of the physicians and Julia, the general's health went on the upswing. "No more blood, thank God," Fred had said to her not long after the baptism. A day later, Maundy Thursday, Fred was able to take his father's arm to help him arise shakily from the chairs, and they hobbled around together. Julia soaked bread with milk and egg, some of which Ulys was able to swallow, and a portion of his strength returned. "I want to live and finish my book," he told more than one person, shaking off discouragement as he had so often done before.

When there was another hemorrhage on April 7, the people in the supportive circle around Grant were at first alarmed, thinking their prior relief had been premature. But the new discharge seemed to continue the positive effect that the one on April 1 had caused. Shrady even let the general puff on a cigar on April 9, which, as Badeau had pointed out, was the twentieth anniversary of the surrender at Appomattox. Although there were no immediate ill effects, the cigar smoking experiment was not repeated. Some writers in the newspapers seemed a little irritated at the general's improvement, suspicious that doctors had misled them earlier. But the public was glad of it, as demonstrated by the many messages that continued to flood into the house, along with friendly demonstrations on the street outside. And the newspapers did also provide positive reports of supportive comments from former adversaries, whether Confederates like Jefferson Davis or difficult colleagues and subordinates like Union general William Rosecrans. Badeau and Fred made sure Grant saw these.

Rosecrans, who these days was a Democratic congressman, had opposed Grant's pension bill. Now, however, he made some more gracious remark. Grant responded in kind, without specifically naming Rosecrans or anyone else, in a statement which he had Shrady insert into the daily medical bulletin: "I am very much touched and grateful, for the sympathy and interest manifested in me by my friends, and by those who have not hitherto been regarded as friends. I desire the good-will of all, whether heretofore friends or not."

The tumor on the right side of his neck, usually concealed by a scarf, was now the size of an egg, and no one—not even Julia—really supposed the turnaround in health was anything but superficial. Grant wrote a philosophic note to Shrady: "It is merely postponing the event. I am ready now to go at any time. I know there is nothing but suffering for me while I do live. I was passing away peacefully. It was like falling asleep." But having woken up, and with strength returning, he went from playing solitaire and other card games to resuming work on the book. Settling down at his desk he felt his bones to be fragile, but he ignored that and his fluttering heart, telling himself, *You've got to live until you die.*

Now, as when his health had been in more obvious decline, he supported the doctors' judgment, and spurned the many quack medicines and remedies sent to the house by strangers. Senator Chaffee falsely told the newspapers on April 16 that Grant was merely suffering from "an ulcerated sore throat" and would "pull though," which prompted unwarranted optimism among the diagnosticians of the press. Yet despite these real and notional improvements, Shrady found on April 18 that the cancer continued to spread. He could not conceal this fact from Julia, whose hopes were accordingly dashed.

Grant was napping in his room one late afternoon in the

third week of April, while Clemens was sitting in the parlor with Fred, Julia, Nellie, Badeau and Noble Dawson, the stenographer provided by the Webster publishing house. The mood was cheerful, in part because of the recently concluded agreement between Century, Webster and Clarence Seward, which had included a modest payment to Grant by Century and settlement of various upcoming publication, royalty and legal issues. Badeau and Dawson were preparing to depart for the day.

Julia still felt a little leery of the shaggy, grey-haired and mustachioed Clemens, who scared her namesake granddaughter and seemed in love with the sound of his own voice. But he won her over now, ironically enough, by bridling at something said by her eldest son. Fred had been talking about the general's intermittent confidence in his own work, and lack of certainty about whether he amounted to a real writer. Clemens looked at Fred in astonishment (although Badeau wondered if he were shamming) and said, "General Grant is concerned about the quality of his writing?"

"He sees you make only minor corrections on the proofs, and do not otherwise comment," said Fred.

"Why does not he, why do not you, take that for what it is," Clemens asked, "for a signal that the writing is so good only a fool would change it? Since my nephew's firm took on this project, I have encountered some men who insinuate that I am writing the *Memoirs* myself, and I tell them they are damned fools." Julia did not bat an eyelash at this language, liking the meaning behind the words. "Grant's plain, clear, vigorous and lively style," Clemens continued, "is much better for the job than anything I could come up with. We do share some points of view, can both tell a story with dry humor, and have little regard for pomp and bombast. But this book is in Grant's own voice."

"I am very glad to hear it," Fred said. "Perhaps you can let him know something of what you feel, or think."

"I can hardly believe he needs it, but will be happy to do so."

Julia, though, was prepared to argue a point with Clemens despite her appreciation for what he had just stated. "I feel," she said, "that Ulys needs rest. He is trying again to do too much, and I fear for the effects, for the strain on his constitution."

"My dear Mrs. Grant," said Clemens, "it gives him a purpose, a reason to keep living, to write an immortal work of history and literature, and restore his wife and children to their rightful place."

"He has told me," Julia said, "that the writing wears him out—to the bone, I think."

"He does say that, Mother," said Nellie, "and I have no doubt of it. But the work also gives his days meaning and purpose."

"Can't we, his family, give him all of that he needs?" asked Julia.

"We help him," said Nellie, "in part, by being the people he is trying to serve, and save."

"We should save his strength," said Julia, "by letting him rest."

There was an awkward pause. No one wanted to tell Julia what she surely knew at some level, but declined to absolutely admit, that nothing in this world could save her husband. Nellie certainly thought her mother at bottom did know that saving his strength would merely be postponing the inevitable. But Julia, Nellie realized, would not say as much even to herself, and meanwhile urgently sought any such postponement. Fred, as usual, felt baffled, though no longer as downhearted as he had been. He was more inclined than Clemens to agree with his mother, for he did think the driving work Grant was doing, in his fragile state of health, could kill him outright in a relapse. While Fred, more than Julia, had accepted the inevitability of Grant's demise, and in other circumstances might not think the precise timing of great consequence, his death right now would damage the book's prospects. But he also agreed with Clemens and Nellie. How could both contrary opinions be right?

Badeau weighed in. "I don't think he will listen, Madam, even to you in this matter. He is determined to work. I had thought a week or two ago that he had worn himself out, and could do no more, but he is stronger than I knew. Now he keeps Fred and Dawson and me as busy as ever, churning out pages, moving into the second volume. It is admirable to see."

"Today I helped him, Mother," said Fred, "by giving him lined paper to write on, which keeps the manuscript neater for us, too." Nellie realized that her father's handwriting had deteriorated, and that Fred's lined paper was an effort to restrain the spidery scrawl, and keep it legible enough for Dawson to transcribe.

It seemed a little thing to be boasting of, but Julia appreciated any assistance given to her husband. It was kind of bitter that they were all against her, even Ulys, but she must yield. She tilted her head like the would-be Southern belle of forty years before, when she gave her heart away to a Yankee, and smiled slightly, to let them know they were forgiven. "I suppose you are all right," Julia said. "It is a labor of love."

Later, Ulys eased her mind by being well enough to get up and join them in the parlor, where he sat with his granddaughter Julia playing cat's cradle. Both of them were so seriously grave in their play work, that Julia the wife could not help smiling. When they tired of the game and turned to her, she said, "When we were girls, my sister Nell and I— long before you ever came visiting, Ulys—we were chasing butterflies and gathering flowers one day in the sunshine. We'd gone around a long way and needed to cross a brook to get home, but it was much higher than it had been the last time we were there, because of the spring rains. And we'd been to church that morning, and the sermon was on how 'if ye have faith, ye may move mountains and walk on the waters.' So I told her—Nell, that is—I would walk across, and started to, and then went in the water up to my armpits. I was quite surprised by that, but got to the other side, and then went back and fetched Nell out too. So you're not the only one in the family, Ulys, to have found the way to persevere at things."

Grant with difficulty restrained himself from breaking into laughter that would likely have been physically painful, but young Julia felt no such inhibition. Ida and Elizabeth came in, the latter carrying her toddler Nellie, attracted by the joyful noise. The grandmother soon left them to look for Fred, found him in the office with his sister Nellie, and sat down to tell them about the scene in the parlor. Julia knew there had been some tension between her son and his daughter, and was heartened now to see him smiling easily at her description, as did Nellie. Julia was proud of the family which she and Ulys had brought into the world.

Fred, however, changed the subject: "I was just telling Nellie, Mother, how I am reading Twain's, Clemens', new book, the *Adventures of Huckleberry Finn*. Perhaps not one you would approve of."

"I am not so judgmental, Fred," Julia replied. "Mr. Badeau spoke highly of it."

"Anyway," Fred continued, "I was telling Nellie I felt that I was like Huck, who floats down the Mississippi, and frees a slave. It's a strange story. But when I was Huck's age, I went down that river with father, who was freeing thousands of slaves."

"I don't think Mr. Clemens had you in mind," said Nellie.

"But the best part," Fred continued, "is when two characters claiming to be an English duke and the French dauphin come aboard Huck's raft, and they stop in little river towns to put on theatrical productions, which I fear you really would not approve of, Mother. But they made me laugh like, like I haven't done for the past year and more."

"I am very glad to hear that, Fred," Julia said kindly. Fred did not mention that he'd talked to Clemens about the book, telling him how the con-men characters made him laugh. The author had laughed a little bleakly himself, and compared the Reverend Newman to the dauphin.

Julia went to see about food for Ulys. Not just milk or cold soup tonight, she thought, but shepherd's pie, with all the color cooked out of the minced beef, to allay his notorious squeamishness at the sight of blood. Nor would her Ulys ever hunt animals, she fondly recalled. He hated to see, or be reminded of, the suffering of any creature.

CHAPTER NINE

LIKE FRED GRANT AND ADAM BADEAU, Mary Audenried
was a reader of novels, although unlike them she had not
yet embarked upon *Huckleberry Finn*. She had been going
through the not numerous works of Jane Austen, some for
the second time, and now was on that author's last published work, *Persuasion*, which was short, but she found
herself reluctant to finish it. Mary had plenty of time for
reading, summoned back to New York by Cump, en-
sconced in a different hotel, and with nothing to do but
bide upon his convenience. It did not fail to occur to her
that that description of her current position could stand as a
metaphor for their whole relationship. While the procedures
she adopted, in consultation with him, preserved secrecy
and discretion for both of their benefits, this time she did
not go through the motions of engaging in innocent activi-
ties for cover.

In Washington, they could be on occasion be seen in
public together, especially when they had both lived in the
city but even now, when Cump was passing through, it
could be done without inciting too much public disapproval. But that did not apply to New York, where neither
of them lived. This time, perhaps as a gesture of affection,
he had booked the adjoining hotel room, with a back door
through which he could come and go to her. She could not
be seen in the company of Cump, and it would not be proper to do much on her own. She was simply parked where
she was, for the purpose of engaging in sexual assignation.

Since Cump's retirement from the Army, and his move

from Washington to St. Louis, their opportunities for meeting were obviously curtailed. He had reacted, she pondered gloomily, by increasing his demands upon her movements so as to bring them together in places like this. Meanwhile, in Washington, she had fallen into another adulterous relationship. Mary knew that Cump, too, had had other lovers, and very likely had them now in his still vigorous retirement, whether in St. Louis or other places. Some of them, unlike herself, were clearly in the theatrical *demimonde*, and unconcerned about the possibility of scandal.

Mary's new lover was the first she'd had apart from Cump himself, and her dead husband. He was a married businessman and banker from Philadelphia who often came to D.C. to lobby Congress and the executive branch. In fact, her Philadelphia friend was in Washington right now, and had been surprised to get the news she was going out of town. She made him wear a rubber sheath, which she did not inflict upon Cump, although she wondered whether her senior and more distinguished lover was really more reliable as a non-carrier of venereal disease. The Philadelphia man was her own age, which had its attractions. She made sure to use the sponge with both of them.

Unlike her plump, bald, late husband Joseph, her married lovers delighted in sexual experimentation, which she had been pleased enough to go along with. Cump arrived today at noon, the daylight itself a stimulant to his aging desire—it might prove a necessary one, since he had also come into her bed the previous evening. He tried nothing unconventional then, had been almost tender in his missionary attentions. He usually preferred her passive and pliant, and today turned her around to enter from the rear, but then went painfully straining on and on before coming with a poor squib, and immediately falling asleep. Now she gazed, naked, at his naked back.

Mary did not feel particularly tender. Cump was full of genuine concern for his old, unfortunate friend, General

Grant (old, that is, except in relation to Cump himself, who was several years the elder). But what was she to him, compared to that? Or the other women who had filled the same role for him, and probably still did, everywhere from New York to St. Louis and beyond? She turned on her back and picked up *Persuasion* from the side of the bed.

The novel's hero, Captain Wentworth, was, like Cump, a military man, and older than the heroine Anne Elliot. But if, as seemed likely, he was going to marry her, then he would do considerably more than Cump was ever likely to do with Mary. Today Cump rather reminded her of Anne's highly unsympathetic father, Sir Walter Elliot. But it would do her no good to quarrel with him. She supposed she should wake him up, or would have to at some point. He was catching a sleeper train west this evening, back to St. Louis and Ellen Sherman. One thing neither of her married lovers worried about, Mary noticed, was conserving their sexual energy for when they returned to their wives. Perhaps neither party in either couple would expect a romantic reunion. These were not, Mary reflected, thoughts that would have crossed the mind of Anne Elliot or, presumably, Jane Austen, for all the latter's sophisticated irony.

She gently shook Cump, murmuring *pro forma* endearments. He woke, reached for his pocket watch, cursed, and went into the bathroom. Mary put on her robe. As Cump dressed, she tried to be cheery, but made the mistake of expressing the hope that he would find Ellen Sherman in good health.

"Not a damned thing wrong with her," said Cump, "though she's forever saying there is." Mary concluded there was more than one woman to whom he limited his sympathy and displays of affection. But she also knew Cump cared for his wife and respected her mind, probably to a greater degree than he did for any mistress, including herself. He had left Ellen the family to manage, while reserving the right to criticize her way of doing so. Cump was, she knew, chronically impatient, which was one of the characteristics behind his success, but also one that was hard on the women in his life, in their separate spheres. He was impatient with everyone, hard not least on himself, frustrated if not yet bowed down by the burdens of aging. Yet now, quickly getting ready to go, he was talking cheerfully about making another trip East soon, when they would meet again. She smiled pluckily, concealing how the prospect failed to enthrall her, although she did not disbelieve his protestations of affection. But she was wondering, *What if Ellen is really sick, or becomes so? What if she were dying? Would you stay and comfort her? What if Ellen died? Would you marry me?*

Of course, Mary asked nothing so counterproductive. Whatever he might have said in response, she was pretty sure she already knew the answer.

CHAPTER TEN

GRANT, BADEAU REFLECTED, was becoming more of a *prima donna*. Last year, the great one had deferred to his aide's literary advice, at first unsure that he was even capable of writing about his own battles and life. In previous years, when turning away requests to write an autobiography, Grant would refer to his aide's *Military History*, saying "It's all in Badeau." He had to be persuaded to tell his own story.

In preparing his first articles for *The Century* magazine the previous year, Grant had taken Badeau's suggestions about adding descriptions and accounts of events, and even on occasion had modified his language as his adviser recommended. Those days were over. Now Grant was more inclined to follow his own counsel, as decisive as on a battlefield. He had come to realize, from the reactions of editors and other readers, including Badeau, that what made the book potentially valuable was himself, descriptions of his own reactions to events, what he had done and thought. That, Grant now saw, would make the book more interesting, both for the reader and the writer. The chapter on the Battle of the Wilderness had been based on the *Century* piece, but now he was moving on to Spotsylvania, about which he had not written previously.

Badeau could hardly object to the general's views of the campaign. His sharper realization was the same as it had been when reading *Huckleberry Finn*, that it turned out people he was inclined to condescend to could write as well as or better than he could. Thus in describing the tactical muddle preceding Spotsylvania, Badeau's book had said, "So manifold and marvelous are the chances of war." Grant's new version went: "But accident often decides the fate of battle." It was plainer, coarser, simple stuff, yet Badeau could not convince himself it was inferior. On the next page, Grant cut through confusion with the simple explanation, "I was anxious to crush Anderson before Lee could get a force to his support," an explanation which Badeau now saw had been lacking from his own account. It was becoming apparent that Grant's book did a better job of putting the war in context with its history and his own crucial experience of it.

Not all these editing events were negative. Badeau knew himself to be a good writer, and did not lose that confidence. Nor did Grant lose confidence in him. As Badeau came to appreciate the general's ability with words, Grant's reciprocal appreciation loomed more significant. Grant read and talked about Badeau's history book in the process of writing his own, taking the opportunity of discussing things with its author, complimenting him on its accuracy and even on occasion the style, and for the most part sticking to its complicated sequence of events. Badeau's book was, in fact, Grant's main source, apart from his own excellent memory —the past rose up vividly in review as he cast his mind back. Their roles were reversed from a few years before, when they corresponded over several years about the Civil War, to assist Badeau in writing his *Military History*. Badeau's role now was coming down to checking his version of events against Grant's newer one, and he still succeeded in inserting the occasional correction. But Grant's version, Badeau was secretly mortified to discover, was boiled down and clearer. The general had even changed the spelling of this battle, cutting out one of the Ts, making it what would surely become the standard Spotsylvania, and making Badeau's Spottsylvania dated and wrong. Badeau had tried to argue this point, only to be dismissed out of hand, ignored rather, by the general, who was supported by his increasingly irritating son Fred.

Grant, too, was free to take blame upon himself that Badeau in his book had been reluctant to apportion. Or at least Grant could seem to accept responsibility. Thus in discussing the failure to exploit a positional advantage held by Major-General Burnside's corps, he wrote: "I attach no blame to Burnside for this, but I do to myself for not having had a staff officer with him to report to me his position." In reality, Badeau realized but refrained from saying, Grant's blame went much deeper than this. There was no real excuse for leaving a beef-witted blunderer like Burnside in command of a corps in a crucial campaign in that the fourth year of the war, no matter "the purity of his patriotism and the loftiness of his public spirit," which Badeau had noted in his own book. Burnside's blunders, and Grant's leaving him in post to make them, resulted in thousands of unnecessary casualties, and neither Badeau's account nor Grant's stated this grim truth. That was a valid criticism of both generals, and both historians.

On matters of substance, Badeau was not convinced Grant had outdone him. Badeau's own history was more detailed, containing some of the grim facts that Grant omitted at Spotsylvania, such as how, after a failed attack and retreat by soldiers from Gouverneur Warren's corps, "the dry woods burst into a blaze, and numbers of the wounded were burned alive." Grant, though, Badeau recalled, had addressed the same phenomenon in his account of the previous battle, Wilderness, in even more precise detail, saying: "The woods were set on fire by the bursting shells, and the conflagration raged. The wounded who had not strength to move themselves were either suffocated or burned to death."

But neither of their versions dwelt on the overwhelming horror of the terrible Overland Campaign, on Spotsylvania's massive, continual close-quarters killing, which was too hard to look at then and remember now. (The two men had served together during the war's last year.) Still, Badeau's account, he insisted to himself, was more complete. But would anyone now bother to read it instead of Grant's? Especially as Grant had for obvious reasons been able to include so much interesting personal history, the writing of which, Badeau had to admit, was done economically and effectively.

He recalled another instance of Grant's literary competence, with reluctant but honest admiration: the description of a meeting with his then superior, General Henry Halleck, on January 6, 1862. Grant had come north up the Mississippi from Cairo to Halleck's headquarters in St. Louis, to pitch his plan to go south and east up the Tennessee and Cumberland rivers, a plan that, as it turned out, would soon bring great victories. However, Grant's manuscript recorded: "I was received with so little cordiality that I perhaps stated the object of my visit with less clearness than I might have done, and I had not uttered many sentences before I was cut short as if my plan was preposterous. I returned to Cairo very much crestfallen."

Badeau remembered Halleck's bulging, balding forehead and goggle-eyed hesitation from later in the war, in Washington, when he rather sympathized with him. By then, Halleck knew his place and deferred to his former subordinate. Grant had gradually discovered Halleck's earlier machinations against him, including spreading inaccurate rumors about drunkenness, but left him in place to function as what Lincoln called "a first-rate clerk." Grant the writer, introducing Halleck into the *Memoirs*, had in one sentence admitted his own humiliation while making the point that his superior was blind to the merits of the plan which laid the foundations of victory in the West. Badeau wondered if the point was fair, if Halleck had really been so blind. Then, in Grant's account, after that plan produces the capture of Forts Henry and Donelson and the Battle of Shiloh, Halleck appears in the field to take command, shunting Grant aside to an advisory role. When Grant presumes to offer advice, "I was silenced so quickly that I felt that possibly I had suggested an unmilitary movement." Again, the brooding Badeau was impressed at Grant's trick, the admission of his own humiliation serving to demonstrate Halleck's foolish arrogance, which he does not need to denounce because it is so convincingly shown.

These realizations of the literary merits of the *Memoirs* in progress, and of the newly-published *Huckleberry Finn*, had served to depress Badeau's spirits, despite his being able to take some credit for Grant's successes. But he took some satisfaction, now that he had finished reading *Huckleberry Finn*, in being able to honestly conclude that Clemens had bungled the ending. He told himself that Grant, too, had only a rough-and-ready-talent, and would need his continuing guidance to finish the book and make it a success.

Still, Badeau's nerves had been further jangled by the reappearance of Clemens that spring after his lecture tour, full of good cheer at the general's improved health and resumption of writing, and anxious to assure the newly persistent author that he was doing a splendid job. Badeau suspected correctly that Clemens had been put up to praising Grant by Fred, and also thought he was laying it on a bit thick, in telling the general his *Memoirs* would rank in value with Julius Caesar's *Commentaries*. (Not that Badeau was very familiar with Caesar's work, but he was pretty sure Grant and Clemens weren't either.) Badeau restrained himself from drawing attention to what Fred had informed him of, that for all the publisher's attentions and promises, Clemens was neglecting to include an index. That appeared to be more because he didn't want to spare the time than the money, anxious as he was to take at least the first volume out of the general's hands, but it amounted to the same thing. In either case, it seemed to Badeau a false economy. Clemens, furthermore, like Lincoln, could rarely resist starting in on one of his own stories, never mind the distraction to Grant from the pressing task at hand.

One day at 66th Street, toward the end of April, Clemens had as usual sprawled his frame around an arm-chair, and as his talk gathered steam, went off on an apparent preamble involving Century, which it turned out was no longer his whipping boy. The magazine's managers had gone up radically in Clemens' estimation by making an offer to have him write something for their "Battles and Leaders of the Civil War" series, which Grant's articles had also been part of.

"I don't understand," said Fred. "Aren't those pieces by generals and commanders?"

"Whereas I," said Clemens, "spent the war drinking with newspapermen, bar girls and miners in the American West, far from any battle? I don't say you don't have a point, Fred, and a good one. It might seem at first blush that I have nothing to contribute."

"At first blush?" said General Grant, with a thin smile, waiting like the rest of the room for the punch line. Clemens didn't smoke in the house, out of consideration for Grant's health, but waved an imaginary cigar as he warmed to the topic.

"It was not, it is true, a successful campaign that I engaged in, but I was a member of an organized armed force in the early days of the war, a small part of a mighty military apparatus, and not far from the sphere of operations of one Colonel Ulysses S. Grant."

"In Missouri?" asked Grant.

"Missouri," Clemens confirmed, "the state of my birth, and one of mixed opinions about slavery and secession. My friends and I changed our positions half a dozen times in those months, it seems."

Nellie, who had appeared in the doorway to take in the entertainment, asked, "And which side did you end up on, Mr. Clemens?"

"I have ended up on General Grant's side, but I confess to you, as I think I will to *The Century*'s readers, that such was not the case," he paused, putting an exaggerated Southern accent on the next three words, "before the war, when I subscribed to some of the same romantic bosh everyone else did. And so in 1861, I served, albeit very briefly, in a state militia allied with the Confederate-leaning governor."

"Claiborne Jackson," said Grant, "who, as I recall, did more than lean that way."

"He did do more," said Clemens, "as did many men at that time. But my colleagues and I—or at least some of them, including me—decided to do less. We decided not to do things, or at least, in my case, to do completely different ones unrelated to warfare and some thousands of miles away from it. And it is the history of that decision, and the very brief preceding campaign, which I propose to inflict upon the readers of *The Century*."

"I seem to recall you wrote a book about those Western days," said Grant, "in which you acknowledged that not every word in the newspapers is gospel truth." He paused, seeming to struggle for breath and speech, the latter of which he was finding increasingly difficult to come up with despite some other improvements in his health. Clemens smiled, although there was a note of alarm, too, behind the faces of him and others as they waited for the general to continue, which he proved able to do. "I found that to be the case in my administration. And now I find the newspapermen make up most of what they say about my health and affairs."

"I am no defender of the modern newspaperman," said Clemens, "even though I may befriend him, and am, too, an old sinner in the same way."

Grant admired Clemens, and liked the way he pricked the pomposity of the successful men with whom they both spent time. And Clemens' admiration for both Grant's character and his writing style was genuine. He appreciated the lack of flummery and purple prose, and the dry humor of it.

Despite his difficulty speaking, especially by the end of the day, Grant's health and spirits remained mostly on an upswing since the April 1 crisis, seeming to reverse the March decline. His breathing tended to be clearer, and in one unalloyed gain, he was no longer getting the migraine headaches that he had been subject to all his life. He realized perfectly well that the improvements were superficial, that the cancer still progressed and would kill him. But his normal state of anxiety, with which the migraines were associated, had been lifted by the purpose of work, of writing a book, that had taken over his life. He was fulfilling that purpose. Nellie, observing all this, resolved to emulate her parents, and not to fall into currently fashionable female neuroses.

The family had also been gratified by the birth of another grandchild and namesake of Julia's, the daughter of Frances and Buck, who was born on April 15. On April 18, the general had stood up straight at the bay window and saluted veterans from the Grand Army of the Republic, parading outside. The reporters, sensing the improvement, and because decline and death would have made for bigger news, were drifting away from 66th Street. To cap off this month of miracles, Grant had even, with the collusion of Harrison and McSweeny, made a triumphant return to sexual relations with his wife, mightily surprising and pleasing her with a post-midnight visit.

One early evening, as Clemens and Badeau were bowing out for the day, Grant saw through the window his son Jesse and granddaughter Nellie looking up from 66th Street. The girl blew him a kiss with both hands, and the general smiled and waved at her.

Nellie Sartoris, meanwhile, sat down with Fred and no others, to tackle the question of Ely Parker and other wartime companions who were known to the general, urging their admission in the next few days. "You see how laughter and camaraderie do him good," she said, "and how much more so he would benefit from seeing old comrades."

Fred smiled weakly and looked through the door where he had last seen his mother. He was still getting used to his sister's reappearance in his life, and her now constant presence. Nellie continued, "What has she got against Ely? Surely not just him being an Indian."

"No," said Fred. "Maybe he seems a little down at heel."

"Are we so high?"

"But I don't really think that's it," said Fred. "At least I hope not. Father does need rest from intrusion, though I know you think Ely and the others would do him good. Maybe Mother is embarrassed about the two of them remembering Galena, when Father was just clerking in his own father's store."

"And the Indian," said Nellie, "the federal engineer, had the much grander job. Father is not so petty as to be bothered by that."

"Nor Mother," said Fred, and continued after a pause. "You know how people cluck about their hard times, Mother and Father's, in the '50s after he left the Army. But she doesn't make it sound like that. More like the ordinary struggles of life. She says they were happy. So we all seemed, and I remember those days."

"They always have been happy, together," said Nellie, shaking off the intrusive thought of her own unsuccessful marriage. "He's just too good a man to drive a hard bargain, demand a pound of flesh. Not at all like his own father, by all accounts."

"Old Jesse had his points," said Fred. "He got Father to West Point, and to Galena."

"It was poverty that drove them there, and Jesse wouldn't bail them out in St. Louis. Those days Mother gets sentimental about, waxing poetic. Didn't she really hate that

log house he built in Missouri, where I almost died as a
baby, and so moved us away back to her father's plantation
—or what they called one."

"Not as grand as your English estates, Nellie," said
Fred, a little unkindly, she thought. "Farming's not so easy,
you know," he continued. "As adults, we never had to live
like that."

"No. We have our own problems. I know Mother
doesn't talk of those days as desperate. Nor these ones,
which are worse. Neither of them lacks courage." After a
pause, she added, "Will you talk to Father about Ely, Fred?"

He smiled, rose, and kissed her on the forehead, saying,
"I'll do it now."

Fred found the general with Harrison, and raised the issue with seeming casualness. Grant cheerfully waved his
assent to the visit.

Julia, it turned out, raised no objections to Ely Parker
coming, when Fred tentatively raised the issue with her. Despite the improvement in her husband's health, she was
distracted by worry. Fretting had never been Julia's natural
state, but her old blithe attitude could not hold up under
current circumstances. It was not just Ulys' illness and their
financial plight, but how the collapse of Grant & Ward had
swallowed up the money and seemingly the prospects of her
sons, Fred, Buck and Jesse. She brooded about Nellie, her
rash marriage that it could no longer be denied had not
turned out well, and her English children thousands of
miles away, without their mother. Was it right to keep Nellie
away from them? Nellie was undoubtedly a comfort to her
and especially to Ulys, but should they be accepting all that
warmth and good feeling on those terms, denying those
needy young grandchildren the presence of their mother?

The newspapers Grant had complained about—and Julia fumed over—were putting him at death's door one day
and declaring him cancer-free the next. In points of fact, he
was able to do more and more work that spring of 1885, but

the doctors also found the cancer spreading in his mouth, which on one side was turning into a pockmarked honey-comb. Fred and Julia managed visitors so that they came in after the main work of the day, to pleasantly distract the general before dinner. Sometimes Fred kept things from his mother, such as a grimly humorous note from Grant that said: "The *Times* has been killing me off for a year. If it does not change, it will get it right in time."

CHAPTER ELEVEN

WHEN HERRON ARRIVED AT POLICE HEADQUARTERS, Ely asked him if he was all right.

"Why, what's the matter with me? No, no, I'm fine."

Ely just gave him a kindly look, and Herron was relieved from further interrogation by the arrival of Tom Sweeny, who'd come in from semi-rural Astoria, Queens County, where he lived with his second wife and their children. The three men, as prearranged, took a hansom cab up to 66th Street, where Grant's greeting was quiet but warm and obviously sincere. Nellie, as facilitator of the visit, sat down with them in the drawing room along with Fred, Clemens, Badeau, and Grant's old friend Matias Romero.

Romero had been a young diplomat working for Benito Juarez in the 1860s, when civil war was raging in Mexico, as it was in the United States. He and Grant had met for the first time in the fall of 1864, when Romero spent several days at the U.S. military headquarters in City Point, Virginia. Badeau had been deputed as a sort of tour guide, taking Romero off to the nearby headquarters of Generals Meade and Butler. But Grant also had made time to listen to the ambassador and give him military advice for the benefit of Juarez and his party of liberal Mexican patriots. Romero was something of a military man, too, having fought for a few months the previous year in the Mexican patriots' war against the two emperors, the Austrian Maximilian, who purported to rule the country with the support of French troops and their emperor, Napoleon III. Now, filling a conversational gap, Romero fell to talking with Herron about those days when, as a young U.S. general, he had been involved in both civil wars on the Texas border.

Badeau had greeted the guests and was now in and out, fussing with some papers in the next room. Julia had greeted the old soldiers formally, not without warmth to Ely as a family friend, and without any hint of the snobbery cited by her detractors. Ely was gracious in reply. Yet it was Romero and Badeau who were her closer friends now. She soon left the company to their own devices. Fred and Nellie helped their father conduct the conversation, to spare his voice. They established that the three ex-military visitors, like the general, were all New Yorkers now, and mention was made of their families and current occupations.

Before they got off on the inevitable Civil War discussion, Nellie brought up the recent memorial service in St. Paul's Cathedral, London, for the British general George Gordon, who had been killed at Khartoum in the Sudan. She related how the British people were outraged that their prime minister, William Gladstone, had not sent a relief expedition in time enough to save him.

Sweeny took the bait: "General Gordon seems to have disregarded the instructions of his government, and I have some sympathy with Mr. Gladstone. Unlike most prime ministers, he is not set on having John Bull rampage everywhere from the Sudan to Ireland."

"Ah, but you are letting your personal feelings of Irish patriotism influence your view," said Nellie, looking to her father for support. Grant duly provided some. "Gladstone did send in soldiers, Sweeny. He just delayed until it was too late to do any good."

Herron thought of an incident the year before, when the American polar expedition was rescued after long delays which had resulted in the deaths of most of its members. General William Hazen was head of the Signal Corps, and he had—perhaps unfairly—blamed Secretary of War Robert Lincoln, for the delays and the death toll. Hazen was a Civil

War hero, while Robert Lincoln had served only briefly on Grant's staff. Herron wondered what Grant thought of the controversy and the role of the late president's son, but decided it was too sensitive a matter to bring up.

"Well," said Sweeny, "count me as a skeptic of the good done by the British. Were not they, including Gladstone, on the side of the rebels in our war?"

"They were," Grant conceded. "But as Badeau knows, Gladstone helped us avoid war later, over the Alabama claims." Badeau smiled tightly, gratified at the recognition.

"Not all the Irish were on our side in the war," put in Ely, "even in this city."

Nellie, though she was growing excited, did not pursue this potentially controversial reference to the 1863 draft riots. She did press on with her case, struggling not to let her voice fluctuate with too much emotion. "Just as our war—your war—abolished slavery, so did Gordon crush the slave power in Sudan."

"Maybe so," said Sweeny. "But wasn't he fighting for the Chinese emperor before that? Chinese Gordon, they called him. These British are always going over to other people's countries and killing them in the name of freedom, to which I've never known emperors to be partial."

"The British caused some problems for my country, too," said Romero, "and set the stage for the French emperor and his Austrian puppet. Even so, now I try to persuade my countrymen to be less suspicious of foreigners, and accept their investments to develop our economy."

"Well as emperors go, I found the Japanese one agreeable," said Grant, cutting any tension.

But Herron stuck to the serious theme, backing the Grants. "Didn't the Mahdi just now massacre 10,000 people who were with Gordon at Khartoum? Negroes, most of them. That was worse than Cromwell in Ireland." Sweeny swallowed his indignation at the Irish reference.

Nellie, warming to her theme, added, "And Gordon died because he would not abandon them, the Sudanese."

"Maybe they should not have put their faith in him," said Sweeny. "And the British in my lifetime caused more deaths than that in my old country, more than the Mahdi did in his, letting millions of my kinsmen, women and children starve. Literally die of hunger. Though I admit Gladstone himself seems to have learned something about Ireland since then."

The discussion, without Julia to restrain it, was becoming uncomfortably intense, so Ely weighed in judiciously, seeking to appease Sweeny while still taking the side of his old friends. "It's true, Tom, that there has been terrible hunger and hardship for the people of Egypt, as well, and it's the British bankers who insist on their pound of flesh that's a big part of the reason why. But Gordon wasn't on their side."

"No," said Nellie, delighted at Ely's unexpected expertise. "I knew he was a good man."

"And even Gladstone," said Herron, who was a thorough reader of newspapers, "seems willing to support colonialism in Africa, as long as it's the Germans who are doing it."

"I hope," said Grant, quieting everyone else, "that we will not follow the Europeans' example and entangle ourselves in imperial wars. Joining together in peace, as I tried to do with Santo Domingo and Hawaii, is much to be preferred." He paused, but seemed not quite finished, so no one spoke. "Some called me a butcher," he said, startling them all. "None of you was at Cold Harbor, I think, except you, Badeau, of course." Badeau, in the doorway, blanched. Cold Harbor, he knew, was on Grant's mind because he had just been writing about it. While, as usual, the *Memoirs* were taking much the same line as Badeau's history, including some aspersions placed on the slowness and lack of initiative of subordinate commanders, Grant had gone far beyond what Badeau had ever ventured in assuming personal responsibility for the Union defeat. On the night of the assault in 1864, he had expressed regret privately in conversation with his staff, but Badeau had not suggested including that admission in his own book—or, more recently, in Grant's. It had been the general's own decision to address the issue head-on.

Now Grant looked at the other old soldiers, who all knew well enough about Cold Harbor, which had come soon after the Wilderness, Spotsylvania, the North Anna River and the rest of the terribly costly Overland Campaign. They knew the criticism by some that this battle, above all, showed Grant as indifferent to the losses of his own side. He asked Badeau to read what he had written about the battle that day. But when Badeau started, Grant prompted him to skip over most of it to the end.

"I have always regretted," Badeau read aloud, "that the last assault at Cold Harbor was ever made. I might say the same thing of the assault of the 22nd of May, 1863, at Vicksburg. At Cold Harbor no advantage whatever was gained to compensate for the heavy loss we sustained. Indeed, the advantages other than those of relative losses, were on the Confederate side."

As Badeau read, Herron was partly impressed. While Grant in his book was saying more than Badeau had dared in his longer history, he had not tried to say enough to appease all those mothers, wives and orphans of the men ordered on doomed assaults against entrenched positions. No sentimental sop was thrown to their agony. Dry, brief, yet powerful, was Grant's confession of error.

But Herron didn't know what Grant meant by "relative losses." While Union losses were higher in every battle of that campaign, in the ones leading up to Cold Harbor Lee took heavy losses, too. That could be a justification for Grant's tactics given the brutal logic of attrition, because he could replace his men while Lee could not. But that logic did not apply to the assaults at Cold Harbor itself, where Lee's casualties were negligible. And Herron remembered Baldy Smith's terrible account of the wounded being left for days to die between the lines, while Grant and Lee postured. Grant blinked first, finally requesting a cease-fire, but by then they were almost all dead—and almost all of them Union men.

The company was quiet for a while. Then Fred, the ex-soldier who had been too young to fight in the war, spoke. "Surely, Father, a commander cannot always know when an attack will succeed, whether it will capture Richmond and end the war, or fail utterly."

"It is his business to know, Fred," said Grant. "But you're right. Only by pressing on did we win and end the war." Grant seemed to have gained strength, able to talk at unusual length. "Two years before that, after Shiloh, feeling slighted by General Halleck, I almost resigned my command. I thought we should have pressed on then, maybe won the war in '62. It was Sherman who stopped me resigning." And, Herron remembered, Sherman had put the story in his own *Memoirs*, published about a decade ago. He remembered, too, a story Grant had told about Shiloh in his piece for *The Century*, and presumably had written in the *Memoirs*, how he had hurt his ankle, and could not sleep that first night of the battle in the drenching rain, and had gone into a log house but found it was turned into a hospital where multiple amputations were under way. Herron recalled Grant's exact words: "The sight was more unendurable than encountering the enemy's fire, and I returned to my tree in the rain." The sounds, too, probably, from what Herron remembered of battlefield hospitals, which served mainly as the setting for amputations.

But Grant had also written that it was after Shiloh he knew that in order to save the Union, the whole South would have to be conquered. Herron remembered the general telling him the same thing when he arrived at Vicksburg the next year. Sherman learned it, too, from Grant, along with a certain amount of ruthlessness and a lot of strategic daring, to go deep behind enemy lines. But Sherman, Herron thought, despite his fearsome reputation, never embraced the logic of attrition, which Grant's confession about Cold Harbor had rather skated over. Sherman was less ruthless in combat, less willing to spend lives. It was their defensive battle on the first day of Shiloh which made them brothers-in-arms. But was Baldy Smith right? What was the value of Grant's admissions of error or expressions of sympathy, and his exquisite sensitivity to the sight of blood or wounded men, when set against the horror of what had been done? What he, what we, had done? *What we have done.*

Now Sweeny spoke again. "I once knew a man named Kammerling, Gustav I think, colonel of the Ninth Ohio Infantry, a German regiment out of Cincinnati. He was one of George Thomas' favorite officers, ever since he led a bayonet charge as a major which broke the rebel line at Mill Springs, in January of '62." Badeau looked sharply at Grant, who had had a checkered relationship with Thomas, and whose great victory at Donelson the next month had completely eclipsed the fame of Mill Springs. But the general did not seem bothered as Sweeny settled in to his story, and Badeau recalled that Grant had mentioned Thomas as the victor of Mill Springs in the *Memoirs.*

"Two years later, Kammerling and I both started off with Sherman and Thomas on the way to Atlanta," said Sweeny. "I was long since a general by then, and so could Kammerling have been, except that he decided to stay with his Ninth Ohio boys—men, rather, some were older, had fought in Europe in '48. But they never got to Atlanta, the Ninth Ohio, and not because they ever lost an engagement. After the Battle of Resaca, I think it was, their three-year enlistments were up, and they almost all mustered out,

Kammerling included. Old Pap Thomas came down for the last parade."

"Why didn't they re-enlist?" asked Fred.

"Well, there was some talk that the Germans were mad at the way they'd been treated, called Dutch and a lot worse, called cowards after Chancellorsville and even Gettysburg— although the Ninth Ohio never served in the East. We Irish heard some of the same damned newspaper nonsense"— Sweeny paused to glare at Ely, presumably in reply to the earlier draft riot reference—"begging your pardon ma'am,"—this last to Nellie, who spread out her hands and grimaced to show she took no offense at the language.

"Although, now that I think of it, it wasn't all nonsense for any race of men. My fellow Fenian patriot Thomas Meagher seems to have lost his nerve at Fredericksburg, and left the Irish Brigade after Chancellorsville. But I don't think that was it for Kammerling. He was a refugee from the 1848 revolutions, like my Polish friend Krzyzanowski; he and his men were all civilians, volunteers. They were at Chickamauga, Mission Ridge, saw a lot of hard fighting. And he felt they'd done enough, the country was safe enough, and he wanted to lead them, those who still lived, back home to Ohio." Herron remembered hearing that Thomas Meagher (whose name Sweeny pronounced something between "mar" and "mare") had died after the war when he fell out of a river boat in Montana, where he'd been appointed governor. The death was ascribed variously to drunkenness or murder.

"I was at Missionary Ridge, Chattanooga," said Grant, taking them by surprise. "It was a battle won by soldiers, without much regard for us generals."

Thomas was Grant's subordinate there, recalled Herron, who like Badeau was aware of the tense relationship between the two generals. But the truth, he realized, as Grant had just said, was that none of the commanders had had much to do with the victory. The troops had captured the rifle pits as ordered, at the base of the ridge, but then, coming under fire, had gone up on their own. For a general to acknowledge this was impressive, although Herron wondered if Grant would say as much in his book.

Badeau thought of his own book, in which, he acknowledged to himself now, he had left the incorrect impression that the battle was fought according to Grant's plan; nor had the general ever objected to that account, or challenged it in his own manuscript.

Sweeny smiled, nodding and grunting agreement with Grant's remark, then continued, "Kammerling knew there would be some hard fighting left, but he was leaving it to the generals, and the newer troops. I couldn't hold it against him. Especially after I got into my scrape not long after and exited the war less gracefully."

The company laughed, and Ely said, "He had seen more fighting than I did, and I don't begrudge him and them going home before me."

They pondered for another moment Kammerling and his Germans, until Grant said, "War, history, can be complicated, Tom. You and I fought in Mexico, though I never liked the cause. I don't think we should have been sent there, but we were and we went. Except those of us who didn't, at least not on the American side. You talk of the English, Tom, and I'm pretty much with you there. But might it have been an Irishman who shot off your arm, one who had maybe deserted from the American army?"

"The San Patricio Battalion," confirmed Sweeny, grimly. "It might have been. I don't hold it against them, as I hope they don't against me. We'll meet up in Purgatory, I reckon."

The captured Irish deserters who had fought for the Mexicans were executed by the American army, as Herron recalled having read.

After a pause, Clemens tried to go back to the previous topic, saying "Kammerling—" but Grant interrupted, saying, "They hanged thirty or so of those Irishmen when we stormed Chapultepec. That's the battle when I placed a gun in the tower of a church. Got commended for it, too. It was all a savage business. If there's a God, I'm not sure he looks too kindly on any of our work down there, Tom."

No one spoke, so Clemens, who knew little of this history or theology, went back, indirectly, to the topic of Kammerling and his compatriots. "It was the Germans who held my state of Missouri in the Union, when I and most of my friends were ambivalent at best. I've spoken to some of you about a piece I'm going to write for *The Century*, on how I served in a Confederate militia for a few weeks, at the beginning of the war." Herron was astonished. He was already a little dazzled to be meeting the famous Mark Twain for the first time, and now all the more so to be told this seemingly scandalous secret.

Sweeny, too, seemed surprised, asking, "How only a few weeks?"

"Maybe just two or three," said Clemens, settling into his story like a country band's fiddle player taking a solo, "before we deserted, some of us. I went to Nevada and west of there, took up the writing trade and stayed well away from the war."

Herron could not resist chiming in. "Your book *Roughing It*, as I recall, describes that time."

"It does," said Clemens. "But before that, in the early days of the war, there was something I have not written about, yet. I served in Missouri, like a certain federal colonel."

"That's me, I think," said a smiling Grant.

"And in the same sphere of operations," said Clemens. "Were you not opposed by my commander, General Thomas Harris?"

"I had thought he was another colonel," said Grant with a twinkle in his eye—something Nellie was glad to see.

"Well, whether or not he outranked you then, we'd all

known the man when he worked as the telegraph operator in Hannibal, no very demanding position, and our military discipline was not all that it might have been."

"Harris is in the book, General Grant's book," said Badeau.

"Yes," said Grant. "I wrote how I was ordered against him, and was nervous about my green regiment. But when we got there, and found him fled, I realized he'd been even more scared of me—which was not a lesson I forgot."

"Or one that McClellan ever learned," said Ely, drawing some laughter. But Herron could not help thinking— though he was careful not to say—that Grant had been overconfident at Donelson and Shiloh in ways that McClellan would not have been. Yet while McClellan might have held on at Shiloh, as Grant did despite his mistakes, would he have had the stubborn ruthlessness to press the counterattack? Herron doubted it, just as he knew McClellan could not have emulated Grant's relentless Overland campaign over two years later, or forced the surrender of Bobby Lee.

Clemens continued. "I learn from your book, general, that you made your regiment march for their moral improvement, which is not something our boys were exercised about. But when we heard you all were coming, we were good and scared. My nervousness took me about a thousand miles away."

"An admirable decision," said Grant.

As the laughter died down, Clemens added, "But there was something else that we did before that. We killed a man." The old soldiers, used to talk about the deaths of thousands, were struck silent by this.

"Who? How?" asked Sweeny at last.

"I don't know who," said Clemens, "but I know how. We used to change camp every time there was a rumor of the enemy approaching, which was often enough, but the rumors never came to anything and one night we grew to disregard them. But then we heard riders—how many I don't know, and vaguely saw one, and someone shouted 'Fire' and we did, I and others, and shot a man off his horse." Clemens paused, and now no one filled the space. "He muttered something, before he died, about his wife and child. We never saw his companions, if he had any. He didn't have a gun."

Again a pause, that no one filled, letting Clemens go on. "I suppose you think me sentimental, worrying about this one man in a war that killed hundreds upon hundreds of thousands. We told each other we were not to blame, were justified by the laws of war—although I have my doubts about that. Some of my comrades stayed in the war, to kill many more men and be killed themselves. But I could not shake, still cannot shake, the feeling that I did not belong there, doing such things."

Another pause, a longer one, until Herron finally said, "I was a volunteer, too, not regular Army like you, Tom, and the general."

"No," said Grant, "I resigned my commission in 1854. I was a volunteer, too."

"Yes, I suppose so," said Herron. "But in some ways I felt more like Mr. Clemens, despite my shoulder stars, which I got soon enough. Through the first two years of the war, I was full of piss and vinegar." He stopped and looked at Nellie, who waved off any potential offense.

"Didn't you end the second year, the end of 1862, by taking Van Buren?" asked Grant.

"We did," Herron replied. "In Arkansas. I'm honored that you remember, but doubt it will go down in history. That was really a successful raid, following up the victory of Prairie Grove earlier that month, December '62." He paused, seemed lost in thought, and no one interrupted. "We had hard marching to both battles, very hard to Prairie Grove, about 120 miles in three days, right in to bitter fighting, some men so tired they could hardly hold up their weapons. Back and forth, we and the rebels went, the guns sounding like hellfire, all to no avail except killing and maiming men."

"Didn't you just call it a victory?" asked Nellie, with some trepidation.

"He and Blunt drove off General Hindman," said Grant.

"Blunt?" asked Nellie.

"Another general," explained Sweeny, "on our side."

"We did that," said Herron, "Blunt and I, he the senior, though it was my division took much the heavier loss. We drove off Hindman. Even though your West Point General Schofield"—Grant and Sweeny smiled at the dig, although the latter was no West Pointer, while Fred looked rather shocked—"back in St. Louis, he seemed to think we shouldn't have done it, or have taken Van Buren, either. Anyway, we did. But before Hindman left Prairie Grove, that first night after the battle, the haystacks caught fire and burned our wounded. I'd seen the same sort of thing at Pea Ridge. This was smolder from our own artillery, some of it our own, anyway, from guns I'd been directing all day. The gunfire was very effective against the rebels, but that night we couldn't save our own men from the effects of it, we couldn't rescue them. Didn't, anyway. I didn't. Then hogs came down among them." They all looked aghast at Herron's story.

"Was that why, general," Grant was asking, "you seemed content with quieter duties as the war went on?"

"Not just that, General Grant," Herron went on, taking no offense at any implied criticism. "At the beginning of the battle, of Prairie Grove, as we arrived after a forced freezing march of three-and-a-half days, our cavalry was driven off. Because Marmaduke had Quantrill's gang of cutthroats as his cavalry vanguard, dressed in our uniforms. I hadn't been expecting to face the Confederate army, thought I was just coming up on Blunt's rear, to reinforce him. The rebels would outnumber our combined divisions, but that didn't worry me. I was badly surprised, though, by Marmaduke, and thought the battle might be lost right there."

There was another pause, broken by Grant. "As General, then Colonel, Sweeny will remember, we were surprised at Shiloh—I was." (That was more than he had said in the book, Badeau reflected sourly. Or at least when dealing with that question, Grant's vaunted clarity of style was not in evidence.) "William Wallace," Grant continued, "the commander of Tom's division, was killed there, along with many other good men."

"He was that, a good soldier," said Sweeny, then adding, with a thin sardonic smile, "I read in the newspaper the other day that General Marmaduke is now the governor of Missouri."

"God help us," said Clemens.

"Yes," said Herron. "He ran on a program of railroad reform to protect the small famers—along with some less savory campaigning that harked back to the war and Reconstruction."

"Yet he and Hindman did not win at Prairie Grove, despite breaking your cavalry and outnumbering you and Blunt," said Grant.

"No," Herron said. "I stopped them." He stopped talking, too, but a miserable wildness in his eyes stopped anyone else now from interrupting. "I mean I stopped my own men, stopped their panic infecting the other troops, the infantry, and more to the point the horses, the artillery horses. It was those guns and troops who went on to win the day. But before that, when our cavalry was in flight, I stopped them by drawing my pistol and shooting one of the fastest riders, one of my own men." No one spoke. Herron had not spoken about this since the war, even to Adelaide. At the time, he had brazened it out.

Herron broke the silence at last. "Dead off his horse as he rode toward me, his supposed friend and commander," turning bleakly to Clemens, "like your man killed in Mis-

souri. I was glad of his death. It would have been worse if
he'd stayed alive, as so many did for some time on those
battlefields. Like you, Clemens, I could justify it if I chose.
Maybe it saved others' lives, his comrades'. That's how I
thought at the time, or pretended I did, and rationalized later. I barely looked at him then, had no time. I decided to
counter-attack. The battle went back and forth all day. Later, though, that man came back—comes back—to my view.
Still does. I only saw him for an instant alive, but it's that I
remember, the moment before I killed him. He was young,
with rather a sparse moustache. Everyone was running
away; he wasn't to blame. Yet I killed him, because I was as
frightened as he was, afraid of our line breaking. No one
blamed me. People didn't mention it. Blunt and I were the
conquering heroes of Prairie Grove, which is now almost as
forgotten a victory as Van Buren. I never found out his
name."

Ely, his face solemn but giving nothing away, was astonished at his friend's story. He wondered if he'd told it before
to anyone in all these after-years. Ely had heard that the
rough-and-ready, murderous rebel general Nathan Bedford
Forrest made a habit of shooting his own men in similar circumstances, but never of a federal officer doing that—
which didn't mean it hadn't been done. Nor that he equated
his friend Frank Herron with any kind of murderer.

Nellie, although rather horrified and with tears in her
eyes, caught Herron's sympathetically.

Badeau, short, stooped and myopic next to the still
handsome Herron, was another civilian-turned-soldier. He
held his tongue. Unlike Herron, he had always been a staff
officer, never holding field command. But unlike his fellow
staffer Parker, or General Grant himself or Fred, Badeau
had been wounded in battle, at Port Hudson. His glance fell
on one-armed Sweeny, whose wound dated from the Mexican War. But that little war, Badeau decided, hardly
counted. His own book proved he knew as much about

warfare as any general. But who would read it now? Badeau determined that in the near future he would take his courage in his hands and seek a new financial arrangement from General Grant. He would write him a letter.

Later, after the guests left, Nellie stayed up with her parents in a little sitting room at the back of the house. She held the hand of her father, who let her know he was grateful for her role in bringing Ely and the others in to see him. Grant had stood to bid them farewell, shaking Ely's hand warmly with both of his, then placing a hand on Herron's shoulder and looking up with kindness into his eyes.

Clemens had left to take the train back to Hartford, to his loving wife and daughters, and Grant, a reader, talked to Nellie and Julia about their famous friend. "He was a rebel and a deserter, yet I feel warmly toward him, and not just because of our present connection. I like his work better than that other westerner's, Ambrose Bierce, who fought for our side. They both have their points, full enough of mawkish coincidence and sentimental twaddle, yet sharp enough, too. But Clemens is the warmer-hearted."

"All kinds of people let themselves fill up with bile," said Julia, who did not like Bierce's writing.

"Not most soldiers," said Grant. "Nellie tells me our writers can't compare to the English—or to the Russians, God save us—for high seriousness. Now Lincoln, he could deliver that, but also make you laugh like Clemens with a country story."

Julia remembered Ulys and others telling her how he had wept openly while standing guard at Lincoln's coffin, but how the assassination had also turned him cold and hard against the rebels. That didn't last, though. His heart, like Lincoln's, was too soft and good. When Nellie was in her teens she was not much for studying, and had been sent away to boarding school, where she immediately started pleading to come home, to the White House. Ulys could not hold out against her. Now she seemed to have become something of a bluestocking in England, a change Ulys had taken in stride. Like her parents, Nellie loved horses, and went on long rides with her father when they visited England.

Badeau, meanwhile, whose family life was irregular, sat alone in a hotel room, drinking whiskey and brooding. He picked up a pen and notebook, wrote out a line, then scratched it out.

CHAPTER TWELVE

HARRIET CONVERSE HAD NOT MADE UP HER MIND about
Herbert Welsh, and that was why she invited him to dinner.
She was suspicious of Welsh's Indian Rights Association,
which he and others had formed in 1882, and she was supporting Thomas Bland's rival plan to form another
association with different political positions on the Indian
question. Harriet, a writer, and her musician husband Frank
(known as "The Father of the Banjo"), were wealthy supporters of Indian rights. They were dubious about the
growing support from their fellow reformers for forced as-
similation—a movement which it seemed Welsh and his
association were part of. She wanted to get her friend Ely
Parker's perspective, so had invited him to the dinner party,
too. But now, before Ely and his wife Minnie had arrived at
the Converses' comfortable home on 46th Street, or Welsh
either, Harriet was alarmed to discover from another guest,
Frank Herron, of another connection between Ely and
Welsh.

Harriet had only met Ely three years before, long after
his glory days, and their bond was a mutual interest in the
Seneca Indians, the Keepers of the Western Gate to the Iroquois Confederacy in upstate New York. She knew, of
course, that Ely was the first Indian to serve as Commissioner of Indian Affairs, and had been driven out of office
in 1871 by an apparently trumped-up scandal—being ultimately vindicated by Congress—because he had cut corners
to deliver emergency supplies to reservations. She had forgotten, however, the name of the man who was the driving

force behind that so-called scandal, the then chairman of the Board of Indian Commissioners, William Welsh, whose nephew was now announced at her door.

Herbert Welsh, a lawyer who was just passing through New York, was aware of his uncle's connection to Ely Parker, whom he had never met. And when they were introduced a few minutes later, Ely himself brought it up without rancor, before moving on to greet Nellie Sartoris, whom he had asked Harriet to invite.

Mrs. Sartoris was accompanied by her friends, the Reverend John and Mrs. Angeline Newman, who had picked her up in a cab on 66th Street. She wore around her neck a burnished, braided, copper-colored golden necklace, from which hung a locket showing a clip of the hair of her dead infant son. She had explained this on the way over to Angeline, a good friend of her mother's, who squeezed her hand, and they also talked about how Julia was holding up. The rest of the Grants had stayed home, as usual. Julia and Ulysses had given up visiting and going to dinner parties like this.

Now Nellie met Minnie Parker for the first time in many years, and the two women immediately took to each other. Frank and Ada Herron joined the conversation, and the three ladies talked about some of the more socially acceptable aspects of nightlife in New York: the new Metropolitan Opera on 39th and Broadway, and a "clean variety" show at Tony Pastor's Tammany Hall theater in Union Square. Frank looked on with pleasure at his wife's animation. Ada, like Julia Grant in Galena, had adapted well to the necessity of leaving lifelong friends and family, and moving North. She found the winters hard, in sharp contrast to New Orleans, and usually became more animated with the coming of spring.

Ely had moved along to talk to the Converses, while the women fell into conversation with Welsh, who was about the same age as Nellie and Minnie. Welsh won Nellie over by talking of his admiration for her father, speaking not just the commonplaces of hero worship for the warrior but intelligent remarks about Reconstruction and warm empathy for the general's current burdens and courage. Frank Herron greeted John Newman.

The Herrons knew the Newmans from postwar New Orleans, where the minister had published a church newspaper and founded schools for the freed slaves, making common cause with the African Methodist Episcopal churches. Herron, meanwhile, was working for the city and federal governments, and as a private lawyer. Newman was in New Orleans before Herron, from 1864, when the war was still going on, and stayed until 1869 when he became chaplain in the U.S. Senate and the pastor of the Grants' church in Washington. Newman moved smoothly into the broad church of American politics and the Grant family circle—one of Julia's grandfathers had been a Methodist minister. A bill was going through Congress then to designate Christmas as a national holiday, and Newman urged President Grant to sign it, which he duly did in 1870. The family celebration which Christmas had become in America was a far cry from what the Puritans had had in mind, which bothered Grant not a bit. Newman even became the distributor of the president's personal charitable gifts to the poor.

Herron had remained South, becoming Louisiana secretary of state before falling out with the governor who had appointed him. After the Grant administration ended and both families moved to New York, the Herrons and Newmans had met by chance a couple of times. They were of different religious affiliations, and Herron was pretty sure Newman looked askance at his family's easy-going Catholicism. Still, the two couples respected each other, and Newman now expressed pleasure that Herron had been in recently to see Grant.

"You know," the minister continued confidentially, with

an effort to suppress, to Herron's relief, his tendency toward bombast, "thinking back to our New Orleans days, I was confident then I was doing God's work." Herron murmured something in agreement, and Newman continued, "In more recent years I have served more prosperous congregations, perhaps acquired some influence with powerful people, which I suppose is what the world calls success. But I admire you for staying down there as long as you did, long after me."

"Thank you," said Herron, rather touched at the compliment. Newman, he thought, showed some awareness of his own pomposity, which made it less offensive.

"It was a hard life down in Louisiana, not without danger, as you know," Newman continued. "I have had softer times since in this rich city, although as you also must know there are many poor people in it, and I sometimes fear that riches may replace religion in the hearts of too many of its people. I see former churches converted into stables and even theaters. As for me, I owe most of any success I've attained to the patronage of our friend General Grant. I also know that some people accuse me, and perhaps I have accused myself, of worldliness in attending that great man. But he is these days a poor man, and a sick one, so perhaps now, even though his fame remains undimmed, I may acquit myself of self-interest in attending him."

Newman's allusions to their mutual idealism did not prevent either of these former carpetbaggers, at dinner, from being impressed at the quiet luxury, excellent food yet easy atmosphere of the Converses' home. This was Herron's idea of civilization.

He was sitting near Welsh and Harriet Converse, who were soon talking politics, deploring together the virulent anti-Chinese prejudice out West, which Congress was slavishly following in the East and enacting into laws. From there they naturally progressed to Indian issues. President Grover Cleveland was in his first months of office, and the country was still getting used to the first Democrat in the White House since before the Civil War—in which he had not participated. Cleveland had just appointed John Atkins as commissioner of Indian Affairs, the office Parker had held under President Grant. Welsh and Mrs. Converse both deprecated Atkins' history as a member of the Confederate Congress from Tennessee. They were apparently not as ready as General Grant to have peace with the former foe.

Herron was soon drawn away into conversation on his other side with a more distinguished guest, Benjamin Bristow, who had served as Solicitor General and Treasury Secretary under President Grant. Since then, Bristow had become a much more prosperous New York lawyer than Herron, and the two had never met. But the war gave them a natural subject of conversation, since Bristow had served at Donelson and Shiloh, where he was wounded, and then as a cavalryman chasing down General John Hunt Morgan's raid into Ohio. Many middle-aged New Yorkers, like the current president, had not served in the war at all; and those who had had generally been in the East with the Army of the Potomac. Herron and Bristow had in common western service.

Herron was a little embarrassed, though. During the war, he had outranked almost everyone of his age or less. Now, in terms of worldly success, Bristow far outclassed him. But he discovered that they both knew Sweeny, from whom the conversation naturally turned to Grant. It occurred to Herron that Bristow in his current prosperity outclassed Grant, too, but the former Cabinet member said he was impressed that Herron and Ely Parker had recently been in to see their old leader at 66th Street.

"I've thought about going," said Bristow, "but wasn't sure I'd be welcome. I'm still not sure."

Herron said, or rather hinted, that Ely, too, had been uncertain—because he had previously been turned away.

"But the general and the whole family could not have been more gracious when we did visit," he added.

Bristow frowned, and said, "I suppose you know there was some coolness between me and the general toward the end of his administration?"

"I have heard so," said Herron diplomatically, although the breakdown in political relations had been anything but a secret at the time, nine or so years before. Bristow, at first with Grant's backing, had broken up the Whiskey Ring, a widespread den of thieves who were stealing federal revenue. But the president had grown less supportive as the scandal moved closer to implicating his secretary Orville Babcock, and Bristow moved closer to becoming a presidential candidate seeking the Republican nomination, which ultimately went to Rutherford B. Hayes. It seemed odd that Bristow pretty much disappeared from public life after that.

"I would like to see him," Bristow said. "I think I will try to do so."

"Perhaps you should talk to Mrs. Sartoris," said Herron, nodding down the table toward Nellie. "Ely did."

"Did he?" said Bristow. "Sometimes women can soften … can ease the way."

"With other women?" suggested Herron.

Bristow, understanding the reference to Julia Grant, who could be a ferocious foe of those she saw as hostile to her husband, smiled wryly. "You know," he said, going back to the Whiskey Ring, "I think Babcock was guilty. But I was sorry to see him drown last year on lighthouse duty. He was not a worthless man. And Grant was—is—a great one."

"You don't blame him then?" asked Herron.

"Not really," said Bristow. "We lawyers see feet of clay all over. Grant never stole a penny, which helps explain why he has nothing now. That and his poor judgment, to trust people like Ferdinand Ward."

"And Orville Babcock?"

"Babcock had more redeeming qualities than Ward"

said Bristow. "He was rough and ready, could be charming. But not a principled man."

Herron contemplated this successful lawyer, the representative of railroads and vast corporations such as Westinghouse, which seemed to be fighting Edison over the electrification of the world. It seemed unlikely that Bristow never misplaced or overlooked a principle in the course of his daily work. But, Herron had to acknowledge, Bristow's Specie Resumption Act of 1875 seems to have been good for the modern economy. And even Lincoln had worked as a railroad lawyer.

"People don't realize how long I've known Grant," continued Bristow. "Not personally, I mean, not as long as Parker and Longstreet who were his friends before the war. I barely knew him even during the war. But those of us who served under him in the early days, at Donelson, we knew we had something, somebody, though he was quiet, very quiet. No speeches, no gestures or posturing, but competent, confident. It was sort of a mystery to us, early in the war, how he commanded. He didn't talk much, but when he did, seemed to know what he was talking about. We knew we were soldiers, under him; he made us believe in ourselves, and in his ability to lead us. Nor did we lose faith after Shiloh, though some of the country did, and had some reason to, surprised as the army had been there. But he was ours and we were his."

"And Lincoln's," said Herron.

Bristow, whose old-soldier eyes had gone far away, refocused and said, quoting the martyred president after Shiloh, when rumors of Grant's drinking and incompetence were swirling around Washington: " 'I can't spare this man; he fights.' " Bristow cleared his throat and continued. "Of course it was us more than him who did the fighting, and I don't need to tell you what kind of business that was. But at Shiloh, we held together. It wasn't that we loved him, as I think some of the Army of the Potomac men did the little

Napoleon. But it wasn't McClellan's flamboyance they loved. I don't think Grant looked out for us like McClellan did for his men. Men threw their coats away in Tennessee, and then almost froze that night at Donelson. We learned, with Grant. And we knew that with him, we would win." Bristow paused, pouring himself some wine, but Herron sensed he was not done, and said nothing.

Bristow continued. "You know, while I was the reformers' white knight in '76, that was just politics, and politics was a trade I took up in the middle of the war, when better men stayed in the Army and got killed, while I made speeches. Donelson and Shiloh helped my career, especially with Grant, and like him I did want to help the Negro. But for all that, I was still just another politician on the make."

"But not on the take," said Herron, and got a wintry smile in return. He glanced down the table at Nellie, whom he was reassured to see was not listening to them. A decanter glistening in the electric lights was being passed around, to men and women alike, and he saw Nellie spurn it with barely concealed distaste.

"No," said Bristow, "there were enough others doing that, at every level and branch of government, far beyond the Grant administration. So many that it seemed to some of the Stalwarts it would be prissy not to join in. I don't defend them. But my point is, in war or peace, it doesn't do to get too puffed up with one's own supposed virtue or dignity, like McClellan, and Sumner."

"Was Grant a competent president?"

"Yes," said Bristow. "He was involved with Akerman and me in the campaign against the Klan, and in passing and enforcing the civil rights laws. He was outraged by the various murders down there. Nor was he a fool about the nation's finances, although I admit I can't say the same about his own. Most of the scandals weren't his. He even backed me on the Whiskey Ring, until Babcock was caught up in it."

Nellie was sitting across from Ely and Herron's wife Ada. The two ladies drew Ely out in smiles talking about his young daughter Maud, who was doing well in school. Nellie was next to Dr. Newman and, at the head of the table, Mr. Converse. She pondered gloomily about all these apparently happily married people, and about the happy marriage of her own parents. It seemed a standing reproach to her, to her and Algy, that they had not replicated this marital success, with who knew what harm in consequence they were doing to their children, whom she now had left to the tender mercies of their English kin. She missed them now with a fierce physical wrench that came upon her in unguarded moments, and that she had thought to escape in a setting such as this.

What about her absent brothers, though? Fred and his impressive American wife Ida seemed able to overcome any marital tensions, and Buck was attentive to his Fannie, although the latter's confinement and recovery after giving birth to Julia meant Nellie had seen little of her. Jesse, though, her rather spoiled younger brother, seemed slow to mature into his marriage, and she hoped he would not go Algy's route. Only Nellie from the Grant family was at this dinner party, where there were few without a spouse. There was Mr. Welsh and Mr. Bristow, and Josephine Shaw Lowell, who was the widow of one slain Civil War hero and the sister of another.

Nellie took a deep breath, and turned to Mr. Converse, a handsome man whose face, despite the moustache, seemed open and to bear out the name Frank which he insisted she should call him. Converse was impressed that a man as famous as Bristow had accepted Harriet's invitation, but was too shy to interrupt his conversation with Herron. Nellie asked him smilingly about the banjo book he was currently writing—she had prepared the way by asking some questions about their host—and was more or less able to follow his enthusiastic explanations about music.

Meanwhile, Ely Parker was talking to Mrs. Lowell, who was dressed in black as she apparently had been ever since the Civil War. Still, she was to his eyes surprisingly young and attractive. She was also actively engaged in public life in the new field of social work, serving on numerous government and charity committees, and, as she told him, these days was engaged in researching the condition of destitute children. She seemed a worthy woman, no social butterfly. Harriet had felt it a coup that both she and Bristow had accepted the invitation. But Ely's eyes had started to glaze over until Mrs. Lowell and he discovered a mutual friend in Jacob Riis, a newspaper reporter with an office near Police Headquarters, who often wrote about crime. Mrs. Lowell, like Ely and Riis, had few sentimental illusions about poor people. She was concerned that handouts would reduce their incentive to work, even though she remained a forceful advocate for the poor and deeply involved in charitable enterprises.

Newman joined the conversation in a flurry of high minded discourse pressing for moral uplift. Mrs. Lowell stated her agreement with him both in terms of religion and in concordance with the high-culture views of the English writer Matthew Arnold. But then she made Newman uncomfortable by talking about prostitution and the need to raise the age of consent for intimate relations from its current level of 10 years old—although he and Ely both hastened to agree with her.

"I also support women's suffrage," said Mrs. Lowell, in a mock conspiratorial tone, "which perhaps my daughter may live to see. But I am rather more concerned at this time to secure shopgirls a decent wage, and the right to sit down behind their counters."

Her male interlocutors declared themselves in support of these latter propositions, and when Herron weighed in, saying he too was inclined to favor votes for women, Newman surprised him by saying that was also the position of

Julia Grant. This caught the ear of Nellie, who did not say anything. She reflected not about the possibility of voting but on her weak position under English law—and perhaps American, too—regarding child custody, in the event of the further deterioration of her marital relations. She was not inclined to sacrifice her children to legal niceties. To a close friend, but not here, she might have said: I am not my husband's equal in law or tradition, although I hardly feel his moral inferior. Nor, of course, were Ely, and the Negroes that Father had tried to protect, inferior to anyone on account of their race, although they might often be regarded that way.

Mrs. Lowell pressed ahead with more potentially controversial points. "In the Smith Carpet Company strike in Yonkers, it is not just pay cuts that the mill girls are trying to reverse. It is work conditions, too; not being able to look out the window without a severe penalty, or to talk, or laugh."

She stopped, and Newman flinched before her quizzical gaze. He felt unwilling to proceed too far down the road of labor radicalism. Ely, somewhat more sympathetic, said, "Regarding the suffrage issue, I think Indians should be able to vote, too, although I'm not sure most of them want to."

The talk at the end of the table between Harriet Converse and Welsh had moved on to a localized controversy at the Pine Ridge Sioux reservation in the Dakota Territory involving the Indian agent, one Valentine McGillycuddy—known, Welsh said, as " 'the friend of Crazy Horse'. But maybe not friendly enough with Democrats to keep his job."

"Nor does he seem to be friends with Red Cloud," said Harriet.

"No," said Welsh, "but McGillycuddy has many Indian supporters. The reason his position there is in jeopardy is a matter of patronage, pure and simple, and shows the need for civil service reform."

"I see you are not a Tammany man," said Mrs. Lowell, and Ely laughed.

"And there I thought things weren't changing much under President Cleveland," said Herron.

"Red Cloud says McGillycuddy is against hunting, and the Sioux way of life," Harriet persisted. Welsh paused, girding for debate.

Ely looked down the table at Welsh, as the attention of the whole dinner party became focused on one conversation. He remembered taking Chief Red Cloud to meet with Grant in Washington in 1870, but did not mention it now.

Welsh said, "McGillycuddy is a good man, and a sincere friend of the Indians. I'm afraid Custer killed the Sioux way of life nine years ago, even as it killed him."

"I hope you are not a supporter of Custer's approach," said Harriet to Welsh, glancing at Ely. "Or should I say Sheridan's?" Philip Sheridan, who had been close to Custer and still was with Grant, now reigned as head of the whole U.S. Army.

"No," said Welsh. "But the buffalo are gone, and the railroad is come. The Sioux, the Indians, cannot go on in their old ways. They need to own farm land, and to have government-funded schools, and to become American citizens. General Parker, was not that your vision? And that of your late friend and scholar of the Seneca, Lewis Morgan?"

If Ely was surprised at the appeal, he did not show it, and took his time replying. Normally, he hated to play the victim, but his personal history was relevant to this point. "I farmed and went to school, then trained to be a lawyer, long before the war, but the State of New York told me I could not pass the bar, because attorneys had to be American citizens and Indians were not eligible. So I became an engineer instead." The whole dinner party waited for him to go on, which he did. "So, Mr. Welsh, with that history and that of my subsequent service, I am hardly likely to oppose U.S. citizenship for Indians. But as Scripture says, on this earth we see through a glass, darkly. Our perspective may change with the years. It may grow … complicated."

"The ways of God may be obscure," said Newman, "but they and truth exist."

"I'm sure General Lee thought as much," said Ely, uncharitably, "but he must have gotten them mixed up."

"Did you know the surrender at Appomattox Court House was on Palm Sunday?" responded Newman. "Our troops sang the doxology."

"Which Father probably didn't recognize—the tune, I mean," said Nellie. Herron saw one or two people who looked puzzled, while others smiled. Most were aware that Grant had no ear for music.

"Senator Dawes," said Welsh—eschewing music along with theology and the Civil War—"and other friends of the Indian are determined to enact a new bill to address the many problems on reservations, to integrate the Indians into American life. The senator and his supporters have been reliable supporters of Indian rights, as well as of the rights of the Negro, from before the war through Reconstruction up to the present day."

"They've covered all the bases then," said Ely, more sardonic than usual, Herron thought.

Newman said, with a hint of disapproval, "I understand Red Cloud has become a Catholic."

"So did I become one," said Herron, "down in New Orleans after the war, Reverend, where you remember our paths crossed. My Catholic wife had something to with it," he added, smiling down the table at Ada.

"Yes," said Newman, deciding not to pursue denominational or matrimonial controversy. "I do think the Christianization of the Indians is part of their civilization. I must say Mr. Welsh's views on the subject seem sensible, and are supported by reliable people. Surely we can do better by our continent's original inhabitants."

Since they all seemed to waiting for him, Ely spoke up:

"Did you ever, Reverend Newman, read any of Washington Irving's *Sketch Book* essays about the Indians?"

"No," said Newman. "I don't believe I have."

"In one of them," Ely continued, "he quotes some other writer, a historian of King Philip's War, who describes the burning of what they call wigwams in one action, and how some of the soldiers were moved by the shrieks and cries of the women and children. I think the passage goes, that they 'were in much doubt then, and afterwards seriously inquired, whether burning their enemies alive could be consistent with humanity, and the benevolent principles of the Gospel.' "

Harriet sat with mouth agape. Newman seemed embarrassed and was silent, with the rest of the company. Herron had never heard Ely speak so harshly about Indian history before. Nellie, restraining her tongue and controlling her facial expression, silently cheered Ely on.

Welsh was apparently the first to recover, saying, "More than *A Century of Dishonor*, to quote the title of a more recent book by Helen Hunt Jackson. I believe she supports our reform efforts, as does Susette La Flesche, who spoke up for her Ponca people in Nebraska as you had done for the Seneca in New York."

"They seem more benign in intent than General Sheridan sometimes was," said Ely, "but don't some of those reformers say, 'Kill the Indian and save the man'? Too often, both have been killed. Forgive my bad taste in raising the matter, but even to this day the subject of massacre is not irrelevant to the Indians, and not just regarding what they did to the Seventh Cavalry, but what was done to them. Although I realize most of their, our, losses came from the diseases of nature, against which we had no immunity. Relatively few deaths came from such as the British general Lord Amherst, who deliberately spread smallpox as a weapon of war."

Ely paused, repressing the disgust, or at least annoyance,

which he partly felt with himself, at his own self-dramatization. As no one interrupted, he decided to continue but with a shift of emphasis. "I am a member of the Episcopal Church. My people were Baptists, and one of their missionaries gave me the name Ely. Yet we also used to talk of the Great Spirit Creator. I suppose I grew skeptical of the old way, the magical way of thinking, following dreams and sacrificing dogs. But some might call it the same God and meaning, whether at the Catholic Mass or the little water ceremony of our old Seneca religion. My grandfather Handsome Lake founded a new Indian, or Iroquois, religion of sorts, and an appealing one, I thought, for preserving our family life. My Uncle Red Jacket was a religious man, but skeptical of Christianity. Still, my first school was at the Baptist mission. Then the Quakers and Congregationalists became our allies in holding on to the reservation against land speculators and politicians. Later, the missionaries helped with Grant's peace policy, served as agents to the Indians, and proved more honest than most of the others, less liable to steal from the Indians and the government. So had the Spanish Catholic missionaries proven better friends to the conquered Indians than the Conquistadors. The Grant administration paid our modern Catholic and other churches for missionary and education work on reservations. But the Christians, like other men, did not, do not, always see clearly what is in front of them."

Ely paused again, but was clearly not finished, and they all waited for him to explain. "I used to think the Indians must adopt the white man's way, including his religion. So did most Indians, so did Grant. He and I did not agree with General Sheridan, or General Sherman either, about these matters. The Indians must adjust, we thought, like the Negroes and the immigrants joining the industrial age, and the white men, too, the settlers. Grant also thought, I think, that human progress would put an end to war. He was an idealistic practical man, although not so practical that he could ever hold on to any money for himself. I thought the Indians should make the whites live up to their proclaimed principles. I fear they have not, do not do so. Maybe none of us do."

"How could we?" asked Newman. "Surely the failure of mortals to live up to Christian principles does not invalidate those great ideals?"

"No. Nor does the fact that Colonel Chivington, who ordered the Sand Creek massacre, was an enthusiast for Methodism and abolition. My point is simply that I would have more faith in the benefits of Christianization and civilization, if I saw more evidence of the principles behind them being applied to Indian affairs."

"I agree with you there, sir," said Newman.

"As do I," said Harriet, and Nellie nodded her own assent.

"Yes of course," said Welsh, "our record toward the Indians has been atrocious. But you, Mr. Parker, helped improve with it with President Grant's peace policy, and now I ask you, is not the vision of Mr. Dawes and others to fully integrate the Indian into American society worthy of our support?"

Ely smiled across the table at his white wife, and considered Welsh's question. "I used to hold that view," he said, "but have grown less dogmatic as I get older. Grant was a doer, not a talker. If you're asking me what I think as an Indian, then I think I'm talking too much." Some others smiled, but he didn't stop speaking. "Grant's appointment of me, an Indian, as commissioner, the first non-white ever appointed to high federal office, was an action which, as actions tend to do, spoke louder than words. In his first term, he made peace with the Sioux, and then the Apache. Peace held, too, with the Kiowas and Comanches, thanks to a Quaker agent and Colonel Grierson. I helped Grant accomplish those and other things to benefit my people, the Indians."

Ely took a sip of water, and the company waited for him to go on. "President Grant did the same with the Negroes —helped them, I mean. The Democrats demonized or at best scorned them. The northern papers and critics, the great and the good in this city, sentimentalized and condescended to the black man, while sneering at Grant, when what he was doing, with Mr. Bristow here, and others," he nodded at Frank Herron, "was passing and enforcing civil rights, and crushing the Ku Klux Klan."

"Did he not issue an order against the Jews, though," asked Mrs. Lowell, "during the war?"

"That was before I was with him," said Ely, "in complicated circumstances. It had to do with his father's business connections in smuggling cotton, which the Lincoln administration was turning a blind eye to. His father's involvement greatly distressed the general, whose order was rashly made and quickly repudiated."

"On Lincoln's instruction," Mrs. Lowell said. "The father seems like a Southern caricature of a money-grubbing Yankee." Herron wondered if she realized that Grant's daughter was sitting at their table.

Newman did realize, and responded in indignant defense of his friend, "General Grant always regretted that order, and tried to make amends for it. He spoke out against racial prejudice, and became a friend to the Jewish people. I was with him in 1876 when we attended the dedication of the Adas Israel synagogue in Washington. No president has had better relations with the Jews."

Ely said, "I had a rabbi as an Indian agent, along with the Protestant parsons, the Catholic priests and the Quakers. They did good work, most of them, genuinely wanted to protect the Indians from being murdered and driven off their land. But in Washington, some of the high-minded clerical types didn't like me, because I wasn't one of their fantasy Indians dressed up in feathers and waiting to be saved. They weren't ready for one who'd saved himself, and had become a regular politician in their world, and knew the Indian part of that world a damned sight better than they did. Excuse me, ladies. Accusations of corruption in this age are often unjustified, and sometimes cynical, but they resonate because the world does seem more corrupt."

Herron thought Ely had an ambivalent attitude toward Wall Street. For a while there, after he left Indian Affairs, he had made too-easy money as an investor, presumably through connections in this Gilded Age. He recalled, too, the racial hypocrisy of the reformers, anxious to blame Negro scalawags or drunken Indians or grasping Jews, Catholic creoles or the brutish Tammany Irish for scandals, when it was white Protestants who stole far more than all of the rest put together. Newman, who was no reformer so far as Herron knew, and to whom he gave some credit for defending the Jews, still seemed to give off some of the same hypocrisy.

"As for the Jews," Ely continued, "General Grant respected them, and all religions. But with due respect to Dr. Newman, I do not remember him as a particularly religious man."

"No," said Nellie, "but not an irreligious one, either. You remember that story about Senator Sumner, how someone—perhaps you, Ely—told Father that Sumner didn't believe all of the Bible, and he replied, 'That's because he didn't write it.' " They laughed politely at the old story, but Nellie continued seriously, "In a way he is skeptical because he respects religion too much, because he can't reconcile it with war, or soldiering, on which his fame is based."

"Your father is no hypocrite," said Ely. Mrs. Lowell's face remained blank, giving Herron no clue as to whether she had only now realized that she was dining with Grant's daughter.

Herron's religious views had tended to fluctuate, not strictly confined by Catholicism, but were not now, he thought, as skeptical as Grant's, whose skepticism must have been reinforced by the chances of war. Bad luck and good courage seemed to kill men whom God or Providence could not or would not save, at least in this world. Yet the war seemed to have moved Lincoln, with whom Grant had so much in common, in a different direction, to the religious, redemptive themes of the Second Inaugural.

"I don't think I agree," ventured Newman to Nellie. "General Grant has Christian ideals, which can come into conflict for any of us. The rebels, after all, were Christians too."

"Stonewall Jackson even more so than Lee, and most of them," said Ely. "More Christian than our side, maybe. Unless you count John Brown."

"I don't count or claim him," said Newman, "after those cold-blooded killings at Pottawatomie. But most abolitionists acted from Christian principles without becoming murderers. And even Brown died courageously. I don't presume to judge the state of any man's soul. Even Bedford Forrest repented at the end, I am told."

"Were Brown's killings worse than Indian killings, or white men killing Indians?" asked Ely. "And the rebels claimed Sherman and Sheridan were starving children to death."

" 'As he died to make men holy, Let us die to make them free,' " said Nellie. "Of course Julia Ward Howe was in no danger of dying. It took practical men, as Ely says, to win the war. Were they ruthless ones, too?" No one answered, so Nellie continued, addressing Newman: "And it was one of your fellow ministers who shipped out guns as Beecher's bibles for the likes of Brown to use in Kansas. Although wasn't it broadswords he used at Pottawatomie?"

"Whose side are you on, Nellie, the English?" asked Minnie Parker, surprising everyone.

Mrs. Lowell spoke up. "It was Beecher's sister's book, *Uncle Tom's Cabin*, which Lincoln said started the war."

"Sherman and Sheridan were soldiers, which Brown was not," said Herron. "They didn't kill soldiers who surrendered, as Forrest's troopers did to Negroes, or murder noncombatants as Quantrill and Bloody Bill Anderson did. Or that other irregular, John Wilkes Booth."

Newman got back to his point. "Grant wanted to help the poor Negro in the South, as General Herron and I tried to do in Louisiana. And I found plenty of Christians down there, both black and white. Religion drove Reconstruction, in part, as it had driven abolition. Before I went, I used to preach about traitors, and I found some bad or misguided men still fire-eating after the war was over. I was a supporter of General Grant's Reconstruction policies. Yet he also wanted, quite properly, to reconcile with his, our, former enemies, the Confederates. It was Grant who stopped President Johnson from trying Lee, and Longstreet and Joe Johnston, for treason, and having them hanged. He ran twice for president on the platform 'Let us have peace,' which might have been said by Our Savior."

"Indeed," said Ely. "Johnson swung from one extreme to another. But to return to Mr. Welsh's topic of the Indians, I have become skeptical about the benign effects of good intentions—which I do not doubt that Senator Dawes and Mr. Welsh here possess. Maybe the Indians would be better off left in peace, now that a U.S. District Court in Oklahoma has ruled that we are in fact persons. My doubts include my own intentions and conduct, my leadership, such it was, of my people. I don't know what they, we, the Indians or the whites, should have done, but sometimes I feel uneasy, guilty, about what I did do. It troubles my sleeping. I suppose in my defense I was trying to prevent their wholesale murder, their extermination, in the West."

Ely was grateful that none of his friends rushed embarrassingly to his defense, and that instead Welsh was persisting in opposition. "Would it not benefit the Indian to learn to farm, and to own land which he can pass on to his son? Isn't that better than leaving them cut off from most Americans on tribal reservations? Should not our civilization include all people?"

"It should," Ely said, "And the policies you propose might do that, benefit the Indians, I mean. Or not. There are no more Cherokee farmers in Georgia or Tennessee." Herron thought of Stand Watie as Welsh started to protest, but Ely held up a hand and went on. "Your bills might weaken the tribes, and their communal life, without creating farmers, and cause the reservations to lose land to outside speculators, who will sell it to white settlers. It might leave the Indians worse off, while doing nothing to really bring them into American society. I don't claim to know, but am not sure that you and Senator Dawes do, either."

"Unless they become regular farmers, like other Americans, they cannot prosper or thrive on reservations," said Welsh. "It is no kindness to leave them there."

Ely's eyes grew farther away, as he shifted gears in the argument. "I have become more humble in advancing age, and have long since left the longhouse of my people. Like the Jew come from his shetl and the Irishman from the potato field, I rent an apartment in the city of New York. Like them, I came voluntarily, but the history of the Indian, like the Negro, is different. I have made peace with the world of those who conquered my people, which you may say the Indian has to do, and I might agree with you, but he does not have to like it. Nor has my progress through this modern world left me particularly prosperous. And there's this: You did me the courtesy earlier of mentioning my Seneca ancestry. When I was young, I helped the Tonawanda Seneca keep some of their land, their reservation. I am still proud to have done that."

Welsh paused with the rest of the company, cognizant that his hostess and Parker were friends, and reluctant to keep challenging the latter. While Welsh in some ways admired Parker, he knew the Indian had been part of the notoriously corrupt Grant administration, and had made money just after that, or seemed to, on Wall Street, though apparently had gone on to lose it. But Welsh doubted he was just a poor apartment dweller now. Didn't he own property in Connecticut? Welsh wasn't sure whether Parker had personally profited from corruption, but felt him tainted by it, and in no position now to cast aspersions on the likes of Senator Henry Dawes. Still, this was not the place to pursue that line. General Herron was frowning at him, presumably out of solidarity with Parker.

"Yes," Welsh said finally, "and the immigrants must give up Yiddish and Gaelic and Italian and Polish, and become Americans, as must the Indians, as you have done."

Minnie Parker suddenly spoke up. "My husband is a proud man, Mr. Welsh, a sachem of the Iroquois Confederacy, which spread for a thousand miles and stood for peace and unity before this country existed, unlike that other white men's Confederacy which he fought against." Welsh smiled weakly, unsure of the point Mrs. Parker was trying to make.

"It still stands, the Iroquois Confederacy," said Harriet.

"Yes," said Nellie. "Ely took me visiting on reservations there when I was a child." The three women and Ada Herron smiled at each other, and at their Indian friend. Mrs. Lowell smiled with them at Ely sitting next to her. Harriet Converse felt glad women were not always obliged anymore to leave a dinner table with the port, and so did not have to miss the interesting conversation.

Bristow had not waded into the general discussion about Indians. After it ended, in private conversation with Herron, he good-humoredly resisted the latter's urging that he resume a political career. Herron, who was a genuine admirer, even compared him to Lincoln as another corporate lawyer, causing Bristow to smile again.

"That is all behind me," Bristow said. "It would have been behind Lincoln, too, but for slavery and secession. God spare us from that kind of crisis again, for we sorely lack a Lincoln. I know my limitations. Now, like other men, like you no doubt, I work to provide for my family. Where I do have public involvements, they are not controversial ones."

Before the party broke up, Bristow did take the opportunity to have Herron introduce him to Nellie, although he had encountered her years before as a girl in the White House. They talked about those days, and how Nellie used to play the piano and sing there, to the joy of her father the president, non-musical though he was. Bristow found her, as did most people, very congenial.

Chapter Thirteen

On April 27, a successful 63rd birthday party was held for the general at his house, the guests in addition to family including Sherman, Clemens, Badeau and the Newmans. Grant's health continued seemingly to improve, including his vocal capacity. He was able to dictate in a low voice to the stenographer, Dawson, about Appomattox and other matters, while continuing to write much of the manuscript in his own hand.

Julia had told her little grandson Ulysses, not yet four years old, to "shout and make a noise" if he wanted anything, and in the middle of one night he proceeded to take her literally, arousing the household because he wanted an apple. Ida and Fred were cross with their son, but General Grant, who had managed to get up to investigate with the others, defended the boy, and Julia fetched him an apple.

On April 29, a story appeared in Joseph Pulitzer's *New York World* quoting Brevet General G. Peter Ihrie, who was not close to Grant but had served him as a staff officer during the war, and had retired as a major in 1873. According to Ihrie and the *World*, the *Memoirs* were being written not by Grant but by Badeau. Ihrie was presumably just trying to sound knowing, which made the slur all the more damaging. Clemens was indignant, threatening legal action against the paper—which had been going from sensationalist strength to strength as its circulation soared. Grant instead wrote a letter to Webster & Company, for distribution to the press, that twice repeated the phrase, "Composition is entirely my own."

Grant and Badeau had a private contract—or rather a memorandum signed by Grant alone—which was drawn up in early February, under which Badeau was to receive as much as $10,000 (depending on sales) for his assistance on the book, including maps which served "as the basis for my maps," according to Grant's note. On March 2, Grant had paid Badeau $250 of this money, in cash, out of $1,000 which he received from Webster & Company. After the *World* article ran on April 29, Fred and Clemens tried to get Badeau to refute it. Badeau, however, was evasive, and declined to sign letters presented to him by Fred that would clarify the matter by saying absolutely that he had had no hand in writing Grant's book. This raised the unspoken suspicion that Badeau was the source for Ihrie's misrepresentation. Badeau, meanwhile, was spending time away from 3 East 66th Street, closeted in his rented room to work on a letter.

On May 2, a few hours after Grant had sent off his letter to Webster claiming sole authorship, Badeau came up to him as he worked at his desk. Badeau, looking fussier and more tense than usual, formally handed the general a sealed envelope, made him something between a bow and a nod, and scurried out of the room and the house. Grant opened the letter.

> Dear General—I beg to lay before you a few views which I am very sure have not occurred to you, absorbed as you have been in your illness and recently in your renewed work. I present them in writing, because I can thus make them clearer, and because you can more carefully consider them and detect if I am in error.
>
> When you sent for me in August last you said that you had always given me to suppose that my work should be the only authorized expression of your views on the war, but that you were now about

to write your Memoirs and to make use of my work for your facts and dates whenever necessary, saving yourself all the labor of research, and that in consideration of these circumstances and of my assistance in preparing your own book, you offered me $10,000 out of the profits, if they should amount to $30,000. The labor I was expected to perform was such as enabled me to revise with you both the Shiloh and Vicksburg campaigns, 250 pages, in a little more than a fortnight, for both these chapters were sent to The Century while I was at Long Branch in August.

In October, I came to you in New York, before I was ready, giving up my own work for yours, and have since devoted myself to your service, happy and proud to aid you.

Your illness first protracted and then interrupted the work, and I have been detained from all other avocations for seven months. I tried once or twice to write for myself, but gave this up as impossible while I was doing such work as your book demands, for I put my whole soul and ability into it. My novel is unpublished today, solely from this cause.

Now that you are happily in some degree restored and able to dictate, an entirely new state of affairs arises. Your book is about half done. The work still to be executed on Volume 1 and the original composition on Volume 2 make necessary eight or ten months more labor. You propose to dictate and I am to piece and prepare and connect the disjointed fragments into a connected narrative. This work is the merest literary drudgery, such as I would never consent to do for anyone but you—five times as laborious as original composition, with none of the interest; five times as difficult under the circumstances as what I have hitherto done with you. It cannot possibly be completed as you want it and as I should do it before 1886. I am to have no pay until the profits of your book come in, at the earliest in March next. In the nature of things I can have no reputation or consideration from my connection with the book. I must efface myself, and yet work intensely hard without increased pay or any at all until a year and a half from the beginning of my labors.

Let me say just here I have no possible desire for the reputation or name of writing the book. The preposterous assertions in the newspapers will refute themselves. I desire the fame of my own book, not of yours. Yours is not and will not be the work of a literary man, but the simple story of a man of affairs and a great general. Proper for you, but not such as would add to my credit at all. With your concurrence I have striven to make it such.

But your book has assumed an importance which neither you nor I anticipated last summer. It is to have a circulation of hundreds of thousands, and the larger its circulation the greater its importance—the more completely it will supplant and stamp out mine. The better I help you to make it, the more effectually I destroy what I have spent my life in building up—my reputation as your historian.

And this nobody but me can do. No literary man has the military knowledge; no military man has the literary experience; no literary or military man living, not one of your old staff even, has one tithe of my knowledge and experience on this subject, the result of twenty years' study and devotion and labor. Besides which no man alive but your own sons loves you so well. No one but myself can destroy my own book. If I don't help you it will retain its place, for you have neither the physical strength nor the habits of mind yourself to make the researches to verify or correct your own memory. If you cannot yourself finish the work, nobody can do it fitly but me.

Dear General, I say this frankly to show you what is expected of me—to give up a year of my life, at the age of fifty-three, to get no shadow of reputation or consideration, to trample on my own fame, to receive no pay at present, and none at all proportionate to my position or claims, for I could easily earn $5,000 or $10,000 a year, with importance and consideration besides. There is only one inducement in the world, and that is to serve you. But I have already written your military history, and I can still write your political history, and earn more, and serve your fame quite as well; while if by any chance your work should be unfinished or ill finished my own could retain its place. Your name sells your work, your deeds are its theme; your own story told by yourself is what the people want. All this is indisputable; but the drudgery is all mine, and the drudgery is as indispensable as your name or as the publisher's part.

Under these circumstances, considering the immense sales assured, the unexpected work put upon me, the unanticipated damage done to my life's labor, is it unfair for me to ask that a new bargain be made?

I am willing to agree to complete the work from your dictation in the first person, with all the supervision you may be able to give, but in any event to complete it, if I am alive and well, within the present year, to claim, of course, no credit whatever for the composition, but to declare, as I have always done, that you write it absolutely.

For this labor I ask $1,000 a month, to be paid in advance, until the work is done, and afterward ten percent of the entire profits. The publishers, Fred told me long ago, have offered to advance any sums you desire, so that you would not be inconvenienced by the earlier payments, and unless you receive enormous gains my share would still be small.

I would engage to help you build such a monument as no man ever yet put up to his fame, and no name would ever appear in connection with it but your own.

Your affectionate and faithful friend and servant, General Grant.

Adam Badeau

Grant was taken short of breath and nauseous after reading this document—he felt as if he had experienced a physical relapse. After so much financial distress and embarrassment in his own family, he could scarcely believe he was being dunned for money by someone he had trusted, whose career he had made for more than two decades. Badeau had already been provided for at the expense of the Grant family, for months in this very house as well as under the terms of what Grant regarded as a generous contract. Family, he thought bitterly, was what life came back to. Badeau had never been the sort of substitute son he'd had in the Army as perhaps Sheridan was, or Horace Porter or Cyrus Comstock. But he had let him get too close. *Now I must cleave to my own real family.*

Grant also felt as he had a couple of times early in the war, most notably at Shiloh, wrong-footed by a surprise attack. He felt this even though the *World* story and Badeau's evasive reaction to it, he now realized, should have been a signal, an obvious warning of what was to come. It was all connected. As at Shiloh and every other battle, Grant grimly, rapidly and forcefully responded. He shrugged off his aide's condescension and insults, and the dishonest proposal to write Grant's book for him without taking credit but grasping at far too much money. Grant's goal now was to clearly demonstrate that Badeau was deluded in one particular above all, that he was very far from being indispensable.

Fred noticed his father's agitation, and was silently handed the letter. Clemens, too, read it, and denounced Badeau in blood-curdling terms before storming off to consult lawyers. There was some question about showing the letter to Julia, who had been a firm ally of Badeau. But when she did read it her past sympathies with the writer now led her to think of him as a traitor, and immovably set her face against him. Nellie also was given the letter to read.

The next day, Harrison announced to Grant, Julia, Fred and Nellie that Ely Parker was at the door, by previous arrangement. Fred, looking from one parent to another, hesitated and did not immediately reply to Harrison. It was a Sunday, which freed Ely from Police Department duties, and only his second visit to the Grant house for at least a year—his first since the memorable evening there with Herron, Sweeny, Clemens and Badeau.

Nellie said, "He knows Badeau," and all of them realized this was true. Ely Parker and Adam Badeau had been among the general's closest staff officers. It also occurred to more than one of them that Ely was the only one of the staffers whose friendship with Grant dated back to before the Civil War.

Julia, who had been badly shaken by Badeau's treachery, said of Ely, "It will be good to see him. We have known each other through all sorts of days, for him and his family, and for ours." So he was admitted. But after greeting him, Julia retired to her room. Fred took Ely aside and asked him to read the scarlet letter, which he did, then rejoined the company. There were in the parlor Fred, Nellie and the general. A somewhat awkward pause in conversation was broken by Grant.

"Well?" he asked Ely. "What do you think?"

"It sounds like extortion," Ely said.

"It does," Grant agreed. "Or blackmail."

"Was he behind the *New York World* article?"

"I don't know. Clemens thinks so."

"So he somehow got this into the *World* so as to get better terms from you," said Ely, "and will not deny the story until you agree to the terms?"

"That's the long and the short of it," said Fred. "He wouldn't sign a letter denying the truth of the *World* story. Clemens thinks he can harm the book, and must be stopped."

"Why don't we meet with him?" Ely asked Fred.

"For what purpose?" asked Grant. "I intend to give him nothing under threat. I can have no further dealings with him. I intend to write and tell him so, tell him exactly why."

"Fred and I can find out what he intends to do," said Ely, "and head him off, if possible."

"I have not been successful in my recent dealings with Badeau," Fred said.

"Then let me go to him," said Ely. Everyone turned to the general.

CHAPTER FOURTEEN

ON MONDAY MORNING ELY WAS UP EARLY but went to Hell's Kitchen instead of his office on Mulberry Street. Fred had given him Badeau's address, which turned out to be a fourth-floor walk-up. He knocked on the door, discovering no servant to answer.

Nor was there any sign of Badeau's wife, whom he had married about a decade ago. He kept his private life private, and could not be expected to welcome this intrusion.

Still, Badeau eventually responded, talking through the closed door, and, after delay, admitted his old colleague Ely Parker. He was apparently living alone, in a more or less disheveled state of affairs which he had had little time to adjust. The aromas of tobacco and alcohol overcame less savory smells, and Badeau was sensible enough to open a window on this May morning—the fourth. He did not offer any refreshment or even a chair, but Ely smiled, gestured with a hand toward a vacant chair, and sat down on it.

"Did Fred send you?" Badeau asked, as he too sat down.

"Yes," said Ely.

"Then why should I deal with you?"

"You and I have known each other for many years, working closely together. Much longer than you've worked with Fred."

"Fred is a little puppy," said Badeau, "lecturing me on something about which he knows nothing."

"About his father's book?"

"Yes. He may think he knows about it, but he knows

nothing really. Nothing about literature, war, even the career of General Grant. He just gets in the way."

While Badeau knew he had seen and suffered more of the real war than Ely Parker, he also had seen the Indian, like Grant himself, exhibit that remote calmness under fire which Badeau and most men found difficult. Was that courage, or lack of imagination? He did not want to be dealing with him now.

"I understand," said Ely, "that General Grant, too, was disturbed by the *World* article, and by your recent letter."

"A letter in which I told him to pay no mind to the scurrilous accounts of newspapers."

"True. But Fred tells me you will not sign a letter disavowing authorship."

"I will not sign anything written by that idiot, stating falsely that I had nothing to do with General Grant's book."

"Is there no way of reconciling you?"

"Of course there is," snapped Badeau, getting up and beginning to pace on the carpet.

"You mean as suggested in your letter?" suggested Ely.

"Parker, you have not been closely associated with the general in recent years, but the fact is I shaped this book, I told him how to write it, guided him in doing so, often changed or suggested wording which he accepted. Those are the facts. Grant is no writer. And I won't sentimentalize the truth, which is that circumstances have changed, and Grant can well afford to pay me what I am due." Ely remained silent, sitting upright in the untidy room.

"Do you know," Badeau continued with a bitter smile, changing the subject back to his *bête noir*, "about the only thing Fred did in the Army? Went on that Black Hills junket with Custer, the one that opened up the gold fields, set up war with the Sioux and led to Little Big Horn? And do you know why, I mean do you know why Grant let him go, let Custer go?"

"I don't know. Maybe the same reason he let him go

back a year or two later, in 1876, because he got tired of trying to stop him, of having to argue about it with Sheridan
and Sherman."

"No," said Badeau. "That wasn't all of it, that wasn't
enough to torpedo the peace policy. Weren't you on Wall
Street in '73?"

"I was," said Ely.

"Which was when the depression started, which as you
know lasted for years, all through the rest of Grant's second
term. That's why he let Custer go in '74, because the money
men, the sainted Bristow and his fellow economists, told
him he needed the gold, the mining, the jobs, the economic
gains. He did it for the money."

Ely was shocked, despite himself. He feared Badeau was
on to something, dragging something nasty into the light
that Ely had not wanted to see. Grant did not do anything
for the money in the sense of being personally corrupt, but
he had become enthralled by the mystique of capitalism, ap-
peasing its dark gods.

"And he was right to do it," continued Badeau. "It was
a bad depression, not like this little one we've had since
Grant & Ward went under. There needed to be a greater
supply of money, hard money. Ask Bristow. When Grant
vetoed the inflation bill, it infuriated the West. He couldn't
stop Custer, too."

Badeau's blow had struck home, and Ely leaned forward
and back, settling himself in the chair, shaking off gloom
and recovering the will to go on advocating for his old
friend and leader. Was this true? Had Grant sacrificed the
Indians? If so, could it be justified as a way to save many
millions of Americans from terrible poverty? Ely could not
justify it, and decided he did not have to believe it. Reality
was too various for simple explanations.

He changed the subject. "Grant always had a way with
words, though, even if people don't think of him that way.
The other day, talking to friends, I said he was a doer, not a

talker. I remember reading about Donelson in the newspapers, when I was still at Tonawanda, and he was only a brigadier: 'No terms except unconditional and immediate surrender can be accepted. I propose to move immediately upon your works.' He had no great shakes of a staff back then, with neither you nor I yet on it. There was no one else but Grant who could have written that. Or a couple of years later, when I saw him at the little table in his tent, cigar in his teeth, writing a quick note to Halleck that ended, 'I propose to fight it out on this line if it takes all summer.' Or just sending a message to Lincoln saying, 'There will be no turning back'."

"He got his teeth in and hung on to the end," Badeau said, "and I don't mean the cigar."

The image might have made others flinch, but Ely merely said, "He did what had to be done," before returning to the point. "You remember the next year, at Appomattox, when he stopped the hundred-gun salute in celebration of the surrender, saying 'The rebels are our countrymen again.' You couldn't put it better than that, although I suppose sending over our rations did more to build goodwill. You know Grant could write his own reports without difficulty. His orders were clearly written."

"Not at Iuka," Badeau muttered, referring to a battle fought by Grant's subordinate, Rosecrans.

"Even in ordinary conversation," Ely went on, "Grant could turn a phrase. Telling Lincoln, soon after he met him, 'I have had enough of this show business.' " This won a wintry smile from Badeau, and Ely, encouraged, continued. "He has a native wit. Remember that line about knowing only two tunes, one was 'Yankee Doodle' and the other wasn't? And that surrender document with Lee which I copied down, saying 'Each officer and man will be allowed to return to his home, not to be disturbed by U.S. authority so long as they observe their parole and the laws in force where they may reside.' Was that ill-written? Did not those words serve to protect Lee from treason charges?"

"Be that as it may," said Badeau, "Grant as a writer had no idea of structure, what to include, to elaborate, what to leave out, until I taught it to him. *The Century*'s editor, Robert Underwood Johnson, rejected—or it would have been a rejection for anyone else—the first piece he submitted last year, about Shiloh, before there had been any real thought given to writing a book. Johnson said it was too dry, and he was right. I rewrote that chapter, and one about Vicksburg, with the general, putting some life into his style."

Ely severely doubted that Badeau's contribution amounted to so much, but now it was his turn not to argue a point. "It's true," he said, "that General Grant never thought of himself as a writer, or had any inclination to tell his own story. And as you know, he had never meant to be a soldier, either, or was ever really comfortable with the pomp and circumstance of military life. But by now, hasn't he learned what you taught him? Isn't he his own man?"

"Only up to a point. A few days ago, what precipitated my letter, was he and Fred handing me a whole new mess of material to put in order."

"His prognosis remains poor," said Ely, taking the opportunity to switch gears again. What really bothered Badeau, he realized, was that General Grant no longer behaved like a halting novice at writing a book, and one who could be easily led, but was in increasingly confident command of the process. "He's fighting it out again now. That is why your old friend, your benefactor and commander, needs your help."

"Yes, and I must be paid for it. Clemens has been telling me the book will pay vastly more than had been envisaged, just based on his advance sales. The general can afford to be generous." Badeau, who had resumed his seat, now jumped up again and plucked at his beard. "It is not dishonorable," he continued, "to seek a new contract to reflect changed conditions."

"Yet your existing contract is not two months old."

"It was written down then," said Badeau, "codified, merely, what we had agreed between us last summer. If I had known then the work involved …" He continued to pace the room.

"The immediate issue," Ely said, "is the *World* article, and the rumors that it is based on, which your letter to Grant has not put to rest."

"I can't control the newspapers, and specifically disavowed them in that letter."

Ely was careful not to contradict him on this point of honor, not to accuse him of being the source for Ihrie and the *World*—even as he approached another delicate matter. "Yet there is a difficulty with your letter coinciding with the rumors in the *World* article, along with your reluctance to sign Fred's letter. You cannot want there to appear to be any connection."

"What do you mean?" Badeau coldly inquired.

"You cannot want," Ely spelled it out, "for anyone to infer that you refuse to deny what was written in the *World* until the general increases your pay." As Badeau's eyebrows went up and he drew in his breath to reply, Ely changed his tack. "Not that I think that. But a man in my position also cannot think the $10,000 provided for you in the contract as unreasonable. It is five times my annual salary at the Police Department."

Badeau, confused, strove to conceal his disdain for the humble condition of his former colleague, who pressed on. "Grant, meanwhile, is in much worse circumstances. He remains in debt to Vanderbilt, I think to the tune of $150,000. While Vanderbilt has offered to forgive the debt, Grant says his honor will not allow that. His children, too, lost their money in Grant & Ward. For one of them you may not care, but this is the general's last chance to earn anything for any of his family, for any legitimate creditor who lost money in the firm, to right the mistakes he has made in managing their money, even though in reality he had nothing to do with the management. It is his last chance, above all, to provide for his widow."

Badeau deflated. His jaw even droppped for a moment. After a pause, he said, "What do you want me to write?"

Remembering a phrase Grant had repeated twice in his letter to Webster & Company, Ely said, "That the composition is entirely the general's."

Badeau walked to a desk, where he sat, found pen and ink, and quickly wrote a short letter. He blotted it and handed it to Ely, who read it carefully.

> Dear General—As I stated to you in my letter of Saturday, I have no desire, intention or right to claim the authorship of your book. The composition is entirely your own. What assistance I have been able to render has been in suggestion, revision or verification.
>
> With great respect, yours faithfully, General U.S. Grant.
>
> Adam Badeau

Ely folded it and put it in his pocket, saying, "Thank you, Badeau. I think this does you honor." He bade farewell, immediately brought the letter back to 66th Street and gave it to Fred, who at once handed it on to his father.

Grant had recovered from the first shock which Badeau's first letter had instilled in him, and, putting the book aside in order to fend off this attack on its provenance, had girded himself to start a lengthy reply in his own hand. He had been hurt by this, by one more betrayal, one more disillusionment about the human condition and its pretenses of friendship and sympathy that serve to cloak greed. At first, sadness at this turn in affairs dominated his feelings, with a little self-pity, but as he began to write the necessary reply those feelings turned into controlled anger and disgust. It was just as well that Badeau had in effect declared himself an adversary, and could be dealt with as such, rather than lurking as a traitor within the tent of the Grant family. Now, interrupted in the act of composing the reply, he regarded the second letter from his former ally with grim satisfaction. Like Grant's old Army friends who went South in 1861, Badeau had turned himself into an enemy, and one who now was showing the first sign of weakness. Grant had learned in the military to press home an attack against the enemy's weak points. He returned with renewed strength and concentration to his letter.

From the beginning, and even as his handwriting wavered toward the end, he came up with adamantine forensic phrases to say clearly and vigorously what he thought about this revelation of Badeau's character, and how he intended to respond to it. And yet throughout the letter, he kept returning to expressions of friendship. For Grant was not hard-hearted enough to cast Badeau out beyond the pale, any more than he had been with once and future friends like Pete Longstreet, against whom he had waged war. Grant's letter showed that he knew this man in and out, for good and ill. But its larger task was to defend the integrity of the great work of history on which he was engaged, and was determined to continue as far as he could. When the letter was done, he had Fred write out a copy, which was taken to Badeau. Grant kept the original.

Addressing Badeau as "General"—which might or might not have been chosen as an irritant—Grant's response was long.

> Since pondering over the contents of your letter, and more particularly over the conclusions I have drawn from it, and reflections based upon what you say, and my knowledge of your temper and disposi-

tion, I understand the letter better than you do. I have concluded that you and I must give up all association so far as the preparation of any literary work goes which is to bear my signature. In all other respects I hope our relations may continue as they have always been, pleasant and friendly.

I shall always regard it as a pleasure to do you a kindness so long as our present relations exist. They will not be changed by any act of mine. But any literary work in which we are mutually interested hereafter must be something to which my name is not to be attached as the author, certainly not further than my personal work bears relation to the whole work. It is not probable, however, that I shall ever be so engaged again. My health is still in a precarious condition, and I shall regard myself as having been almost under the care of a special Providence if spared to complete the work I am now engaged upon.

In order to answer you I will take your letter by paragraphs. Commencing with paragraph 2, I would say it is a little overdrawn, at least, in the ideas it would convey. Your first volume was prepared in my office while you occupied a position on my staff, with the rank (temporary) of Colonel. This gave you pay three grades beyond your actual rank and access to papers and documents that other writers at the time could not attain. You also had the assistance of several very intelligent staff officers to aid you in hunting up data, relating incidents, furnishing military terms, with which you at that time were not familiar, &c., &c. Your remaining volumes were written abroad while you were holding office under the government. I was President at the time and had control of all the Executive departments. You were furnished material which you called for from time to time until your book was completed, compiled under the supervision of my secretaries, the same officers who had assisted you before. You had possession of a copy of the records of my headquarters (my work really) kept for my special use, until you were through your work. I also read every chapter of your book before publication and corrected the facts. I knew what care had been taken to get the facts of history correct. I naturally would take your dates and figures before those of any other writer, for I know that most of them are right. The data you give cannot be excluded from public use and certainly not from me, for years ago I stated in writing how your data was obtained and made myself responsible for it, but in terms denied all responsibility for your reflections, deductions, comments and judgments. There is nothing in your book that I ever objected to so much as I did to your continuous praise of me personally.

In paragraphs 2 and 3 I disagree with you in your statements. But if it is correct that you have spent seven months in work for me, you are not nearly up with the manuscripts which I have composed and written with my own hand. Besides this Chattanooga was put in the hands of The Century magazine without your seeing it, as I remember, to say nothing of the manuscripts—more than a hundred pages—in the handwriting of the stenographer, of which you have made but little. At this rate you would not be through my book in the time the contract calls for; in which case the loss would fall upon my house and it would include not only what you demand, but the expenses incurred by the publisher in various ways.

In paragraph 2 you say I offered you $10,000 to help me. I said I would like your assistance, because

I had never written a book and there was much work connected with such an undertaking that I was not familiar with. When I said this you replied that I knew what a pleasure it would be to you to serve me and that you would take nothing if it were not for your circumstances, which I knew. It was out of respect for your sensitiveness that I enumerated as I did the details of compensation in the paper which I long subsequently handed you, so that in case of my death you could still get what I promised on the fulfillment of your part of the work.

I did not contemplate your writing anything except in case of my death, but I expected you to help me arrange it and to criticize my work, so that I could correct. I knew how much disappointed you had been in the reception by the public of your own work. I knew that you needed employment for your support, and I was suffering greatly in body as well as in mind.

The work which I wanted you to do I did not think would take over two months of your time, working on an average of four hours a day, six days in the week. It would not take longer if done by an expeditious writer and as I want it done, and I thought and you thought the compensation large at the time. My name goes with my book and I want it my work in the fullest sense. For your work, it being understood by me as above, I proposed to give you $5,000 out of the first $20,000 received from its sale and $5,000 out of the next $10,000. At that time $30,000 was supposed to be a large amount for me to receive for my book. About that time it was reported that a publisher in this city would give $50,000 for the copyright. I was advised by a friend to accept this offer. If I had done so your share of the profits would have been twenty percent.

In paragraph 5 you say the work wanted of you calls upon you to connect the disjointed fragments into a connected narrative, &c., the merest drudgery you would not do for anyone but me. I do not admit that disjointed nature of the matter you speak of, except of that part I wrote after I became so ill that I could write but little at a time, and that often after long intervals and when I supposed someone, whose name would necessarily be given to the public, and that name yours, would finish the book. I would occasionally think of something in the way of incident, reflections upon some phases of the war, estimates of character of some leading officer of one or other of the armies which I would deem it important that I should write myself; and, sick as I was, I wrote them. They were disjointed in the particular that some of these scraps will go in one part of the book and some in another.

For the compensation you ask I could get very able work done by persons who would not regard the work as either drudgery nor as degrading. It would be degrading to me to accept the work from you as you regard it.

You say the work cannot possibly be completed before 1886. If not, General, I fear its completion would depend entirely upon both the prolongation of my life until the work was done and that I should retain strength enough to push the work. To be frank, I do not believe the work would ever be done by you in case of my death while $1,000 per month was coming in.

Here, now, is where I understand you better than you do yourself. You are petulant, your anger is easily aroused, and you are overbearing, even to me, at times, and always with those for whom you have done or are doing literary work. Think of the pub-

lishers and others you have quarreled with. As an of-
fice-holder you have quarreled with your superiors
until you lost your office.

You say that your novel has not been published
because the publishers would not take it. You have
tried several and they would not take it on account
of the theme.

If I had died leaving the unfinished work upon
my book to you to complete, with $1,000 a month
in advances, you would have become so arrogant
that there would have been a rupture between you
and my family before many days had elapsed. I will
not give any other reasons why advanced payments
would defeat the completion of the work. They do
not reflect upon your honor.

I will not notice at length any of the other statements contained in your letter. But you dwell upon
the 'drudgery,' the absence of fame, the sinking
from sight of the work of your life if my work is
completed, &c., the better you do my work the
deeper you sink yourself or your work into obscurity, &c. Allow me to say that this is all bosh, and is
evidently the work of a distempered mind that has
been growing moody by too much reflection upon
these matters. The fact is, if my book affects yours
in any way it will be to call attention to it.

You say that I am a man of affairs, &c., and can
tell a simple story, &c. You imply that a literary man
must supply some deficiencies, and that you are the
only man that can do it. If this is the case, General, I
do not want a book bearing my name to go before
the world which I did not write to such an extent as
to be fully entitled to the credit of authorship. I do
not want a secret between me and someone else
which would destroy my honor if it was divulged. I
cannot think of holding myself as dependent upon

any person to supply a capacity which I am lacking. I may fail, but I will not put myself in any such position.

You say 'no one but myself can destroy my own book. If I don't help you it will retain its place, for you have neither the physical strength,' &c. In answer to this I have only to say that for the last twenty-four years I have been very much employed in writing. As a soldier I wrote my own orders, plans of battle, instructions and reports. They were not edited, nor was assistance rendered. As President, I wrote every official document, I believe, usual for Presidents to write bearing my name. All these have been published and widely circulated. The public has become accustomed to my style of writing. They know that it is not even an attempt to imitate either a literary or classical style, that it is just what it is and nothing else. If I succeed in telling my story so that others can see as I do what I attempt to show, I will be satisfied. The reader must also be satisfied, for he knows from the beginning just what to expect.

Your letter affords an abundance of other reasons why you should not help me in my work which is to bear my name. But these are sufficient. I add only what is necessary to make a part of what has been already said plain if others than yourself should ever read this letter. You ask for a contract and demand $1,000 per month in advance until the work is completed and ten percent of the entire profits arising from the sale of the work after it is put upon the market. This would make you a partner with my family as long as the book found a sale. This is preposterous. Not for one moment has your proposition been entertained by me. This, with the statements enumerated in this letter and others contained in yours, makes it impossible for us to be associated in a work which is to bear my name. It would be a degradation for me to accept honors and profit from the work of another man, while declaring to the public that it was the product of my own brain and hand.

I write frankly, because I want you to know why I cannot receive your services now on any terms. I hope that it will not disturb the relations which have heretofore existed between us in all particulars. I hope sincerely that you may be able not only to realize with your pen the $5,000 to $10,000 a year which you say you can earn, but twice the larger sum. Your prosperity in life will gratify me. You can always be the welcome visitor at my house that you have been heretofore. This correspondence between us may be unknown to the world if you choose. I do not ask secrecy, but the necessity for publicity will not occur through any fault of mine. Repeating my assurance of the best wishes for your success in life and health and happiness to the end, I subscribe myself as ever,

Your friend and well wisher, U.S. Grant.

P.S.—In your letter you speak of a contract. There is no contract, but simply a memorandum I gave to you, signed by me alone, and was intended to let my family know what I wished in case of my death, which was expected, and would prevent any disagreeable discussion arising about what my wishes were. Although this bound no one I should have regarded it as binding me.—U.S.G.

Harrison Terrell was dispatched to deliver the letter to Badeau, who was shocked by its contents. Because the copy Badeau received had been written out by Fred and signed by General Grant, he assumed incorrectly that Fred had written the whole thing—or at least he purported to think so.

But Grant, Badeau realized, must have had input, especially where the letter scored points against him personally in a manner too intelligent for Fred to have come up with. Some of the lines struck home, particularly the accusations and examples given of his petulance, overbearing and quarrelsomeness, and how these had shipwrecked his career.

Badeau knew himself to be both quarrelsome and out of employment, and that the latter was in part a result of the former. Grant, he recalled, deprecated other cantankerous personalities who had dared dispute with him, such as Generals Gordon Granger and George Armstrong Custer, and even Edwin Stanton, Lincoln's chief of the War Department, although Stanton eventually returned to favor.

Sherman and Sheridan were of the same personality type, but directed their wrath at others, not at their superior Grant, even when they strongly disagreed with him, as over Indian policy. So they remained in Grant's good graces. The truth was, Badeau thought, that Grant was vindictive, as he had been to other Union generals in the war, such as Rosecrans, Thomas, John McClernand, Gouverneur Warren and Benjamin Prentiss. Some of that vindictiveness came out in the *Memoirs*, although, Badeau had to admit, there were also words of praise as well as criticism for some of these officers, such as calling Prentiss "a brave and very earnest soldier."

When Sherman did defy President Grant, over Reconstruction and Indian policy, he found himself frozen out of power, though he retained his rank as head of the Army—and now was back as Grant's close friend, a friendship he had never entirely lost. Badeau knew that he himself would not be extended any such special dispensation. Apart from anything else, there was not enough time left. Sometimes a man needs to stand up for himself. But that didn't mean there was anything to be done about the current situation.

On May 9, Badeau wrote a reply, his third letter to Grant that month.

Dear General—I have received your letter of May 5, and shall make no attempt to change your views. I laid my own before you and they have not been accepted. You do not recognize the services which I supposed I had rendered, and you reject the idea of increased and peculiar remuneration for what I thought increased and peculiar work. You look upon my assistance as that of an ordinary clerk or literary hack; I thought I was aiding you as no one else could in doing a great work.

I took it for granted that if your answer was unfavorable my connection with your book would cease, but I left it for you to sever the connection.

I still, however, intend to write on the theme which has engaged so much of my life. I have not changed the views or feelings of twenty years, because it seems to me that in one instance you are unjust, and, though it is hard to believe that I am the one, of all others, selected to receive injustice at your hands, I can not and I would not recall or unsay my past, much less yours. Since I am not to help you build up the monument on which I have already done some labor, I will attempt another, and strive to make you and your family, for whom, as well as for yourself, I have cherished so deep an affection, appreciate the effort.

As the occasion for remaining at your house is at an end, I will send for my trunks and boxes as soon as I have secured lodgings, and pay my respects to yourself and family when I return to town.

With great respect, as ever, your faithful and affectionate servant and friend, General Grant.— Adam Badeau

While quite aware that he had lost the game insofar as

securing more money to work on the Memoirs, Badeau made sure to hang on to the February contract. He had every expectation of at least securing the $10,000 it referred to —although that was not a suit to be pressed for the time being. Meanwhile, there was the publication of his two books to attend to—the English and Cuban ones—and the writing of a third, on Grant, the one he had referred to in that last letter. Just what that book would include, Badeau considered, would depend to some extent on what the *Memoirs* would get around to covering—and leaving out. But it would be a saga covering twenty years of considerable interest and drama.

Badeau never saw Grant again.

THE GRANTS RECOVERED from Badeau's treachery, a process aided by the astounding news from Clemens about advance sales for the *Memoirs*, which were on track to produce some $300,000 in royalties. Badeau did not learn this news until later, when it did not surprise him.

Nellie had not forgotten Benjamin Bristow, and her half-promise at the end of the Converses' dinner party to ease his way back to her father's side. Now she found a cheerful Julia quite amenable to a visit from him.

"Why should we hold on to old grievances?" the mother asked the daughter. "Let him come. The only reason I ever was suspicious of Mr. Bristow, or anyone else, was when I thought they might do harm to your father. He is beyond all that now."

Bristow did visit 66th Street, where he and the general were glad to see each other for the first time in nine years. They did not dredge up old quarrels, recognizing their common values and ideals. Grant more or less apologized for giving insufficient support to his Cabinet member, without getting into the details of the Babcock case. Turning to current events, Bristow mentioned the state legislature's recent action in Albany establishing a vast Forest Preserve upstate, which he compared to Grant's creation of Yellowstone National Park in 1872. The general smiled to express appreciation for the gracious conduct of his former aide.

The next day Grant met with a delegate who was headed for a convention of the Grand Army of the Republic, the chief Union veterans group, and said to him (as the newspapers reported): "Tell the boys that they will probably never look into my face again, nor hear my voice, but they are engraved on my heart and I love them as my children. What the good Lord has spared me for is more than I can tell, but it is perhaps to finish up my book which I shall leave to the boys in blue."

Yet a few days after that, on May 23, when he did write out a dedication, it was "to the American soldier and sailor," without distinction of uniform whether blue or gray, or of rank. When Fred questioned whether he should change it to specify those who served for the Union, Grant declined to amend the wording. He recalled seeing a badly wounded Union lieutenant and Confederate private after Donelson, and how the Yankee was trying to give the rebel a drink. Grant, as he told Nellie, had made the stretcher bearers take the rebel private, too. Clemens put the handwritten, signed dedication at the beginning of Volume I.

The pain was becoming stronger in Grant's throat, tongue and jaw, and speaking became harder to do. His hours were more irregular, and he often wrote now at night. On May 30, he stood at the window to salute the Decoration Day parade.

Nellie's wedding anniversary had passed on May 21, with no one, including she and her husband, paying any acknowledgment to it. It was also the date of the death of her first child, ten-month-old infant Grant Sartoris, nine years ago.

PART TWO

GRANT IN PEACE

CHAPTER FIFTEEN

"The fact of the matter," said Tom Sweeny, leaning forward confidentially between Frank Herron and Ely Parker, "is that the mad Cossack or Russian or whatever you want to call him changed his name when he got here, into what people could call him, Turchin, instead of whatever it was he was known as on the steppes of the Don or wherever he was from, a name which I was told once but can't for the life of me remember, while Vladimir here never did change his Polish name. So Turchin became a general, despite getting into that little bother in Alabama in 1862, while Kriz had to settle for being a colonel throughout the war, even though he commanded brigades, because no one, let alone those geniuses in Congress, could pronounce, never mind spell, Krzyzanowski."

"I thought Kriz was a rebel against the Russians," said Herron.

"So he was," said Sweeny. "But the Turchins are hardly agents of the tsar—although come to think of it, he fought for the tsar in '48 when Kriz and some others we know were on the other side. But now the Turchins are some kind of agents for Polish immigrants in Illinois, or at least he is, and they live among them in some kind of farming community or colony, probably a sort of socialist experiment, and as you can see they speak the language." Sweeny's own language had taken on a broader Irish brogue as he became more voluble, with a hint of mockery as he drew out the word "socialist." He was using the plural because John Turchin's wife Nadine—the former Nadezhda L'vova—was

now talking animatedly at the side of her husband and
Krzyzanowski among a sea of Polish-American picnickers.
Mrs.—or Madame—Turchin had been with the general during most of the war, sometimes issuing orders to the troops,
which was not at all the way more conventional military
wives behaved.

"I too have changed my names and language," said Ely.

"I thought," said Herron, "that Ely Parker has been
your name since childhood?"

"Yes, but also as a member of the Wolf clan I was
known as 'Hasanoanda,' and later 'Donehogawa,' as I still
am among my people. Donehogawa means 'Keeper of the
Western Door of the Long House of the Iroquois,' or rather
of the Haudenosaunee. The Seneca, or Onondowaga, are
the westernmost of their Six Nations."

Herron found Ely unusually talkative and confusing.
But then he had also talked a lot about complicated matters,
and more clearly and seriously, at the Converses' dinner party, which was more than Herron had ever seen and heard
him say about such subjects. He increasingly wanted to
speak about his Indian heritage. Even as he did so today in
Central Park, Ely kept an eye out to the east, and was re-
warded by the sight of Nellie Sartoris walking toward them
from the Fifth Avenue side.

Fred Grant had been a little alarmed at Nellie's plan to
walk on her own in search of the picnic, and had accompanied her with little Julia until they saw Ely. "It'll be a break
for us," he had said, and the girl chatted happily to her father and aunt on the way. As Nellie now bade them adieu
and ventured by herself toward this somewhat exotic company, she thought of her father's tale—Fred had shown her
the passage in the manuscript, after she'd heard Clemens tell
his version—of nervously leading his Missouri regiment
against the rebel Tom Harris early in the war. Modern wom-
en could walk in the park in daytime, she had told Fred.
Women office clerks and garment factory hands were walk-

ing all day on their own through the city. So were some ladies known to society, such as Mrs. Lowell.

Fred was not enthralled at the prospect of plunging into a New York ethnic event, and they had decided he would not wait. Ely Parker would take care of her, Nellie said. She acknowledged to herself that Fred was not wrong to be concerned, for across much of both New York and London, and doubtless many smaller places, it was still possible for a lone woman's intentions to be disastrously misconstrued, although that was more likely after dark. Yet she did not really take such alarms seriously, compared to the real sorrows she buttoned under a British stiff upper lip or her father's phlegmatic courage, to do with the loss and absence of her English children.

Nellie was reassured at the sight of Ely, with his fellow old soldiers Frank Herron and Tom Sweeny, coming forward to greet her. She waved her rolled-up parasol in greeting, and they all stopped and talked together for a while on the path, Ely asking after her father.

"His health seems to be holding up," she said, "although we are worried about the increasing heat." It was a fine, warm day in the late spring, ideal for this Turchin-Krzyzanowski picnic.

"And his book?" asked Herron.

"That holds up, too," said Nellie, "despite the departure of General Badeau, which has added to Father's burden. But these days he has been caught up in the drama of twenty years ago, writing and rewriting the Appomattox campaign." They all turned with affection and admiration to Ely, who had been at the surrender with Grant. Nellie continued. "He writes of a sick headache going away with Lee's message, and how General Lee was taller, impeccably dressed with a sword and new dress uniform, while my father came in in his muddy private's garb."

"We had ridden hard for days to get there," said Ely.

"General Grant didn't feel the need for a sword, or for taking Lee's. He let him keep it."

Krzyzanowski, whose guests they all were, came up to greet Nellie, and the introductions resulted in some commonplace banter about the difficulty of Polish and Russian names. The picnic was a sort of fundraiser (a detail which Ely had taken care not to tell Nellie) for a Polish aid society that Krzyzanowski was helping to organize for his immigrant community. Eastern Europeans were the newest immigrants, especially Poles and Russians, both Catholics and Orthodox, as well as Hasidic Jews. They were fleeing from poverty along with repression and pogroms, following the assassination of the fairly liberal tsar Alexander II. Along with others from other countries who were crossing west over the Atlantic, mostly Irish, Germans, Scandinavians and Italians, they were overwhelming the Castle Garden processing center, operated by the state and city at the southern tip of Manhattan.

Nellie walked bravely with Krzyzanowski back to the bright and bustling scene, where pitchers of beer and blackcurrant juices were on the tables, along with pots of pierogis and varieties of sausage broiling on the grills. Minnie and lively little Maud Parker came up to greet them. They took Nellie under their wing, joining Adelaide Herron, her daughter Augusta and grandson Frank. Maud was six or seven, and Frank a year or two older, and they got on well enough together under the women's care.

Passing in the other direction were the Turchins, who joined Ely Parker, Sweeny and Herron, Mrs. Turchin having long been comfortable in the roughest male company. Herron judged she was in her late 50s, no beauty and with her curly hair gone gray, but with lively eyes, a witty looking mouth, and prominent bust. Herron and Sweeny had met General Turchin before, but reminders-cum-introductions were made. The Turchins were on their first trip east for several years.

"So that is Nellie Grant," said Nadine Turchin in an exotic Russian-French accent, looking over to where Mrs. Parker and Mrs. Herron sat with Nellie—while Frank and Maud darted around—along with other women and children, including three nuns. "I am glad to see she does not confine herself to the English aristocracy or American robber barons." Herron restrained himself from lifting his eyebrows at this barbed comment.

John Turchin was a balding, distinguished looking man despite his modest garb, whose gray beard was turning white. He looked vaguely embarrassed when his wife made tactless remarks, but far too used to them to mount any kind of protest.

"She is the people's princess," said Herron, embarrassed in his turn at what had just come out of his mouth.

Mrs. Turchin snorted derisively. "We left princesses and tsars behind in Russia, and all Americans should do the same, not make an ordinary man like Grant and his family into icons. And he, too, he makes icons of his plutocratic friends. You see these people," she went on earnestly, with fire, looking down the slope to the picnickers, "that our friend Vladimir wants to help, these are the people America is for, whether they have been here two hundred years or came off the boat last week. And too many of them are terribly, desperately poor, here in New York as all over America, while the rich build mansions on Fifth Avenue, in Saratoga, Newport, wherever they go, like the so-called nobility of Europe."

"Grant's poor enough now," ventured Ely.

"Pah," said Madam Turchin. "Does he live like a poor man? Even like us?" Her gesture took in the picnickers and perhaps the rest of Central Park and New York City.

"I remember Grant when he was poor, before the war," said Ely. "He was a friend to me and tried to be one to my people, and to the Negroes, who are even poorer than these Poles."

Nadine Turchin said, "I do not doubt, Mr. Parker, that Grant did some good things, despite his tendency to be dazzled by the mysteries of money. He did hold out for the Negro and Reconstruction longer than the rest of the country, longer than all those liberal Republicans"—she put a menacing, strongly accented emphasis on the adjective—"who had such tender concern for the civil liberties of lynch mobs. Horace Greeley, pah!"

"Wasn't that the Democrats?" asked Sweeny. He and the others knew Mrs. Turchin, at least by reputation, and had seen enough of the world not to let show any shock they may have felt at her words.

"The Democrats were Confederates and Copperheads," said Mrs. Turchin. "We knew where we stood with them. Greeley was their candidate, but he wasn't one of them. He was a Republican traitor, an intellectual like those oh-so distinguished Adamses, Charles Francis and his whining son Henry, who was too delicate to fight rebels but wanted to hang Lee. And Senator Sumner, another drawing room prig, who proved that he hated Grant more than he loved the Negro, and wanted to fight the British and conquer Canada. Maybe they despised Grant because he wasn't a hangman, he wasn't the butcher they called him."

"The revolt of the stuffed shirts, eh?" said Herron.

But Mrs. Turchin countered, "Not just them. Our friend Krzyzanowski's fellow immigrant and commander, General Carl Schurz, was just as bad a politician as the Adamses. He was worse, a soldier turned disloyal who wound up in Hayes's Cabinet. And at the end of it all, what is left for the Negro, for whom the war was fought? Abolition, yes, but what beyond that? The former slaves have been abandoned to the scant mercy of their former masters, who deny it to any they deem lacking in servility. And all the dreams of Reconstruction are left in the dust. The politicians and the plutocrats got together to blame the Negroes and Indians and immigrants for corruption, holding them to a standard they had no intention of applying to themselves. Not Grant, he was not crooked; but he was in awe of money and the rich. And when the depression started on his watch, he lost the support of the people." Her sentence structure, like her carefully articulated accent, came from Europe, yet was mesmerizing to the old American soldiers at this picnic.

Or at least it was to Herron. We talk of Grant in the past tense, he thought, as if he were already dead. He looked at Ely, who had been notably silent, perhaps willing to concede that the Grants' fascination with the rich explained their neglect of him. Sweeny, too, was holding fire, but Herron felt both the lawyer's inclination to argue the point—or at least to make a case of some kind for a client's mitigating circumstances—and the resurrected feelings of his own past during Reconstruction. But as he drew breath to speak, he was forestalled.

"I have some sympathy for the Adamses crying decline and fall," Ely said, "and for the do-gooders who decry corruption. But the real reason they called themselves reformers is because Grant wouldn't give them the grand jobs they felt entitled to. I can even feel for those who lament the old lost South. Before the war, when I spent time on the Mississippi River, southerners sometimes tried to make common cause with me, as an Indian, against the Yankees. But we oldest Americans are poor, like the Negro. They thought we were the Noble Savage, but we're more like the new Italian immigrants moving in now to New York, south of my office on Mulberry Street."

"I once talked in this city with Senator Roscoe Conkling," said Sweeny, "who as you know is no angel. But he said he needed Negro votes to win Congress, which made him a better friend to the black man than any number of New England humbugs out to improve and educate and preach to 'em."

Herron got a word in: "Surely, Madame Turchin, it is the achievements of rich men, say the railroads they build to bind the country together, and which employ the Chinese, the Irish and the Negroes, any man who wants to work and build a stake in America, it's all that which General Grant has admired, not the money itself. And it is not the rich but the Knights of Labor who are trying to bar the Chinese and other immigrants from our shores."

Mrs. Turchin snorted again, and said, "The soldiers who were killed, most of them, were poor enough. Is it for those rich and riches you speak of, that they gave up their lives? Or have they been betrayed by the chiselers who took their place at the trough? And it is hard on the Negroes that America can no longer be bothered with them. They will have to take your railroad and emigrate out of the South."

"Which they can do," said Sweeny, "because the war abolished slavery."

"Maybe the Negro will do better just working his way up, out of the limelight, like the immigrants," said Ely. "Maybe the Indians would do better that way, too. President Grant hired some of us. One of his first proclamations guaranteed all federal workers an eight-hour day with no pay cut."

Sweeny would not let the slavery issue go. "And is that freeing of three million or so people, is it such a little thing? They say we Irish were anti-black, but even the Confederate general Patrick Cleburne, a fine soldier as you know who was killed at Franklin, and came like me from County Cork, he wanted to enroll the slaves as rebel soldiers and give them their freedom. And there were more Irish on our side than his, and other immigrants too, Frenchmen and Jews and God knows what, could also be found in both camps, but more in ours. I sent him a message, you know, Cleburne, in the Georgia campaign, across the lines, that said we should team up after the war to liberate Ireland. And he wrote back, too, but said we'd have seen enough fighting by then. Maybe I should have listened to him. But my point is I saw some of slavery's tools in the war, like neck yokes with the spiked prongs in 'em. I'm just glad that it's gone. Slavery couldn't hold up in our New World."

"That's about the only place it did hold up," said Mrs. Turchin. "It's where they'd made it pay. Slavery never faded away, like Jefferson hoped it would, but knew as he grew older that wasn't happening, so he spent his time ignoring it, founding a university for white boys instead. It became stronger and crueler, as they sold the Negroes downriver and restarted the slave trade with Africa. They came up with new and shameless justifications. So, yes, it was a huge thing to end slavery. Other countries abolished it peacefully, but that did not look like it would happen here. I, too, remember what it took. Yet now in the South, the position of the Negro is again becoming worse, worse than in other countries. In the border states, too."

Sweeny looked vaguely shocked at this unflattering, downright unpatriotic view being bruited about here at an American picnic. As Mrs. Turchin was drawing in her breath to speak again, he shook his head and interrupted, "I came up through the ranks, you know, where the men were what the Duke of Wellington called 'the scum of the earth.' But we Americans don't look at our soldiers that way, especially the Civil War volunteers. I helped some of them write letters home, full of religious notions and love for their families and country, some just before they died. And some wrote better than me. I don't like to see that all changed now. Now when despite all the reunions and speeches, for all the sententious cant of politicians and preachers waving the bloody shirt, it seems you're a sap to care for anything but money."

Herron was surprised to hear Sweeny use that phrase, "waving the bloody shirt," which he associated with the Democrats and anti-Grant Republicans who opposed Reconstruction. But then most Americans had long since given up on those policies to which he and Grant had devoted the postwar years. He was also a little surprised to hear the Irishman sounding idealistic about money.

"Although now I think of it," Sweeny continued, "even during the war there were the Shoddyites getting rich at home."

"You're right there, Tom," said Ely. "If old soldiers live through the fighting, they can get lost in the world they made. Grant too."

"They miss what they mostly hated, what we went through together," Sweeny said. "But I don't want to get too pious about it. As you know, I've been devoted to the cause of Ireland, but that doesn't mean the Irish will be governed by incorruptible angels, once we drive the English out. I don't think it has worked that way in New York, where money greases the way, builds the city, gets things done. And England may sneer at them, at us Irish or New Yorkers, but those proper honest Englishmen have got the whole world in their pocket to service their stately homes, so to that extent I'm with you, Madame Turchin. But I don't think Grant's scandals were as bad as they were painted."

"Well," she replied, "I hear the current mayor of this city is reasonably honest, and he's an Irishman."

"A lot is lost," said Herron as the somewhat uncomfortable laughter faded, returning to Ely's theme of soldiers after the war. "I remember ingloriously hiding with my wife and her children in New Orleans in '74, when the White League rioters killed dozens of people. I held no public office at the time, but was a marked man nonetheless. Longstreet and his state militia—mostly blacks—didn't hide. They tried to stop the rioters. He was wounded, lucky not to have been lynched when they pulled him off his horse. I knew him well, Longstreet. We had been allies against a backsliding governor, Henry Warmoth, who was selling out the Negro to the Democrats.

"I remember before that," Herron continued, "the New

Orleans riot of 1866, when a number of Negroes were killed, and another in 1872, and the terrible Opelousas massacre in between. I remember the Colfax and Coushatta massacres, also in Louisiana, which President Grant cited in a message to Congress in 1875—although Congress had by then, as you say, Madame Turchin, lost interest in the subject. The Democrats won a landslide in the congressional elections of '74, and Republicans, except for Grant, were running scared. More than seventy blacks were murdered at Colfax, and more than that number at Opelousas. These are not indifferent matters to me."

Mrs. Turchin literally tipped her hat to him, but said nothing.

Sweeny asked, "Were you not United States marshal down there for a while? That was no picnic, I'll wager."

Herron smiled, touching his head in his turn to the Irishman, and continued. "After the 1874 riot, when Longstreet was injured, Grant had to send in five thousand federal troops, and three gunboats. By then, as you know, the people of the North were tired of what they saw as endless strife. But despite the Republican political defeats that fall, Grant sent Sheridan back to Louisiana in early '75. And he didn't stop there, nor in that state. In October '76 he sent troops to South Carolina to protect black voters, after the massacres there, and back to Louisiana too. No, he wasn't an idealist or a socialist or any kind of 'ist', but he was about the last man in America to insist on executing the law in the South."

Mrs. Turchin gave him a long look and an ironic smile, and said, "I salute him, and you, and Sheridan. Still, in early '75, as I recall, Grant sent troops to Mississippi to support a Negro sheriff in Vicksburg. But when the sheriff was killed that summer, and other Negroes were executed, I mean murdered, some of them in Vicksburg, and many more were prevented from voting, the president did not act. And Governor Ames, another onetime soldier like yourselves, was driven out of office."

Herron considered making the point that the Mississippi Negro leader Hiram Revels, a former U.S. senator, did not support Ames, but Mrs. Turchin's diatribe was rolling along. "I have heard it said that Grant did not help Ames because he thought it would lose the Republicans votes in an election that year in Ohio. And then in 1876 the Republicans lost the presidential election but kept the White House anyway for Hayes, handing over the southern Negro to the Democrats and the Klan, or the White Leagues, the Red Shirts, whatever they have taken to calling themselves."

"That arrangement was not Grant's doing," said Herron. "In his last two years as president, it was not just the Democratic majority in Congress but Hamilton Fish and others in his own Cabinet who opposed their own president's Reconstruction policies. Even before that, when I worked for the federal and state governments in Louisiana, and for the city of New Orleans, I found enforcing the law there not quite as easy as you seem to imagine. Who more than General Grant has acted in support of Negro rights?"

"I am sure you did your duty," Mrs. Turchin said.

"I tried to. And when I wasn't working in government there, I was a private lawyer. Unlike much of the South, Louisiana had prospered after the war, and I found work enough. But when the Democrats took power, there and in Washington, it became obvious we could not safely stay in New Orleans. Even though my wife and her children had spent their whole lives there, we all had to move north, to this city, where few care for idealistic politics or dwell upon the past."

"The question," said Mrs. Turchin, "is what did we fight for and have we won it, or have we rather lost the peace?" She turned to Ely. "And what of your Indians? What have they gained from all these American ideals, or from the railroads either?" She paused, and as no one answered her, continued, "I am sorry. I get het-up. And I don't really believe we can afford to be distracted by the Indian, the Negro, the Jew, the Chinese, Russian or Pole, or the women's issue, either. We must be united, all the people, in and with the labor unions, against the rich who keep us down."

"Frederick Douglass would disagree with you, Madame Turchin," said Herron, returning to the previous point. "Douglass said: 'To Grant more than any other man the Negro owes his enfranchisement and the Indian a humane policy'." Herron was too middle-aged to stay angry long, and was actually rather impressed at Mrs. Turchin's command of issues such as the political opinions of Henry Adams and Charles Sumner, and the fate of Mississippi Governor Adelbert Ames. Ames, as she had noted, was a general during the Civil War. After it, he married Ben Butler's daughter and became a politician during Reconstruction, and a more successful one than Herron.

"But Grant has freely admitted his own political errors, notably in his last message to Congress," Herron continued smoothly, until he was brought short by the inconvenient thought that maybe it was a real failing of Grant that he hadn't held the support of men like the Adamses and Sumner, because it was their absence and opposition which helped doom his second term. Running out of arguments, he asked, "Are you a nihilist, then? Or do you really think that socialism is the answer?"

"Nihilism is indeed an invention of us Russians, yet we have there many more interesting writers who are not nihilists—who are socialists, anarchists, pacifists even, like those former soldiers Tolstoy and Kropotkin. Most soldiers want peace, as Grant did. I am an American now, and have no time for nihilism, or bomb throwing. Socialism is a different matter."

"Will it lead us to the promised land?" Herron persisted, although immediately feeling unhappy about the ponderous irony of his own remark. "Or are you a Marxist?" he blundered on.

"Marx is too dogmatic," she replied, "like a Calvinist with his predestination. But socialism? Why not? Better than believing in survival of the fittest, as Marx did, and which is also a fashionable opinion among the capitalist oligarchs. I like Frederick Douglass, but he relies too much on the Republican Party Stalwarts who have grown uninterested in his cause—while the Democrats just go from bad to worse."

Ely finally spoke. "But could we have kept federal troops in the South forever to enforce the law? People naturally grow tired of great causes."

Mrs. Turchin smiled darkly. "Better to have kept them there in the South than sent them West under Custer, don't you think? And in the end, didn't Grant, like the rest of them, give up on the Indian peace policy?"

"I suppose he had to do something after Little Big Horn," said Ely.

"How about before it? And didn't he give up on Reconstruction, too?" continued Mrs. Tuchin, who saw Herron open his mouth in protest to resume the argument, and held up a hand to forestall him. "But we do need new thinking, gentlemen. And maybe you are right, and the Negro will do better out of the spotlight."

"Or it could be worse," said Herron. "I concede."

"The Indians, too," Mrs. Turchin went on, waving an arm. "A new wave, new people. Here they are." She gestured, smiling again, at the happy crowd of mostly Polish-speaking picnickers. "New parties, new ideas and new ways to act," she added. "In the West now, the farmers and the Knights of Labor—who may not be perfect, General Herron, but are on the right side of this issue—they are uniting against the railroad barons."

Ely said, "General Grant never would retrace his steps; he was always looking for a new way forward."

"I'm not so sure if he's in step with us now," said Mrs.

Turchin. "Or if he's more in tune with his rich friends. But I am talking too much."

"Your conversation reminds me of General Sherman's," said Herron, and got a frown in return.

John Turchin looked at his wife with eyes still shining with good nature and affection, and she caught his gaze and softened. She also caught a quizzical long-distance glance from Nellie Grant, down among the picnickers with the rest of the women, looking up at this heated conversation which she presumably—Mrs. Turchin hoped—could not actually hear. The now-rueful Russian lady smiled more broadly, and said, "Ah, I do not mean to be so harsh about General Grant. I can feel sympathy now for him, too, like a normal person."

"Not like Henry Adams, you mean," said Sweeny.

Some laughter broke the tension, and Herron said, "Someone should tell Adams that Grant is the wrong man to cast as a villain, or a fool. The taint of this modern age doesn't stick to him."

"Nor to us, I hope," said Sweeny, "although didn't I hear Adams is a friend of Badeau? I think Grant will do better at book writing than some of his other civilian jobs."

"At Appomattox," said Ely, "the day after the surrender, Longstreet came to our lines on some business, and Grant went up and greeted him, said let's have a game of brag like the old days, Pete—that was a card game they'd played in St. Louis before the war, when Grant was selling firewood on the street. I used to play euchre with him. But that day after the surrender, I saw tears fill Longstreet's eyes, at the generosity of his old friend—who had also sent rations over to the starving rebs, and let them keep their horses. He let them ride the railroads home, too, or go south on Navy ships, and draw rations just like our troops."

Mrs. Turchin said, "Perhaps I should let you old soldiers talk, of General Grant or other things. So many generals I see. How could one war produce so many?"

"It was a big war," said Sweeny, smiling back at her, and taking the cue to change the subject. "Nellie mentioned Badeau being gone from Grant's house. I think there's some bad business there." He looked at Ely, who held his tongue.

"I met him by chance," said Herron, surprising them all. "Just the other day, in a restaurant, or tap room I suppose you could call it. We were both alone, and I went up and reminded him we had met at General Grant's, and sat down with him for a while." Herron was slightly uncomfortable bringing this up, wondering if some might think he and Badeau met in a more disreputable establishment. Brothels, and bars that might as well be, were thick on the ground in New York, but Herron did not frequent them.

"And did you talk about General Grant?" asked Ely.

"We did. At first he seemed reluctant, or maybe that was just a pose, but soon he was asserting the right of his position. He said he had done much work on Grant's book and deserved to be paid for it."

"The newspapers," said Sweeny, "say he claims to have written it."

"He did not say that to me," said Herron. "Quite the opposite. In fact, he grew almost maudlin, saying he would do nothing to harm the general or his family."

"Let us hope he will live up to that," concluded Ely.

CHAPTER SIXTEEN

As MAY TURNED INTO JUNE, Julia saw Ulys' health and energy begin to flag again. He had shrugged off Badeau's
betrayal. The work Badeau had been doing was taken up by
Grant family members, especially Fred, along with Noble
Dawson and Clemens. In reality, Badeau had not been doing that much toward the end, which left him time to plot.
And Grant, despite his failing health, was—as Badeau had
come to recognize—no longer in much need of professional guidance.

Ulys himself, Julia also realized (to her surprise), had become a literary man, exercised about details which he had
avoided before. He had never meant to become a soldier, or
ever felt really comfortable in the Army, nor in any other
trade except military command. After being a general he became a generalist, statesman, tourist and business visionary.
Now he was a writer.

But the work was tapering off again, and his breath became more labored in the great city's growing heat. His
post-midnight visits to her room had ceased. As the cancer
spread in his mouth and throat—and Julia knew it spread,
while she still avoided talking about it—his ability to speak
became increasingly constrained. Ulys was now constantly
using his little notepad for routine communications. On the
bigger pads of paper he added, when he could, to the manuscript of the *Memoirs*. No longer able to dictate much, he
was writing the book by hand. This had changed Dawson's
role to that of a copyist, who was able to read Grant's writing and transcribe a neater version.

Grant also found the strength to write other things, such as, on June 2, a letter of reference which he gave to Harrison.

> Harrison Terrell: I give you this letter now, not knowing what the near future may bring to a person in my condition of health. This is in acknowledgement of your faithful services to me during my sickness up to this time, and which I expect will continue to the end. This is also to state further that for about four years you have lived with me, coming first [as] butler, in which capacity you served until my illness became so serious as to require the constant attentions of a nurse, and that in both capacities I have had abundant reason to be satisfied with your attention, integrity and efficiency. I hope you may never want for a place. Yours, U.S. Grant.

The two men had become inseparable in the last year, with Grant willing to show pain before Harrison that he concealed from his family. Harrison had been born a slave in Virginia, and was freed at the age of ten before the war. He was now forty-five. Last year his son Robert, whom Grant occasionally asked after and had helped find summer jobs for, graduated from Harvard College. Robert Terrell was now teaching in Washington and hoping to go to law school. The rest of Harrison's family, including his wife Louisa, had remained in Washington when he went to live at the Grant house in Manhattan. But Harrison told the family he would stay on in New York as long as they needed him, and his sacrifice was recognized and appreciated.

With his increased difficulty in speaking, Grant did ever more listening than talking, and was today hearing Julia and Nellie converse with Clemens, Dr. Douglas and Matias Romero. Twenty years before, as a youthful Mexican diplomat, Romero had gotten Grant to provide crucial support, behind the back of U.S. Secretary of State Seward, to the patriotic revolutionary movement of Benito Juarez. The patriots were fighting the Austrian, French-backed emperor of Mexico. They had wound up winning their civil war, with the Emperor Maximilian being overthrown and executed in 1867. Since then, Romero had served as a legislator and finance minister in his country, and then again as Mexican minister to the United States. He had maintained his relationship with Grant, in recent years working with him on an unfulfilled project to build railroads in Mexico. They were even designated by their respective governments as negotiators for a trade treaty, and had agreed on one, but that too had not yet come to fruition in the two countries' legislatures.

Last year, Romero had been personally generous in alleviating the general's financial plight, earning the strong gratitude of him and Julia. Like Tom Sweeny, he had a shovel-shaped beard to compensate for a lack of hair on his head, but he was a somewhat younger, much slighter, sad-eyed and fashionably dressed man, who overcame nervousness at the cost of a poor digestion. He was from Oaxaca like his Indian mentor Juarez, and the half-Indian new president, Porfirio Diaz. Romero had an American wife, the former Lucretia Allen. He remained a frequent guest at 3 East 66th Street.

Grant had shown what he had written in the *Memoirs* about Mexico to Romero, who was greatly impressed. Early in the same chapter there was something about Grant's courtship in Missouri, and Romero was struck by the sentence, "One of my superstitions had always been when I started to go anywhere, or to do anything, not to turn back, or stop until the thing intended was accomplished." This, he realized, did not just apply to journeys on horseback or troop movements, but to the determination with which the general was working on his book.

Romero also was stuck by a personal detail, not to do

with Mexico *per se*, but about U.S. Representative Thomas Hamer, who had recommended Grant for West Point. Hamer went on to volunteer when war came with Mexico, became a general and served there with Second Lieutenant Grant. The two of them talked and became well acquainted before Hamer died in Mexico. Grant speculated in the *Memoirs* that Hamer would have become president had he lived, and how his own career in the Army might have been affected: "Neither of these speculations is unreasonable, and they are mentioned to show how little men control their own destiny." The very young American officer had fought throughout the war with great distinction. Romero admired the vividness of the book's descriptions of Mexico, knowing that Grant's impressions of the country had been reinforced by recent trips there which they had taken together on railroad business.

Romero's shock came at what his friend said about the causes and justice of the Mexican War. He knew from their long and close association what Grant's views were about it, but was very surprised that the *Memoirs* attempted no diplomatic hedging about his thorough disapproval of the American claims. But then Seward was the man for diplomacy, not Grant. In fact, after clashing with Seward in 1865, Romero had gotten on better with him even while stirring up opposition to his policies. It had been Grant who bridled against Seward on Mexico's behalf—although the general obviously felt that he was also advancing the interests of the United States more effectively than the Secretary of State was.

In the *Memoirs*, Grant wrote about the injustice of the American cause in the Mexican War in much stronger terms than Romero himself would ever have used in this country, saying it was an unjustifiable campaign of conquest, and explicitly linking that cause to the ensuing disaster which fifteen years later engulfed the United States: "The Southern rebellion was largely the outgrowth of the Mexican war. Nations, like individuals, are punished for their transgressions. We got our punishment in the most sanguinary and expensive war of modern times."

The Mexican raised the issue now, asking Clemens what he thought of the passage.

"People will be shocked by it, perhaps," Clemens said. "Which is all to the good. General Grant can afford to tell the truth. His doing so is among the great strengths of the book."

"Lincoln said the same things," Grant managed to say. "In the '40s. And in his Second Inaugural." Grant's thoughts drifted to Robert E. Lee's father, Light-Horse Harry, a Revolutionary War hero who had been almost beaten to death in 1812 by a pro-war mob that called him a traitor. Grant, like Lincoln, wanted no part in judging who had committed treason. *Was I wrong to fight in Mexico?* Old man Lee had gone off after his beating to the West Indies, where he stayed for years and never quite made it back home, leaving his wife to raise Robert E. and their other children with scant resources. That behavior Grant was more inclined to judge, even though he realized all too well the difficulties attached to man's role as a provider. He looked up, realizing that by sinking into a reverie he had stopped the conversation.

Julia, in part to spare her husband's voice, changed the subject. "Dr. Douglas, I believe you and Dr. Shrady think the general should move out of the city during the summer season."

"We do, Mrs. Grant. He will be more comfortable elsewhere."

"But not Long Branch, I think?" persisted Julia.

"No," said Douglas. "While the ocean breezes in New Jersey would be helpful, the air would be as hot, and even more humid." He did not say that the humidity, whether here or there, might precipitate coughing, hemorrhage and death. Julia did not say it either, though she realized more about the medical condition of her husband than she let on. She also flushed in embarrassment upon remembering that they'd agreed to rent out the Long Branch house this summer, having been unable to sell the place at a reasonable price.

"Where, then," asked Nellie, "shall we go? And how?" The questions were delicate. The family's chronic cash shortage continued, and they were in no position simply to rent a cottage in the mountains. On the other hand, according to Clemens, Webster's had taken sixty-thousand pre-orders for the book. So the long-term financial prospects were steadily brightening—both for those who would live to see their full fruition and for Grant himself, who had been heartened by Clemens' report.

"The general has many friends with houses in more suitable positions," said Romero.

"And the newspapers have gotten ahold of these matters and questions," said Clemens, "which means hotel keepers may want to court publicity by inviting this famous guest without charging him."

"Mr. Clemens," said Julia, "I fear you are too cynical. We have received an invitation from Joseph Drexel, who has an interest in the Balmoral resort in the southern Adirondacks. He is also a friend."

"I know his brother better," said Grant, but did not pursue the point, and not just to spare his voice. Julia, he realized, was reluctant to accept charity from strangers, even though she also felt the country should have done more for the family. He was growing beyond such concerns, and had recovered more than she from the shock of their bankruptcy, for all his determination to erase it.

"Balmoral is on Mount McGregor," said Douglas, "which would be a suitable spot. Its elevation is not so high as to make breathing difficult, while it would be cooler and less humid than this city, or Long Branch."

"And it's near Saratoga," said Nellie, "where we have spent some time. But out of town."

"Mr. Drexel's kind offer," continued Julia, "as I understand it includes our whole family, and we would not actually be in the hotel."

"That's right," said Douglas. "There is a separate large cottage on the mountain top, owned by Drexel, that I think predates the Balmoral. It is to there that you are all invited."

"Free of charge?" asked Grant bluntly.

"Yes," said Douglas.

Grant nodded and Julia said, "Perhaps, then, we had better accept."

After Julia left the room, Romero brought up the subject of the French novelist Victor Hugo, who had died on May 22. The newspapers were describing a huge turnout for his funeral in Paris, which had been held on June 1. Grant wrote a note which Romero read aloud: "I admired *Les Miserables*."

Clemens said, "I liked the will he wrote, Hugo, rejecting the prayers of all the churches, but saying he believed in God."

Grant smiled thinly and nodded slightly at his friend. "I am not in a position to reject any aid," he rasped.

On June 12, Lieutenant Colonel Richard Napoleon Batchelder, a deputy quartermaster-general, arrived from Washington to collect a whole mass of memorabilia that was to be donated to the Smithsonian, pursuant to an agreement between William Vanderbilt and Grant to satisfy the latter's debt in an honorable way. Grant, unwell, nonetheless was pleased to see Batchelder, whom he remembered had served under General Rufus Ingalls in the Army of the Potomac. He spoke with him briefly about his own sometimes grim quartermasting days, in the Mexican War and then later passing through Panama in 1852.

Julia, while pleased to witness the conversation, was nonetheless melancholy at the need to deal with the task of packing up in order to dispatch all those swords, busts, coins, medals, vases, portraits, pens, golden trinkets, jewels, even elephant tusks. Her children helped, but she more than they appreciated the personal as well as historical meaning associated with most of the items, many reminding her of happier days on her and Ulys' very long trip around the world.

In the absence of these objects, the house seemed emp-ty, which did make the decision to leave it easier. Grant was continuing to weaken, the swelling getting larger on his throat, his voice almost gone. Douglas and Shrady decided that he must be moved upstate before he became too weak to go, and the date of departure was moved up. Julia felt none too well herself, with the accumulated stresses of the past year and more. She was putting on weight.

When Romero came back to 66th Street two days later, arrangements were well under way for the move to Mount McGregor. Nellie, who had grown fond of the foreigner— and almost felt like one herself—sat in a corner and talked to him in near privacy, receiving his assurance that he would come visit them upstate.

"The Hotel Balmoral, I hear, is a delightful place to spend the summer," he said. "It will be no sacrifice at all to spend time there in such honorable company as your family and friends."

"Now you are talking too much like my English rela-tions," said Nellie, "as no doubt these hotel developers do, who must have named it after Queen Victoria's Scottish palace. They are probably the sort of snobs who build vul-gar, garish would-be *palazzos* in this city, while the poor are crammed into stinking tenements. Not that I am accusing you of doing that, Senor Romero. But in Saratoga, I bet they would go to the casino, which the Grant family will be in no position to frequent, although it might be useful for us to break the bank there."

"I think you are harsh toward your host," said Romero,

trying to keep up. "And I like some of those *palazzos*. Perhaps the Balmoral on Mount McGregor will be in tune with your father's Scottish ancestry. And while I take your point about the poor, are they any better off in London?"

Nellie, however, wanted to move away from political or architectural banter, and was wondering if she were reckless enough to tell him something of the truth about her own life. She felt a slight chill these days between herself and her mother. Nellie had tried to tell Julia a little about the reality of her married life, and felt she was rebuffed. This had caused her to pause in confiding not just to Julia but to other members of her family, and she did not want to inflict her problems on friends like Clemens who were caught up in the wider business of her family's affairs and their own, and should not be distracted from these necessary pursuits. The Reverend Newman and his wife were too conventional, seemed too likely to disapprove, and she rarely saw Ely and Minnie Parker. Romero appeared a distinguished man of the world, but not a predatory one like her own husband. He was married, although his wife rarely came with him to the house, and—notwithdtanding his deep-set, soulful Latin eyes—unthreatening. While not as old as Grant, and definitely a foreigner, he seemed a suitable, sensitive and sensible confidant.

Nellie had taken Julia's hints, and not taken offense at her withdrawal. Her mother, she realized, could not take on board the additional stresses of knowing unambiguously about Algy, how his womanizing, drinking and abusive behavior had gone from bad to worse. She did not want to inflict all this on Romero, or anyone. But she knew that shutting it all up inside, while growing increasingly panic stricken at the thought of her absent children, was not good for her or them or anyone.

She started with the children, talking to Romero about how much she missed them, and her uncertainty over whether it was right for her to stay here with her father in America while they remained so far away.

"Could not they come over here?" he asked, reasonably enough.

"Their father would not permit it—continues to not permit it, as I discovered from one of his rare communications today." As Romero did not say anything, Nellie continued, "It is unfortunately the case that my husband and I are not on good terms."

"I regret to hear that," said Romero, his English not quite idiomatic, whereas hers had a mid-Atlantic overlay. "What does he do?" he continued.

"He would regard such a question as vulgarly American. The truth is," she went on, looking around to see that they were not overheard, "I should not have married him. I was too young. And a married woman has few rights that a bad husband is required to recognize. Even fewer in England, I think, although my mother-in-law and her sister both managed to have famous careers. And now there are three others, our children, whose needs I must put first—although my husband's family might sneer at me for doing so."

"I am very sorry for your situation," said Romero, who had only the vaguest notions about Nellie's in-laws. This was not something Grant discussed. "Can nothing be done?"

"I am alone over there," said Nellie, "apart from my children. And over here, too, without them. I don't want to inflict these sorrows on my stricken parents. Nor can they truly understand a bad marriage, their own being so good. My mother would tell me, the children need their father. And can I deny that? To her, a woman's life is home and family, even though she changed homes many times. But wouldn't almost anyone else tell me the same thing? Yet if a father fails his children, don't they need their mother all the more?"

"Is there no hope of reconciliation between you and Mr. Sartoris?"

"I suppose there must be," Nellie said. "What other hope can I have? But I don't really think so."

"There is not another woman in particular?"

"No. Algy is not at all particular in that regard. And, to be equally blunt, there is no other man on my side of the equation."

Romero swallowed uncomfortably. "Can no influences be brought to bear on his behavior, from his parents, perhaps, or a churchman?"

"My mother-in-law died last year," said Nellie. "She became a writer, after she was an opera singer. Perhaps you have heard of her, Adelaide Kemble? She was famous in her youth for singing *bel canto* all over Europe. She wrote a poem, *When I Am Dead*, which I can recite some of:

Lay no stone above
My lonely head.
Lay no stifling tombstone there;
The flowers will spring up thick and fair;
The violets love
The early dead.

"An opera singer and a poet?" said Romero, bemused yet impressed in spite of himself.

"Yes," said Nellie. "Though I think my own parents' marriage had more of the grand operatic passion about it than anything in the Sartoris or Kemble families. Certainly more than Algy's and my shipboard romance. For Father and Mother, it was Julia keeping the home fires burning, and Ulysses warming himself there. My own husband spurns my sputtering flame. He has not reciprocated my loyalty, my fidelity."

Romero tried not to let show how uncomfortable he felt, as Nellie's English-style rhetoric continued to flow.

"My mother-in-law's equally glamorous sister, my husband's aunt, is the actress and writer Fanny Kemble. She still lives. She spent much of her life in America years ago, and detested slavery as we do. As a girl, or a young married woman, I was something in awe of the whole family. Next to them, I knew I was a boor—something my husband was always ready to remind me of, whether with humor or merely contempt. I mistook their bohemianism for nobility, in both senses of the word."

"You do not seem the awestruck type," said Romero.

"They made me realize my own ill education. I have had to become less of a dull, scared stick and more of a sophisticated woman, as well as better read."

"I remember you as a girl full of life. And still you are lively, in a different way."

"I froze some in England," Nellie said, to which Romero had no response. "Father is a reader, too, you know. And we've both read his friend Mark Twain, who is now my friend, too, whom the English consider frightfully *déclassé*. I find it easier to make friends over here, and I like Clemens more than your average duke or dissolute artist."

"How about the duke in *Huck Finn*?" asked Romero, and won a smile in return.

"But Algernon does not listen to his father," she continued, "nor would he to mine, when mine was well and the most respected man in the world, or to his own relatives or to anyone of good character. My own father, you must know, Mr. Romero, is not a religious man, and people spread rumors about his drinking—although maliciously, I think, since I have never seen him drunk. I concede that it may have been an issue in his younger days. My husband's family is not religious, either, and I was willing enough to wear my faith lightly with them. But my husband's irreligion, and his drinking, and his romancing, are not like my father's."

Nellie paused, and Romero waited for her to go on.

"My father drank when he was two thousand miles away from his family, on a barren coast. My husband does it wherever he chooses, sometimes in front of me, making himself a spectacle, or in other places, from where reports sometimes reach me. His vices lead him down paths that my father never took, nor any good man. To idleness, gambling, and, to be blunt, faithlessness to our marital bed, along with violence and threats to myself. He has never found a manly occupation, but tries to prove his manhood by seducing any actress or serving maid or flirting wife who happens to strike his fancy. My romance was a snare and a delusion. I must tell the truth to someone."

Nellie's unconvincing attempt at a brave smile turned into a grimace as she met Romero's attentive eye, but she refrained from weeping and breaking down, as he continued to refrain from speech.

"Not that I am so perfect," she continued. "I find myself finding the Madeira bottle too early in the afternoon. Not here, not now, although I am unmoored enough without my children, and don't know if going back to them and England will fix it because it was there I started drifting, down into helplessness, though I trust it will be good for them. About the rest, about my husband, I do not know what to do. He is often absent; his letter today indicated he was away from the children. He would argue, I suppose, if anyone bothered to press him, that he is behaving according to the standards of his class. He could point to American women, like Jennie Jerome Churchill, who have embraced some of the same views—and in her case the Prince of Wales, among others. He might even suggest I emulate that behavior, which I am not inclined to do.

"These are things everyone knows but are not to be spoken of, not outside the charmed circle. I am not in it, but I know its rules and values. In my husband's clique, they scorn virtue and piety, disparage work and what they would call middle-class morality. They take nothing seriously but adultery, and are inclined to be insolent to anyone gauche enough to bring up their bad behavior. Manners trump morals, and are the sole definition of a gentleman—if he even bothers to still call himself that. I am just an annoying nag, a Puritan, an uncultivated, ill-bred nuisance, according to their lights. A traitorous gossip, too, if they could see and hear me now. And God knows I cannot speak of such things to my mother, or people here. I cannot live up to their standards."

"But your mother loves you," said Romero.

"Yes. And I cannot argue with her now. I don't want to. But hers is not my life."

"Have you no allies there?"

"No," said Nellie. "Some people are kind, but I am driven to make friends with servants. I am the outsider, even though I have learned to appreciate England's art and architecture, its history and literature. Your New York looks quite raw to me now with English eyes, and I am no more at home here than there. But my youthful spirit of adventure is gone, and so are romantic illusions."

"You think divorce out of the question?"

"No, unfortunately, not for me or my husband. His Aunt Fanny Kemble divorced. I am not so advanced as to advocate it, but perhaps must accept its necessity. We, Algy and I, are often apart, and I don't just mean in my present situation. But how can I raise such a matter, of divorce, here and now?"

"I suppose," said Romero, steering the conversation away from the apparently insoluble, "that the father of Jennie Jerome is in no danger of losing his popular title as the King of Wall Street, now that Ferdinand Ward has been dethroned and seems likely to join James Fish in prison."

"I met Mr. Jerome with Father at a horse race track in the Bronx. Jerome owned the track, I believe. And I think Mr. Fish, at rather an advanced age, has married a star of operetta. Things all seem to be connected in strange ways.

But an American without money has no value to my husband's circle."

"Nor much in this New York," said Romero, "where scandals among rich people and artists are hardly rare. Doesn't Jerome have open mistresses?"

"I suppose he does," said Nellie.

"Politicians, too, like Roscoe Conkling, your father's friend, and his paramour Kate Chase Sprague." Romero saw Nellie grimace at this, but she said nothing, and he decided to press home the point. "I apologize for my bluntness, Nellie, but you have been frank with me, and I feel I should be no less so in return. Let us be honest with each other." Even as he said this, he glanced briefly around to make sure they could not be overheard, before continuing, "I do not really think that houses of prostitution are any less common in New York than in London, or other cities, for all classes and prices. We are a long way from the Garden of Eden."

Nellie looked pained and said, "I am no friend to white slavery any more than black, in any place. As for Messrs. Jerome and Conkling, there are limits to my—and I think my parents'—willingness to support the American ruling class. In England, I think it is the avoidance of scandal that is the religion of Society."

Romero softened his tone. "When I was young, I supported the patriotic revolution in Mexico, and read Darwin, and was of the anticlerical party. I thought the Catholic Church was on the side of the rich and the colonialists, and that in this country it supported slavery—at least compared to the many Protestants who were strong abolitionists. But in my dull middle age, I have grown more appreciative. The church does help the poor, in Mexico and in New York. I believe it is Roman Catholic nuns who take care of most of this city's destitute children—the ones who are not running wild."

"Some nuns were nurses in the war, Father says."

"Yes," said Romero. "And the children on their own

here, in the streets, no one was caring for them before the Sisters of Charity came along. Most of them the sisters don't get to are left to die—or to Darwin."

"I wonder if Mrs. Josephine Shaw Lowell approves."

"I think so. If the street children live, it may be through vice and crime. Polite society does not want to think about child prostitution. But now the city has gotten in league with the nuns, and for once I think Tammany is backing the right horse."

"God bless them," said Nellie. "But is not the current mayor an anti-Tammany man?"

"Yes," said Romero, "although an Irish Catholic, and I don't think an opponent of the nuns. I see you have become an adept at the politics of New York."

"I also suspect you are simply approving of religion because you think it does good. Building schools and orphanages and such. Not that preachers like Dr. Newman don't do the same thing, when they talk about it reducing crime and vice. God knows we can use all that, in London as much as here. But I think you're dodging. The question is, is it, is religion, is any of it real? Is there a world to come? I think I believe so, like my mother, but fewer men seem to. I am not ashamed to have turned to God when I needed to, when left desolate by the failure of my marriage. But surely you don't think one can adopt Christianity on some kind of utilitarian basis. Doesn't it have to be true? And might it not demand of me duties impossible to bear, for my own sake or my children's?"

"I suppose your mother might say the truths of religion and a good life support each other." Romero paused, not wishing to be further drawn into religious or sexual argumentation, but realizing his words could be heard as judgmental criticism. Before he could elaborate, Nellie said "I can't argue with her."

Romero merely waved away over his shoulder any potential negative interpretation, before proceeding. "That's how your father and I think of trade, and business, that they contribute to progress, and raising up the poor. Maybe we think religion does the same thing, which is a more positive view of it than I used to have. It's not that I think my softening toward it has made me a better man, Nellie, but might not your husband become one? Might he not grow out of this folly?"

"And viciousness?" inquired Nellie brightly. "I suppose that must be my hope. But it is a frail reed to support my life and my children's. And since we, unlike your countrymen, are not Roman Catholics, I suppose divorce might be a possibility in the future. But I would have to have the children live with me, which as you can see from my current state is easier said than done. All I can do to mother them now, all I have been doing since March, is writing letters." Nellie stood up suddenly. "I suppose my family history, here and in England, shows how all our futures are uncertain, and precarious."

Chapter Seventeen

The trip upstate on June 16 went pretty well. Onlookers cheered the now almost white-haired general—although their cheers tended to fade as they noticed his obvious weakness and frailty, and some saw the large tumor on the right side of his neck—as the family left 66th Street that morning in a carriage, and then made their way through Grand Central Station to the Hudson River line. They were ushered into Vanderbilt's private railroad car. Into the baggage car were hauled the armchairs Grant had come to rely on, and a load of research material he had been using for the book. The manuscript itself came with the family in the passenger car, where it was held by Fred or Nellie.

On the journey Grant dozed through the heat, which continued to gather despite their northward progress along the river. While Julia was pleased to see him at rest, she decided to wake him anyway to point out West Point across the Hudson, and the general gazed at it hungrily until the view was left behind. He was looking backward, down the river, to avoid soot blowing in on his face through the windows, which had been left open to reduce the stifling heat. No one expected him to speak much now, and most of the family knew some of the old West Point story.

He had arrived there not long after turning seventeen, an undergrown youth called Hiram Ulysses whose name had been mixed up by the congressman who recommended him for a place, and the West Point bureaucracy. So they bequeathed Ulysses S. Grant to posterity. But Grant wasn't thinking of that, or of the cadets he met there whom he wound up fighting with in Mexico, and again with or against during the Civil War. He was thinking of Winfield Scott, his commanding general in the Mexico City campaign of 1847, old Fuss and Feathers who, as he'd noted in the book, was such a contrast in style to laconic, undemonstrative Zachary Taylor. Grant had served under General Taylor in northern Mexico, earlier in the war, and had been impressed by his "rough and ready" style which did not often extend to an actual uniform.

As a young second lieutenant, he had seen more of that war than either of the famous generals. Taylor and Scott were equally successful commanders, and the latter had cut loose from Vera Cruz and his supply line the same way Grant did sixteen years later before the fall of Vicksburg. Scott remained in command of the U.S. Army at the beginning of the Lincoln administration, and retired a few months later to write his memoirs at West Point, where Grant visited him in 1865, just after the end of the war. Then, the next year, he'd come up again for Scott's funeral, and the Fenian crisis broke while he was there, and he'd had to dispatch General Meade north to the border to arrest Sweeny and the other Irish would-be conquerors of Canada. He smiled now to remember.

As West Point drifted away behind the train, Grant wondered idly if he would ever see it again. He remembered they had some of his paintings displayed there, and the unfolding landscape of the river valley and Catskill Mountains before his eyes reminded him of the Hudson River School. His thoughts drifted away to a portrait of Scott, which had been one of the items taken away the other day by Colonel Batchelder, and then to painting in general, and specifically the Old World masters. Grant, who was famously indifferent to music, had been a painter at West Point, although the fact that some of his works were still on its walls was not likely entirely due to their artistic merit. His West Point colleague and future subordinate Truman Seymour was a better painter, but an inferior military commander. Still, Grant had become a connoisseur of art, a gratification he had eagerly indulged in many galleries and churches on the long European leg of the very long round-the-world tour that he and Julia made after leaving the White House, a three-decades-delayed sort-of honeymoon. He smiled now toward Nellie, remembering how the three of them went around the National Gallery together in London's Trafalgar Square.

Julia, too, had been an enthusiastic tourist and traveler, though it was finally her insistence which brought them home from that trip after almost two-and-a-half years. Now she was looking up the river, dotted with sails that still easily outnumbered the occasional smokestack of a steamer. She saw her husband lost in thought, and was glad that waking him had not meant an immediate return to the constant suffering of pain and the ever growing weariness.

They made good time, not stopping at Poughkeepsie or Hudson or the other stations on the Hudson River line, where they nonetheless saw from the windows well-wishers who had come together to wave at them. They arrived early at Albany before any large crowd had gathered. At Saratoga Springs, where they disembarked at 1:55, the reception committee included their host at Mount McGregor, Joseph Drexel. He was a good-natured, soft-looking man, but not as plump as Grant remembered. The honor guard from the Grand Army of the Republic applauded, but had the wit to let the exhausted general go by without requiring him to take the time and energy to inspect them, although he managed to raise his cane in salute.

They boarded a smaller train for the forty-minute run up to Mount McGregor. The narrow-gauge railroad had been built for the Balmoral. The smoke was worse now, and the ride rougher up the winding mountain route, with the mostly deciduous forest seeming to press in on either side. When they finally arrived at the station near the mountain-top, Grant found he could not walk the short distance up to the Drexel cottage. He had to be carried in a chair by two strangers, policemen who were part of another honor guard of Union veterans. He did manage to walk up the steps and in the door. Fred and Harrison, meanwhile, struggled with the two leather armchairs brought from New York.

The rest of the furniture was supplied by Drexel and the Balmoral Hotel. Workmen from Troy had been gussying up the cottage, which was really a handsome, albeit rustic, sizable, two-story, yellow-painted wooden summer house. They were making it fit for the great man's family, and had even constructed a large and handsome porch. But Grant's arrival was some days earlier than anticipated, and the porch trim and railing supports were not quite finished when the train arrived, and the workers were shooed back up to the hotel.

Harrison Terrell and McSweeny helped Grant bathe, and Douglas cleaned black soot dust and cinders from his throat, along with other detritus. Then the general settled into the leather chairs which had been brought into the ground-floor back room, soon asking for prayers to be said so that he could retire early to bed.

There was no question of Grant having the strength to walk upstairs, where the bedrooms were being parceled by Julia out to the family members. He would sleep on the chairs in the back sick room, with the valet and nurse sharing a small room next door. And he did sleep that night for ten hours. Julia at first picked a ground-floor room on the other side of his to sleep in, but soon decided against it. This corner room, well lit from two large windows, was converted into an office, and she moved upstairs with the rest of the family, though spending much of her time on the first floor at the side of her husband. But the family took meals at the hotel and the children played outside while Grant spent almost all his time at the cottage, much of it working. He accepted that Julia's move upstairs meant the end of any prospect for sexual intimacy, meaning he would husband his remaining energy and time for the book.

Grant began to revive in the cool mountain air, although no one thought the death sentence had been lifted. Yet the whole family was pleased with their new cottage, prospect and provisions. The next day, he sat on the spacious porch and read in the newspapers that while he had been riding north on the train, the Statue of Liberty had arrived from France in New York Harbor. In the days of his prosperity, Grant had contributed to and helped raise money for the fund to build a huge, carved-stone plinth and pedestal for the statue. He felt a modest pride at his share in the great event, along with gratitude and sympathy for the French Republic as he never had for the Emperor Louis Napoleon, who had invaded Mexico and favored the Confederacy.

Grant was able to walk down to what they called the eastern overlook, and even managed to spit *en route* like a normal man, without excessive coughing and expectoration. At a cleared area on the hillside, there was a large wooden gazebo and a view across the Hudson Valley to the Green Mountains of Vermont. That was, Grant realized, the scene of "Gentleman Johnny" Burgoyne's campaign in 1777, the British invasion from Canada whose defeat at Saratoga was the turning point of the Revolutionary War. Behind them, out of sight on the west side of the mountain, must be the Mohawk and Schoharie valleys, which the British and their Indian allies had raided throughout the war, with the Americans inflicting revenge on the natives. A grim business, soldiering, and not a trade he had meant to follow.

W.J. Arkell, who with Drexel owned the Balmoral, pointed out a recently constructed monument in the distance marking Burgoyne's surrender to the American general Horatio Gates. Grant smiled thinly to himself at the recollection of who really won the Battle of Saratoga and the whole war in the North. It was Benedict Arnold, who had had the drive to set men in motion, let loose the energy of American farmers and mechanics against pressed men, Hessians, aristocrats, until he switched sides, for what bauble, compared to what he could have had in the New World? Was it a bad wife's influence, jealous of English aristocracy? Yet maybe Gates should get credit for encircling Burgoyne, bringing it to a less bloody conclusion, as Washington did five years later at Yorktown, as Grant himself did at Donelson, Vicksburg, Appomattox.

He could make out the Saratoga surrender monument with binoculars, but soon put them down, and looked instead at the farms and forests, and felt peaceful. Some of the woodland was growing back, Arkell told him, as farmers pulled stakes and went West. They go where I came from, Grant thought. He recalled Bristow telling him recently that the New York state government had just created a Forest Preserve to protect much of the Adirondacks and Catskills from logging, which had often denuded their slopes and polluted their waters. While it sounded like a pragmatic, pleasing measure, he wondered what would become of the loggers and other workmen who had tried to make a living from the forest, and whether it was wise to discourage them, since farmers were finding it hard to continue cultivating the soil here. It was a relief no longer to have to make those kinds of decisions. When he turned to go back he found it a difficult slog from the overlook back up the hill. He was exhausted again by the time he made it to the cottage.

Newman arrived the next day, and though he soon had to depart for a Sunday preaching engagement in Philadelphia, promised a speedy return. Day-trippers from Saratoga Springs began showing up in large numbers, mostly keeping a respectful distance in the wooded areas still prevalent on the mountaintop. Grant paid them little heed. While his exhaustion from the trip to the Overlook made him realize anew how little time he had, he did recover strength in the clear mountain air. He was even able to take an occasional glass of sweet wine, at the urging of Julia and Fred, who obviously felt no concern at potential abuse of alcohol, and valued its stimulating yet soothing effect. The energy Grant took from his temporarily improved condition he devoted to work—on the *Memoirs* and, to a lesser extent, on preparations for his demise, embarking on letters to Dr. Douglas, Fred and Julia.

Clemens was anxious to publish, to take the book out of Grant's hands, but when he came to visit he did not get it. They both knew that Grant lacked the energy and time to write a third volume about his presidential years. Still, having reached Appomattox, the manuscript was eminently salable—indeed Clemens' drummers had already racked up extraordinary sales. The two volumes would make a big book, a large body of work. Grant was pleased with what he'd written about his meeting with Lee, respectful of that great soldier "who had fought so long and valiantly and had suffered so much for a cause," and even happier to have appended, "though that cause was, I believe, one of the worst for which a people ever fought, and one for which there was the least excuse."

Now, though, he was determined to finish a concluding chapter, and write a preface. He also kept making corrections and additions to the text. Dawson, Fred, or Clemens himself when he visited (as he did twice that summer) would find the right places to insert them. Dawson also kept ink in Grant's pens and sharpened the thin, short pencils he was using more often. Grant was doing all the composition by hand now, sometimes outside on the porch and sometimes through the night in the back room, as the spirit moved him. Dawson was able to decipher the increasingly illegible script, recopying it for the publisher.

Grant's physical condition slipped back into decline. He could barely swallow anything because of the increasing pain in his throat, was losing the ability to walk, and only

sleeping now for an hour or two at a time. He worked inter-
mittently but consistently, hardly ever leaving the cottage,
although the rest of the family ate at the nearby Balmoral
hotel, which had opened for the season after their arrival.
Grant just had a little mush, or maybe tapioca or apple-
sauce, in the back room. Long gone were the days when
Julia could prepare for him favorite recipes like breaded veal
rolls with onion and spinach, and sweet potato fries. For a
while he had regretted this, longing to eat without pain even
a cold chicken sandwich. Now, perhaps mercifully, his ap-
petite was sharply diminished. One dish still in Julia's
repertoire for him was rice pudding, now made with eggs,
cream and vanilla. Some months previously, she had adapted the recipe to make the dish smoother and less acidic,
omitting the lemon juice and peel, and the slivered almonds.
But even this version he now found difficult to swallow.

When sitting outside on the porch, Grant often had his
work interrupted by well-wishers. Fred tried to discourage
them by deploying Sam Willett, a sturdy local bootmaker
and Union veteran in his mid-sixties who had camped himself out back to be of service to the family. Willett was
posted in front of the cottage to keep strangers off the
porch, telling those who dallied to "move along," although
at Grant's request he did not dress in the military uniform
which he had at first put on. Despite these precautions, the
general would sometimes tip his hat to sight-seers, and occasionally wave them up anyway, although he couldn't talk.
When Fred protested, his father wrote a note saying: "I do
not wish to be exclusive. Let them come."

The cheerful, clean-shaven Willett made friends with the
family, including the grandchildren, and swore that camping
in the mountain air had cured his rheumatism. He told a reporter from the *Albany Evening Journal* how he had first
encountered the general in 1864 as a member of a fatigue
party, to which Grant had personally demonstrated a better
way to haul up bags of oats.

While Grant sometimes worked on the porch, he spent most of his time on the two chairs in the room at back, which the others had taken to calling the sick room. He worked, slept and ate there, and was bathed by Harrison and McSweeny (who also helped him with the chamber pot). His digestion improved in the latter part of June, and he was able to get some food down—even the occasional small cup of coffee. The pain in his throat and mouth, however, was more or less constant, and he often struggled for breath. He wrote in a journal, for the benefit of Fred and the doctors and perhaps for history, how "I can feel plainly that my system is preparing for dissolution in three ways: one by hemorrhages, one by strangulation, and the third by exhaustion." Nellie read this too, and gasped. Would he choke or bleed to death, or just give up the ghost? Then she remembered the worse loss of her own Grant, the first-born child whom no one here but herself had known. Like her father, she must accept the ordinary yet terrible nature of death, despite the bewildering circumstances of this particular departure. Grant had written to Clemens asking him to come, which he did on the evening of June 28. Clemens was anxious to get the proofs finally done for Volume 1, which went up to the fall of Vicksburg in July 1863. But Grant had been revising the article on Vicksburg he was preparing for *The Century* magazine, so Clemens and Fred worked on putting the same revisions into the book manuscript. Clemens had started correcting the galley proofs for that volume in April, but Grant had never conceded that he was finished with it. Now, at Clemens' suggestion, Grant turned his attention back to the beginning of the book, and a new preface.

"Man proposes and God disposes," he wrote. "There are but few important events in the affairs of men brought about by their own choice." The preface told of how he came to write the book, mentioning the collapse of his finances and health. But Grant felt the truth of that opening line as a commentary on his whole life, how much he was really the shuttlecock of events, rather than the commanding figure. He knew his decisions had mattered, that he had been, apart from Lincoln, the only indispensable man in the winning of the Civil War. But he also knew—as did the world—how that war had lifted him from deepest obscurity, a clerk in his father's store, an almost failed middle-aged man who had struggled against drunkenness and poverty. He had consistently declined to view negatively that period of his personal history, choosing to dwell on the good things that happened then, especially with his family. Long before then he had chosen Julia, which had made all the difference, and she thought the same way.

That afternoon, as she leaned over to wipe his face, the smell of her reminded him sharply of the sexual act, now lost to them, even as she turned her head and said to Nellie, "We were Missouri farmers when you were born. That was a happy time." What she smelled, he pondered ruefully, might be a good deal worse, his rotting breath, but she gave no sign of that. Together, they had been invincible—and still were, despite their losses, at least while life lasted.

Romero stayed at the Balmoral, like Clemens and other visitors, and except for the medical men and Sam Willett, spent more time with the family than any other outsider. Small of stature, he made himself unobtrusive. At the cottage on the early evening of June 29, he was talking to Fred in the parlor, the main reception room, while most of the family was eating up at the hotel. Fred showed him two notes Grant had written about potential burial sites, in which he ruled out any place where Julia could not be buried with him, and suggested the states of New York, Illinois or Missouri.

"That means not West Point or Arlington," Fred said, the latter place being the former home of Robert E. Lee, which had been seized by the federal government and turned into a military cemetery.

Romero, whose regular work involved close observation of U.S. cultural changes, had paid attention two years ago when Lee's heirs won a lawsuit in the Supreme Court, and received $150,000 from the U.S. government for the Arlington property. But what did that have to do with Grant's burial?

"Why not there?" he asked.

"Wives can't be buried in the Army cemeteries," said Fred, adding, "I wonder why he doesn't mention Ohio. Most presidents are buried in the state of their birth and childhood home."

"The same reason," said Romero. "Your mother. He did not know her in his Ohio days, but lived with her in Missouri, and Illinois and New York."

Meanwhile, Grant was working in the sick room, while in the small kitchen behind it Harrison heated beef tea on a tiny cast-iron, kerosene-fueled stove. He mixed in a little milk and egg. Grant managed to gulp it down, and paused to recover from the pain and strain of swallowing.

Then he set the unfinished preface aside, and took out a new sheet of paper. Perhaps the pain of swallowing had reminded him of this task left undone. It was a farewell message to Julia—not something to give her now, but to be found after his death.

My Dear Wife;
"There are some matters about which I would like to talk but I cannot. The subject would be painful to you and the children, and, by reflex, painful to me also. When I see you and them depressed I join in the feeling.

I have known for a long time that my end was approaching with certainty ... the end is not far off ... My will disposes of my property ... I have left with Fred a memorandum giving some details of how the proceeds of my book are to be drawn from the publisher.

Look after our dear children and direct them in the path of rectitude. It would distress me far more to think that one of them could depart from an honorable, upright and virtuous life than it would to know they were prostrated on a bed of sickness from which they were never to arise alive. They have never given us any cause on their account. I earnestly pray they never will.

With these few injunctions, and the knowledge I have of your love and affections, and of the dutiful affections of all our children, I bid you a final farewell until we meet in another, and I trust better, world.

Grant felt the note a little stiff. It was somehow easier to write for the world than to this woman who would feel his loss so deeply. With the letter, he put into an envelope his wedding ring, which he could no longer wear because his fingers had gotten too thin. Also, he put in a locket of Buck's—Ulysses Jr.'s—hair entwined with Julia's. The boy had been born in 1852 in Ohio (the "Buckeye State"— hence the nickname). Julia had been staying there with her in-laws while Grant was serving in Oregon. Julia sent him the hair locket which he held on to for two increasingly unhappy years out West, before he resigned his commission and finally came home to rejoin the family, and met his son. Grant had kept the memento with him ever since. In Oregon and California, his efforts to make money on the side to supplement his small Army pay had ended in failure, and so he was never able to afford to bring out Julia and the boys. Left alone there and brooding, he had drunk more than was good for him.

Yet he had also loved the West, the new city of San Francisco, and the majestic Columbia River in Oregon,

mightier than the Hudson here. It was grand, the West, as
well as lonely. A promising country. By the time he'd returned from California, Julia was with her parents in
Missouri. She had never been much of a letter writer, and
Grant, coming from New York, had gone first to his own
parents' house in Ohio. Then he approached St. Louis as a
thirty-two-year-old, flat-broke would-be provider whose
skills were in the field he had abandoned. He lacked a civilian trade. Yet Julia's greeting was warm and genuine, and
Nellie was born nine months later. Despite what proved to
be his precarious livelihoods in civilian life, her affection
never flagged, and they soon had a fourth child, Jesse.

The convicted banker James Fish, Grant read in the
newspapers, had been sentenced to ten years, and was going
to the Auburn prison in upstate New York, which was the
town where the Sewards were from. Ferdinand Ward remained in a New York City jail and had not yet gone to trial,
even though Fish blamed him for everything. But others,
apparently, were too embarrassed to testify. Grant wondered about his sons. That farewell note to Julia implicitly
defended their conduct, for love overrides all, but he wondered why they, too, like him, had been so foolishly trusting
of Ward. Lured in by easy money, the Grants seemed to
have been. He wondered if his sons thought Ward had been
trading in lucrative government contracts. That's apparently
what Ward told Fish, although he told Grant the opposite.

And, it turned out, Ward had partly been telling him the
truth, for there were no government contracts that might
have created a conflict of interest. It turned out that instead
of investing clients' money in such contracts, Ward had
been putting it into his personal accounts, to spend on himself. There were essentially no investment contracts of any
kind, government or private. It was all a farce, in which he
and the boys had played their roles as gulls. (While Nellie
had lost some money, it was less than her brothers, and she
had had no contact with Ward or the firm.) You could be

blinded, lulled and seduced by money, by greed—which could take the simple form of signing up for high returns on investments—the same way you could be by politics. Grant hoped his sons now realized, as he had done, that money must be earned, and was not to be acquired so easily as they had supposed. If only he himself had learned that earlier, before others, including his sister, were led astray by his folly.

He put the envelope with the note for Julia into the pocket of his robe and looked at the draft of the preface again, scratching out a sentence that apologized for the truncated nature of the book. *Let it stand on its own.* He set the manuscript aside, and managed to smile up at Harrison, saying he was ready to eat. He was able to swallow without choking a little of the mush held ready for him, that had been crushed in a special metal device kept at the cottage. At last, Harrison and McSweeny lifted him into the parlor, where he hailed Fred and Romero just before the rest of the family returned from the hotel. Grant, tired and content at what he had accomplished, beamed to see them come in, little Julia and her brother Ulys and their cousin Nellie, Jesse's girl, among the first up on the porch and through the door to greet him.

Chapter Eighteen

A BATH WAGON was a fancy wheelchair named after an English city frequented by invalids. One was delivered at the Mount McGregor station on June 25. It offered Grant some revived freedom and gave Harrison and Fred relief from carrying him. He was wheeled up in the new chair toward the hotel, and when Harrison joked about becoming a draught horse, he wrote him a note saying, "For a man who has been accustomed to drive fast horses, this is a considerable come down in point of speed." While he enjoyed himself at the hotel, this was a rare excursion. He mostly remained at the cottage. Before Clemens left at the end of June, Grant let him have Volume 1.

Back working on Volume 2, the general was adding significant material on Appomattox, and a final chapter skimming over its twenty-year aftermath. "Wars produce many stories of fiction, some of which are told until they are believed to be true," he wrote to debunk one common fable about the surrender.

He described the terrible blow of Lincoln's assassination, how he knew the man's fine character, "and above all his desire to see all the people of the United States enter again upon the full privileges of citizenship with equality among all." The phrase was shorthand—because time was running out—for his and Lincoln's shared belief that it was necessary to do two things at once: restore the rights of the former Confederates so as to welcome them back without rancor into the American family, and protect the rights of their former slaves. It was necessary to reconcile those goals, a "consummation devoutly to be wished," in Hamlet's words, but not one necessarily achievable in the absence of Lincoln. Grant had done his best, but John Wilkes Booth had done more in opposition.

The beneficial effects of the mountain environment could not last, being overwhelmed by the progression of cancer rotting deep into his mouth and tongue, throat and tonsil, growing larger by dissolving flesh, spreading through his body. When his scrawny limbs refused to work, and pain gathered strength behind the drugs, Grant felt as if the machine which undergirded his identity was breaking down. But he did not feel like a machine when he held the hand of his wife or daughter, as he took the rest he increasingly needed. While everyone was very attentive, he was nonetheless pleased to catch glimpses of his children and grandchildren going about their lives without reference to himself. It was good that the world would go on without his being in it, although he still could affect their future lives by what he was doing now.

So Grant continued to work, despite any amount and degree of difficulties. Sometimes there was nuance to be added to the text, as when he felt his somewhat harsh remarks about the slowness of General George Thomas needed tempering. In the same way in March, following the publication of the first *Century* article, he had scaled back its criticisms of General Lew Wallace at Shiloh. Now when he wrote one of these additions, he left it to Fred or someone else—usually Clemens or Noble Dawson, with Grant's other children sometimes helping by looking through the manuscript—to find the right place to insert it into the book. But he was not prepared to alter the truth as he saw it, no matter if some feelings might be hurt.

Grant had time for nothing but the truth, which permitted him to say of General Thomas, a man with whom he had had little real personal or professional sympathy: "Thomas was a valuable officer, who richly deserved, as he has received, the plaudits of his countrymen for the part he played in the great tragedy of 1861-5."

It was a family tragedy for Thomas, too, Grant now recalled, that had pursued him even after death, to his burial not far from this place, in Troy, New York, in about 1870. Thomas had not spoken with his sisters in Virginia since 1861, which was their choice, not his. They refused all contact, even after the war was over, because they never forgave him for sticking to the Union. Nor did they come to the funeral. Thomas' wife was from Troy, and Grant vaguely recalled that her side of the family had a plot in the cemetery there, which was in the countryside north of the Episcopal church in town where the main service was held. President Grant and his whole Cabinet had attended, and there must have been 10,000 people at the grave site.

Grant reflected that one thing he had in common with Thomas was lack of an obvious site for a burial place. Thomas had died suddenly, on duty in California, and the wife hadn't made it back home for the funeral. They had no children. Grant thought there must have been concern about the Klan or some random vandal desecrating a headstone in Virginia, or perhaps just fear of sisterly insult. An advantage of his own slow death was that he had had the opportunity to write to Fred about his wishes for a burial place.

In the manuscript, Grant had mentioned briefly in the Wilderness chapter the death of Alexander Hays, who was a friend, and one of many generals in the war who were now obscure and unremembered by the public. James McPherson, another, younger friend who was killed at Atlanta not long after Hays' death in Virginia, was now represented by a grand equestrian statue in Washington. So was Thomas, who had died after five years of peace. Grant had wept in his tent after that first day at Wilderness, when Hays died, and then again in the summer when he heard the news about young, bright, gallant McPherson, who had a warmly humorous twinkle in his eyes, and was killed before he could marry his *fiancée*. He wept again, years later, visiting the grave site of Hays. But Hays' sad bearded face was now forgotten by the world, and perhaps his friend Grant was to blame. Unlike McPherson, Hays had been killed when under Grant's direct orders. He had actually been demoted from division command in the military reorganization when Grant came East, just before the battle. Hays would still, though, have been leading from the front as a division leader, like Sheridan, McPherson, Longstreet.

Grant added the short paragraph: "I had been at West Point with Hays for three years, and had served with him through the Mexican war, a portion of the time in the same regiment. He was a most gallant officer, ready to lead his command wherever ordered. With him it was 'Come boys,' not 'Go.' " He wondered briefly if that was too obscure for the general reader, but decided he liked it anyway. Readers would figure out the meaning, that Hays went into the fight with his boys, and so died. *While I stayed back, and lived, to die now.*

Grant wrote a Conclusion, since it was quite obvious he lacked the strength to embark upon a third volume about the presidency and the rest of his postwar history. "The cause of the great War of the Rebellion against the United States will have to be attributed to slavery," it began, since he was determined to refute the Southern special pleaders who were saying the late unpleasantness was all about states' rights, and sought to minimize the significance of their peculiar institution. The book as a whole was an unvarnished statement of the rightness of the Union cause, and however much it also called for national reconciliation, there was no question of its condemnation of secession and slavery. He had never wanted to engage in controversy about the war, but was now prepared to state what previously had been buried under his customary reserve.

Earlier, in the Chattanooga chapter, Grant had referred

to slavery as "an institution abhorrent to all civilized people not brought up under it." Now in the Conclusion, a defense of Negro rights discussed how "the colored man … was brought to our shores by compulsion, and he now should be considered as having as good a right to remain here as any other class of our citizens"—but then got sidetracked into a defense of the presidential effort to annex Santo Domingo. Grant had always thought of that project as a wedge against the remaining slave strongholds in the Western Hemisphere, especially Brazil, and as a way to enhance the economic bargaining power of blacks in the United States. But he lacked the will and energy to explain this failed effort. He did write a note about "our duty to inflict no further wrong on the Negro," but that phrase did not make it into the manuscript. The shadow of the unresolved Negro problem lay behind, but did not eclipse, his vision of national progress, in which reconciliation with the former enemy did not quite equate to forgiveness.

The Conclusion skipped around some of the events of the past twenty years and opined about them, but always came back to the Civil War. Reading it, Clemens was reminded of Badeau's cutting phrase about "disjointed fragments," but found it rather beautiful withal (although he took care in public to use more vigorous praise words than "beautiful"). The chapter made some positive remarks about the result of the war, only to undercut them: "This war was a fearful lesson, and should teach us the necessity of avoiding wars in the future." His handwriting had become shaky and spidery, but Dawson was able to follow and transcribe it. And for all his disdain for the secessionist cause, Grant wrote:

> I feel that we are on the eve of a new era, when there is to be great harmony between the Federal and Confederate. I cannot stay to be a living witness to the correctness of this prophecy; but I feel it

within me that it is to be so. The universally kind feeling expressed for me at a time when it was supposed that each day would prove my last, seemed to me the beginning of the answer to 'Let us have peace.'

The expression of these kindly feelings were not restricted to a section of the country, nor to a division of the people. They came from individual citizens of all nationalities; from all denominations —the Protestant, the Catholic, and the Jew; and from the various societies of the land—scientific, educational, religious or otherwise. Politics did not enter into the matter at all.

This passage reflected recent events, for as his life slipped away, Grant had been especially touched by messages from his former Confederate enemies, seeming to fulfill his yearning for inclusion, for peace.

His ability to speak had at first returned at Mount McGregor, but then fell into decline with the rest of his health. His tongue was being eaten up by the cancer. Julia fought against the realization that she would never hear again the clear, musical tenor of her husband's voice, which soldiers had told her could quietly command their attention and action across camps and fields—like Lincoln's high voice over crowds. She still drew life from those liquid blue eyes of his, and she and he could still demonstrate, with touch and look, their love for one another. She took a little comfort that neither McSweeny nor Harrison, nor the famous nurses Dorothea Dix or Clara Barton had they been present, could do as much.

Grant wrote more and more notes to hand to people as his primary method of communication, sparing his diminished capacity to speak. He called this "pencil talk," and seemed almost possessed by the writing bug. One note to Dr. Shrady on June 24 said the lower dose of morphine he had taken the night before had worked satisfactorily. But a few days later he wrote to Dr. Douglas: "The fact is that I am a verb instead of a personal pronoun. A verb is any thing that signifies to be; to do; or to suffer. I signify all three." This caused the physicians to resume injecting morphine, which they had not done for two days to spare the general's much punctured arms and thighs. Grant was usually content not to receive the drug or to minimize the dosage, so as to keep his mind clear for work, but now recognized its necessity.

A note to Shrady on July 2 said:

> If it is within God's providence that I should go now, I am ready to obey His call without a murmur. … I am thankful for the providential extension of my time to enable me to continue my work. I am further thankful … because it has enabled me to see for myself the happy harmony which has so suddenly sprung up between those engaged but a few short years ago in deadly conflict. It has been an inestimable blessing to me to hear the kind expressions towards me in person from all parts of our country; from people of all nationalities; of all religions and of no religion; of Confederate and national troops alike. … To you and your colleagues I acknowledge my indebtedness for having brought me through the 'valley of the shadow of death' to enable me to witness these things.

The doctors, nurse and valet, along with Julia, Nellie and the rest of the family, sought to relieve the patient's pain and make him comfortable as far as they could—which they knew, despite all their efforts, was not far. He was building up tolerance to the cocaine hydrochloride, which became less effective at numbing and paralyzing the inflamed flesh and cancerous growth, tending rather to irritate it further. Grant wondered if he should just drink the cocaine in water, as Shrady had had him do before. At least it didn't dull the mind, and permitted him to work. Yet too much of the cocaine could prove confusing, as no drug was without its mental costs. That price, though, was sometimes worthwhile to prevent the constant dull background pain rising, advancing unchecked to sting and choke, or latch like a limpet on neck, mouth, through bones in bleak connection, duller or sharper, more or less ungovernable, unless drugged by dangerous doses of opium.

Still, Grant often joined the family in the parlor, sometimes smiling and seeming happy to listen to their talk, sometimes joining in card games. Jesse was an indefatigable card player, who could also make his father laugh—physically painful though that could be, these days. The younger women—Elizabeth, Ida, Nellie—occasionally helped with the manuscript, perhaps reading back to him what he had written so that he could correct it. Buck was going back and forth between Mount McGregor and New York City, and brought back galleys from the publisher.

To Newman one day in early July, Grant said he had "many friends who have crossed the river before me."

"Yes, General, that is so," said Newman "They have taken the journey before you and now stand ready to receive you."

"It is my wish that they may not have long to wait," said Grant, and Newman was not shocked to hear it. It was painful now for the general to speak, which gave Newman more scope to talk to him about Christ suffering along with us here below. Grant had him read aloud instead, from the book of Job and the Gospel of Matthew.

To Julia, out of Grant's hearing, Newman ventured to speak about the events of the past year and their inevitable outcome, casting Ferdinand Ward as Judas Iscariot, and the general's book and illness as a redemptive burden that he was carrying for his family and country. Nellie, listening somewhat skeptically, had to concede the point that the *Memoirs* would not have been written had her father's good fortune continued. But for neither her nor Julia did the achievement seem worth the cost.

They were getting on well now, mother and daughter. Both naturally vivacious women, they now were quiet together. It occurred to Nellie that Julia seemed to have recreated the plantation of her youth, with everyone at her beck and call. For a family without money they were living, and her father was dying, in luxurious surroundings. She did not dwell on or share such uncharitable thoughts, yet one evening upstairs at the cottage Julia surprised her daughter by bringing up the subject of her own upbringing.

"You know," Julia said, "I was so happy in those days, in the Old South, I almost feel guilty about it. We did look on our darkies as friends, not really slaves, but I know that's the way unreconstructed rebels speak, so I don't now. And I know perfectly well that slavery was wrong. But my mind isn't as strong as yours, dear."

"Yes it is, Mother."

"Oh, maybe for housekeeping. And even there, when we were first married, I nearly bankrupted your father. We had such fine old servants at home that I sort of thought the house should keep itself, which it never got around to doing. So I had to learn on the spot to do things, like cooking. Before that, at White Haven, I was a sillier girl than you, believing in fairies and such. They used to come out, I thought, on midsummer nights like this, as the fireflies do here. And later, when you were a baby, and your father had built that log house on land which my father gave us, our lives were hard and constrained compared to what they had been. I no longer had Papa and Mama and our people around me, nor the other officers' wives. I remember one night there, at about this time, I was in a funk of thinking this is my sad lot, feeling sorry for myself."

"I have never known you like that," said Nellie.

"No, thank God," said Julia. "I wouldn't let you feel my fear. I know it sounds silly to people when I say 'Up and be doing for your dear ones,' yet that's what some fairy, or angel maybe, told me that night at Hardscrabble, driving off the dark clouds, giving me courage and determination to be happy and grateful, to make the best of things. I still try to do that."

Nellie smiled, and was grateful that her mother merely took her hand, not pressing for talk about impossible subjects like the death in dreadful convulsions nine years ago of ten-month-old Grant Sartoris, about whom she had had to endure so many expressions of formal comfort, leaving an emptiness in their wake which she filled up with new births. Nor did she want to speak about the threats now lowering over her little family three thousand miles away.

While Nellie was by no means as close to Newman as was Julia, she did not share the antipathy to the reverend which was held by Clemens and others. The next evening, as they sat quietly together on the porch, she said, "You seem curiously uncertain for once, Dr. Newman. I think I like you the better for it."

"I was thinking about the Roman Catholic doctrine of Purgatory," he replied, "for which, as you may know, there is no biblical sanction—it's just papist mummery. But it would solve the problem of what to do with people who don't seem good enough for Heaven or bad enough for Hell."

"Ah, I know some of them," she laughed.

"I am not really uncertain about my religion, Nellie, about what I believe. The scoffers do not shake me. But I see it as an entry to a great mystery. There is grace, and sin, and we get better than we deserve. I know I'm no saint, but if only saints can preach, then the Devil will drown out Scripture." He smiled ruefully. "I don't seem to be able to resist the temptation to sermonize. Your father, though, has seen so much of life, from the tannery to the battlefield, that

I sometimes think he does not sufficiently acknowledge that mystery. Yet he is full of grace, and goodness."

"You could remind him of those Thanksgiving proclamations from the White House," said Nellie, "which Mother treated like the prayers they were."

While Grant berated himself for his naïve approach to human relations, which had allowed confidence men to take advantage, he did not fall prey to a disillusioned cynicism. He retained a belief in the goodness of many people, such as those who had helped the family after the collapse of Grant & Ward. He was still humbled by that turn of events, and turned around in his mind how he had been at fault. Perhaps it was a sort of squeamish, snobbish idleness, not wanting to bother himself with the mundane business of grubbing for money, so setting up himself and his dear ones —in Julia's phrase—to be robbed. These days he tolerated Newman's talk and prayers, but still preferred to have him read aloud. If the preacher was right about Heaven, then there might be an opportunity through those pearly gates to clear up some trivial questions that he had about earthly things—but then again, one presumably would have more elevating preoccupations, in the event that a world beyond this one actually existed.

While Grant mused in the sick room and Nellie talked with Newman on the porch, Ida and Elizabeth were putting the children to bed. Julia sat with Fred in her room upstairs and, at first tentatively, talked quietly about Nellie, how she was worried about her: "Has she said anything to you to give you … doubts … about how happy she is? Not here, not with us, but in England, with …"

"With Sartoris," said Fred, and got a "Yes" in response.

"I never thought much of the fellow," Fred continued, sounding a bit like an Englishman himself, his mother mused. "Too much the aesthete—dilettantes, the whole bunch of them, that family. A gaggle of actresses and women writers and opera singers and God knows what. No wonder he's not amounted to much."

"We must have civilization, Fred," said Julia, keeping her voice down. "But is he ... good to Nellie?"

"God knows, mother. I don't see him as beating her, or locking her in the attic."

"No. But that is hardly the limit of a woman's aspiration."

"I don't think he's an ideal husband," said Fred. "But he's acceptable enough that she's stuck with him."

"Young people talk about marriage so cynically," said Julia. "It is supposed to be a woman's refuge, and her work and achievement. But for Nellie ..." The two of them stared gloomily out Julia's window at the darkness.

The next day, July 3, when Grant lay down for a nap it brought on an agonizing coughing fit, and there was another one following a rare visit to the Balmoral hotel in the Bath chair. The pain was not just the very sharp one at the site of the spreading cancer, but seemed to spread up behind his nose to the top of his head, and continued as he then struggled to draw in air, often bringing on more coughing. It was decided to have him rest on the Fourth of July, and cancel the planned celebration which would have included the birthdays that day both of Nellie, who turned thirty, and Fred's son Ulysses, who was four, along with that of the United States of America. The Emperor of Japan was among those who cabled greetings. Julia, reading his lines to her husband, thought of the neat quiet gardens and lovely mountains of that country, where they rested after two years touring the world. Grant recalled the peace treaty he had helped broker then between Japan and China.

"Birthdays are for the young," said Nellie to Fred and Ida, dismissing her own role but sympathizing with the disappointment of young Ulys. The public, too, were disappointed when Grant stayed indoors and they could not catch a glimpse of him on the porch. The birthday boy wanted to be a soldier like his father and grandfather. In April in New York, Grant had written a letter to whomever would be president in 1898, recommending his grandson for a place at West Point. Her father used to tell her, Nellie now told the four-year-old, that the fireworks on the Fourth were for her. Now they would be for young Ulysses, too, as well as for Gettysburg and Vicksburg.

Nellie told no one that she had received no birthday greetings from England, but it added to her melancholy. She continued to write conscientiously to the children, receiving the very occasional reply, but hardly expected them to notice her birthday. Algy might have bothered, but did not. Her birth on this national day, and her father's victory on the date at Vicksburg, made her a sort of patriotic *cliché*, yet her own country was half strange to her, and not the land of her children. This mountaintop felt like a combination of prison and refuge, a beautiful bright shadowland, suspended over the real world. She was happy that her American family was getting along, and happy she could be of use, sometimes relieving Fred, for example, of his constant attendance on their father, and allowing him to get some sleep. And to her broken father her love could flow clear, not dammed and muddied up as it was between her and Algy. She was grateful for the presence of friends like Romero, although rather embarrassed to recall her last conversation with him in New York, when she had been perhaps too forthcoming about the state of her marriage.

Still, brooding a little about that here on the mountain, she reminded herself that not all men were like Algy, and how extraordinary and distasteful it would be if they were. If he were here now, would he not be hanging around the hotel for the purpose of sexual adventuring, cozying up to tourists or scullery maids? Or even if circumstances caused him to restrain himself from that, he would be settling instead for the relief of alcohol. And what must it be like to be him, under the constant strains of such a life, difficulties different from hers but by no means negligible? No wonder he sought sympathy no matter the circumstance, and was indignant at its refusal. Yet she could not quite harden her heart against the father of her children, and the memory of his attractions. She thought of her own father, how his hardest times, harder even than now, were when he was away from the family. She could not really believe that Algy's motive in now depriving her of the children's presence was his own distress at being separated from them. Yet she supposed—at least hoped—that it was not simple malignity, either. In any case, she needed enough of her father's strength, and gumption, to live her own life.

Newspapermen on death watch, along with hotel guests and day-trippers wandered by the cottage. Julia was glad Sam Willett and Fred kept them away, because Ulys could not spare the strength to deal with their intrusions. Nellie, too, thought the almost permanent mass display of onlookers was a bit ghoulish and undignified, and was at first made uncomfortable by the photographers. But she didn't mind ordinary people paying their respects, and she and her mother both liked the ex-soldiers, including Willett himself. Despite any qualms, the two women were honored and gratified at this and other visible evidence that the world was at last giving General Grant the honor he was due. It was not a brand-new phenomenon. A flood of supportive messages from all types of people had been pouring in to New York for the past year, and continued to find their way up Mount McGregor. Grant, too, did not cease to humbly appreciate displays of the public's affection. Nor did it fail to occur to family members, including the general, that all this publicity would be helpful to Clemens' sales efforts— just as Arkell, and perhaps Drexel, too, hoped it would buttress the future business of their hotel.

The reporters used the telegraph line at the Balmoral to keep the country and the world informed of every development in the general's condition, and what they could observe him doing. But for the most part, people left the family alone. Nellie often spent time with the children, sometimes picnicking in the woods with them and their mothers, her sisters-in-law, or paddling in little lakes on the hotel property. The hotel had a sleepy boat launch on the biggest one, Lake Bonita, and once she went out rowing with Elizabeth and little Nellie on the uncrowded lake, navigating around little islands of reeds. It was as if they were in a German fairy tale, surrounded by evergreens and silence, until a wind came up to dapple the water, making them nervous a storm might come, so they paddled to shore.

Another day she, Ida, Elizabeth and Jesse brought the children on an excursion to Lake George, about fifteen miles to the north, and took their carriage part way up Prospect Mountain, discussing on the way the names of wildflowers—Queen Anne's lace and black-eyed susans, and the pale blue cornflowers also known as chicory. They stopped at an outlook, gazing northeast to the lake and northwest over the rolling peaks of the Adirondacks, where Ida said John Brown and his wife were buried.

Occasionally Nellie persuaded Fred to come along with them on excursions, or at least on local picnics near the Drexel cottage (already becoming known as Grant Cottage). She was heartened these days to see his tender sympathy with young Julia, and hers with him, while his son little Ulys and Jesse's daughter Nellie, cousins of the same age with the same family names going down the generations, played happily enough together and made a sweet scene. They all agreed that the Saratoga mineral water—a case of which had been delivered to the cottage—tasted terrible, and should be kept away from General Grant, although it turned out there was a more palatable Vichy water version.

Visitors kept coming. There was a Roman Catholic priest from Baltimore, whom Romero introduced with a twinkle in his eye, recalling Grant's occasional offhand derogations of "priestcraft" in Mexico, and in the second term his controversial speech calling for public schools to provide education "unmixed with sectarian, pagan, or atheistical tenets." But if Romero supposed his old friend was holding on to any anti-clericalism, or cared to refight political battles about Catholic schools and the separation of church and state, he would be disappointed. Grant listened respectfully to Father Didier's assurance that "We are all praying for you," and wrote him a gracious note thanking "Catholics, Protestants, and Jews, and all the good people of the nation, of all politics as well as religion," for their prayers and good wishes. "I am a great sufferer all the time," the note said. "... All that I can do is to pray that the prayers of all those good people may be answered so far as to have us all meet in another and a better world."

Romero noted that the Methodist Reverend Newman had absented himself from this meeting, and suspected anti-Catholicism was the cause (although to be fair he wasn't sure if Newman was currently on the mountain). He also wondered whether Grant really hoped to find another and a better world after death, no matter what he said to those, such as his wife, who did believe in one. Previously, Romero, like Clemens now, would have openly doubted such protestations of conventional religiosity coming from Grant. Now, he was not so sure what his friend believed, and did not plan on pressing him.

On the same day as the Catholic priest, July 7, in the afternoon, Romero brought up on the cottage porch a group of twenty Mexican journalists. They were of exotic appearance to many of the Americans on the mountain, but Romero was acquainted with several of them, and Grant was not put out at all, relishing the distraction. While the American newspapermen had been kept at bay, reliant on secondhand news, Grant met with the Mexicans and sat patiently through their speeches—though Romero could see he preferred it when they fell to bantering about politics south of the border, even if he couldn't catch all of the

Spanish. He did grow tired. Grant was never a man for speeches, although he'd had to sit through plenty. He had sought when possible to avoid inflicting them on others, whether soldiers or voters. But now he found strength to write a gracious note that Romero read to the newspapermen, regarding "my great interest in Mexico," the "outrage on human rights" of the French invasion, which had sought to conquer "a civilized people without their consent," and what seemed to be his realistic hopes for the future of the country.

For three days Grant and the doctors had given up applications of cocaine as a swab, because of its diminishing efficacy, but when they were resumed on July 8 he found the application did work again, almost as well as before. Grant allowed himself to be distracted for a time by writing another, shorter and even blunter letter to Badeau than the one he had sent in May, containing particular criticisms of his character and conduct both over the years and recently. But at the bottom of it he wrote, for Fred's eyes: "Note. I do not want this mailed but at your leisure copied and retained so that if advisable it can be sent." He had merely been preparing a defensive position for his heirs to use, if necessary, after his demise.

A more positive distraction were notes of thanks to well-wishers. He had asked Fred to write to Charles Wood, a stranger who had been the first to send a loan (or what Grant insisted on treating as a loan) after the previous year's disaster, inviting him to visit. When Wood came, Grant said in his pencil talk: "I am glad that, while there is unblushing wickedness in the world, there is compensating grandeur of soul." The pencil now was gripped by fingers comprised merely of skin and bone.

The *Century* editor Robert Underwood Johnson came up, ostensibly to meet with Fred about proofs for the Vicksburg article which the magazine was running. Grant was gratified to establish that Johnson bore no ill will for losing the book contract to Clemens. Indeed, the young, full-bearded editor was fighting back tears as he bid farewell to the general. Their relations were enhanced by his firm's voluntary decision to pay an additional $1,500 in royalties, a sign of confidence that its upcoming articles by Grant would boost circulation.

Working on the *Memoirs* and fighting the disease, the general was often up at odd hours, turning on the kerosene lamp at night, or going out on the porch at dawn to write by the light of the rising sun. He was down to less than a hundred pounds by now, any paunch long since vanished along with the lassitude and prosperity of his semi-retirement. He had spent the last year working on the book, in increasing weakness and pain, under sentence of inevitable death, and was not quite finished. A newspaper photographer caught him early one morning in mid-July, sitting in his regular wicker chair on the porch. He was in a robe, with scarves and blankets to keep the slight chill from his brittle, sometimes painful bones, a wool skull cap on his head and a towel concealing the tumor at the right side of his neck. He was oblivious to observation, photographic or otherwise, sitting mostly upright and working at a lap desk on the manuscript, with grim determination. Normally, he was properly dressed when he went outside, in a suit and top hat. Julia, when she got up and came out onto the porch, delivered a friendly kiss and then shooed him inside.

Grant complied easily with Julia's requests, and if he experienced an occasional irritation it would vanish at the next thought or sight of her, in the overriding reality of love. Even as in his terminal sickness he profoundly missed their sexual relations, he still felt his warm affection for her grow stronger and deeper, as it had throughout their experience of marriage.

Nellie went on an excursion by train with Fred and Ida to Round Lake, a new but quaint Methodist camp meeting village of summer cottages, which was a few miles south of

Saratoga Springs. President Grant, it turned out, had delivered a keynote address there in 1874. Nellie surmised that
her brother and sister-in-law thought she was brooding
about her absent children, for on the journey out they got
her to talk wistfully about them. When she dropped vaguely
gloomy hints about the state of her marriage, Fred sought to
say pleasantly reassuring things until she responded, "I am
not fishing for compliments," and then apologized for snapping at him when she knew he was doing so much for
father, and then experienced the further sweet pain of Fred
saying, "You are most like him, you know." Their mutual
embarrassment had no ill effects. She did feel a little inferior
as a wife to Ida, or unluckier, anyway. But she was impatient
at herself for complaining about her marriage, even though
the pain of separation from the children did not diminish in
intensity. And her relations with Fred and Ida, and with the
rest of the American family, were now on too solid ground
to be affected by little squalls.

At the village, they toured the new Auditorium, a rather
grand wooden structure soon to be dedicated by none other
than the Reverend John Newman—as he had mentioned in
passing the other day. The houses were much less imposing,
pretty little wooden structures that Ida objected to for the
reason that they seemed very close to one another. Nellie
humorously replied that it must mean the Methodists are so
well behaved that no one minds the proximity. A reunion
was being held there of the Grand Army of the Republic,
and mingling with the Union veterans was the Confederate
general Simon Bolivar Buckner, an old Army friend of their
father's from West Point and Mexico. They talked with him,
and Buckner accepted an invitation to visit the Mount Mc-
Gregor cottage, and on July 10 he did come up there.

In 1854, Buckner had guaranteed the New York hotel
bill of the semi-disgraced Captain Sam Grant, who had just
resigned from the U.S. Army. Buckner had helped Sam recognize reality, and the need to write to his father in Ohio,

asking for money to get back home. Meanwhile, until Jesse came through, Buckner had helped keep his friend's head above water. They'd next met in 1862, when Buckner, now a rebel general, complained about "unchivalrous terms" at Fort Donelson—meaning Grant's "unconditional surrender" demand that had sent a frisson of excitement through the Northern press. Buckner, like Grant in '54, had agreed to recognize reality and signed the surrender (since his two superior officers had fled). He was imprisoned and exchanged, then went on to fight through the war until May 26, 1865, when he provisionally surrendered all Confederate troops west of the Mississippi to Major-General Francis Herron. This was the first time Grant and Buckner had met since Donelson, and while they didn't say much, they communicated enough to show they were now on terms of warm friendship.

The next day, a grimmer Grant told Douglas, "I feel as if I cannot endure it any longer." But he did, and mostly in silence, continuing to set an example of stoicism for the family. Sometimes he refused morphine to keep his thoughts clear, and accepted injections of brandy to spark him back to life and work. He told Fred he doubted he would live through July. "Any hour may prove my last," he wrote, echoing a phrase he had just put into the book.

Clemens' last visit followed Buckner's. He left the general, who was somehow reviving a little, still working on the second volume, revising the account of the 1864 Overland Campaign. Not Wilderness, he reckoned he had gotten that right, but Spotsylvania and after. Clemens was on the one hand gratified by this flurry of activity, thinking Grant might conceivably still have months to live; but he hoped that did not mean the delivery of the manuscript for the second volume would be indefinitely delayed. He left before the Sunday, July 12, religious service at the hotel which was presided over by Newman. Nellie, Fred, Ida and others in the family attended, though the general stayed at the cottage.

Afterward, Grant came out and sat on the porch in the evening air, joking to Drexel and Arkell that he didn't feel as bad as he looked. Newman came over too, and thought Grant looked tired out. After the general went in, Newman urged the doctors to bar further visitors. They were noncommittal, and when Newman left, Shrady said to Douglas, "There went the voice of one who crieth in the wilderness." Grant had resisted, as Shrady was aware, Newman's suggestion that he attend the service at the hotel and take communion there. As to the general's personal religious beliefs, they were a mystery to Shrady and about everyone else.

On July 16, after Douglas carefully inspected the growing, ulcerous hole at the back root of Grant's tongue, the patient looked into the doctor's sad eyes and wrote a couple of notes, the last one saying: "The disease is still there, and must be fatal in the end. My life is precious, of course, to my family, and would be to me if I could recover entirely. There never was one more willing to go than I. ... I first wanted so many days to work on my book, so the authorship would be clearly mine. It was graciously granted to me ... and with a capacity to do much more work than I ever did in the same time."

Grant no longer felt he had to keep up a false front of medical hope in front of his wife, which was a relief. It made her constant presence more comforting than ever. Also comforting was, had always been, Nellie's presence. When his daughter sat next to him and held his hand, Grant felt at peace through the pain, even the increased agony of coughing, and through whatever medical crisis impended. He had felt guilty, knowing Nellie was unhappy separated from her children, not just as he had been unhappy in Oregon in the '50s, but in a way alien to his experience, in a context he did not fully understand. The English husband did not seem to respect women, for all his family's fashionable feminist ideas, and Grant felt himself at a disadvantage. Sartoris did not stay in touch, Grant gathered. Yet even Julia had not written as many letters as her *fiancé* and husband had done, and had wanted in return, when away in Mexico, Oregon and California.

Guilt and folly, he wondered (his mind flitting around), is that what religion amounts to? Or what if Newman is right, and we'll be judged for everything at the end—or is he one of those who claim to be justified by faith alone? Grant let the guilt go because he knew Nellie's separation—from her children, at least—would last only as long as his own life. That would not be unduly prolonged, as he knew she knew. Anyway, you can't protect people, only strive to do your best for them. He had never needed to talk to Nellie to communicate deeply with her. Now she sometimes told him about her day, how she spent time with the children not her own, but Fred's and Jesse's, they went to pick flowers on the mountainside and make daisy chains. She stirred in him smiles, and the occasional wink which called for no explanation. He knew her sorrows, too, not just the marriage gone wrong, but the death of her first-born, named Grant, when she was far from home, like a soldier on a battlefield, no stranger to loss. A stranger in a strange land. He remembered in Missouri when Nellie as an infant had been so sick, and he had walked up and down, back and forth for hours, cradling her in his arms. He had been spared what she had suffered with the child named after him. As a father he still felt some guilt about her unhappy marriage, which he had not striven to prevent, and later had been too embarrassed to honestly discuss. But their loving compassion for each other now flowed sweetly back and forth, not needing either of them to speak.

His remaining words were put into the work. Once the Conclusion was done, Grant made a few more notes for the book. His last addition concerned the beginning of the Petersburg campaign in June 1864:

Colonel J.L. Chamberlain, of the 20th Maine, was wounded on the 18th. He was gallantly leading his brigade at the time, as he had been in the habit of doing in all the engagements in which he had previously been engaged. He had several times been recommended for a brigadier-generalcy for gallant and meritorious conduct. On this occasion, however, I promoted him on the spot, and forwarded a copy of my order to the War Department, asking that my act might be confirmed and Chamberlain's name sent to the Senate without any delay. This was done, and at last a gallant and meritorious officer received partial justice at the hands of his government, which he had served so faithfully and so well.

Chamberlain had been a civilian volunteer, a college professor who became the hero of Little Round Top. After the war, the two of them became friends. At Petersburg, Grant recalled, Chamberlain had continued standing after he was shot, leaning on a sword to wave the troops on, although the wound proved so bad it was thought to be mortal, and plagued him in subsequent years. Nevertheless, General Chamberlain had returned to the Army of the Potomac to play a key role in the Appomattox campaign. And immediately after that, knowing his chivalrous sprit and seeking to promote reconciliation and honor the volunteers, Grant had put the professor-soldier in charge of the Confederate surrender ceremony.

Lately, it seemed like he had been revising the manuscript in the intervals of his death-bed scene. Now Grant decided to surrender the whole manuscript to Clemens, to let the publisher have the book at last. Volume One would be published in December, they told him, with the next one coming in early spring. Then his wandering thoughts returned to Chamberlain, about what he had not gotten in the book because he had not witnessed it, being away in Washington: Chamberlain exchanging salutes at the formal surrender ceremony with the rebel general Gordon. Grant half smiled as he recalled the conversation that spring with Ely Parker, Frank Herron and the rest about another general in other wars, "Chinese" or English Gordon. Chamberlain had been dealing with a different man, another volunteer, a Georgian Gordon who would turn out to be no supporter of Reconstruction. Gordon had led the last rebel attack before the surrender, stopped by Sheridan, who was breathing fire and wanted to go in and destroy the rebel army. Like the Confederate artillery general Porter Alexander, as Longstreet told him after the war, who had wanted Lee not to surrender but to break up the army and disperse it into the hills.

Nor did Chamberlain, for that matter, turn out to be a supporter of Reconstruction, nor most of the country, by the end of it, the end of the Grant administration. Yes, the rebels were our countrymen again, they had become so right after Appomattox, but so were their former slaves deserving of full citizenship. The country had grown weary of it all, wary of him because he stuck with it, kept demanding justice for Negroes in Southern backwaters—vainly, as it turned out. The country had been wrong to abandon the blacks to gangs of murderous whites, yet he too had turned away with the rest, gone around the world for years to forget. Politics can confound any position, infiltrate and overrun justice itself, and memory. Let this book be a record.

Grant's mind went back to Wilderness, earlier in '64— Chamberlain wasn't there. The invisible enemy made our big guns useless, and Gordon led the rebels on a flank attack in the evening, near the end of the battle. That had caused some panic in the Army of the Potomac, staffers warning him about "Bobby Lee" with fear in their voices which he had to quell sharply. And then turn south down

Brock Road the next day—but only eight miles, to Spotsylvania. It was Pete Longstreet whose attack caused real trouble at Wilderness, rolling up Hancock—under whose command Hays had been killed the day before. The gunfire and burning trees made it hard to see anything, and Pete was shot off his horse by his own men, a few miles from where the same thing had happened to young Tom Jackson, whom the rebs called "Stonewall," at the Battle of Chancellorsville the year before.

At Wilderness, Hancock rallied his corps. Then fought well at Spotsylvania, or his men did, capturing thousands of rebels and two generals, Colonel Upton serving under him, through the Mule Shoe's trenches to the bloody, muddy angle. No such break at Cold Harbor, the slaughter there of none but our own. All those dead soldiers on all those fields. And still living men whom the bearers could not reach, left where the mud infected their wounds. Was the cause, that eventual victory, worth the cost? He had left the attack at Cold Harbor to Meade, sparing his tender feelings of being displaced from command, and so left how many thousands on the ground, in the ground? Can't put the blame on Meade, who had his strengths. And his limits, as at the Crater. But who left him there to act, or fail to act? And left in place Burnside, too, to fail there, after he wanted to keep attacking Cold Harbor. Our men left in the Crater like sitting ducks. Lee should have listened to Longstreet at Gettysburg.

Pete was a good horseman, like me. But so was Lee, for that matter. And for all his spit and polish, with no demerits at the Point, Lee said late in life that he was sorry to have chosen a military career. We weren't so different.

Unlike Jackson, Longstreet recovered from his Wilderness wound to go back to the war, as far as Appomattox, and then to become as true a friend as he'd been before, a patriot in Reconstruction. Hancock had gone the other way after the war, became an ally of President Johnson, like

Custer and Gordon Granger. Hancock asked to be relieved toward the end of '64. Still, he was just worn out, with that old Gettysburg wound. He had been a good soldier.

Grant was disappointed there would be no third volume of the *Memoirs*, which meant, among other things, nothing about Longstreet as his Republican ally in Reconstruction. But he recalled with pleasure something he'd just finished writing, in the Chattanooga chapter, about Longstreet and his feud with another, less competent Confederate general, Braxton Bragg—a passage that included a jab at the military pretensions of Confederate President Jefferson Davis. One reason his book was better than Badeau's, Grant thought, lay in the stories he knew and had told about himself and others, people like Bragg, who had been a favorite of Davis and was Longstreet's commander in the Chickamauga and Chattanooga campaigns. It wasn't originally Grant's story, but one that circulated in the old Army, coming allegedly from the commanding officer of an understaffed frontier post. This unnamed joker, Grant had written, told Bragg he had "quarreled with every officer in the army, and now you are quarrelling with yourself!" Then in his own words, which came back to him now, he described Longstreet as "brave, honest, intelligent, a very capable soldier, subordinate to his superiors, just and kind to his subordinates, but jealous of his own rights, which he had the courage to maintain." His smile as he recalled this turned into a laugh and a painful cough. That gave old Pete his due.

While Grant retained a low opinion of Davis' conduct and judgment, he had, as head of the Army after the war, tried to help Varina Davis when her husband was in prison, and he held no grudges now. But old Jesse Grant had held one for him against Davis, who as Secretary of War spurned Jesse's request to set aside Captain Grant's resignation from the Army. Jesse's son had contented himself with naming one of his Civil War horses Jeff Davis. That small but game and loyal mount had been liberated from the plantation of the Confederate president's brother, in Mississippi.

There was something about Rosecrans in that chapter too, Grant recalled a little guiltily, a jab, when he'd written about the need to open up the cracker line to besieged Chattanooga. On his way there in 1863 he met Rosecrans, who was on his way out, and the departing general "described very clearly the situation at Chattanooga, and made some excellent suggestions as to what should be done. My only wonder was that he had not carried them out." Grant now allowed himself a flinty smile, as he also recalled Lincoln's description of Rosecrans in Chattanooga, after the defeat at Chickamauga, being "confused and stunned like a duck hit on the head."

To celebrate the completion of the book, Grant wrote a note suggesting another trip to the Overlook, and on that July 20 sat reading a newspaper on the porch while Fred and Harrison made preparations. Now, of course, he was far too weak to walk there and back, which he had been able to do the month before. But they could take him in the Bath wagon. It turned out to be a rougher ride than he had anticipated, and when they arrived he was uncomfortable, in pain, so they didn't stay long. Being hauled back uphill a different way on a loop trail, he contemplated the lush exuberance of summer vegetation, before the fall. When Fred came to a pile of coal being stored by the railroad, which was lying across the path, Grant was able to help by getting up and walking around it. For a few seconds he was climbing Mount McGregor, before collapsing back into the chair. By the time they reached the cottage he was completely exhausted, his face drained of blood.

He was no longer up to writing notes, or going onto the porch. The next day, standing in the cottage supported by Julia (who was able to hold up her feather-light husband) he suddenly let go of his cane and fell back into a chair. Nellie telegraphed for Newman in New York, who arrived on the evening train.

A day later, July 22, the grandchildren were brought in to say good-bye, although that purpose was not stated openly. Buck arrived, too, summoned back from the city. Grant had become too weak to keep sitting up in the chairs in the sick room, or in any chair, and asked for a bed. Some of those who heard him exchanged meaningful looks. Shrady and others had sometimes been using a cherrywood camp bed when they spent the night, or part of it, at the cottage. It was normally kept folded up against a wall, out of the way, and now was unfolded in the southwest corner of the parlor for Grant, under a lithograph of Lincoln on the wall. It was a little cooler in the cross-ventilated front room. Asked if it felt good to lie down, Grant replied: "So good. So good."

He seemed too weak to cough much now, which was a blessing, even Julia thought, since coughing had brought on the worst pains. She resisted thinking it through, although others did: that if he were too weak to cough, he would soon be unable to breathe, especially in his current prone position. When he asked for the bed, his family realized, he was not expecting to arise from it. The question whether writing the book had undermined his strength or kept him alive was now moot. Now that the book was done, or at any rate he had done all he could on it, he had no reason to struggle to stay alive.

Noticing their sad countenances, Grant was able to say, "I don't want anybody to feel distressed on my account." Later, when asked by Fred if he wanted anything, he croaked, "Water," and as Nellie held his head up and Harrison the glass, was able to drink a little of it without much pain. God's or nature's mercy, he supposed. When he tried to speak again, he found he could not, nor sit up, nor hardly move. They tried to use the suction device to remove the phlegm and puss at the back of his mouth to stop it choking him, with indifferent success. He did not try to listen to the occasional conversation around him. Grant's thinking, though, remained partly clear—surprisingly so, it occurred to him. He was gratified at Julia squeezing a sponge of cold water inside his lips.

On the evening of July 22, the family went two by two to the hotel, to take a quick evening meal in a private room they used there. Then, except for the grandchildren, who were tended by a nursemaid and put to bed, they gathered around the short camp bed. Julia sat next to her husband, holding his hand, sometimes kissing his face and wiping his brow. Asked if he were in pain, Grant was able to shake his head in the negative. He deduced they were waiting for him to die, although they all drifted away before dawn at Douglas' suggestion, going to their own beds.

Grant remembered Romero's look the other day when the priest visited, and wondered what, if anything, would happen after his death. If there was something, would it involve God's judgment? He did have an uneasy conscience for sending so many to their deaths, sometimes in error. Providing free embalming services, as he had done for slain soldiers, made up for nothing.

He could have died too, at Belmont, say, in '61. Some generals did, like Hays and McPherson, his friends. Still, their, our, risk was on the whole less, and the reward much greater. His had been. He had not gone—could not have gone—with the men who attacked the lines at Vicksburg, or Cold Harbor, when some fool—when he had ordered them. Their names lost, soon their memory, and no time then for their comrades to mourn. When we did mourn, was it not tempered by relief that it wasn't us lying dead on the ground? And guilt for that feeling. For them, no ridiculous mountain-stage setting of a deathbed scene. Their parents left to grieve at home. "I feel how weak and fruitless must be any words of mine which should attempt to beguile you

from the grief of a loss so overwhelming," Lincoln had written to Mrs. Bixby, mother of five dead soldiers.

I could have been killed in Mexico, when I left the supply train behind for the front, and then in battle time
seemed to both slow down and speed up, and you'd notice
things. Like these last months of dying and working, it was
all mixed up. If he had been killed at Monterrey, Julia would
have mourned her lost *fiancé*, and married someone else.
That was the real yet ghostly burden for the battlefield dead,
who never had a chance to live real life, past youth. Not that
everyone did much with it. What of Julia's brother Fred
Dent, who had been up to visit them at Mount McGregor?
They first met on the way to West Point, and became
friends, and in 1847 Grant had tended him wounded at
Molino Del Ray. Raised with slaves on that Missouri plantation, Dent stayed loyal in the Civil War. Later he was on
Grant's military and White House staff, serving 40 years in
the Army—yet despite it all his life seemed, the dying general mused, to have been curiously uneventful. *Still, he has been
loyal to us, the family, as well the United States, done no disgrace; a
good friend and man.*

The general thought of the fearful burden on the parents of dead children, something he and Julia had been
spared. Not Nellie, though, she was not spared, with her
firstborn, little Grant, long dead in England. Or Mary Lincoln gone mad—so her surviving son said—after the deaths
of his three brothers. Or Mrs. Bixby. Lying in this unfamiliar bed and position, he saw across the parlor a print of a
painting by William Bouguereau. It depicted the Virgin
Mary consoling a distraught mother who was sprawled
above the dead body of her son. We are all chastened eventually. He had noticed the painting previously, with his
artist's eye. Further to the right, where he could hardly see it
now, was another Bouguereau, a portrait of Charity as a female figure. The room was full of artworks that must be

part of Drexel's collection, or taken from the rooms of the hotel.

Grant knew that in addition to military blunders he had made political ones—more of them—although there were also some peace-time achievements. It was good that he'd made up with Bristow in New York. Grant still didn't think his dead friend Orville Babcock had been a villain like Mc-Donald, but he knew that the Whiskey Ring had started as a way to raise political money for his own re-election in '72. Then it turned into a secret slush fund for its controllers. He as president had not kept a grip on things, which allowed corruption to damage the country and his own reputation, and the great causes and modest decency to which he had tried to dedicate himself. It was hard to admit this, and also to acknowledge that he had failed repeatedly to be an effective provider for his beloved wife and family. He had put his faith in weak men and thieves like a credulous child.

But here they were now, his wife and children, despite all his failings, and the book should help them. Now, broke, he was receiving luxurious medical care, though soldiers had often died, their wounds untended, between the lines. Or burned in brush fires, forest fires at the Wilderness, wounded men leaving bloodstained clothes in the bushes as they crawled desperately away. *I put them there.* Trees shot down, great branches crashing onto the heads of soldiers. Or dying from lack of a coat, or tent, or boots on some winter's night, life eluding their grasp. Or in spring, at Shiloh, and Wilderness, men and horses, dead and wounded. Through the remembered carnage of the Overland Campaign came the hint of a smile as he thought of Totopotomoy Creek, not the fight with the rebels there but how he had stopped a teamster from abusing a horse. A horse needs love along with firmness. Just a few years ago, when they'd somehow gotten him to go to a bullfight in Mexico City, he'd walked out because of what happened to the horses. Into his mind flitted Herron's tale of Prairie Grove, which was not even Grant's battle, shooting his own soldier off a horse. Not just enemies. Not just soldiers. No man or woman escapes death, sometimes children, too. As bad as any memory was crossing peacetime Panama in 1852, as regimental quarter-master leading a convoy of mostly women and children. More than a hundred of them had died in his care, from cholera.

That outbreak could have killed his son and pregnant wife, had they not stayed home in Ohio and Missouri. So even their separation had been a godsend—a blessing, he supposed Julia would say, although at the time, in 1852, she with sweet courage had wanted to accompany the regiment. He had felt their connection even more than she did, be-cause he was a needier, weaker person. His father had been right, he was foolish to resign from the Army. *Yet she wel-comed me home, never blamed me for the money running through my fingers, ungraspable. It's the spur of necessity that gets a man going, to win a woman, or a battle, write a book, reach safe harbor. They say there's more than $300,000 of subscriptions sold already. That num-ber means provision, debts repaid, honor saved; it has the ring of true romance.*

The assiduous attentions of doctors and nurses to clean his mouth could not dislodge the detritus, or dispel the foul odors his prone position brought out from belly to mouth to nose, or do more than dull the abiding pain. *Julia or Nel-lie, Harrison or McSweeny, Douglas or Shrady, washing my pus, phlegm, blood, vomit from beard, throat, rotted stump of mouth. Sans teeth, sans taste, sans everything. And the cancer gone far beyond, rid-ing the blood like Forrest upriver to smash into organs, my body turned traitor, defenses all gone. Pain beneath drugs. I can barely gur-gle, will I manage a death rattle? What's done is done. The words of Lady Macbeth. Start off where you are. I did not follow Jesse into the stench of the tannery, but found worse with blackening, bloating bodies on fields of human slaughter. Maggots no fit subject for a book. Too many, many dead. Thank God I cannot talk, and scare the children in delirium. You can only live your own life, going forward. Mine has gotten to be enough, coming to the stop. I must take what comes, or does not come, whatever it will or will not be. No fear for the middle-aged, the old, no fear for what must be.*

Julia did not share her husband's doubts about his soul's destination, although her faith would fall short of comforting or mitigating her loss. They said prayers aloud at midnight, and Grant rested in the warmth of his family's embrace. Buck was back now, all the children here.

The thought of grudges and political disputes seemed light beside the war, and his dying, and he let them all go. Why not be magnanimous? He had written the history as he saw it, not sparing the truth, but had he really found it? *Was I not sometimes too hard on others' arguments, too anxious to vindicate what I have done, too harsh against their failings while minimizing my own, with vision blurred by what I wanted to see?* Such were common failings of anybody's memoir. But was the book grudging, ungenerous, say to Rosecrans at Iuka and Corinth, battles in which, after all, Rosecrans had actually fought, while Grant himself, the superior officer, had somehow missed his way to?

It was nothing personal. The trouble with Rosecrans, and Thomas, and the Army of the Cumberland, and with McClellan and Hooker and the Army of the Potomac, was military. They did not understand, as Sherman and Sheridan did, that the way to end war was to win it, keep driving hard and let nothing stop you, and, as you could hardly say in polite society, to keep killing men, and crushing their will to resist. Then, when it was done, you could make peace as at Appomattox. When to be hard, when mild, he had known that then. But no one could agree later, in the world of politics. And he had been too soft with Ward.

Sherman was right; war is unrefined hell. If hell exists, it was at Spotsylvania. Or Cold Harbor, where the wounded lay in long agony before they died, my fault more than Lee's, the cost they paid for my blunder, the point I was making, no acceptance of defeat, no relenting.

Sherman lost far fewer men. Yet the survivors do not blame me, honor me too much, my fame their symbol, how many of our comrades in unmarked graves?

At least as president he had mostly avoided war. He caught himself reflecting sourly that McClellan like Halleck had spread those rumors of drunkenness, and Little Mac the new major general had refused to see the civilian Grant who came cap in hand in 1861, waiting vainly in the office reception room. Grudges among generals looked petty, set against all the dead soldiers in their command. His last view from the Overlook came back to him, as he looked out to the past, present and future, to the people he had known, living and dead. He remembered in gunnery calculating, as from the center of a sphere, the azimuth of fire. "Azimuth" was the kind of word he had kept out of the book.

George Thomas was an artilleryman, Grant recalled, and suddenly remembered, to his chagrin, something he should have written in the *Memoirs*, how his late addition about Thomas at Nashville in 1864 still hadn't gotten it quite right. He had written about his concerns before the battle, how he'd started west by rail to replace Thomas because that general kept delaying a planned attack, but turned back *en route* when he heard the attack had at last got under way. He should have included the line from his report after the war, how Thomas' "final defeat of Hood was so complete, that it will be accepted as a vindication of that distinguished officer's judgment." Well, it was too late now. He brightened at the memory of Clemens saying, that for at least some of the editions, he would include Grant's postwar report as an appendix. But didn't that document also criticize Rosecrans' handling of Price's raid in Missouri? *Let it go.*

They hadn't been on bad terms, he and Thomas. The Virginian had escorted Julia at the inauguration in '69. Thomas was Lee's good friend before the war, which proved Lee did not have to turn disloyal. Lee was no fire-eater, a decent man following his conscience, but he should have stayed true. And after the war, when Thomas fought the Klan, there were other southerners like him who stood up for the Negro. Some Confederates, too, not just Longstreet but another friend, John Mosby, and Amos Akerman, Sam Clemens and his friend George Washington Cable; maybe Henry Wise and Little Billy Mahone, who inflicted that terrible defeat on us at the Crater.

Now, Grant thought, let any soldier—Joe Hooker, Baldy Smith, John McLernand, Hancock, Granger, McClellan, Halleck, even Robert Buchanan, the martinet C.O. at Fort Humboldt who had forced him out of the Army in 1854—let them all have the benefit of the doubt. He hadn't sought revenge on Buchanan when he came to command him, and every other Union man. *Spare him, spare them all humiliation, as he had been spared by Lincoln, Sherman, Julia, as I spared Lee. Someone must spare Nellie, tell her nothing that fool of a husband does can humiliate her, as she carries her burdens, raises her children in love.*

He remembered the miserable winter at Humboldt, the wool uniform never dry, the beauty of the giant, thousand-year-old redwoods in the mist, and the different western light, yet all the sunsets over the bay doing nothing to salve his wretched loneliness—all for ninety dollars a month. There was a poor Wiyot Indian village at the foot of the bluff, some of whose residents, like the white miners and soldiers, like himself, were inclined to drink too much whiskey. Grant, though, had not shared the widespread hatred of the Indians by the local white men, which helped propel him away from there, deciding to give up the Army and go home.

Only now, though, was he really cutting loose, as he had from the Mississippi River in early May of '63, away from Halleck and Lincoln both, away from orders and any putative supply line. No going back, nor south to join Banks in Louisiana, but east, into the void, behind enemy lines to the city of Jackson, where Joe Johnston was headed from the other direction. Lincoln's later message about that turn, how he'd thought it had been a mistake, but it wasn't, how he, the president, had been wrong—kind of an intimate message, sent to a general he hadn't even met yet, and wouldn't until the next spring. *Both Midwestern, border-state men, from the people. Lincoln's faith in me, his tenderness, his hardness. The way he talked about Providence. But back in May '63, a thousand miles east in Virginia, Tom Jackson was getting shot as he beat Hooker at Chancellorsville, crossing over the river to rest under the shade of the trees. Those days were the real hinge of the war, two months before Gettysburg and Vicksburg, what I decided and did.*

Spare the rebels, too, reconstructed or not, if they in return will leave the Negro be. And spare the politicians. Let us have peace with Elihu Washburne, even if he cost us the presidency in 1880. What of it? When Garfield was shot, I went to comfort his wife in Long Branch, and later sat with him when he was brought there to die, as he did like a man. What profit in holding grudges? Even Badeau's treachery, let it go, let go of James Fish.

Even for Ferdinand Ward, the deliberate defrauder of the Grants, he declined to hold on to his bitter indignation which had curdled into hatred. It was not an explicitly religious decision, for the general was not an explicitly religious man. But he let go the balls of resentment he had been grasping; and they growing light and floating up, could be blown away easily enough even by a man *in extremis*, whose lungs were clogged and gradually ceasing to function.

Around 7 o'clock in the morning, not long after retiring to her room, Julia and the grown children were roused by Harrison as their husband and father weakened further, and they came downstairs in night clothes. McSweeny had remained by Grant's side, and Harrison had heard him tell Douglas he thought the general was "going."

So he turned out to be. The sun rising through the window lit up Grant's face, as Julia sat holding his hand, which grew cool, sometimes stroking and kissing his head and face. He appeared unresponsive, but his mind flit back sixty

years, to the shadow over the gap within his relations to his
Methodist mother Hannah, a woman much like himself except somehow colder, and his difficult yet warmer father. At
least they gave him his head with horses, didn't try to force
him into the tannery. And Julia had warmed to his mother,
and warmed her. *Before she did that, forty-one years ago now,
spring in Missouri with white fragrant locust blossoms, and a pretty
eighteen-year-old girl who could keep up with me on horseback, a sweet
charge of connection and movement running down from riders to horses
to each other. Then walking, she calmed a flighty palomino by blowing
in his nose.* The young soldier's urgent wooing, on his way to
war, had won her tentative consent to their engagement. He
felt her loving presence now sitting alongside him, and Nellie and the boys—young men—standing around the camp
bed. Buck waved a fan over him. Nellie took his other hand,
noticed it had grown cool, and spoke into his ear, "Papa, if
you know my voice, will you squeeze my hand?" She felt a
slight squeeze in response, which was the last sign of consciousness.

Grant died after the rising sunbeam, filtered by a cur-
tain, had passed over his face and up to Lincoln's picture.
His breathing had grown fainter, but then there was a
strong sighing exhalation, and the family waited for the next
breath, which did not come. "It is all over," said Dr. Douglas, tears rolling down his face. Julia started to protest and
Nellie said, "Poor Mamma." She stressed the first syllable
this time in her old American way, reaching out a comforting hand, but then brought both hands up to her own
weeping face. Fred stopped the hands of the clock on the
mantel, while Julia kissed her dead husband's face. Shrady,
walking out, saw Newman returning from breakfast at the
hotel, and said, "He is dead." To Newman's chagrin, he had
missed the great event, but now he went in and led Julia
gently to the sofa.

Grant had died, Shrady thought, from exhaustion and
malnutrition along with the cancer. The morphine he inject-

ed had been enough to avoid pain and sometimes induce sleep, but was not the cause of death. As Nellie led Julia weeping from the room, Karl Gerhardt, Clemens' sculptor *protégé*, entered the cottage and immediately set about preparing a death mask.

CHAPTER NINETEEN

MUCH OF THIS INFORMATION was in the newspapers, where the progress of Grant's dying on Mount McGregor was followed avidly across America, including in New York City by the general's old comrades. His death on the morning of July 23 was soon telegraphed and noted at length in special editions of the city's numerous newspapers. Herron had become more diligent lately in attending to his by no means glamorous legal trade, but he was willing and able to give it up today. Along with Tom Sweeny he sought out Ely Parker at the Police Headquarters, where others too had gathered around the Indian, of course knowing of his connection to Grant. At lunchtime Ely gave up work and repaired with Herron, Sweeny and a couple of police detectives named Albert Mattison and Daniel Joyce to a table at a nearby tavern.

Ely, Herron knew, picked and chose his friends in the department, not wanting to associate with those on the payroll of vice lords and who tried to avoid bothering themselves with the investigation of crimes against the poor. For a while the five men passed newspapers back and forth between them and spoke little, which Herron recalled was what the writer Walt Whitman and his mother had done in Brooklyn after Lincoln's assassination twenty years before. This occasion was not so solemn, and Ely consented to have a beer or two while unbuttoning his waistcoat and taking out his collar stud, which slightly alarmed Herron. The joint was below street level, in a half basement which made it a little cooler, while overhead fans worked to dissipate the still substantial heat.

Two men carried in a block of ice from a delivery wagon outside, and took it into a back room to keep the beer cold. It prompted Ely to say, "At least Grant had it cooler up in the mountains. I miss that beautiful, peaceful land of lakes, of upstate New York."

Ely was drinking Bass Ale, an English import, while the detectives, mindful perhaps of the Irish domination of their department, or just to save a buck, preferred American lager. When Mattison and Sweeny went to the bar to get another couple of jugs, Joyce vigorously dispatched tobacco juice into a spittoon and began telling Herron the story of how Ely had once gone on a police call to a domestic dispute. An Indian woman, apparently a Seneca, had been beaten up in one of those teeming, grim rear tenements at Mulberry Bend, along with some other trouble, and Ely was brought in to translate. He wound up doing more, dissuading her from throwing a pot of boiling water and otherwise keeping the peace. Ely's face remained impassive, and Herron did not think it a particularly uplifting tale. Like most New Yorkers, he avoided that notorious, evil-smelling neighborhood, and could imagine the small apartment, the desperately poor conditions.

Herron did not ask what occurred to him, if they knew what happened to the family, but took the opportunity of changing the subject back to the obvious one. He had not, he told Ely, in fact been following the Grant story in great detail, instead getting caught up on work, even though willing enough to take this afternoon off.

Ely smiled. "You're like me, Frank, a horny-handed son of toil."

Sweeny, overhearing as he came back with Mattison and the beer, said, "Like the Young Napoleon of Wall Street," referring to the still jailed but as yet untried Ferdinand Ward.

"It's the way we live now," said Herron into the laughter, wondering if his friends would catch the reference to the title of Anthony Trollope's modern novel about a crooked financier.

"Well I've given up work as a bad business," Sweeny continued. "But General Grant seems to have kept it up until the end. Does it not feel decadent, boys, to be drinking on an afternoon when the rest of the world works." While he laughed with the rest, Herron thought it did feel a little that way. For all the undercurrents cited by Madame Turchin at that picnic, this was a staid Victorian age, far from the hard-drinking one of his youth—or, even more so, of Grant's youth.

"If they bury him in New York," said Joyce, "Byrnes will have us round up all the pickpockets." Ely frowned slightly at this reference to Chief Inspector Thomas Byrnes, ally of Tammany and enthusiastic practitioner of the third degree, with whom he had a strained relationship. But Joyce and Mattison soon enough said they had to go interview a witness in an assault case, leaving the three former soldiers in the basement barroom. Herron smoked a cigar.

Sweeny said, as if in reply to Herron's thoughts, "Yet Grant wasn't really a drinker like this, not one for the bars, despite all the talk about him."

"No, he did what they say we Indians do, went drowning his sorrows. We grow out of that, if we're lucky. He did."

"Aye. The Irish, too."

Herron said, "For God's sake let's not be lachrymose. Do you think he finished that book?"

"Enough of it," said Ely. "I hear Clemens has been racking up sales." Catching the waiter's eye, he asked for a glass of water.

"The papers say he was still writing up on Mount McGregor," said Sweeny. "It's a gutsy thing to have done."

"Died with his writing boots on," said Herron, feeling a

little under the influence himself. He stubbed out the cigar. Ely, observing, wondered if it was tobacco, which the Seneca took for incense, that had caused Grant's cancer.

Sixteen days later, on Saturday, August 8, Samuel Clemens was smoking with rather more enthusiasm. Little clouds from his black cigars drifted out of the windows of the Union Square offices of Webster & Company, over a mass of firemen, engines and marching bands going from Broadway west to Fifth Avenue, comprising a fraction of the seven-mile, uptown-heading funeral procession for Ulysses S. Grant. There were of course veterans of Grant's armies, including Negro soldiers. Yet near the front had marched some ranks of Confederate veterans, dressed in their rebel uniforms. It was said there were a good million-and-a-half people on the streets to watch the somber parade, most of them clad in black, along the route north to the edge of the city and the banks of the Hudson.

Four days before this massive funeral, there had been many thousands lining the train tracks as the body was brought south from Mount McGregor toward New York. The train stopped in Albany and a procession took the body up State Street hill to the Capitol. On that and the next day, August 5, upwards of seventy thousand people had gone through the new Capitol building, which looked like a huge French chateau, to pay their respects. There were several thousand an hour for much of the time, in double file, with a somewhat slower pace in the middle of the night. The body was laid out again at New York City Hall, where per-haps a quarter of a million filed by.

Now, on August 8, many tens of thousands were marching behind the catafalque, which was drawn by twenty-four black horses, with Union and Confederate generals —Sherman, Sheridan, Buckner and Johnston—marching alongside. General Hancock was in charge of the military funeral, and had limited the number of marching men-at-arms to sixty thousand, most of them joining the parade from side streets. The railroads had added so many extra cars to trains coming in to the city, that most had to be pulled by two locomotives. Extra ferries were put into service to Manhattan, starting at five o'clock in the morning. The city was swathed in black crepe—at least it was all over the funeral route, while more modest black cloths decorated the side streets—with flags at half staff and busts of the general displayed in shop windows. The vast crowd was hushed, speaking little and quietly, although many lads perched themselves on trees, poles, even statues, to get a better view. The newspapers said there would be thousands of other, no doubt smaller memorial demonstrations that day at locations across America, from cities to villages, including the South. The carpetbag novelist Albion Tourgee was addressing one gathering at the Chautauqua Institute in western New York, according to one of the papers that Clemens was looking over.

General Buckner was interviewed in a piece from a Midwestern paper picked up by the *Times*, on his way to the funeral, where he would be a pall bearer. He, like many other Southern voices, praised Grant's generosity at the end of the war, but added, "During his Administration he was in the hands of other people." Clemens snorted, but kept reading. Buckner told of Grant at Mount McGregor saying "the war had been over with him for a long time." Yet the former Confederate general had praise for Grant's conduct as a "great soldier ... persevering, tenacious and kept right ahead. When he thought he was right he could not be moved. I go to help bury him as one of the Nation's great men. I cannot speak further of him. He may have made some mistakes—all men are liable to do so—but they are buried in the past and must remain so."

The occasional report about an African-American memorial for Grant, Clemens noted, tended to put more stress on emancipation both during and after the war, with the general as Lincoln's strong right arm who upheld his legacy. Overall, these ceremonies far eclipsed Lincoln's funeral, in terms of numbers, although Grant's death was obviously less shocking and traumatic. But it had prompted demonstrations of mourning beyond anything ever seen in the history of the United States.

Despite his abounding self-confidence, it was hard in a way for Clemens to realize that he had actually known the man whom the whole of America was eulogizing, known him in an intimate connection enduring until the end, in the important work of his last days. He felt that this concluding saga of Grant's last year was as heroic as a tale of battle, and was in awe at his friend's tenacity up to the end of his life. In the same way he had hung on and kept moving forward during the war, and before it. Now this mass adulation, greater than for Lincoln, for anyone, seemed like a miracle —had Clemens believed in such phenomena. The scandals of the presidential years had faded away to nothing, seen as either the creation of political partisans or the normal detritus of any administration. Grant was flawed, human, which made him the more beloved by the common people, from whom he, like Clemens, like Lincoln, had come. He had sought the common good when others were lost in bitterness, and loved his wife and children like a good-hearted man. Clemens' only regret about the book was that Grant had not addressed the issue of alcohol, the hold whiskey seemed to have had on him, and how he overcame it. It was not something he had ever felt he could bring up when Grant was alive; nor would he now.

Julia, whom Clemens credited with helping Grant stop drinking to excess, had stayed up at Mount McGregor after his death. She was resting there along with the preacher Newman's wife, while everyone else came down to New York for the funeral. But his own family, Clemens thought fondly, Livy and their three girls, Susy, Clara and Jean, had remained in Hartford. Were they too much like hothouse flowers? He reflected with satisfaction that he would be home with them tonight. Clemens' mind drifted to his own writing, which he had been neglecting for business pursuits, and the essay for the *Century* that he had been working on haphazardly. There was the shadow of a doubt on him that his creative well, fed by the Mississippi River, was running dry. Grant had read and enjoyed *Life on the Mississippi* a few years ago, he knew, although he didn't think the general ever got around to *Huckleberry Finn*. Clemens shrugged off the shadow—he had confidence he would be able to write again when he paid attention, heading in new directions.

He and Grant had been able to do business together, and remain firm friends, with the result that both their families, but especially the general's, would prosper. The title of the *Century* essay, "My Campaign Against Grant," would have to go. The humor in the piece was warm, but it was not all humor, and such a title would be too jarring for mourners. He was determined to keep Grant in it, even though, upon further consideration, he rather thought his own desertion from the Confederate militia in Missouri had occurred before Colonel Grant came upon the scene. The piece worked better with Grant in it, though, and no one was going to nit-pick. For a title, he thought, how about: *The Private History of a Campaign That Failed*. He wrote that down on a scrap of paper which he put in his pocket.

Clemens smiled, and couldn't help basking once more in recollecting the artistic and commercial success of his most recent book, *Huckleberry Finn*—then checked himself because of the solemnity of the occasion. Still, while it was sad that his friend was gone, he could not help feeling good about the last year of Grant's life and the role he himself had played in making it so productive and admirable. Grant's conduct over the past year seemed to Clemens as glorious as when he was a newly hatched brigadier-general, and saw his troops back onto the boats after the Battle of Belmont, Missouri, near Clemens' home turf—although by then Clemens had struck out for the West, for Nevada and

California. At the end of the battle, Grant had ridden his horse over a plank onto the last boat to leave, when it had already cast off but not yet begun to steam back up the Mississippi. Clemens had never heard of this event, and barely of the Battle of Belmont, before reading Grant's remarkable book.

This vast crowd at the funeral filled him with good feeling, which spread out to include America and the world. The era of wars was coming to an end, with democracy, prosperity and progress moving to cover the globe. The Europeans were still at their wicked colonial games, but they could not last. Even the Catholic pope, Leo XIII, seemed less like a force for obscurantism and more a fellow toiler for justice and peace. Better than that unctuous holly roller, Newman, who had wormed himself into a role saying prayers at today's ceremony uptown. Webster & Company, Clemens happened to know, had a shot at publishing the pope's memoir to follow Grant's, which should further buttress the firm's and his own prosperity, with all the Catholic immigrants now populating this city and the rest of America. Then he remembered Grant himself, how prosperous and healthy he seemed a year-and-a-half ago, how quickly that all collapsed. Which was a melancholy thought, redeemed only by the recollection of Grant's behavior in adversity, when Clemens had really gotten to know him. The melancholy also was relieved by the happy fact that Clemens himself, who would turn fifty later that year, was enjoying good health and success in all his endeavors.

On that day about two hundred miles north of Manhattan, Julia was still on Mount McGregor, with only Angeline Newman for company along with Harrison Terrell. She was looking over the posthumous notes which Ulys had written her. One said: "I am sure I will never leave Mt. McGregor alive. I pray God however that [I] may be spared to complete the necessary work upon my book." She gathered his prayer had been answered, and was content with that. She was doing little these days, still grieving and gathering her strength. She did not regret letting go, letting everyone else depart for New York and the funeral without her. Harrison said he would stay as long as she needed him, but Julia knew he would have to be going back before too long, as he should, to his own family in Washington. She would see Nellie again before she departed for England. They had not really talked yet about the difficulties of Nellie's life in England, which Julia realized were real. Perhaps they should have done. After Ulys died, they had mostly communicated by tears and embraces. Whether they talked bluntly soon or not, Julia vowed to herself to become a better correspondent. Ulys used to complain she did not write enough when he was away serving as a young officer, and now their daughter—God bless her—would need to hear from her more.

It turned out—they had lots of time to talk—that Angeline was from Saratoga County, which encompassed Mount McGregor. She had been born in Stillwater, the daughter of a Methodist minister in nearby Mechanicville, and was familiar with the Methodist village of Round Lake, where Nellie and Fred had met General Buckner. That local knowledge made her a good guide on the Overlook, when Julia could bestir herself to go there, breathing in the balsam-scented air and looking out over the peaceful and beautiful upper Hudson Valley. Julia's distance vision was not good, but Angeline tried to make up for it in her descriptions.

Although she was to stay behind on the mountain, it was Julia who had made the decision for New York. The night after Ulys died, a great thunderstorm had burned out the electric lights and scared the children. Then offers for a burial site had come pouring in, including a telegram and letter from the mayor of New York City, William Grace. He offered sites in Central or Riverside parks, and Fred and Jesse went down to the city to meet with Sherman, Horace

Porter, Senator Chaffee and other family friends to discuss the matter with city officials. Fred and Jesse came back and talked to her, after which Fred cabled the mayor: "Mother takes Riverside Park"—a site off what would be 122nd Street if the city ever built up that far north, on a hill over-looking the Hudson. Some day she would go see it, before she was laid to rest beside him. They had already built a temporary tomb to lay his body in, but people were also mentioning future plans for a grander one with pillars and a dome to arise there one day. Money should not be a prob-lem, thanks to her Ulys—although perhaps she ought not to commit herself to spending any of the royalties. She made a point of thanking Fred for all that he had done and was do-ing now.

On August 4, Julia had been woken at dawn by a can-non fire salute. Later, just before they took Ulys' body away from her on his final journey, there was a somewhat more private funeral service on the porch of the Drexel cottage, presided over by Reverend Newman. Sherman had come up, along with General or Colonel Horace Porter and Gen-eral Hancock, a Democrat whom she vaguely recalled Ulys had had some issues with after the war—but all such was forgotten now. Also there was Julia's young sister, making one more Nellie in the family party, and Ulys' sister Vir-ginia.

The service had begun with one of the other clergymen reciting the 90th Psalm, beginning "Lord, thou hast been our dwelling place in all generations." They sang "Nearer My God to Thee." Newman eulogized Grant for one-and-a-half hours on a theme from the Gospel of Matthew, "Well done thou good and faithful servant, enter thou into the joy of the Lord." He talked about Julia, too, about her and Ulys, their marriage: "He, the oak to support; she the ivy to en-twine. He, unhappy without her presence; she, desolate without his society. ... She shared his trials and his tri-umphs, his sorrows and his joys, his toils and his rewards.

... Lovely and pleasant in their lives, and in their death they shall not be divided." It was all true. She knew Ulys' love for her and the children was stronger than anything else in his life, and that if he could believe in immortality, it would have been from a desire for them to be together.

Her heart was touched by Newman's tribute, which also got the attention of Sherman, who had been trying not to listen to most of what the preacher said. He would write Julia a letter, he decided, along the same lines, to convey his genuine admiration for her devotion, and mourning the brave death of his old friend. But life, Sherman's own life, must go on. Maybe he would write the letter tonight in his Albany hotel room, where he would not be distracted by the charms of Mary Audenried, who had remained in Washington. But he thought he would be able to find a substitute for the companionship of Mrs. Audenried, if not tonight or tomorrow then immediately thereafter, in the arms of a successful New York actress with whom he had been striking up a friendship. He wondered if this lady could suggest a method whereby a visitor might be permitted to enter her house without being observed.

Large floral displays, representing crosses and swords and such, had arrived at the Mount McGregor cottage, and some, their freshness frozen by wax, remained there now. One depicting the Gates of Heaven was sent from California by Leland Stanford. In all the fuss and ceremony, a soldier, Private Timothy Allman, had been killed in Saratoga when a cannon misfired. That was enough of funerals for Julia. She would carry her loss with her.

A few days after they'd all gone, Angeline took her to a little weekly vespers service organized by the hotel guests and employees. The others smiled in welcome but did not bother them. Julia prayed for the repose of Ulys' soul, not quite confident of his faith, but trustful that his good character merited the infinite mercy of God. She prayed, too, for Private Allman.

For all her simple religious belief, Julia did not hold with the stricter kind of self-satisfied preacher who talked endlessly about the depravity of ordinary decent Christians, and how only the elect were saved by faith alone. Her friend Newman was not a minister of that type, whatever heathens like Clemens or Sherman might think of him. He was aware of his own human failings, including a tendency toward pomposity, and, like Angeline, was a true help in her distress.

Lieutenant Colonel Batchelder had written from Washington, offering to send back a sword to place on the coffin, or some other memorabilia for the funeral or interment. It was thoughtful of him. Vanderbilt—or rather the Smithsonian, which was why it fell to Batchelder to make the offer —was in possession of all Ulys' military effects. But Julia did not reply. She and her Ulys were beyond all that, and he had never been one for uniforms and swords and such. His body was dressed in the coffin in a civilian suit. She first laid eyes on this some days after his death and embalmment, when she had gathered enough strength to go downstairs and look. Fred had slipped his daughter's wreath of oak leaves in with the body, and put the wedding ring back on his father's thin finger.

Now, with them all gone to New York, Julia drank in the quiet and peace of the mountain, while still taking a little pleasure at reports of the vast state occasion the funeral had turned into down below. She read in a newspaper and appreciated General Hancock's prayer at the interment in Riverside Park: "God of battles, Father of all. Amidst this mournful assembly we seek Thee with whom there is no death." She also appreciated the federal and New York City governments paying for all the funeral arrangements.

Many thousands of messages—letters and telegrams— from all ranks of people had arrived at the cottage in the past few weeks, and many more were coming in for Julia now, from people common and famous, the latter including

Queen Victoria and Prime Minister Gladstone, Generals Longstreet and Sheridan. Fred had been handling the correspondence since well before his father died, often reading it to her and responding. Now, in his absence, she occasionally dipped into the letters, at least the ones from people she knew, which Angeline helped sort. But mostly they were piling up by the thousands unread, awaiting Fred's return.

From the second floor of the cottage, the view to the east was almost as good as at the Overlook, and Julia enjoyed looking through the open window over the farms and woodlands to the Green Mountains of Vermont, catching a little breeze. She felt close to what Ulys might have called the spirit of Providence, but to her was simply God, to whom she could still be grateful for the goodness of his creation, and in whom she found hope. One day when they were walking to the Overlook, she saw two men cutting down a dead tree, and start sawing it up for firewood. It reminded her of Ulys before the war, not when they lived so far north upriver in Galena, but before that in Missouri, when he cleared some of her father's land to raise crops on, but the only crop that ever paid was firewood. He'd haul the wood into St. Louis and sell it on the street. She was never really afraid about money, not even when he had to sell his watch in 1857, to buy Christmas presents. She wasn't really afraid of anything, except when there was sickness. They gave each other courage. It was still in the first half of August, which apparently was not too early for these men to start preparing for winter in a northern latitude. Ulys' spirit was not chained to this rock. It lived in her heart. She would leave the mountain by the end of the month.

The others had departed with the general's body on August 4, stopping at the New York State Capitol. When they left Albany the next day to continue the train ride south, Fred and most of the adults had looked out the eastern windows, sometimes touching their heads in returned salute to the many mourners standing by the tracks. Many houses, all the stations and the train itself were draped in black. On the other side of the river at West Point—near where on the way up, Fred remembered seeing a veteran amputee approach the stopped train to express his devotion to the general—there were cannons firing and a band playing, with the cadets on parade. Fred was feeling better—relieved, to be honest—that his father's ordeal was over, and that the *Memoirs* were already giving every indication of being financially successful, with a good prospect of bailing out the whole family. He was also happy that his own labors and status as head of the family no longer seemed actively absurd. Further, he was getting on better with his family, including, crucially, Ida. He looked forward to resuming their marital relations in less cramped and inhibiting environments than the jam-packed upstairs of the cottage on Mount McGregor.

But Nellie Sartoris, feeling a little like her mother left behind on the mountain, had sat with nieces and nephews on the western side of the southbound railway carriage, gazing at and sometimes pointing out the beauties of the Hudson River, and the Catskill Mountains beyond.

Chapter Twenty

NELLIE WENT BACK TO MOUNT MCGREGOR after the funeral. She spent the next month with her mother, working their way slowly south, leaving the mountain for West Point, and from there going to stay with Jesse and Elizabeth in Westchester County. At last they returned to Manhattan, as Nellie prepared once more to say *adieu* to her native land.

The day before her ship was scheduled to depart from South Street in New York for Liverpool, England, Nellie met with Ely Parker, Frank Herron and Matias Romero for lunch in a modest restaurant near the Grant house. It was a somewhat odd grouping, since Herron did not know either Romero or Nellie well. The day before, talking on that new-fangled telephone contraption—he had learned not to shout into it, but it remained as one more reminder of a changing world where he was no longer the dashing officer of yore—he asked Ely if he should really come, saying: "Surely Nellie has more important farewells to make than mine."

Ely responded, "You can be our token white man." Herron looked down at the still unfamiliar telephone mouthpiece, before realizing that his friend had made a joke.

Nellie had told Julia she was glad to be have spent this time with her parents. But she was also very relieved at last to be leaving for England and her own children. She knew her father had needed her, and that she provided him with something no one else could. Eleven years ago, she'd used her youthful will against him, to marry in haste, but now she had made some amends, and had gotten, she thought and hoped, new strength from him. She would need it to deal with the consequences of what she had done years ago in ignoring his wishes.

So the three middle-aged or older men came to say goodbye to the still young—if faded—daughter of General Grant, as she prepared to leave her homeland once again. Herron had chosen the uptown restaurant, one a couple of blocks south of 66th Street where a woman would not be out of place. He came early, so that Nellie would not be uncomfortable arriving on her own. Ely and Romero also arrived in good time, whereupon Herron went out into the street to wait for the guest of honor. He was feeling good. The day before, he had gone to Ward's Island and resolved the case of Elias Watson to everyone's satisfaction. The troubled but nonviolent veteran of the Wilderness and Spotsylvania would be able to leave the insane asylum, and live with his comrades in the Eastern Branch of the National Home for Disabled Volunteer Soldiers, in Togus, Maine. Herron's smile when he saw Nellie coming was broad and sincere.

Inside, Ely and Romero had proceeded to get better acquainted by talking about the status of Indians in Mexico. When Nellie walked in with Herron, she cut short with thanks their expressions of sympathy, and urged them to continue the conversation.

So Ely brought up the famous patriot President Benito Juarez, under whom the young Romero had served during the 1860s, when both countries were embroiled in civil war. "Wasn't he an Indian?" he asked.

"Yes," replied Romero. "A Zapotec. So is our current President, General Porforio Diaz, on his mother's side. I fought under him for a few months in 1863." Romero felt annoyed with himself at this boasting before men who had done real soldiering. Or at least Herron had for a while, and then did his best to help the Mexican patriots when stationed on the border. "The Zapotecs," Romero continued, "live in Oaxaca in southern Mexico, where they predate the Aztecs. They are supposed to be descended from celestial beings known as cloud people."

"We Seneca people," said Ely, "say everything came from a tree of life with white blossoms in the center of the sky world, and back then this world below was all covered by water. The tree of life was uprooted somehow and Skywoman, or First Woman, who was pregnant, fell through the hole it made out of heaven but was caught by geese, or at least they broke her fall, floated her down, and the animals in the sea which covered the world brought up mud from the bottom, and put it on the back of the Great Snapping Turtle to receive her, or maybe just a muskrat did that, but she, Skywoman, spread around the earth and it grew into Turtle Island, or America, or the world. A cynical friend of my youth asked what was holding up the turtle, and maybe it all does make the Christian religion seem more sober and sensible by contrast. But does Mr. Darwin's explanation make any more sense?"

"Why doesn't it?" asked Romero.

"I don't say he's wrong," Ely said slowly, "but it doesn't seem to me, taken all in all, an adequate explanation of the very odd and large facts of life."

"It may be religion that can keep the Indians and Irish sober," said Herron, "but with Grant it was Julia." The men laughed briefly, looking askance at Nellie.

Ely said, "When I was a young man, and unmarried, I had a cousin, a serious Christian Seneca, who disapproved of the way I lived. I guess I made fun of him some, at least in my mind, but now I don't think he was wrong."

"What do you mean?" asked Nellie.

"I mean I regret the way I treated some women then. Not all of it. I can't regret all of it, and haven't gone over entirely to my cousin's, or Mr. Newman's, way of thinking. But they seem more right than they used to. It's also been a long time since I was young."

"I think Mr. Darwin's a cold doctrine," Nellie said. "It appeals to superior people who think themselves sophisticated because they sneer and believe in nothing. It's more than that, I know, and I should not sneer at *them*, either. But Darwinism reminds me in a way of Mr. Audubon's paintings."

"The bird man?" asked Romero.

"Yes. Such colorful, sharp, active images. Virile somehow. Alive. Yet Father told me the birds were all dead when he painted them, Audubon, after he killed them."

"You may be right about Darwin," said Herron. "But I hated those southerners who used the language of redemption, not for religion but to celebrate the murder of blacks, and taking away their votes. They said a state was 'redeemed' when they'd won back power for the kind of fire-eaters who started the war, who had made slavery their religion, and after it was lost turned their energies to keeping the Negro down. I guess they've won back almost the whole South by now. That's colder than Darwin."

"I suppose Darwin won't let us have the Garden of Eden," said Nellie. "But it does seem to me that the whole world is Eden, ruined by human vice and folly. And while I know Father wasn't a religious man, he seemed somehow redeemed these last months."

"Rescued from riches, to find the meaning of life," said Herron, as Nellie gave him a puzzled glance. He continued, "I don't think your father was meant to be someone who did a little work on Wall Street. When he was forced out from there, and his health collapsed, he was able to do one last great thing, to write the book."

"I'm not sure greatness is worth the cost," said Nellie.

Ely moved back a topic. "So was Madame Turchin right about the war?" he asked Herron. "And the South is winning the peace?"

It was Romero who answered. "They can't bring back slavery, and the Confederacy would have entrenched it, expanded it. We Mexicans abolished slavery before you *Norteamericanos*, but the Confederates would have plagued us with it again. They wanted a slave empire."

Herron weighed in. "Lincoln was talking about redemption, too, though I don't know that he used the word. 'We here highly resolve that these dead shall not have died in vain—that this nation, under God, shall have a new birth of freedom.' But do his brave words ring true now for us? Or did they sugarcoat the killing?"

"I think my father thinks—thought—like Lincoln, about many things. There's that other, late speech by him, by Lincoln, about both sides reading the same Bible and praying to the same God, and the horror of the war somehow redeeming the nation from the sin of slavery."

"If the war was part of God's plan," said Romero, "it doesn't make me think well of God. Your father read me something months ago from his book, about how some in the South thought there was divine sanction for slavery."

" 'Let us judge not, that we not be judged,' " said Nellie with a smile. "And, 'With malice toward none, with charity for all, with firmness in the right as God gives us to see the right, let us ... bind up the nation's wounds.' Words can show us the way."

"The Seneca said I was marked from birth as a peacemaker, descended from Jigonsaseh, the peace queen, leader of the Corn Way. We gathered in the broken tribes after General Sullivan's raid. And our family healed the British prisoner, Gaylord Parker, and took his name."

Herron remained confused by the details of Ely's family and military history. The year after Sullivan's expedition, in 1780, weren't the Seneca part of the Mohawk Joseph Brant's force, allied with the British in the Burning of the Valleys upstate? But his friend was continuing. "The Iroquois had a Tree of Peace as well as a Tree of Life, and a Great Law of Peace. They buried their weapons under a great pine, so the roots of peace would spread out through the peoples. In war, though, they often tortured their captives, which shows why, perhaps, they needed such a law. Why we all do. And your father said 'Let Us Have Peace,' when God knows we all needed it. Maybe we need more than evolution, too."

Nellie sang lines from a Protestant hymn, "They all shall sweetly obey thy will, Peace, peace be still."

"Like they played on the melodeon, in the church of my youth," said Ely.

"But what if we can't get what we need?" she said.

"He kept the peace abroad, too, as president," said Herron, "when people wanted war with Spain, or England, or even Mexico. Like Washington, he knew war, and knew to avoid it."

"Yes," said Romero. "He was a friend of my country, and of its people, their freedom and prosperity."

"So he knew war and stood for peace," said Nellie, and smiled at her older friends. "What do we modern people know or stand for?"

"Your father's administration had an Indian peace policy, which lasted a while longer than I did," said Ely. "But it fell apart in the Black Hills and Little Big Horn." He paused, then continued on a different tack. "People think I'm a full-blooded Seneca, but I had a white grandmother. And a daughter who I sometimes think might as well be. A half-breed, some might call her."

"Some malicious fools," said Nellie.

"Why, Ely," said Herron, "you call her beautiful flower in your Seneca tongue. How do you say it?"

"*Ahweheeyo.*"

"In Seneca culture," said Nellie, "don't daughters follow their mother's way?"

"They do," said Ely, looking at her sharply. "Not just daughters, either. We are matrilineal, as my anthropologist friend Morgan used to say. But I guess I left the way of the peace queen, went off the reservation." He smiled rather bleakly.

"In Mexico," said Romero, "we intermarry easily."

"Less so in the United States," said Ely. "Some of my Indian friends do not like to, fearing, rightly, that it means we cannot survive as a people."

"Just as people, then," said Nellie, "like the rest of us."

"And of course many whites object to intermarriage, too," continued Ely. "Are we so sure they are wrong?"

"Your daughter must be," said Nellie. "My father hated race prejudice and violence. But does an Englishman count as intermarriage? Mine seems more with a different species." They laughed uneasily, and she continued seriously, "Did you know General Thomas, Ely? George Thomas?"

"Sure. I met him at Chattanooga, and later."

"He's buried not far from Mount McGregor, and father was writing about him there. It made me think of you, of what you said at the Converses, how you'd joined the world of your people's conquerors. Isn't that what Thomas did, and other southerners who stayed loyal to the Union?"

"I suppose so," said Ely. "But I don't think Thomas ever questioned that decision, once he'd made it."

"And you have?"

Herron said, "When they dedicated Thomas' monument in Washington, I don't think Grant or Sherman was there."

"Grant was on his trip around the world," said Ely.

"Yes," said Herron. "But I remember something Sherman said around then, that Thomas would come to be seen as a hero in the South. The trouble is, I don't believe it. The Lost Cause southerners, Jube Early and his crew, can't deal with Thomas, or other loyal white southerners like Admiral Farragut and General Newton, or even Longstreet, for that matter. They'll malign or forget them. They can deal with Frederick Douglass or Grant, but not Thomas."

"Why not Thomas?" asked Romero.

"Because as a teenager he had to run away and hide from Nat Turner's slave rebellion, and in his middle years he was a good friend of Robert E. Lee. But his life showed that Lee didn't have to join the Confederacy, and that a Southern white man didn't have to keep the Negro down. Even though he and Grant never quite got along, they were both defenders of the Negro in Reconstruction, when Sherman and Halleck were not."

"In the war," said Ely, "Thomas asked Bragg for a truce once, I forget why, but Bragg refused to deal with him because he said Thomas was a traitor to Virginia. And the two of them had been friends; they fought together in the Mexican War. I guess you're right, Frank. They haven't forgiven him yet."

Nellie went back to the previous topic. "I don't really know what Father believed about religion. He wrote to me in February telling something about his condition, which made me realize I had to come over, over here to America. In that letter, he said: 'Philosophers profess to believe that what is, is for the best. I hope it may prove so for our family.'"

"He and your mother always made the best of things as they were," said Ely.

"And as a general," said Herron, "he did the same thing, with the men he had on hand, going on from where he was, not whining to Washington about why he couldn't."

"When he was awake at night," said Nellie, "we, his family, could comfort him. But he soon went back to working, writing."

"Most old men get insomnia," said Herron, "but they don't use it as well. Though come to think of it, my grandmother would bake bread in the middle of the night. I guess your father was doing the same sort of thing, doing what he could to be useful."

"What matters for those of us who won't make history?" asked Nellie. "Family? What if our peace is not found there? My husband's family are always talking about what they do and don't believe, but I'm not sure they even convince themselves. The problem isn't that they're English. Aren't we beyond all that? Union or Confederate, slave or free, woman or man, no more. Isn't that something like a prayer, from Saint Paul? Dead or alive. While I'm more religious than he was, I'm not as sure of it as Mother. We can hope, I guess. Isn't that a virtue?"

"What are you going to do in England, Nellie?" asked Romero.

" 'Aye, there's the rub,' said Hamlet. I can take courage from my father, but to do what? It seems like foolishness and conceit, but my little life seems more complicated, less clear than his, harder in some ways. I can't live up to their, to my parents', example, but I have to carry on with what I've got. Protect the children as best I can, from their parents' failings and unhappiness. See what happens. What else can I do?"

"Are things so bad?" asked Ely. "I am sorry."

"You are not powerless, not without friends," said Romero.

"No," said Ely. "And when the Seneca must part from a friend, we say I will see you again."

"Thank you," said Nellie, and achieved a brave smile. "Sufficient unto the day is the evil thereof." The men smiled, recognizing the quotation from the Bible, although Herron for one thought it sounded grim, and could not immediately pin down the context. Nor did he know what she meant by the phrase, although Ely seemed to.

Romero walked Nellie back to 66th Street, while Ely and Herron headed downtown, separating without much enthusiasm to go back to their offices in late afternoon. Later, as Herron walked home from the El station on an almost deserted street, he recalled Nellie's line of a hymn about peace, and sang quietly to himself a different song:

We are tired of war on the old camp ground,
Many are dead and gone,
Of the brave and true who left their homes,
Others been wounded long.
Many are the hearts that are weary tonight,
Wishing for the war to cease;
Many are the hearts looking for the right
To see the dawn of peace.
Tenting tonight, tenting tonight, tenting on the old
    camp ground.

He paused, looking up in the gathering dusk with a smile at the lit apartment of home, in a five-story building that stood out amid vacant lots, that seemed to be waiting for the city soon to surge up around it and beyond, in the direction of Grant's new tomb. Out the front door and running down to meet him, calling a greeting, came his grandson Frank. Herron's smile grew broader.

The next day, as Nellie stood on the second-class deck taking in a pleasant breeze under a grey sky, gazing forward across the vast ocean, Adam Badeau remained back in New York. His desk overlooked a couple of sumac and alianthus trees, wilting from the late-summer heat of the back alley, toward which he gazed without seeing.

Badeau took some satisfaction that he was navigating and steering his way through difficult territory. His novel *Conspiracy: A Cuban Romance* was being published in New York by Worthington, and also had an English publisher. And another book, the long-delayed *Aristocracy in England*, would soon be coming out, too, courtesy of Harper and Company. It was business, much of it with publishers and lawyers, that kept him in the city.

The Grant controversy was distressing, and it was possible that he would be unable to come to civil terms with the family. He might have to sue Mrs. Grant for the money due him, which would look bad in the newspapers, but would at least remind the world of his existence. While he felt partly guilty about Julia and his falling out with the general, it was not healthy to dwell on such emotions. And as P.T. Barnum might testify, there's no such thing as bad publicity—especially when there were books to be sold.

It would all look less bad when he won in court, as he was confident would be the case if Julia were foolishly advised by Fred and others not to reach a reasonable accommodation. She would still get the lion's share of the proceeds of what was obviously going to be a very successful publication. There would be plenty of money to go around, and in the long run, it was in nobody's interest to keep airing dirty linen. It would never get into the books, certainly not into his own. Badeau was a genuine admirer of General Grant, and would follow in his footsteps as a writer. He anticipated, one way or another, getting paid, and along with the royalties of the two new books, reckoned he had enough prospects of money to avoid having to seek employment.

Instead, Badeau would be free to focus on his next book, about Grant. The general's *Memoirs*, he gathered, stopped, or at least the main narrative stopped, in 1865. That left twenty years of the life, including two terms in the White House, covered neither in Grant's book nor in Badeau's military history. Grant as a writer was fortunate that he died when he did, for he would not have been able to deal so clearly with the political years, their failures, embarrassments and muddles, along with some success. That left a large subject for Badeau's next book, which would be no vindictive piece of gossip—and perhaps vindictive was not the right word for Grant, either—but a generous, majestic treatment of the elder statesman. It would cover the reunion and revival of America at home and abroad, chronicled by his closest aide. Scandals there would have to be, but also new triumphs of the great man, including the terrible struggle of his last year to write the *Memoirs*, along with portraits of his famous associates, all of whom Badeau had known. While not dwelling on the negative, and being fair to all parties, the book would tell untold truths—such as the antagonism that existed between Grant and Seward, both of them great men. More interesting than dreary details and disputes about the Indian peace policy or Reconstruction would be the emergence of America, under Grant, into its rightful place at the front of the world stage.

Badeau recalled how a few months ago, when discussing Cold Harbor, Grant had shocked the room by using the term "butcher," showing his awareness of what some people called him. Lincoln had been called a baboon. Yet the baboon and the butcher had saved the country, and it now fell to Adam Badeau to finish the latter's story. He would pay tribute to his mentor, while also bringing order to his own life, and fulfill all the promise of his literary endeavors.

Badeau's eyes were dreamy, facing the alley but not focused there, for he was in work mode—which also meant dream mode, as he remembered Secretary Seward and Senator Sumner and all the men he had never been able to deal with as equals. He took up his pen and wrote at the top of a blank sheet of paper the title: *Grant in Peace*.

AUTHOR'S NOTE

Among a great many historical works consulted, I mention here biographical studies of Ulysses S. Grant by Bruce Catton, Jean Edward Smith, Frank Scaturro and Hamlin Garland; and six books about the last year of his life, *Grant's Final Victory* by Charles Bracelen Flood, *The Captain Departs* by Thomas Pitkin, *Many Are the Hearts* by Richard Goldhurst, *Grant and Twain* by Mark Perry, *U.S. Grant: American Hero, American Myth* by Joan Waugh, and *Grant's Last Battle* by Chris Mackowski. Several participants in these events left their own recollections, including both Julia Grants, George Shrady, John Newman, Adam Badeau and Mark Twain. Such accounts often differ, leaving it to the conscientious reader, or perhaps the historical novelist, to try to figure out the truth.

For Ely Parker, I relied on biographies by Arthur Parker and William Armstrong. There is a biography of Grant's wife Julia by Ishbel Ross, and a long essay in Carol Berkin's *Civil War Wives*. Michael Fellman's *Citizen Sherman* provided evidence for one rather scandalous relationship, while Geoffrey C. Ward's biography of his great-grandfather, Ferdinand Ward, shed light on a different, definite scandal. Among the many other writers I have found useful are Edmund Wilson and Brooks Simpson. I am grateful to my fellow colleagues and volunteers with the Friends of Grant Cottage, including Samantha Dow, Dave Hubbard, Steve Trimm, Hady Finch, Jerry Orton and especially Bill Underhill, whose numerous email links over the years have provided great insight into the period. Thanks also to my wife Barbara Conner and editor-publisher Richard Vang at Square Circle Press for reading the manuscript and suggesting improvements. Barbara wants me to include the fact that Grant's grandson and namesake, a very minor character in this book, did grow up to go to West Point, and became a general.

I first wrote a play about Grant's last weeks on Mount McGregor, but abandoned it in part because I heard that the celebrated playwright John Guare had taken up the theme of the dying Grant in *A Few Stout Individuals*. Years later, after writing the biography of another Civil War general, I decided to write a novel instead of a play about Grant's death, in part at the suggestion of my daughter. This time I followed much more rigid historical rules. Much of what happens in the book is historical fact. All quoted written material, such as the letters of Grant and Badeau, is genuine, and the references to the Civil War are to actual events; nothing from the war is made up. All the main characters—in fact virtually everyone mentioned in the book—were real people, who spent time in New York in 1885. With one minor exception (discovered too late), no one does anything they could not in fact have done, as far as I know. Guare's play and those historical rules helped persuade me to move most of the action to New York City; but this is a very different work from his, with none of the fantastic elements.

Robert C. Conner
Saratoga County, N.Y., 2018

ABOUT THE AUTHOR

This is the first novel by Robert C. Conner, a longtime journalist who won two first-place writing awards from the New York Associated Press Association for newspapers with circulation between 50,000 and 200,000. His previous book, published by Casemate in 2013, was a biography, *General Gordon Granger: The Savior of Chickamauga and the Man Behind Juneteenth*. Conner has a Phi Beta Kappa bachelor's degree from New York University, and an associate's degree in chemical dependency counseling from Hudson Valley Community College. He serves as a volunteer at Grant Cottage in upstate New York, and as president of the Malta Sunrise Rotary Club. He and his wife Barbara have three grown children.

CPSIA information can be obtained
at www.ICGtesting.com
Printed in the USA
FFOW02n0840190318
45702151-46572FF

9 780998 967011